MW00770378

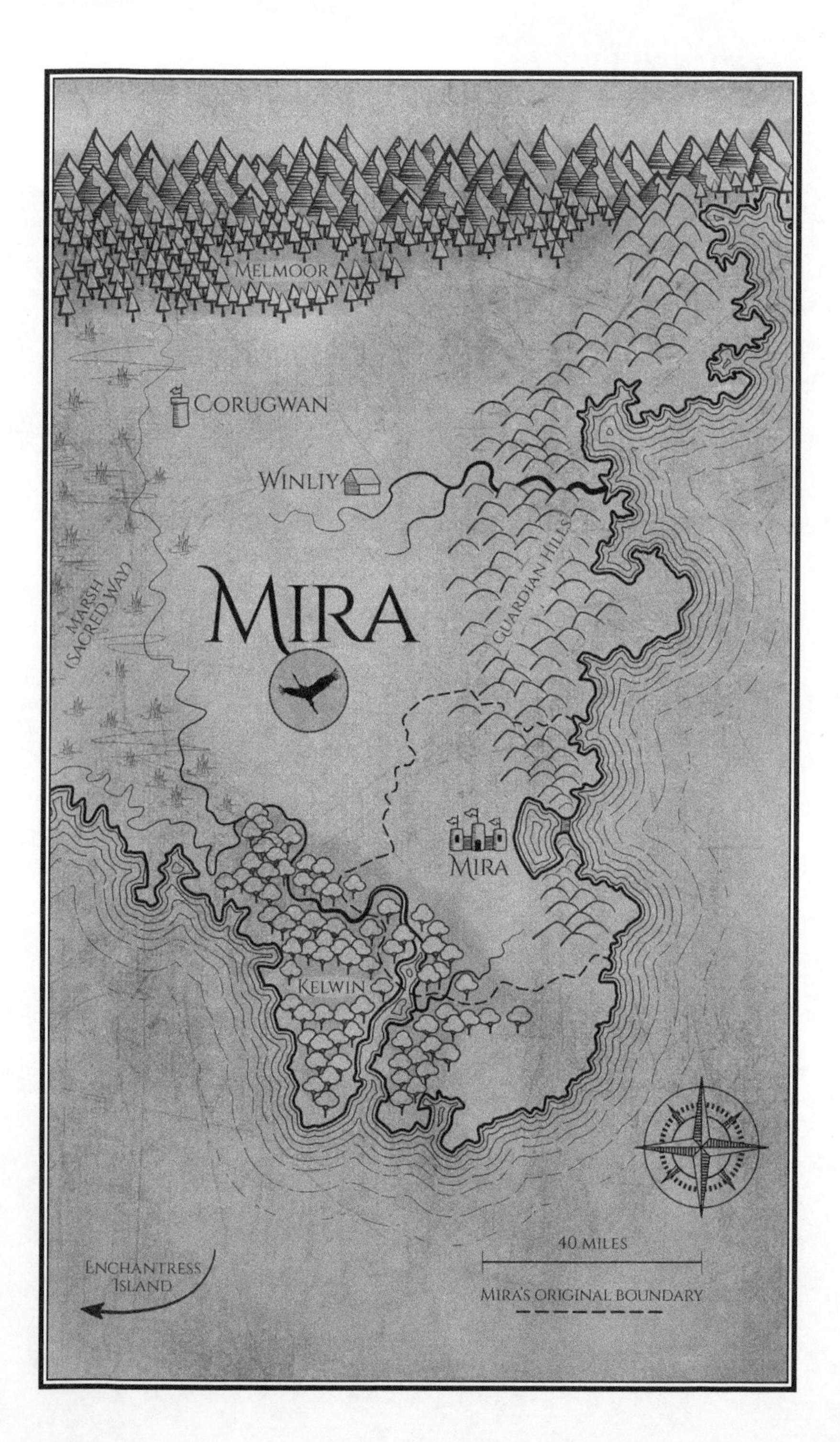
Melmoor
Corugwan
Winliy
Mira
Marsh
(Sacred Way)
Guardian Hills
Mira
Kelwin
40 miles
Enchantress
Island
Mira's original boundary

Diane,
May you find joy in all your talents

THE SAVAGE WAR

- [illegible] Wallace

THE SAVAGE WAR

BY

ESTHER WALLACE

The Savage War
The Black Phantom Chronicles (Book 1)

Cover design by Mark Gerber

Books published by Emerald Lake Books may be ordered through your favorite booksellers or by visiting emeraldlakebooks.com.

ISBN: 978-1-945847-05-9 (paperback)

978-1-945847-06-6 (ebook)

Library of Congress Control Number: 2018964890

For my dear sister, Lia,
even though you may
never read Arnacin's story.

Cast of Characters

Arnacin . . . . An islander and the protagonist of this story.
Bozzic . . . . . Arnacin's father.
Carpason . . . Lord of Tarmlin, first Miran friend of Arnacin.
Cestmir . . . . A Miran duke.
Charlin . . . . Squire to Lord Carpason.
Charlotte . . . Arnacin's sister.
Cornyo . . . . One of Duke Cestmir's knights.
Darien . . . . . A councilor to Miro.
Erlund . . . . . Another councilor to Miro.
Firth . . . . . . Son of Gagandep.
Gagandep . . . An adopted native and a skilled healer.
Garak . . . . . A Miran earl.
Hadwin . . . . A Tarmlin knight.
Krisno . . . . . A councilor to Miro.
Memphis . . . High Councilor to Miro.
Miro . . . . . . King of Mira.
Raymond . . . Arnacin's childhood friend.
Rosa . . . . . . Princess of Vemose, neighboring kingdom of Mira.
Samundro. . . A Miran sailor.
Sara . . . . . . Valoretta's nurse.
Shashidha. . . A native boy.
Tevin. . . . . . Arnacin's childhood friend.
Valoretta . . . Princess of Mira and heir of Miro.
Voninath . . . Master swordsman.
Wilham . . . . Captain of a rowing vessel.
William . . . . Arnacin's younger brother.

Prologue

Dust blew into the air as Arnacin's father, Bozzic, carefully brushed his hand over the crackling parchment. Beside him, his son watched, eyes round with wonder and anticipation.

"Do you remember, Arnacin," Bozzic almost murmured, "the day you convinced a group of older, rowdy boys to cease their mischief? That was the first time I thought this had been saved because of you."

"What is it?"

Slowly unrolling the parchment onto the table, Bozzic replied, "My father gave this to me on my wedding day, as he received it on his. The fear was, I suppose, that we would run off if it was given to us before wives kept us accountable."

As Bozzic finished flattening the parchment out, Arnacin stepped near, beholding the faint scratches of an ancient plan. "It's a ship," he breathed after a second.

"Yes, it is the only documentation of an ocean-faring vessel in all of Elcan. See how different it is from the coastal vessels you grew up with? It has been passed down from father to eldest son since its creation nearly a thousand years ago. This is the best representation anyone could make of the enchanters' ship as it was carefully ripped apart, beam by beam. And now, it is yours, to recreate the ship drawn here or to save it for your first son."

Brow furrowed, Arnacin looked up at his father. "Why are you giving this to me now?"

Sinking into the nearest chair, where he could look his son squarely in the eyes, Bozzic placed his hand on Arnacin's shoulder. "I believe this was made for a purpose and that it came to me for a reason, as have you. You might only be eleven, Arnacin, but you are marked with leadership in your humility, compassion and intense feeling of responsibility, whether you are responsible or not..." He smiled. "Yes, even in your pride you show leadership–nothing can make you surrender unless you are completely convinced it would be wrong not to. If it stopped there, I would just think you will make one superb father and villager, but it doesn't. There are your stories.

"So, Arnacin, why don't *you* tell me why almost all your stories are of men and women who frequently die for honor, love and complete dedication to righteousness?"

"I don't know. The stories just come and I tell them. If other stories did come, I don't think I'd find them worth telling. But if there was a reason... I guess–I guess I want to be those men. I want that test of trust in the Creator's authority and power, and I want the triumph of knowing I did not fail."

"If I asked you today to pick a career on this island, which one would you choose?"

His gaze moving toward the open door and the village beyond, Arnacin inquired, "Must I?"

"If you can picture yourself as anything here, what would it be?"

After a long silence, the boy nearly pleaded, "There's nothing... costly. It's all... village life."

"If you think there's nothing important, Arnacin, you should remember that we have no government here. We need each other to keep us all accountable to morality, to provide every aspect of village life and, if ever it's needed, to supply our own defense. Is that not service enough?"

"Father, I..." Arnacin sighed. "It's too easy. Where's the triumph in that?"

Nodding as if he had known the answer long before he asked, Bozzic concluded his pursuit. "Then if you could pick a career out of all the ones you know exist, what would it be?"

Somber blue eyes flicked to Bozzic, yet they roiled in churning thoughts–thoughts that were likely far too serious for a boy Arnacin's age, yet needed to be thought.

"A martyr," the boy eventually replied, causing his father to bark in laughter despite the fact that it had been said with the deepest amount of conviction.

"Oh, Arnacin," Bozzic sighed. "That is the last thing I would ever want for you." Despite the pain that joined that fixed gaze, the seriousness did not waver and, leaning forward until their eyes were only an inch apart, the boy's father asked, "And if that option were given to you, would you take it, even if it meant separating yourself from your family for as long as you lived?"

Sinking into those dark pools in his son's eyes, Bozzic read the full understanding of the question, the knowledge of the sacrifice, and also the sincerity as Arnacin slowly nodded.

Straightening, Bozzic rolled the parchment back up. Placing it into his son's hand, he exhaled. "Then it is time, Arnacin, we prepare to send you to sea. Only out there will you discover the reasons you were given all your passions and talents and yet were not born in a place that could use them."

Arnacin grew while he and his father, along with his younger sister and his closest friend, Charlotte and Raymond respectively, toiled at building a sea-worthy ship. Just as the ship neared completion, his father died.

Suddenly, Arnacin held responsibility as man of the household, a task that halted any voyage for life. Darkness descended on him, a darkness of lost hope and emptiness, until the day Charlotte and Raymond secretly pulled him back into finishing his ship, thereby rekindling a hope that stirred in the depths of his now fifteen-year-old heart...

Chapter 1

The Runaway

SLEEP REFUSED TO COME FOR Arnacin of Enchantress Island. Beside him, his brother's warm, toddler body was a sticky reminder of what he was about to abandon. From the other side of their one-room home, he could easily hear the whispered conversation between his mother and sister as they finished drying the dishes.

Their words were the only barrier between him and the guilt, fear and anticipation pounding through his veins. He was leaving. It had to be tonight, lest he lose the courage to ever leave his family. Even after his mother fell asleep, he lay there, staring undecided at the toddler beside him. As usual, William slept with his fist in his mouth.

It had not been uncommon for Arnacin to be suddenly whacked in the face at night by that wet fist. This night, he just shook his head, whispering so low that he hardly heard his own words as he used his mother's fond name for her youngest. "Farewell, Bluefire. I don't know when I'll return, but I know you will not be the same when I do." With sadness and love, he ran his fingers through the thick black hair on top of the toddler's head, and slipped off.

Arnacin jumped as he nearly ran into Charlotte, who stood in the doorway. She, however, only turned silently and he led the way to the ocean, where the small ship awaited him.

Charlotte did not speak until they stood by the water, where moonlight cast over them in an almost eerie light, like the last glow of a funeral pyre.

"Arnacin," she called softly. She paused uncertainly as he turned to her before smiling innocently. "You know how I hate you."

He did not answer, but stared off to where the moon shimmered across the sea.

"Why must you go?" His sister's teasing suddenly broke loose into temper. "While I'm told I can't because I'm a girl, you know you will be told the same thing for another reason! That is why you are sneaking away in the black of night like a criminal!"

Turning to her in surprise, he snapped back, "Were you not the one who insisted that I had to go, that I was meant–*called*–to leave, when I said I couldn't?"

"Not like this!"

Nodding in comprehension, he jibed, "You're just jealous."

Charlotte flicked her head hotly. "Perhaps I am jealous. Jealous that, unlike me, your bow is not your truest companion. But more than that..." she released her temper in a long sigh. "I have the feeling I will never see you again. We fight, I rebel, but I love you anyway."

Those words pierced him with a sick feeling that even then he knew he would never forget, but he answered, "I will return, I promise. If I'm out there so much as ten years, it will be excessive. Besides, my leaving will give you the freedom you want. Someone has to look after the sheep. Raymond promised to take care of anything else Mother can't. Who knows, in a few years, you might not even care," he shrugged, "...when you're married."

She laughed, a sound of deep hatred and malice bubbling out of her. "I'd murder the first person who tried making me."

Arnacin stared at her in disbelief. Was she the same girl who stroked William's head at night and rocked him to sleep, who drifted silently through the woods alongside wild deer?

"Charlotte, I would never betray you or Mother or William, but I need to go. You know how it calls me, its mystery and..." His voice dropped off as his gaze sought the open sea, whose whispering waves sounded like a beckoning. Turning back to his sister, he implored her, "I'm nothing here. Father thought this adventure would reveal my purpose. As long as I stay–"

"I know," Charlotte whispered. She glanced away. When she looked back with a forced smile, her voice was commanding once again. "Go. Find your meaning."

Arnacin briefly threw his arms about her before climbing aboard his small ship. He did not dare tell his young sister to wait until the right man came along, for on that day, he was sure, she would be only too happy that she had not set sail with her brother. He simply wished for her heart's healing.

Arnacin's original thought was, by allowing the wind to guide the ship wherever it would, he would soon hit land. Obviously, many lands existed. Yet summer's warm winds turned cold. Storms blasted the ship, tossing it about. Still, Arnacin persevered, caring for his vessel as much as he knew how, marking down each day as one less to travel, all the while calling himself an optimistic fool. Only his need to succeed kept him going, while he watched his stores shrink.

Finally, he again traveled through warmer seas. If it was not technically spring back home, he still thought of it so. With fewer storms, he spent his days on deck, cheered despite the small amount of food left.

One especially warm day, he slid his arms under his head and closed his eyes against the brightness of the sun. There he dozed until thick raindrops slapped him awake.

Dark clouds blew overhead, leaving him only seconds to move. As the black spray lashed, Arnacin slammed the cabin door shut against the storm. His last image of the outside world was that of enormous waves amid the crack and roar of thunder.

Throwing his blanket around his shoulders, Arnacin could still imagine the sky spilling its evil contents into the dark abysses that the waves formed time and again. The sea thrashed in torment from the biting hail, driven by the whim of the wind whipping about it. Caught without aid inside those rearing whirlpools of water, his ungainly little ship careened through the waves that forced it onward with unrelenting demand.

In the background, he could hear the creaking and groaning of the ship, a sound so inferior to the might of the tempest. With every heave, Arnacin braced himself between the wall and his bed to keep from rolling around the floor like the objects that were doing their own clinking dance as they knocked into each other. Yanking the blanket more firmly around his shoulders, the boy sighed in frustration.

How long had he been out here? He had lost track. Several weeks, a few months, half a year, a little bit more... It did not matter. Day in and day out, it had been the same constant routine, now only altered by the lack of food and water and, of course, by the current storm–only the fifth during his voyage. Still, nothing had broken the endless sight of sky and water. His book, created for navigation purposes, had become a mixture of navigation and doodles of sheep, wooded mountains, and cloud formations. At least his constant sketching had replaced his artistic ineptitude with a tiny bit of skill.

The ship lurched onto its side. Slammed into the bed, Arnacin could feel the ship rise upward, a sensation like it was about to leave the earth entirely, and then... he was thrown off his feet, his back hitting wood while his pillow, blankets and other objects rained about him. Something broke with a loud crack and Arnacin looked up just in time to see water rushing in from every crack around the door, the cabin stairs now above him.

In a flash of reflexes, the islander shot to his feet, ignoring the deluge of unyielding saltwater as he fought his way to the door. It would not open or budge for the pressure heaving against it, yet the water had already filled the cabin to the boy's waist and was still coming, raining down over his shoulders and head, swirling about his ankles.

He felt his feet slip from the force against them. With a splash muffled by the roar of water, Arnacin seized the only option left to his panicked mind. Rising into the disappearing space between the new roof and water for just a second, the boy drew air, coughing up the water he had swallowed. Inhaling as deeply as the rising water would permit, he plunged back into the torrent, clawing for the cracks between the slats of the door.

As he felt the swirling of the water decrease around him, he knew then that his cabin had become a large fish bowl, without air pockets. With one last futile yank as the burning in his lungs shot to his head, he felt the wood give way beneath his fingers. Desperately, he kicked upward, bumping his head into something hard. His ship's deck blocked his escape and blackness started to descend. Only the waves rescued him, sweeping him from beneath the ship. Surfacing, he gasped, just catching his foot on the rail so as not to be dragged away.

There, waves pouring over him, he shivered, spluttered and choked. The storm threatened to rip him from his hold however, while his ship continued to float like a giant, overturned basket.

Arnacin dipped back beneath the surface, finding one of the trailing sail lines. It took several submerges to twist it around the top of the rail, fighting constantly against the waves. Then, with fingers too stiff to work anymore, Arnacin climbed onto the bottom of his ship with the assistance of the waves, slid down the other side and found another sail line.

Using the last of his ebbing strength, he once again gained the bottom of the ship, now armed with both ropes, and tied himself to the boat. His mission finished, he let the darkness envelop him.

In the early hours of the following morning, sunlight beat onto a sandy spit escaping the wooded coast. For the first time since dragging himself there earlier, Arnacin painfully stirred. He trembled in the light breeze that ruffled the tangled shreds of canvas on the wreck of his ship, beached nearby. Stifling a cough, Arnacin finally pushed himself slowly into a sitting position, sand sliding off him as he shifted.

Pulling his sodden clothes about himself, he dropped his chin onto his knees, glaring at what remained of his ship. It lay there on its side, its broken mast dug into the sand as if trying to impersonate a lean-to, its railings and cabin smashed through, stripped by the sea of many of its possessions.

There was no way around it. Despite the care and logic put into the boat's creation, Arnacin was stranded. Now, there was no way to return, as far as he could see.

"Charlotte," he croaked amid shivering hisses. "Fine, I concede defeat. I can't return."

If honest with himself, however, he never considered defeat an option. With that reminder, he lifted his head. He had barely begun to lurch to his feet, though, before he looked again at his ship and reality washed away his renewed determination.

Even if he found some form of food and water, he had no way to rebuild his ship. By himself, he could never replace the mast. Furthermore, he did not know if he had even built it correctly and, if he had not, another storm might completely sink the thing if he rebuilt it.

With that thought, he dropped back onto the sand.

For hours, Arnacin sat there, trembling and coughing, beyond all care for his own well-being. As the sun set, to be replaced by night's full moon, the only difference was that he lay on his back in the sand, his eyes closed and his tongue pressed between dried lips. The only sound came from the pounding of the surf and the wind in the trees.

A scream shattered the night. Arnacin jerked up, his face pale. More screams followed, or perhaps shouts. It made little difference to Arnacin. To his sheltered ears, those sounds were the most blood-curdling, horrible noises he had ever heard or even imagined in his sixteen years of life. As if only to add to his terror, the din, now from tens of voices, drew closer. Then, almost as quickly as they had arisen, the sounds ended, leaving only the hiss of the waves in their wake.

Momentarily distracted from his cold, starvation and thirst, Arnacin slowly climbed to his feet. Heart and blood pounding, his gaze never left the dark of the redwoods where the screams still seemed to echo.

Like a coyote that prowls noiselessly through the forest, he set off in the direction from which he'd last heard the sounds, led by that morbid desperation to know all dangers. Before long, he saw a spark of light in the distance and he angled toward it. Almost as if mocking his hearing, crickets chirped in the underbrush and, somewhere, an owl hooted.

It was as if nothing had happened, and yet–the normal noises were almost a façade. Somewhere, un-pinpointed, the woods still retained a deadened sound, as if the crickets were simply putting on a brave front, while the owl–

As a hoot came again, Arnacin stiffened, realizing that it did not quite sound authentic. Only a few feet away, the light flickered like many torches.

Just as he realized that the hoots could be a signal of some kind, a dark shadow rose from the base of a nearby tree. Before he could move, the shadow grabbed him around the neck. The arm tightened, forcing him forward. In his weakened state, that was all it took. Blackness descended. He could remember no more than the feeling of his attacker's grip slackening.

Lord Carpason of the ruined city of Tarmlin looked up as a commotion erupted along the edge of his troop's encampment in the Melmoor forest. The sounds of shock and exclamation, even slight exasperation, piqued his curiosity, prompting him to investigate. Several of his cloaked men stood around a sickly-looking boy in his mid-teens, with the deepest dark hair. It was that hair that caused Carpason's eyes to widen as his gaze shot to his men for explanation. All the men around him possessed golden to light-auburn hair–he had never even imagined hair could be brown, much less black.

Meeting his lord's gaze, one man, Sir Hadwin, shrugged. "He was sneaking through the woods by our camp. I almost didn't see him."

"But–where did he come from?" Only the same confused hum of speculation met his question. "Could it be dyed?" Carpason asked, looking again at the dark hair.

"If you're asking if it could be a savage ploy, my lord, it no longer matters. This boy's as good as dead."

"You're not supposed to attack without cause."

"I didn't do anything. He just fainted."

Ignoring his lookout's defense, Carpason knelt, taking the boy's wrist between his fingers. A fast beat pounded under them, easily felt beneath the meatless skin covering sinew and bone. Thoughtfully, the lord looked again over those pale, flushed cheeks and parched, swollen lips.

Sighing, he ordered, "Give him some water, but don't jostle him. In his state, he needs the rest. We'll take him with us back to Mira. The king can decide what to do with him once we have time to interrogate him. At the moment, I'm not going to disregard the fact that he might be one of our enemy's cleverer ploys. Death might lie in such an assumption."

"Should we bind him?" Hadwin inquired, causing the lord to pause before turning away.

Looking again at the boy, however, Carpason shook his head. "Should he be a spy, he is still no threat physically. Do watch him, but should he truly be innocent, I don't wish our caution to create instant enmity."

As soon as the first rays of sun splattered through the canopy of trees, Lord Carpason commanded his men to break camp. Only the perimeter patrol and the mysterious boy, unconscious in the middle of the encampment, did nothing to help.

Sudden shouts of alarm from the patrollers caused Carpason to whip out his sword. Around him, the hiss of swords leaving scabbards echoed. Yet the men of Tarmlin had no time to organize before they were rushed by savages.

Carpason had one glance of their bright yellow hair, vengeful faces, and pillaged spears, swords and axes before his need to defend himself cut off his peripheral vision.

Freeing himself, he leapt onto a horse, calling to his sub-commanders, "Hadwin, Alten, Lindan! Gather your divisions! We mus–"

Above his enemies, he had an advantage, but he was forced to wheel his steed toward an attack. Atop one of Tarmlin's horses, a savage rammed the beast into Carpason's own, lunging at the lord. Carpason instantly sidestepped his mount, but proving their reputed horsemanship, the savage moved with him.

Still, there was a second's respite and in it the lord dropped to the ground, fleeing to a weapons cart. There, he yanked out a spear and flung it into his attacker's throat.

A glow on the edge of the camp caught his attention as the savage fell off the steed. Carpason barely registered that it was a large fire before a blazing arrow whooshed overhead. Crackling, it embedded itself into the weapons cart next to the lord, the first of many.

"Water!" Carpason cried while more arrows found other supply carts. Men rushed to fight the fire, yet smoke soon filled the air, blinding and choking everyone. Coughs and terrified shouts sounded around the lord. His own lungs clenched in pain.

Suddenly, the attack ebbed.

Taking advantage of the lull, Carpason renewed his assault while one of the knights nearby ordered, "See to the wagons! Shovel dirt over the fire!"

Wordlessly thanking the man, Carpason also gathered a group, found the remaining savages still fighting, and cut them down. Only when the sound of battle no longer echoed through the smoke and the lone shouts were of those trying to save the supplies did the lord call his men together. As one, the men attacked the fire that roared over their supplies and filled both lungs and air with its stench.

Afternoon sun shone through the last of the smoke as Carpason helped his blackened troops load the surviving supplies onto the salvageable wagons.

"Don't worry about the rest," he rasped. "Our water's gone along with half our supplies, if not more. Line up."

His order, although hardly heard, was spread through camp and, little by little, men began assuming their traveling formation.

It was not until the lord hauled himself back onto his horse that one knight questioned, "We must leave the dead behind, of course, but what of the boy?"

"B...?"

Carpason turned sharply back toward what remained of the camp. The dead cluttered the bases of trees and blood soaked the leaves, but there, buried under a savage corpse, Carpason spotted the stranger's black hair. Huffing, the lord snapped, "Retrieve him."

Finally, with troop readied and motionless boy safely in one of the mounted men's arms, Carpason started them back toward the capital in the long-rehearsed practice of infantry, followed by knights, then the remaining carts of armor, weapons, tools and tents, more knights, and then Carpason, followed by the same pattern in reverse order.

They stopped once by a small trickle of water to clear their throats of smoke. There, the lord approached the dark-haired stranger, whose unconscious form rested on the ground. It seemed almost ominous that the natives had not attacked him as well, yet that chest continued to rise and fall. Perhaps the enemy simply had not paid attention to unmoving lumps on the ground.

Stirring as the noble watched, the boy opened his dark blue eyes to stare at the trees overhead. Carpason stepped nearer, crouching beside the weak newcomer. "Our attackers do not wait for a proper introduction. We must be on the move before the hour. Can you ride?"

A sharp, indiscernible croak answered him, while the boy attempted to sit up. Every muscle quivered, yet he somehow managed. Watching for only a moment, the lord hailed one of his men, asking softly, "Are there any canteens remaining that can be filled?"

"There are spare canteens on the saddles, my lord," the soldier replied. "Would you like me to fetch some?"

Carpason nodded and a minute later he was gently supporting the boy to prevent him from choking while he sipped the reviving water.

"We're ready, my lord," someone informed Carpason from behind, receiving a nod.

"Line up, then." As the man turned to relay the order, another brought the lord's steed forward. Helping the boy to his feet, Carpason eased his support away only when he felt his charge steady beneath his hand.

"Come, you may ride," the lord began to offer, halting in surprise as the boy shook his head.

"I don't know how to ride." Although still hoarse, the words came across clearly. Those words were contrary to the savages' horsemanship, but it was the boy's foreign accent that convinced the lord that his fears of a trap were unfounded.

"You don't need to," Carpason said. "I don't think you are capable of walking beside the footmen, however."

The boy's eyes flashed and, with a slight flick of his head, he corrected the lord, "I walked here from the shore, and I prefer to be in full control of my direction."

A minute passed in which the lord considered the boy. Carpason's command had never been refuted before, however politely. Could the boy be that ignorant of authority, or that obstinate?

"Very well," the lord finally decided. "We shall see if you can keep up with the pace. If not, the choice shall be taken from you. Is that fair?"

Once again, while his words were stated partly as a question, they were anything but. The boy's dark blue eyes fully registered that with a challenging reply, but he simply inclined his head. Seconds later, they were again on the march.

The world seemed to tilt around Arnacin. He had counted on walking with difficulty, yet it proved even harder than he imagined. Concentrating solely on each laborious step, he noticed little else.

A horse's piercing whinny was his only warning before something rammed into him. His knees gave way and he landed with a gasp in the leaves. The world turned black and he was only aware of what felt like hundreds of feet rushing around him.

As consciousness returned to him, he heard shouts, screams and whinnies amid the crunching of disturbed leaves. Slowly raising his head, the islander noticed a swarm of hide-bundled, thickset opponents all hurrying directly toward the army's commander, ignoring everyone else in their path. His horse lay dying a few feet away, an arrow in her neck, while her rider fought for his life. The rest of the army engaged a wall of attackers both behind and in front of the commander and Arnacin, who remained unnoticed where he fell.

Despite the horrific skirmish writhing about him, unreality seemed to pass over the boy. He felt like one watching reflections in water. The daze broke as, with a scream that seemed to echo directly in his ear, a body thumped to the ground beside him. Blank eyes stared into Arnacin's and, with a gasp, he jerked away, wincing as something bit into his side. A blade lay beside him, blood trickling down its edges and running into the leaves.

Closing his eyes to the hideous sight, Arnacin turned back to the commander's struggle. The attackers were forcing their victim into the depths of the woods. Without backup against the mass pressing upon him, he could do nothing to gainsay their attempts at swift and easy murder. With a hasty glance at the rest of the troop still struggling futilely to break through their enemies, the islander knew he was the only one in any position to aid the commander.

With that in mind, Arnacin heaved himself to his feet and, lifting the cumbersome sword as best he could, he stepped toward the nearest ambusher.

Realizing that he was stepping farther away from the center of the fray, Carpason dropped to the ground and rolled toward the rest of his army, locked in battle with their opponents. This threw his own assailants off fleetingly, hardly allowing him to regain his feet, let alone free some of his men as he had intended. Now, trapped between the savages attacking him and those mutilating his men, Carpason used his position to the best of his advantage, sidestepping in order to force his enemies' thrusts upon each other.

In the confusion that ensued when his attackers accidentally collided with their own men, Carpason dispatched a few more of his attackers, leaving him with only two. Yet it did not free his men.

His glance toward them betrayed him, as his feet were knocked out from under him. Swiftly, he blocked the sword flashing downward. The blades clashed inches from his neck. No room existed for parrying the next attack, which struck for his stomach. Death had arrived.

Mid-swing, the savage turned sharply, whirling his slashing blade with him. In a flash of green and black, the savage dropped to the ground, his turn unfinished. A blade protruded at an odd angle through his stomach. Scrambling to his feet to attack, Carpason paused. There stood the strange foreigner. Using the killing sword's hilt as a crutch, he was striving to keep himself on his feet.

"It's idiocy to keep routines–tells them exactly where to attack," the boy breathed, just before collapsing over his fallen opponent.

Ripping his gaze away from his unconscious rescuer, Carpason searched for the second attacker. That savage also lay dead with a jagged, faltering slice across his throat.

Glancing only once more in disbelief at the still boy at his feet, Carpason sought out the rest of the battle. His questions had to wait.

Night had fallen once again and the army had been forced to quit their hard march, light fires, and set guards. The attacks had not abated throughout the day. There, by a stream, they finally had the opportunity to look after their injured, although nothing could be done about the many bodies left where they fell during the day. Canteens were refilled at least, and the troop's thirst quenched.

"It's a treacherous business, my lord," one knight sighed, wincing as their field surgeon prodded his slashed shoulder. "I wish the savages would find a less effective method, but every time, they create a ruckus simply to entangle us and then launch their real attack. At least it's likely safe to say that they had not prepared their normal poison today."

"I think they have lost their supply for the time being, during this manhunt for our group," Carpason said in weary agreement. "Once we return to the city, that respite shall be at an end. We can count on it. They will regrind whatever it is they use, mix it with whatever else–I don't even wish to know... But today..." He puffed in slight amusement. "Today, someone protected us."

Smiling himself, the knight joked, "After we lost about ten Lord Carpason's this afternoon..." He received a guilty glance from his lord but plowed on anyway. "I dare say, *someone* protected us. You say it wasn't your idea to switch the order and put other men in your place?"

"Not entirely," Carpason whispered, glancing over his shoulder to where the surgeon was now bending over the still, dark-haired boy. "I wonder where he came from and how he wound up on our shores."

His musing was not really meant to be answered, but, following his gaze, the knight shrugged. "Why does it matter, my lord?"

"Idle curiosity. Yet if not for him, I would lie dead. Some may call it 'luck,' but I wonder. He has no skill at swordplay and seemingly no knowledge of... politics or warfare. Yet he can sense a weakness in a plan without thought, so it appears, and possesses all the lightness of foot and keenness of eye that most of us lack without training. How so, I ask myself. How so? What distant land, homeland of the black hair, breeds such natural skill into its men, and why do they know nothing of the world?"

"I'm afraid he's the only one who could possibly answer and, somehow, I doubt he will," the knight supplied.

Noncommittal, Carpason groaned as he pushed himself to his battle-aching feet and joined the surgeon beside the motionless boy. "Is he all right?"

"I think so, my lord. He's starved and extremely dehydrated, but under careful and patient ministrations, I think he will be as good as new within a month or so."

"Will it be safe trying to feed him?"

"We'll work up to it, I expect." That said, the surgeon moved on to help other injured men.

Carpason watched him go and, when he turned back, found two dark blue eyes coming into focus on him from the haze of unconsciousness. Pain crossed those foreign features as the boy tried to push himself up.

"No, don't," the lord whispered, gently pushing the boy back down.

Too weak to protest, the boy submitted to the light force, closing his eyes again. Regarding him, Carpason attempted, "I realize I don't have a name for you, or know anything of who or what you are..." He left the sentence invitingly open, waiting.

Almost contrary to his expectations, the boy breathed, his voice clearer although just as soft as before, "Arnacin. I'm a shepherd boy."

Carpason could feel his eyebrows rise in surprise as he replied, "Really?" With a teasing smile, he added, "I suppose your flock was stolen and so you hired the first ship in hopes of finding them. You must own good wool."

A slight smile flickered on his face as Arnacin admitted, as if it were simply a fact, "The best."

Those dark eyes again met the lord's, this time with a sad or scared glimmer Carpason could not discern. "The ship I came in is my own, though–and it's lying off the coast... of wherever I was last night... if it was last night."

For another minute, the lord was stunned speechless. Then he muttered, "Captain of your own ship!"

"Not really." Arnacin smiled. "Not in those terms, just sailor of my own ship–but you're not likely to understand unless you see it."

"Still, Arnacin, son of..."

"Bozzic, of Enchantress Island."

Carpason nodded his gratitude, finishing, "Son of Bozzic the shepherd. You are the most unfathomable boy I think I have ever met. Shepherd boy, sailor, captain and not captain, and whatever else. I have the feeling I've only broken the surface."

Blushing slightly, Arnacin mentioned, "My sister would instantly add 'fool' to that list."

"Well, she's wrong then," Carpason mused and Arnacin glanced away.

Silence fell for a minute, while the lord continued to regard the boy thoughtfully. Then he pulled his short sword from his belt, offering the weapon. "Here, this may help you."

Glancing at the gift, its gold-covered sheath patterned with a canopy under which the long-necked bird of Mira stretched its wings, the boy shook his head. "You should know from earlier that I cannot use one."

"On the contrary..." Carpason started before, grinning, he compromised. "More or less. But to my knowledge, shepherds don't protect their flocks with their bare hands."

"My family is comprised of archers."

"Quite skilled ones, I'd guess."

"Well, my sister and I pride ourselves as such, if that is any answer from people who think too highly of themselves."

Unsure if the boy was joking or not, Carpason laughed uncertainly. "Trouble is the day a girl counts herself good–"

"Deadly, sir," the boy swiftly corrected, a sudden coldness in his eyes and tone. "Her skill is not to be taken lightly."

Again regarding the boy, Carpason nodded. "As you wish, Arnacin, son of Bozzic. Perhaps I can see your view." Indeed, looking at the boy, a deadly sister did not seem all too unlikely. "I'll bring some water and then you should go back to sleep. When we reach the capital, I'll see that someone retrieves the remains of your ship."

Chapter 2

Valoretta

ARNACIN SHIVERED, FEELING SOMETHING COLD blow across him. As a stronger gust whipped his hair into his face, he jerked awake, sitting up and looking around. He sat in a bed, larger than any he had ever seen, covered by soft, thick blankets. The room itself was fairly sparse, as though no one had ever claimed it. Outside an open window, storm clouds twirled about the sky, darkening the unfamiliar room. That was the source of the frigid air—storm wind.

Slowly, he slid his legs out from under the covers. The cold floor met his bare feet and he shivered. Just as he did so, the door swung open and an older man, stooped and careworn, bustled in.

"Well," the man wheezed, catching sight of the boy. "You seem stronger. The drugs don't seem to knock you out completely anymore at any rate."

At Arnacin's wary stare, he laughed throatily. "No harm was intended, dear boy. I simply wanted you to rest while you needed it. King Miro has generously offered you housing while your—" He broke off, laughing, before controlling himself and forcing the next words out between a grin that seemed near to cracking. "Your ship is in need of repair. In another day, I'll allow you to leave my care—if that agrees with you."

"What if that doesn't agree with me?" Arnacin wondered, knowing the answer before the man spoke.

Smiling as he placed his tray on a nearby table, the man said, "I would suggest you agree. I will simply be forced to drop my thoughtfulness if you don't, lest my honor as healer be tarnished."

To that simple reply, Arnacin had no response.

Finding his ship was not as straightforward as Arnacin had first imagined. Although he could see the harbor and his broken ship from many of the windows he passed, he could not locate an exit from the castle itself. He dared not tread where the windows disappeared, since they alone guided him. Yet no stairs opened on the corridors he traversed.

Beaten into practicality, he took a preparatory breath and, with one last look at his destination through the nearest window, he headed down the corridor before him. This gallery only led to a circular sitting room at the end, with benches running along the walls and a large, circular mosaic filling the center. After examining the floor art for a minute, the boy turned down the only other passage he had seen off the hallway.

Stubbornness and a touch of timidity kept him from asking any of the people he passed for help. Yet a spiral staircase, sixteen corridors, and countless corners later, Arnacin began to wonder, as he glimpsed another alcove that looked exactly like every other one, if he was now traveling in circles.

With that concern, he turned around, yet could not recall from which passage he had entered the current one. He passed six that seemed to stir his memory, yet in choosing one, he found himself eventually at a tall mirror he knew he had not seen previously.

Feeling just a tiny bit of desperation, he once again turned around and attempted to retrace his steps. Instead of returning to his starting point, however, he found himself staring up at another staircase, wondering if he could return to his original level by using it. Forcing his doubts away, he started the ascent. As it turned into a circular staircase, continuing to climb ever higher, now with thin window slits spaced above his head every five steps, he paused.

“Oy, what are you doing?” someone barked from behind him. He whirled to see an aging man panting up the stairs. “This is my staircase, or don’t you know that?”

“No, I didn’t know that,” Arnacin refuted. The man halted abruptly, his expression turning quizzical.

“What are you?” This was said while the man took another step forward, his groping hand extended toward the boy. It was only then that Arnacin noticed the cloudiness of the man’s eyes.

All the same, as that hand reached up to his face, he slapped it away. “A human, or don’t you know?”

“Ah ha,” the man barked, “but not from around here. I’ve never heard an accent the like of yours, nor the impudence.” Almost mumbling to himself, he continued, “Impudence, impudence… Ha! Not in words… The late king. Oh, the late king.”

“What about him?” Arnacin wondered.

“Mira used to know how to treat those of prophecy,” the man snapped. “We held the seats of councilors, barons, princes.”

With each word said, he grew more hysterical.

“Yet does Miro remember me or ever ask my opinion? Never! The most he does is give me a tower all my own to rot in. Ha! And then he sends impudent youths to bother my stairs.” He paused for a second and then inquired as if realizing something, “Or are you, in fact, lost?”

“Lost?” Arnacin repeated, sliding past the man with all the dignity he could muster while those sightless eyes followed him. “I wouldn’t answer that if I *was* lost.”

And with those words, he dashed back down the stairs to relative safety from hysterical madmen. Any king had a right to disregard that fellow.

Half an hour later, he was wishing he had admitted he was lost. Insane directions were likely better than none at all.

Asking the next person to cross his path–a middle-aged woman in green silk–Arnacin received directions to the harbor. Those took him through a garden courtyard, springing forth in new bloom, briefly into the castle again to the main keep’s doors, and then he was in the inner bailey.

Walls entirely surrounded it. The only entrance was underneath the archway with both its own portcullis and wooden doors beyond that. Both were currently open. Horses walked through with their handlers. Ladies followed with baskets of produce. There was a wheelbarrow full of barrels already in the cobbled bailey where men trailed back and forth carrying the kegs into a side door.

Everywhere the islander glanced, people were busy, chattering happily, as if everything he remembered of the woods were merely a dream. Yet he let that thought slide, hurrying down the steps, across the large cobbles, and into the outer bailey.

This one was grass-filled, though walls encircled it too. It was also quieter despite the same trickle of people coming through the outer gates and entering the inner bailey. Arnacin merely passed them, yet many of their gazes followed him and some even stopped to stare. He yanked his hood up.

Finally, he stood on the pier staring at the remains of his ship, which someone had kindly towed through the open sea walls into harbor while he lay sick.

Looking at it, he hardly knew where to start and, for some time, he simply stood there, holding his cloak closed against the cool air. The ship's mast was cracked and missing, part of the cabin's side had been smashed through, and ropes dangled off everything. Sitting next to the harbor's more elegant occupants, the ship simply looked like a scrapheap.

"I know," someone stated from beside him, laughter in his voice. "That thing is the picture of pathetic. What a graveyard it must've been hauled out of."

Glaring at the sailor, Arnacin snapped, "It wasn't in a graveyard. It is in fact mine, and it has been quite seaworthy for some time."

"Yours?" the sailor repeated, peering beneath the boy's hood. "Everyone—" He broke off, seeming to see something. "Ah, but you are not from this territory, are you?"

"No," the islander whispered, looking again at his ship. Without another word, he leapt from the pier through the hole in his cabin's wall, where the floor was level with the dock. He began opening the remains of his drawers, finding what had been ruined by saltwater and what could be saved. Although the medicine remained in place, water had destroyed everything, from the pastes to the alcohol. Sighing, he placed the damaged items on the stripped bed and moved to the next drawer.

Since he had made the upright chest part of the wall itself and always locked the drawers during storms, all were still intact, yet their contents were beyond repair. Sadly, he pulled out his journal, carefully turning the crumbling, ink-run pages. No longer were there intelligible words or shapes.

Laughter made him look up from the book to see that an audience had gathered on the dock. Sailors stood there, slapping their companions' backs and shaking their heads. Although no words were discernible, the boy knew they were poking fun at him for even trying to save anything off what they considered something only fit to be burned.

Exhaling, Arnacin ignored them and resumed his work. Once all the drawers were empty, he moved to the closed hatch beneath the bed. It was a slight, cheering discovery to find that his bow and arrows were mostly unharmed except for the replaceable bowstring.

Dragging the bow out, he fingered the stained wood. Not since the island had he touched it and his eyes found again, as if they were new, the engraved designs along the tips. Only an islander would recognize those marks for something close to an emblem, their enchantress's name in her native writing. Little would she know, if she even still existed, that most of the islanders, when fiddling with lines or strokes, would find themselves creating her name.

Removing the salt-eaten string, he replaced the bow beneath the bed, just as a shadow fell over him. He jumped to his feet, facing the sailor who stood there. Like the Mirans, he was blond-haired, yet unlike them, his eyes were brown, and he only came to the islander's shoulder despite the thickness of his build.

"What may I do to help?" Pity filled the sailor's tone.

"I didn't ask for help. Nor do I think I need it yet, and not at all from the likes of you." Arnacin nodded to the group on the pier.

"This is quite a job for one person. If you are to make her fit to sail again, she needs some estimating, as well as cleaning. I and my friend, Belo, know how to tally those things up, if you'll allow us."

Although Arnacin wished to say that he could do it himself, he knew it to be a falsehood. Something in the design had failed its builders, he guessed, and he had no idea how to find the flaw or change it.

Smiling slightly, Arnacin nodded. "Thank you, sir. I could use someone's greater knowledge."

Blushing at the title, the sailor shrugged, "It's just Samundro."

Hours later, in the red light of the late sun, everything had been cleared, swept and scrubbed down in order to better see what they were looking at.

"You'll likely have to rip up the deck entirely," Samundro commented as the threesome stared at the splintered stalk of what had been the mast, rising out of the floor. "That's always the best thing to do when replacing a mast. Usually, only portions of the deck are removed, but this flotsam doesn't have enough wood."

Arnacin ignored the insult to the ship, and the sailor continued, "If you remove the planks carefully, they can be reused if they're still good. Your biggest problem that I see is your flat hull."

"Meaning?" the islander wondered.

"Boy, listen to reason. No one builds a flat-bottomed hull. It tips right over in the first storm."

"Is there no way around that?"

Sighing, Samundro pushed his cap farther back on his head while he and his companion shared raised eyebrows. Biting his tongue, Arnacin waited for them to answer.

"Not likely," Samundro said. "As far as I know, every ship with a flat bottom is uncontrollable, floats aimlessly, and then sinks. End of story. Smarter people never take flat-bottomed ships anywhere. Therefore, your largest task is the redesigning of your entire hull."

Arnacin felt like he had been hit. Something of what he was feeling must have shown, as the sailor clapped him on the shoulder.

"Sorry to upset you. I have one suggestion. Find some sort of plan for a properly built ship."

Exasperatedly, the islander watched them leave before swinging a kick at the remains of the mast.

Arnacin's room was located in what the servants called the "elevated corridor." The cooks told him the main hallways were designated for servants, nobility not directly related to the royal family, and then the elevated, or in other words, the knights.

These rooms were located before the servants' corridor and after the nobles', since they were neither one nor the other some said. Unlike the rooms belonging to the servants, the elevated rooms were spacious, if unadorned–their furnishings sparse, yet fine.

In answer to why he was placed there, they said, "That's where the physicians want all charity cases receiving our hospitality. Your only difference is we can't send you home in a week or two."

This information came from the kitchens, located deep beneath the southwestern tower. There, smoke and steam vented through undetectable holes in the high vaulted ceiling–the reason for the pleasant aromas and constant haze to the south of the capital.

Having received permission long before Arnacin found the kitchens, the head cook insisted that he try everything. Every time she passed, she placed a new morsel before him, pronouncing him the best-mannered boy she had ever met because of his soft thanks, questions and, undoubtedly, his honest compliments of her cooking.

Beaming, she would tell him of all the places their food and recipes originated, since they were such a large trade center. It made Mira's banquets the finest and most varied in the world.

Arnacin only smiled. Though he could not argue with the varied part, he remembered the excellent feasts back home, including the fisherman's seaweed cakes that routinely took the villagers by surprise. That thought would always feed his restlessness while he struggled to find something to help with his ship repairs.

Therefore, sitting in one corridor's window, Arnacin strove to salvage as much as he could of his journal's useful tidbits. Hearing footsteps nearing, he hastily stuffed his charcoal stick and journal out of sight. Laughter told him the movement had not gone unnoticed and he looked up to see Lord Carpason's broad grin.

"Well, well... Secrets, is it?" the noble chuckled. "Perhaps we should worry about spies."

"Spies?" Arnacin repeated, innocently. "Where would I be finding my information?"

"The kitchens, perhaps," Carpason commented, resting his foot on the window's sloped sill and leaning against his knee. "The right question is: what do you have to hide if you are as much a nothing from nowhere as you claim?"

Meeting that gaze—now only inches from him—Arnacin said, "I am a no one, and I prefer to stay that way. My home is afraid of foreigners knowing about them."

Studying him, the lord wondered, "Is that title serious, by any chance?"

"What title?"

"Enchantress Island?"

Quickly looking down, Arnacin bit his lip. Carpason, however, did not seem to be fooled. In the silence that stretched between them, the islander looked back up nervously to realize that the lord was appraising him warily.

"Your sister, a girl, is deadly, you say," Carpason finally mused aloud. "And you know nothing of the sea, yet you sail. Still, you're all shepherds. Are you magical, Arnacin son of Bozzic?"

Smiling in amusement, Arnacin jerked his head slightly. "No."

"Are you ruled by a sorcerer, then?"

"Not anymore," the islander admitted, his words just as soft as the noble's question.

"Anymore? What happened?"

"They perished in an earthquake."

"They?" Carpason's tone was one of shock. "Yet your kind survived?"

"It wasn't a normal earthquake," Arnacin added, shifting now in discomfort.

"I should say not. Who conjured that miracle?"

"As far as anyone knows, they did. I wasn't born then." True as this was, it was a lame attempt to escape the questioning, but the lord did not press further.

It seemed hours before Carpason shook his head, sighing, "You're more mythical than I first imagined, Arnacin. Perhaps I can understand your secrecy. Most would put you in the place of a god or kill you for dealing in sorcery."

His mouth dry, Arnacin breathed, "And you?"

"Me?" Carpason shrugged. "Frankly, I'm stunned beyond thought. I was under the impression all my life that those things simply did not exist, that everything could be explained with—a friend would say 'sight.' Since your arrival, you have been testing all I thought I knew. Be that as it may," he said briskly, straightening, "it appears you are helpless to become seaworthy once again."

"How did you guess?" Arnacin grumbled.

"I have contacts in the city, as well as outside of it. They've doomed your vessel. So it is my guess you are trying to decide whether to ask around until you can find out how they make their ships so you can start over again, or you are thinking of finding passage to take you home. However, after our conversation, I had better cross off my second guess."

"You better cross off your first guess, as well," Arnacin laughed. "I am too fond of my ship to let it burn so easily. I just don't know how I can help fix its... imperfection."

"What exactly is the problem?"

"According to the sailors, no one sails a flat-bottomed ship without sinking." The islander's gaze went to the harbor where his ship rocked on the swells. He shrugged. "Yet it took me here in one piece through five storms. Only on the last one did it fail."

"That it did." Carpason nodded, his gaze also drifting to the harbor. "Well, I don't know anything about the craft, personally. However, I do know they're not completely correct. No one *now* sails a flat-bottomed ship without sinking, yet those of us who have had to sit through dry history and war strategy lectures as boys know that Mira was first colonized by sailors of flat-bottomed ships. We also know that this castle holds all the histories, journals and plans of that time in its chambers."

As Arnacin's eyes lit up, the lord grinned. "Come, I've been given permission to show you, now that I have once again made sure you are not a foreign spy." The last was said with a smile and the islander returned the look of humor.

Arnacin followed Carpason along passages very much alike to every other one. Yet then, they came to a series of wooden doors segmenting the corridors. The islander counted three such doorways and then abruptly the hallway widened. Open to the air, high windows lined the passage to Arnacin's left, yet the flagstones lacked the weathered look of the window sills. Out of those fissures, he could see the hazy outline of mountains in the distance.

His gaze was so captured by the view outside that he jumped when Carpason directed his attention to a pair of strong doors they were passing on their right. "Beware those doors, Arnacin. Only immediate relatives of the royal family and their personal attendants may pass through those without meeting death. It is their living space, and even I have never been beyond those doors."

Looking back over his shoulder at the doors that had gained an ominous air, the islander nodded. Nothing more was said about them, and he dared not ask if the lord even knew more.

The end of the corridor, however, stopped at two immense, carved double doors, the likes of which Arnacin could well picture guarding a treasure house. Oddly, as Carpason opened one door, it did not groan as the islander thought for sure it would, but instead swung with ease, revealing a dark expanse.

Stepping just inside, the lord lit the lanterns hanging there, and Arnacin inhaled sharply as the void took shape before them, filled only with shelves upon shelves of parchment receding away from them into the darkness. Light allowed sight of the domed roof far above them, and the islander bumped into the wall behind him trying to follow the shelves upward with his gaze.

Beside him, Carpason chuckled, handing the islander a third lantern. "Be careful. If I judge your character rightly, I have the feeling you will become far more lost in here than anywhere else in the castle."

As he started to leave, Arnacin mentioned, "This seems quite a bit of information to reveal to someone you question as a spy."

Halting, the lord appraised the boy. "Honestly, Arnacin, did I not tell you I have contacts in and outside this castle and even through the rest of Mira? Considering your hair color, there is nothing you could do that I would not know."

"So I'm watched," the islander whispered, feeling suddenly very alone indeed.

Clapping the boy on the shoulder, Carpason admitted, "If I could let my heart rule my head, Arnacin, there is no one I would trust more. I would sooner trust you than myself. You have something about you... But I am a war general, and so reason tells me I cannot take such a chance." With a comforting smile, he departed, leaving the islander to wander the cavernous room alone.

Despite returning several times, Arnacin found that the library had little to offer him. Mira's linear marks were entirely different from the island's alphabet of curving letters, even if they did speak the same language. His only hope was to find one of the plans of an original Miran ship and then make sense of it without the aid of words. Therefore, he continued his pursuit.

It was on the third day of combing the library that Arnacin stumbled upon someone else. A young lady sat huddled in a corner. Atop the desk beside her, a small candle cast its slight glow upon the book covertly hidden between her up-drawn knees. Leaning against the bookcase, Arnacin laughed inwardly at her obvious attempt to hide.

Then, slowly, her red head lifted. They stared at one another for a split second without reaction and then her pale blue eyes widened and she slammed her book shut, hastily pushing herself into a more ladylike position.

Laughing aloud, Arnacin folded his arms. Before him, the girl's expression began to change from annoyance to puzzlement. For his part, the islander let her stare, while he in turn used the time to fully appraise her. She was about the age of his sister, he guessed, though her softer features and wider eyes made her seem even younger. Her slender, pale fingers, which gripped her book, looked like they had known little work and less sun, as did the rest of her. He could see the edges of three other skirts peeking beneath her heavy and bejeweled dress. Adding to his guess that she was more than any plain castle occupant, someone had carefully threaded pearls through the gently-restrained auburn hair that fell down her shoulders.

"I thought you might reprimand me for reading," the girl said finally. "But you can't, can you? You're dark-haired."

Ignoring another exasperating comment about his dark hair, Arnacin wondered, "Why should I ridicule you for reading?" He could not quite remove the laughter he knew showed on his face.

Pursing her lips in a coy smile, she shrugged, reopening her book as she said in a rush, "I knew someone would agree with me someday." Her voice grew slightly distant, if not slower, as her eyes once again skimmed a page. "Everyone around here says it is uncouth for a noble to read as a hobby and uncivilized for a girl to read at all, much less to read stories."

Imagining his sister's expression if she heard words like those, the islander felt his laughter rise into his throat. Though he did his best to restrain it, he only succeeded in making it sound as if he was choking. This seemed to make the girl feel that she needed to defend herself, though she did so with an open smile.

"I think of it as a vacation, soothing all types of hurts, but I always must do it in the dark, so no one knows. My nurse, Sara, says it's a bad habit I picked up when mother died." Arnacin dropped his gaze in understanding and she continued, "I only started to read–well, Mother begged Father to teach me to read, which he did while he would work on–" She glanced more guardedly at the boy before her and then, her voice smoothing, she shrugged.

"I started reading stories after she died, but now, even Father couldn't order me to stop. You won't tell, will you?"

Slowly, Arnacin shook his head, still smiling as the girl dived back behind her book. A moment later, however, she looked up, her face flushed bright red. "Father would kill me if he knew I forgot all my court training in favor of a story." Regally, she rose, extending her free hand as she introduced herself with a new air in her tone. "I'm Princess Valoretta of Mira. Whom do I address and from what place where the hair is black?"

The fact that she was princess came as no surprise and, politely, Arnacin took the tips of her fingers, shaking them slightly. He turned red as she laughed, "I see I had nothing to worry about. You know nothing." Seeming to recognize the angry flush in his cheeks, she stumbled, "I mean... of course, in the matters of court. I'm sure you know plenty of things in reality..."

As she reddened herself, Arnacin felt his smile return in slight apology. With a relieved grin she pressed, "But who are you?"

"Arnacin," the islander replied simply in his open and yet least informative way. "I'm stuck on this... island, continent, whatever it is, until I can fix my ship."

"It's a continent," the princess supplied. "You still haven't said where you're from. Certainly, you're not from around here. Even the savages possess lighter hair."

Finally conceding, Arnacin admitted, "Enchantress Island. We're not all dark-haired, although..." He paused to consider the truth of his thoughts. "I suppose most of us are, now that I think about it."

"I've never heard of it," she mused, "but then, I've never heard of anyone with your coloring." Even this did not seem to appease her curiosity and she asked, "Who is your king, that you don't know court etiquette?"

"We proudly proclaim independency there."

"How strange! Are you then savages?" Before he could reply to this seemingly odd question, she remarked musingly, "But no, even they have chosen leaders. How does such a system work?"

Arnacin shrugged, averting his gaze from her questioning eyes. Regardless, the princess pressed on with the conversation.

"Well then, just to say I have not slacked in my duties, Arnacin of Enchantress Island, for your own sake, if a noble lady ever holds out her hand to you again, take it lightly and bow, at least slightly. Always bow to any noble, actually, at entrance and exit." Quickly she added, "Don't do it to me, though. I would prefer a change. Do I need to tell you the proper titles to use when addressing a noble?"

Arnacin shook his head and, as she started to add something, he finished for her with a smile, "But don't use them on you."

"Exactly." She grinned back. "And never finish for a noble either. They think it's impudence."

"Then I'll do it always," Arnacin said, already hating the sound of courtly customs, "simply to aggravate them."

Laughing, the princess slapped him across the arm and then froze, her face whitening. "I'm sorry. I've been too open with you. Don't think anything of it, please."

Soothingly, the islander shook his head, saying, "I prefer openness. It speaks from the heart."

Embarrassment flushed Valoretta's cheeks as, swaying from side-to-side, she muttered, "Do you mind if I return to my book now?"

Guessing she was acting completely outside of her training, Arnacin grinned, shaking his head. As she hastily dropped behind her book, he slipped off into the corridors of laden shelves.

Carpason departed early the next morning, the one person with whom the islander felt comfortable enough to ask about Mira's alphabet. Not able to surrender, however, Arnacin simply returned to the library. After all, codes were unraveled through vowels. What was so different about Mira's characters?

The islander did not know how long he tried, striving to make sense out of the tallies with long lines drawn across groups of them, before he found himself only flipping through random, usually smaller, books.

One thin book had drawings throughout it that caught his attention. Most of the illustrations were of people acting in very peculiar manners, like the man in a handstand with his head in a small hole. One illustration was of a lady washing clothes in a cauldron; yet dark shapes seemed to be rising out of it with the steam. Although he could not decide whether it was just places where the ink had run, a shiver ran down his spine.

He could not pull his attention away, however, until another light penetrated the darkness around him. Startling, he slammed the book closed as someone passed the other end of the row he occupied. A low gasp told him that he was not the only one to jump. At the end of the row, the princess Valoretta unfroze, exhaling in relief.

"Arnacin of Enchantress Island," she breathed, approaching. Spotting the book he held, she halted midstep, asking, "You're not reading that, are you?"

Turning the cover back to look at the unreadable title, the islander wondered, "What is it?"

"Don't you know? I thought, you being here, you surely knew how to read."

"I do," Arnacin stated flatly, his cheeks once again burning. "Your characters are completely different from mine."

"But how can that be? We speak the same language."

Cocking his head and raising his eyebrows, Arnacin remarked, "Yes, I could ask the same."

A humble smile brushed the girl's face as she conceded, "We're from different lands."

"So, what am I supposedly reading?"

"*Savage Superstitions*. Is that interesting to you?"

"Does that mean uncouth superstitions or those of your natives?"

"Our attackers' superstitions, of course. That book is only a few years old. I forget the writer's name, but he found out as much as he could of their beliefs in the hope that we could use it to manipulate the war to our end."

"It hasn't worked, has it?"

"No," Valoretta answered, exhaling in defeat. Looking back at him, she redirected the conversation. "So, if you cannot read our writing, what brings you here?"

Sighing himself, Arnacin shoved the book back on the shelf. "I'm stuck here until I can fix my ship and, although your father apparently granted me the use of your records, my ship is flat-bottomed."

He left the rest unsaid, figuring the princess could finish it herself, but her face was blank with a lack of understanding. Facing her, the islander explained, "The secret to crafting flat-bottomed ships is lost in your past, I'm told, and I never really knew the secret, so I was pointed in this direction."

Light dawned in Valoretta's eyes and she nodded. "You want to find our ship diagrams and descriptions from those days." Hopelessly, the islander nodded. Her next words made him start as much as her sudden presence had before. "Well then, I'll simply need to teach you."

"Your nurse complains at you simply entering here–"

"Arnacin of Enchantress Island," the girl said regally. "Father agreed to support your departure. Therefore, Mira supports you. I am Mira, as much as he, so it is my responsibility to aid you in this dilemma."

Smiling, Arnacin shook his head. "Very well, My Lady. Your help is accepted."

Teasingly, the princess laughed, "For your own sake, that's good, but you didn't have a choice."

The first thing the princess did was lead Arnacin to where their historical documents housed the ship designs. There, they went over the drawings. Valoretta read the notes for the islander and, where she did not understand the terminology, Arnacin pointed out the parts of the ship. Unfortunately, those documents alone did not tell him what he needed to know, so they moved on to the histories of the first journey to Mira. This meant the islander simply listened to the fragments the princess read.

It was agonizingly tedious. As Valoretta muttered, "This would be a lot faster if you knew how to read."

Arnacin did not bother to correct her, sliding down in the chair and dropping the last unreadable book she had passed him over his face.

"Arnacin, *listen*," the princess insisted. "I'll summarize this for you. Before they founded Mira, our ancestors decided to escape their homeland, Carta, because the government... um, how do I condense this? Random people would suddenly be grabbed as slaves. The rations were terrible. No one was allowed to come or go. The government spied on everyone, so when these twenty men decided to escape with their families, they chose to make a ship that didn't look like a ship, or at least, what everyone expected of a ship. Therefore, they were able to hide it better."

"Is this supposed to help?" Arnacin asked, straightening again and resting his chin in his hand.

Valoretta shrugged. "This one's all very vague, actually. I'm trying to see if it will go into more detail."

Groaning, the islander again slipped down.

The next day found them sitting at one of the library tables, a list they had written of both lands' alphabets before them. Rubbing her hand over her forehead, Valoretta sighed, "There's nothing in common. I can't make any sense at all of yours. In the first place, you only have twenty-seven characters out of thirty."

For the past hour, Arnacin had simply watched her hopelessly scrutinizing the list, a knowing smirk on his face. Now, however, he leaned forward, stating, "There's nothing in common with the shapes, but we're speaking to each other."

Slowly, Valoretta looked up at him, her face blank. Laughing, the islander finished, "What sounds does each of your characters represent? Don't they represent the same things mine do?"

Throwing a book at him, she exclaimed, "You've been sitting here the whole time with the answer!"

Mischievously, Arnacin shrugged.

Within thirty minutes, they had the two alphabets translated into each other, although the books with the information Arnacin needed were written in still another language. Not ready to go into that subject yet, Arnacin practiced with Mira's modern sea poetry, while Valoretta hunted for translations of their histories.

Arnacin woke early the next morning and returned to the hall of books. Valoretta had finally located one modern translation of some portions of Miran history before she needed to rush off the evening before. Finding a seat, the islander found the place he had left off in the book and dove back in. He might not have been learning what he needed, but he found it fascinating all the same.

Some hours later, he looked up, hearing the door open. Valoretta rushed in at that moment, slamming the door behind her, and briefly rested her back against it. Before Arnacin could ask anything about her behavior, she dashed over and dropped down on the floor beside him, hiding against his chair.

"Sara wants to know where I've been," the princess panted, looking up at him. "If someone comes in, hopefully I'm well hidden here."

"Why not wait until a couple of days later, if you can't stay?" Arnacin wondered, trying to discreetly brush her auburn waves off his leg.

"Keep reading," Valoretta ordered. "I'll tell you why. I found a book that will probably help, as it documents the first attempts at leaving Carta. There is no translation, so if you are serious about leaving within a reasonable amount of time, you'll have to learn our older language quickly."

Taking his gaze off the pages to give her a sideways look, Arnacin teased, "How are you going to help from down there?"

In answer, she smacked the back of her head into his arm. "I'm only staying here long enough to translate important nouns for you to study. After that, Sara will probably be in here to look for me, and I want to be gone before she gets here."

Smirking at the back of her head, the islander returned to his book without comment. Within a few minutes, the only sound was the scratching of Valoretta's pen on the piece of parchment she held pressed against her knees.

Two hours later, a soft gasp of pain emitted from the princess as she shifted against Arnacin's leg. "Finished?" the islander inquired.

"For now," Valoretta nodded, wincing as she slowly pushed herself up. "If I don't leave now, Sara is bound to discover I'm gone. Until tomorrow, you can study those."

Arnacin shrugged, "If you wish."

"I wish." The princess' words were a groan as she took one hobbling step and had to catch herself on the chair.

Watching her, Arnacin inquired, "Would you like some help?"

"No." So saying, Valoretta regally pushed herself away from him, straightened, and promptly landed on the floor.

Stifling his amusement, the islander turned back to his book, stating unconcernedly, "If you're sure."

"I changed my mind," the princess laughed hopelessly, holding out her arm. "I would appreciate your help, son of Bozzic, if you will give it."

"Oh, no," Arnacin teased wickedly. "I agree with your first statement. You don't need my help."

"Arnacin," Valoretta moaned through her teeth half in exasperation and half in amusement. Putting his book down, the islander arose and helped the girl to her feet. As she slipped her arm over his shoulder, she admitted, "I could likely crawl to the hall myself, but if I want to save any dignity..." She left the rest hanging.

Taking up the slack, Arnacin joked as they began stumbling toward the doors, "If that's what your dignity's based on, I should just leave you to lose it."

"You really don't believe in thinking normally, do you?"

"Why should I? If everyone thinks it, nothing's unique."

Missing his teasing tone, the princess exclaimed, "Oh, so you worry about being unique?"

Laughing outright now, the islander shook his head. "I just don't worry about my dignity."

Her laughter joined his as they pushed open one door and hobbled through, right into a smallish woman quickly approaching. They froze in surprise and the woman shrieked. Arnacin instantly dropped his arm from around the princess' waist, feeling her stiffen beside him.

The woman was the first to break the silence with a reproachful gasp, "My Lady!"

"Sara," Valoretta inclined. "Arnacin has been nice enough to offer his assistance."

"You... you've been reading in front of a stranger."

"She actually wasn't reading," Arnacin muttered, feeling his cheeks warm.

"That is not the point. My Lady, do you know nothing of proper conduct?"

"Do you, Sara?" Valoretta intoned. "Do not forget, you stand before a foreigner, chastising royalty."

It was the nurse's turn to redden. Curtsying, she turned away—but not without a last, lethal glance toward the islander. Only as Sara's back vanished around the corner did Arnacin inquire, "Why is it such a problem that you read?"

Looking at him, Valoretta turned along the corridor. "I'm not just a princess, Arnacin. I'm the heir and future queen of Mira. It makes the crime even greater, from Sara's viewpoint."

"Should that not make it detrimental for you to be unlearned?" the islander asked in quiet astonishment.

"In Mira, Arnacin," the princess recited, "traditionally queens are important, and not just for the children they bear." She exhaled. "Apart from that simple fact, we are no different from any other kingdom. A fair-complexioned, idle queen means that Mira is strong and powerful, that its nobles can simply take life at ease. A queen that toils in any form or publicly works her own mind is the sign of a crumbling kingdom, one where anyone can swoop in and take over. Therefore, queens have long done little to nothing, not even raise their own children. Hence, Sara."

A brief pause followed before her voice rose in pride. Throwing back her head, she scoffed, "But I will not be a puppet queen. I will accept the authority granted me and lead my people to their best advantage. So let the wars rage when I become queen. Let the world throw itself on spears if it's stupid enough to defy my authority and scoff at my intelligence. I shall end that vision of queens. That, I vow."

Turning aside with a distant smile, Arnacin's thoughts fled the castle.

Apparently noticing, Valoretta snapped, "I'm deadly serious, Arnacin. Mira is mine and it needs my intelligence. Even if it didn't, I could not live without more meaning than I ever saw in Mother's life. I want to know—I must know—that the world needs me."

The islander turned back to her. "I wasn't laughing at you." As they continued walking aimlessly, he told her of his sister, of whom the princess' last words had reminded him. He told her of his brother and mother, and of how his father's death had devastated him.

And he didn't stop there. Strangely, he even found himself sharing how he had searched for hope and a light that had not appeared in his home until the thought of high seas adventures had returned some life to him.

Valoretta's understanding lay in the hand she had slipped inside his as they strolled the corridor.

Chapter 3

The King of Mira

Days passed while the outside world almost disappeared. Arnacin spent all his time in the library, searching, studying and sometimes even sleeping there, for he intended to be on his way home by spring at the latest. Only Valoretta kept him in touch with reality while she continued to help him read through informational tomes written in Mira's ancient language. Even when he did not need her, she would sit beside or across from him reading her own interests, which, to Arnacin's amusement, grew increasingly to be the same things he would read.

"Arnacin?" Valoretta wondered, looking up from the book she was reading when she wasn't helping the islander decipher the book of Mira's beginnings. "You said your sister is the best tracker on the island. Didn't the villagers have a problem with a girl being a tracker? Was your family considered odd or even crazed?"

"I expect the villagers did," Arnacin admitted with a shrug as his mind drifted back home. "I remember..."

He paused, but the princess leaned closer in a silent request for him to continue. Grinning, he obliged. "When I was eight, there was this red spruce tree, two trees grown together actually. At their base, before they connected, they formed a little tunnel of sorts, an archway into the ground and, when the sun set, its light would strike one side of that arch, casting part in shadow and making the rest glow, dark brown on one side and lit red on the other.

"I liked to stare at it sometimes and to imagine how a tiny dragon slept beneath that arch, waking at sunset. And as it rose from beneath the leaves, its fire would waken with it, burning the underside of the tree with its colors, red-hot yellow and dancing russet. That was my wild imagination, anyhow... but we, boys around my age or so, were playing in the spruces at sunset, and one of them asked me what I was looking at as I watched that little archway begin to glow and thought about my dragon.

"So I told them, and one thing led to another in this... tale. Our legends of dragons as beings of evil merged with my little dragon and I found in this story that the dragon grew out of the village's greed and concealed itself as the small thing it started from during the day. When nothing changed in the village after many years, it reached the size of its forefathers. By night, as the sky darkened around us in reality, it woke with that light beneath the tree arch. Crawling out, it spread its black wings, creeping and crawling up the tree. As it did, however, it kept growing as if a snake was stretching. Once it reached its full size, it attacked and burned down the village, slaughtering and devouring everyone—all due to their greed."

Arnacin paused in his tale, remembering those days, but then, apologetically, he shrugged. "The next thing I knew, women kept pounding on our door, telling Mother that I had given their sons nightmares, and that they couldn't sleep and were too afraid to enter the woods. Some of them said I possessed a sick mind and that they wouldn't allow their children to associate with me anymore. For a week, it continued to worsen. Parents whispered about how Mother and Father didn't raise us right, about how Charlotte was sure to grow up even more demented than I since she helped Father with bow-making among other things.

"Finally, it died off and I continued to play with those boys, but I'm not sure the gossip ever completely ended. I sometimes overheard whispers about how we had to be part enchanter ourselves, owning bad blood, as they liked to say—"

"Wait," the princess interrupted. "Are enchanters bad and only enchantresses good? After all, your island is named after an enchantress."

Laughing slightly, Arnacin shook his head. Remembering Carpason's warning, however, he said as truthfully as possible, "My home's named after our legends, which are as old as the island itself, particularly the one about the enchantress who survived when evil was destroyed. In all our legends, though, enchanters, dragons and the like are evil. The enchantress was just of a different make."

Nodding, Valoretta asked, "So, despite the villagers' whispers, you were accepted?"

"I suppose it didn't matter too much as I grew. I had friends, like Raymond and Tevin—I wasn't too odd. Little by little, I was looked at as more common, and just another boy with my own set of flaws and strengths. Charlotte was never accepted, though. She never became their expectation of a young lady, and so was often ousted from the rest of the village. I only hope it didn't destroy her as it sometimes appeared it might, but I don't know."

As he trailed off in thought, Valoretta asked, "Did she not love her family, at least?"

"She loved us," Arnacin stated, "but it seemed at times that was all she loved. She could say the darkest things when certain subjects rose. Not that any of us could really blame her, but... well, she didn't even enjoy the things common girls did—at least not most of the time. She liked to sew with us when it was a family thing, but otherwise thought it a bore, and the rest of many girls' interests were simply scorned by her." The islander shrugged, "I don't do her any justice..."

"I think you do, though you might not know it," the princess whispered. "It's both tiring and hate-spawning to have people trying to force you into an ideal of what they think you should be like, what you should do, how you should dress, what you should enjoy... The list can just go on, but we don't fit it. Sometimes, we don't fit any of it and, when that is the case, they try to kill our spirit." Looking back down at her book, the princess whispered, "I know. I think I could easily like your sister if we ever met."

Smiling bittersweetly as he thought of his sister's reclusiveness, Arnacin knew friendship with Valoretta would unhappily be harder than it appeared. The laughter he had heard emit from his sister last they spoke seemed to ring in the corners of the room and, sadly, he returned to his own book.

Valoretta was not done probing however. After a moment of silence, she asked, "What is your extended family like?"

"Extended family?" Arnacin distantly repeated, slowly pulling his focus away from Mira's records of the first flat-bottomed ships.

"I was asking about your extended family. Do you have any cousins?"

Marking his place, he closed his book to give her his full attention. "Well, not any that I'm extremely close to. On my mother's side, there were no other siblings, and..." He shrugged, turning back to his book.

"No, tell me, please," Valoretta begged. Meeting those blue eyes, Arnacin recognized the hope for freedom in them—the freedom brought by tales of worlds nothing like one's own.

Conceding, he started, "My grandfather—when he still lived—was a carpenter. I never met him, but Father's favorite story about him was how he waited until his son was married to reveal that he possessed plans to a ship."

As the princess laughed appreciatively, Arnacin continued, "Anyway, Father had one brother, who, despite being the younger, inherited the carpentry work because of Mother's sheep. I heard that he raised a very successful family while he lived, with four children, only one of which was a boy."

"You say that like you don't know. But wouldn't those be your cousins?"

"Technically, yes, but I'm fifteen years younger than my first cousin once removed. That gives you an idea of how close we are, not to mention how my remaining cousins all moved after they married. They left their father's work to their brother, naturally, and found husbands in other villages."

"What happened to his family then, unless you're saying he didn't marry?"

"Oh, no, he married and had a son as well, but when their son was only two..."

He once again stopped, but Valoretta finished for him. "They died?"

"Falling logs killed both parents in a timber accident, but that was the last of the carpenters in our family. One of the boy's aunts took him to live with her in another village, since she was closer of kin. He didn't come back either. Last I knew, he aspired to be a potter, of all the boring tasks–" Valoretta's laugher cut him off and he grinned back at her, knowing what she must be thinking.

"Yes, the *shepherd* says it's boring," he conceded. "Sheep have personality. There's none in whirring a wheel around until it makes you sick."

Returning to the point, the princess pressed, "And did he not marry? What about your remaining cousins, who you said married, and illegitimate relatives?"

"What type of relatives?" Arnacin wondered.

"You never have those?" Valoretta's tone was both curious and bashful. "My only extended relative that I can honestly say I know about is illegitimate, which means his parents weren't married when he was born. For that matter, they never were." She turned bright red as Arnacin simply continued staring at her. "Well," she shrugged, "my great aunt was banished for... being found pregnant when she was not wed. When it was discovered that her companion was a foreign squire, his master had him beheaded."

Arnacin stared at the princess in speechlessness. Then, deciding not to comment at all, he threw his book back open and attempted to resume reading, yet his concentration had been ruined and after three seconds he looked back up at the princess in annoyance.

"They banished her and executed him?" he finally repeated. "One crime wasn't worse than the other."

Sighing, Valoretta dropped her gaze to her fingers, entwined in her skirt. She shrugged. "The same people didn't invent the penalty. The squire's master alone was responsible for his servant's punishment."

"Is that all he was to whatever type of brute *the master* was—a servant?"

"I don't know, Arnacin, but I do know politics dictated some sort of like response." At his incredulous gaze, Valoretta patiently explained, "He was a foreign lord with a servant who had just dared to tarnish nobility. War could ensue instantly over such an occurrence unless he made the squire pay the price and, even then, everyone would be pacing for months afterward, waiting to see if Mira's wrath had been aptly appeased. Moreover, he was responsible for his servant's actions, so..."

"If so, he should have *taken* responsibility," Arnacin snapped, causing Valoretta to regard him strangely.

"He did. That's why he had the squire beheaded."

"No, that's shifting responsibility, and it's cowardice—pure cowardice. If someone under your charge does something wrong, you must pay the penalty, and you alone."

"In other words, you think he, a noble himself, should have been beheaded? That could start a larger war and certainly would never solve anything, since he wasn't the one to commit the crime in the first place."

So the argument went until Arnacin said, "Then you should have made it abundantly clear that you had no intention of going to war over the crime from the start. Otherwise, their fear of your attack aided their murder."

Opening her mouth, Valoretta just as quickly shut it. Coolly, Arnacin retrieved his book, burying himself behind it. He could feel her watching him, but he did not look up to read her expression.

"Sire." Carpason bowed upon entering the great hall, which was adorned in gold, blue lapis and opal.

The king stood beside the windows. Miro would stand out in any crowd of Mirans. Both wisdom and age shone in his pale blue eyes, his bearded jawline spoke of his determination, and his powerful shoulders revealed his past on the field, still maintained after all the years on the throne. He was no spoiled, flabby, bejeweled monarch. The only ring he even wore was the signet, the crane with its piercing ruby eye. Miro was a king who could still defend his people.

"Our armies are returning in pitiful numbers, Lord Carpason," the king warned, still watching the lines of soldiers pouring through the gates.

Sighing, the lord confessed, "The savages' ambushes are picking us off with absurd ease. Unless we find some exceptional new soldiers or many new reinforcements, we're going to run out of men before next summer."

"There are no more men to spare," Miro sighed resignedly. "All the other nobles' estates have been deserted and their men sent out. Now, only this city's guards remain exempt from being sent onto the battlefield."

"No," Carpason sadly agreed. "We would not want to see this citadel razed as all the rest." His gaze went to the harbor as his thoughts traveled there. "It may be time to evacuate, Sire."

"We cannot, and you know it." Miro's reply was a low growl. "Should we lose face to other kingdoms, they will rip us apart as quickly–and more effectively–than any savage."

The lord slowly exhaled, refusing to say the words of defeat on his tongue. They were dead without a miracle. It was as this thought took him that the small, broken ship in the harbor caught his attention and he thought again of the dark-haired stranger.

"There is someone I think could help, at least," he mused aloud and the king turned to him in surprise. "Have you met Arnacin, son of Bozzic, yet?"

"Who?"

"The boy you gave permission to stay until his ship is fit again."

"Ah, the one my daughter likes to talk to in the library. Yes, Sara has complained that he encourages her bad habits and that I should evict him." He was quiet a moment, a slight smile on his face. Looking up, he demanded, "What help could he be, a boy so innocent he would seem younger than three-quarters of the squires and knowing not a tenth of what they do. To send him out would be slaughter and would serve nothing."

"We may be surprised, Sire. I have not spoken of this, but he rescued me in an ambush single-handedly, and he possesses all the raw, undeveloped skill of a mythical hero."

"He's a foreigner," Miro insisted obstinately.

"Then ask him if he will. I remember him as fairly obliging."

"Very well," the king snapped. "Bring your sailor here and I will ask him." Bowing, Carpason went to find Arnacin of Enchantress Island.

When Carpason stepped aboard Arnacin's vessel, the islander lay on his stomach with several diagrams spread out before him, a piece of blank vellum under his elbows. Not a scratch marked the hide, however.

For a moment, the noble simply took in the calm sight, with the healthy-looking boy in the midst of the wrecked ship, a gentle breeze rippling through cloth, hair and the parchment held down by rocks.

"Well, is this the same boy from a month ago?" Carpason teased, causing Arnacin to jump. "Except for your black, unruly curls, which no one else I know could possibly own, I would doubt it."

Grinning, Arnacin said, "I thought you were still away in the war zone."

"We return once a week for supplies, rest and to report, unless hindered. There is no communication while we are out there, so our comings and goings are very necessary. At this point, we would be annihilated if we stayed out longer." Nodding to the parchment, he changed topics, "I see you are already at work."

"Not really," the islander admitted. "I've cleaned a little bit and emptied all the ruined supplies. Other than that, I've just been reading–what I could anyway. I can't read much of your alphabet."

"We do have several languages in that library and more variations on our alphabet besides. I see you mostly picked diagrams for your research."

"For now," Arnacin admitted. "Someone's been helping me work through the rest."

Carpason quickly hid his knowing smile, imagining the uproar that tidbit about the princess would create if it became known. Apparently, the boy also had some idea of the unseemliness of it since he had simply brushed over names. Instead, the lord sincerely apologized, "I'm sorry I can't help. As I said, I know nothing of this skill."

The islander laughed. "Until a year ago, neither did I. Even now, I'm still learning." He nodded to the diagrams. "That's where the research comes in. Something went wrong when we built it at first, and I think it's the balance. I need to figure out where before I can even begin to start rebuilding."

Shaking his head, the lord replied, "I see you are more reckless than I realized. Most men don't become captains of their own ships within a year of plying their trade." Arnacin did not reply, simply dropping his gaze back to his work, and Carpason informed the boy, "The king has requested to see you."

At the look of concern that passed over the islander's face, the lord hastened to soothe him, "It's nothing you've done, I assure you."

Sighing, Arnacin rolled up his work and deposited it in his cabin before following the noble back into the castle. Moments later, king and islander met for the first time.

As the lord and boy entered the splendid hall where the king awaited them, they bowed. Straightening, Arnacin met the king's assessing gaze and withdrew his own. Slowly, Miro circled him. It was with a nervous pulse that the boy stood there, unmoving, mentally ticking off the firm, purposeful footsteps.

Finally, the king stopped in front of Arnacin, stating briskly, "We have no more men to rely on. I would not make such a request of a foreigner if there were any other choice, yet even if you aided inside the castle to free another man from his binding duties, there are no able-bodied men to send onto the field, other than you, apparently, and our guards.

"Arnacin, son of Bozzic from Enchantress Island, Mira makes the request of you to aid its side until the war ends, foreigner though you are. In repayment for your aid, it will provide the gold for repairs and supplies for your ship. Will you do so?"

Licking his suddenly dry lips, Arnacin could not think of an answer. A small part of him whispered that not only did he owe it to them, it was likely that if they fell, he would also perish, but... "I know nothing of war, Your Majesty," he finally forced out.

"Yet you would say you possess skill in such areas?" the king inquired.

"If I did, it could not be trusted as anything but pride speaking."

With a slight quirk of his lips, the king replied, "I am told that you do by authorities I trust in this matter. You will pick it up swiftly enough."

"My skills are not enough to end your war for you, Your Majesty."

"My Lord Carpason appears to think you will change something, heaven knows what. I have learned to trust his feelings."

The king said no more, seeming to await the answer. Only one response could come, the boy knew. In spite of himself, he knew that he feared the answer–that the horrors he had witnessed in battle would only be repeated should he agree–the sight of blood dripping from blades and pouring from figures on the ground, of hate-filled faces, and of the sightless eyes of the dead.

Finally, he asked, "May I ponder my answer for another day?"

Tapping his fingers together, the king contemplated Arnacin for another second. Then he waved his consent, and the islander departed.

"You know what that says," Valoretta groaned in exasperation. "You read it at the top of the page."

"Sorry," Arnacin whispered.

Running her tongue over her teeth, the princess studied him, yet she did not probe, allowing him to struggle through his lack of concentration. A moment later, however, he met her eyes, asking, "Why is Mira at war?"

Laughter colored her cheeks, as if the answer could not be more obvious. Recognizing his sincerity, however, she closed her book and her gaze drifted far away. "Well... It's just..." She shrugged. "I guess the natives are sick of Mira claiming their land, growing ever larger. They want us off Mira—or our lives. I've heard some say we should just leave, but there is nowhere else to go. On neighboring continents, the land is claimed by other kingdoms and they would never give land to us without a fight."

"What caused the sudden distrust?"

"I don't know. No one does. Perhaps one of their mediums is motivating the entire thing to gain power. I do know there was an uprising when my grandfather had the throne. He thought a larger population would make Mira more defensible. So, he parceled out farmland and built new villages to encourage larger families. But... when he ran out of land to give, he just ran right over our border into savage lands—practically claiming the whole continent as Mira's. Prior to him, whenever Mira's population outgrew its boundaries, if the king did not wish to send some away, he sent generals to talk to the natives, and they chose whether to grant more land or refuse. A few battles arose when they refused, but they always resolved things fairly peaceably. Not so after my grandfather's action.

"The uprising did die down once Father ascended the throne, but because the many hundreds that Grandfather had allowed to stay were all Mirans, he felt he could not ask them to leave. If I were to pick something that truly sparked this war, it would be that. It stirred the natives' resentment and, for years, it has long grown under the surface. But why ask?"

"The king asked me to fight for Mira," Arnacin softly admitted. At her disbelieving stare, he shrugged, "Apparently, Lord Carpason believes I will make a difference."

"Father does take his thoughts very seriously—more seriously, in fact, than he takes his councilors' thoughts. In the first place, I believe Lord Carpason respects his authority, while the councilors simply try to persuade him to their own thinking. In the second, Lord Carpason is father's closest friend and is said to possess a large amount of foresight." When Arnacin only continued to run the nearby inkwell between his fingers, Valoretta stated, "Even so, no one would blame you if you refused. This is not your war, after all."

Sighing, the islander finally voiced, "What choice do I have? Mira has supported me with shelter, food, knowledge..." He helplessly shook his head. "I possess nothing to give in return, other than what the king has asked."

Opening her palm on the table, Valoretta suggested, "Wool. You're a shepherd. You could help open trade with Mira. If it's good enough, it would benefit both lands."

"I couldn't promise that. It would not be my choice, but the entire island's. To add to that fact, we are not a seafaring people by nature. It would likely never happen even if I strove with my very being to keep my word."

"Then tell them it is not your war. We'd all understand."

"I wouldn't," the islander confessed. "I cannot remain here and give nothing even when asked unless I *know* your side's not worth supporting. I would simply be using Mira, and that would be the same as stealing. Right now, I still don't know my answer."

A sad smile brushed Valoretta's lips and she breathed, "For your consideration, Arnacin, thank you. May you not suffer the fate of many."

Finally accepting that he could no longer concentrate, Arnacin slipped off to his ship. The parchments from earlier that day still lay curled up on his bed. Unfolding the diagram of the ship, the islander exhaled slowly. Not thirty seconds passed before he allowed it to roll itself up again. Tossing it on the bed, he stepped back outside to watch the sky turn purple from the setting sun. Soon, a commotion on the shore caught his attention.

A long procession of horses and men wound toward the castle—a war party returning home. The knights did not ride the horses, however. Blackened, human forms slouched over the steeds' necks, and those who would typically be riding were all carrying smaller bundles than the ones adorning the mounts.

"The last forest town was burned to the ground!" one man cried and his words sparked similar pronouncements of doom all around.

"The savages slaughtered them all!"

"They would have, except for the king's army coming at the last minute."

"It won't make any difference! Those poor wretches are as good as dead!"

Arnacin shuddered as he caught sight of one boy, possibly of two years, his blackened skin blistered, his exposed throat bloated and bubbly, and his lips peeling while his head hung over his bearer's arm.

None of the other survivors of the savage attack had fared any better, dead-looking indeed, but the sight of that boy in particular caused a strange heat to seep up Arnacin's back. Valoretta had said the savages would massacre Mira, if allowed. And so they would.

"Will you aid?" the king repeated the question the following morning and, slowly, Arnacin dipped his chin in consent.

"Do you swear?" Miro demanded.

"Swear?" Arnacin repeated in disbelief.

"Yes, swear. It is not broken so easily and, should it be, the least it brings is the death of all honor."

"Your Majesty," the boy returned, unable to control the regal lift of his head, "I gave my word. One wordless nod is all it takes, and I will not break it. Is that clear?" Beside him, Carpason placed a hand over his eyes, yet a smile just showed beneath his hand's shadow.

With a glance at the lord, Miro also grinned, conceding, "Very well, Arnacin of Enchantress Island, I accept your nod as token of your deep commitment and pardon your unfitting tone and unmeant insolence. You may leave with Lord Carpason when his troops move back out this afternoon."

"War's not all young men make it sound, Arnacin," Carpason warned as he led the boy to the outer bailey where men massed in preparation. "You'll grow tired of the bland food, damp nights, uncompromising ground, insects, hunger, thirst and, most of all, the blood."

The islander shrugged. "I really don't have any expectations."

"Well, I thought I'd warn you, since you sometimes have that youthful gleam of adventure about you. War is no adventure. Try thinking that way now and it will be easier once the grisliness starts." Arnacin simply nodded in apprehension as they stepped out into the midst of the battle preparations.

Horses hitched to carts bearing all kinds of weaponry, food and tools pawed the ground impatiently while men dashed around them with barked orders. Through the hustle, Carpason took his charge over to one elderly man buckling on his sword.

"Arnacin," the lord introduced. "This is our master swordsman, Sir Voninath."

"Don't dare repeat that name," the man growled. "Leave it at 'Master Swordsman.'"

Smiling, the lord added, "He will be training you while on the field."

Politely, the boy nodded, watching the swordmaster's pale eyes flick sharply over him. That introduction was it, however, as those with horses mounted. Others clambered onto the carts and the rest fell into file on foot. With that, they started on their journey.

Sitting beside the swordmaster on one of the carts, Arnacin looked up when the man finally growled, "And what do you know already, boy?"

"In what field?" the islander asked.

"A boy of your age?" the man harrumphed. "You should at least know the basics to everything."

"Everything in swordplay or weaponry in general?"

"Warfare, swordplay, archery, spear-throwing and so forth."

Smiling, Arnacin shook his head slightly. "I am well advanced in archery and nothing else."

"Ha, you're a deprived sailor." He again glanced at the islander, "Strange, though, that you know archery. Nevertheless, we shall see how well you know *that*. Half these men could use a refresher in that area. We will test your skill tonight before it grows dark. I have already discussed our travel time with his lordship."

Dipping his chin in acknowledgment of that challenge, Arnacin said no more and neither did the swordmaster.

It was with little patience that Arnacin endured a long description of the bow that evening: its construction, strengths and weaknesses in battle, and possible dangers to the careless user. It was with even less patience that he remained silent as the master swordsman instantly ridiculed him for taking the bow in his left hand when he was finally handed the weapon.

"I thought you said you knew the basics!" the trainer snapped, shoving the weapon into the islander's right hand and positioning the boy's left fingers around arrow-shaft and string. "Now, take careful aim before you release the arrow."

Although an easy shot for his trained hand and eye, the cart with the target drawn on its side beyond the campsite taunted the islander's left-handed ability. Biting his tongue, Arnacin pulled back and, aiming, released the arrow. To his frustration, it embedded itself in the ground beneath the cart. He instantly yanked out another arrow, notching it on the string, only to find the master swordsman's hand on his arm.

"Take longer before you let go," the man advised.

Slowly exhaling, Arnacin lined his shaft up with the direction it was to go, as near as he could make it. It still did not land on the target's field, but at least it hit the wood of the cart. Five arrows later, he still had not hit that target, however, and he could hear men beginning to snicker behind him.

"Yes, his sister's deadly, in comparison to him maybe," someone whispered jovially.

That was all it took. Whipping another arrow out, Arnacin switched hands, pivoted on his foot and, before anyone could blink, sent an arrow into the center of the target, where it landed with a soft *thunk*. Dead silence fell all around as every eye except Arnacin's was glued to that arrow.

Without even a nod of acknowledgment the islander calmly returned to practicing left-handed.

"He just bested you, men." The light-hearted challenge made the islander turn. "Are you going to let that stand?"

The speaker was a tall young man, around his mid-twenties, with dirty blond hair and an easy, impish grin.

Arnacin responded with his own smile and cheekily returned to his practice. From the crowd, however, he heard the master swordsman growl, "Don't start anything, Charlin, or I shall need to report you."

"Be my guest," the young man replied as his footsteps approached the islander. As Arnacin turned to his jaunty challenger, the young man held out his hand. "Squire Charlin. I was home, sick with the winter curse, the day you arrived in Lord Carpason's camp, but I've wanted an excuse to meet you."

"Why is that?" Arnacin questioned as he shifted the bow to his left to accept the squire's hand.

"Keep practicing." The swordmaster's warning growl forced Arnacin back to the target.

Charlin was not perturbed, however. "My lord often speaks of you, and your stubbornness concerning your ungainly ship is the talk of the town."

"I know. Any logical sailor would either purchase another or take passage on someone else's ship," Arnacin flatly parroted. "Why has your lord talked about me, though?"

"My lord is the Lord Carpason of Tarmlin—or what once was Tarmlin." A note of bitterness crept into the last words. Feeling it was not the time to ask, the islander simply nodded in understanding while he notched another arrow onto the string.

Looking toward the cart himself, Charlin offered, "Well, Arnacin of Enchantress Island, since the men here either lack the courage to appear stupid, or they just fear the bully training you–"

"Huh," came the comment from the swordmaster.

Both young men grinned. Looking back at Arnacin, the squire finished, "I will challenge you, your left to my right, and the reverse when we grow tired."

"Or the sun beats us," Arnacin laughed, releasing his arrow.

Indeed, the sun quit first, as it gave way to the moon and stars. After a brief acknowledgment of how terrible he and the islander both were, and how neither could pick a winner because of that, Charlin drifted back into the camp.

Despite the hour, however, the swordmaster simply pulled his charge under the light of the camp's fires and began showing him the basic attacks and defenses in sword fighting.

One thing the master swordsman pressed. "Always watch the eyes, boy. Only amateurs watch the blade itself. Eyes convey intent and, while something as large as the blade cannot be missed with peripheral vision, you will never see the eyes if you watch the weapon. Never forget that." So the night passed in training until the islander was ready to drop from the harshness of it.

"Why did you even suggest him?" the swordmaster snapped at Carpason. Secluded in the lord's tent, the two bickered over the swordmaster's insistence that they spend a week in the plains for training time before reaching the battlegrounds.

Sighing, Carpason admitted, "Because we need him. Therefore, he needs to learn and he needs to learn now, while we still hold something of the high ground. That said, we can't be out here an entire month. The village will move."

Folding his arms, the swordmaster growled, "You want the moon, my lord, and it's not possible. Allow me to say when you enter the battlefield, or send me and the boy back to the capital. It–"

He broke off as Charlin entered. As the squire made a hasty apology and began backing out, the lord waved him inside.

"Sir," Carpason continued without further ado. "I fear I must be frank. I gave the king the impression that Arnacin knows more than he does. Should you have trained Arnacin at the capital, no matter how hard you pushed, Miro would not believe the islander capable and he would wonder why I feel the way I do."

"For that matter, why do you?" There was a suspicious warning in that tone.

Glancing at Charlin, who watched the older men with quiet curiosity, Carpason tapped his thumb against his lips. "Feelings, sir, are not always explainable, yet I have learned to trust mine."

Raising an eyebrow, the swordmaster pressed, "Yet it is illogical enough that you endanger a boy's life to hide the stupidity of your feelings from your king."

"I have every confidence in your ability and his." Yet the swordmaster continued to stand there with his arms folded, his chin jutting out and, sighing, the lord surrendered, "As you wish, you may command our progress. Just let me know when we can abandon this crawl."

Chapter 4

War and Training

Arnacin gasped sharply as the sword bit into his flesh. The army was camped that day, still a mile from Melmoor, and the master swordsman used the relative safety to the best of his pupil's advantage.

"You forgot to watch the eyes, boy," the master swordsman growled, stepping back. "If I had not stopped, you would have lost your arm."

"Sorry," the boy panted, trying to ignore the blood trickling down his arm. After a week of practice, the master swordsman had moved to live blades. Yet the moment he had, Arnacin had found the flashing steel far too distracting to keep his attention on—as his trainer said he must—his opponent's eyes.

With only a grunt, the man swiped his blade clean, slid it back into its sheath, and grabbed Arnacin's arm. Deftly, he ripped a strip off a piece of cloth ready nearby, poured some wine over it, and bound it tightly around the slice. "It's a clean cut. By tomorrow, it will be better. Rest it for today."

Leaving it at that, he walked away and Arnacin sighed in frustration.

"Some of us don't agree with the king..." In the camp that evening, Carpason paused, glancing again at the boy across the small fire from him. "Not that I should tell you that."

Shrugging, Arnacin asked, "In what way don't you agree? Do you not think he should wage war?"

"No, we simply disagree with his view of the enemy. As to this war, we have no choice but to fight. They attacked and, unless we take a stand, they will wipe us out. I, however, cannot deny they had some reason to attack." He waved a hand. "Not that I know what we could do about it, considering Mira's constantly growing population."

Arnacin did not answer, running his hand down his bandaged arm thoughtfully, while the lord studied him.

"What are you thinking, Arnacin?"

"What am I thinking?"

"Yes, what are you thinking? Your mind works so differently from the rest of ours. Do you disagree with our war?"

"No, but who could think war was such a large trap, a corner impossible to avoid?"

Nodding slightly, the lord allowed, "That's life, Arnacin. It's harsh and cruel." He motioned toward Arnacin's arm. "Don't worry about that, by the way. He's trained most of us the same way. First, he'll drive the importance of watching the eyes by nicking us. Then he'll slow down a bit to let us focus on the warning flickers. The only difference with you is that he's attempting to train you within a fifth of the normal amount of time. Most of us started, as a matter of fact, at nine and ten..." He smiled. "At dances."

"What?" Arnacin choked.

Carpason nodded with a smile. "When he trains, he trains first in every possible way not involving weapons, turning out the best duelists you could imagine. When foreign visitors arrive, it's almost always Mira that wins the tournaments. A few kingdoms can still flatten us though. Ursa is our greatest challenger."

Carpason's men entered the Melmoor forest the next afternoon. Instantly, tension filled the troop with a waiting readiness. Sticking between Charlin and the lord's horses, Arnacin asked in a whisper, "Why do you constantly go to find them? If they are a danger to you, why not let them fall into *your* traps?"

"Behind us are the fields of farmers, the homes of the unprepared," Carpason replied. "Melmoor was also once completely in Mira's domains."

He pointed northeast. "My home, Tarmlin, was once in that direction, yet the savages attacked, beating us back. Should we not take the battle to them, they will indeed take the battle to us and kill many more than just our fighting men in the process. We also guess that they are trying to reclaim Melmoor as theirs and thereby gain access to the Guardian Hills on our east coast. For some reason, they seem to fear the marshes on our west coast."

"Is there any strategy to where and when you go beyond your safe boundaries?"

"Our plan for quite some time has been to hunt down the temporary encampments they have hidden and force them out of Melmoor. Therefore, we send out scouts to find the areas where their presence is the thickest, which means they're protecting something. Then, when one group has discovered such an area, they return with the location and another troop goes out to infiltrate those guarded perimeters and remove their battle village, much as we are doing now.

"We–"

A cry resounded from the front lines. "Savages!"

Arnacin heard the alert only a second before arrows started whistling down toward them. Instantly, Carpason kicked his horse forward and, within moments, all his troops stood in a tight, shielded huddle.

On his orders, they pressed forward. Such a move forced the enemy to abandon their perches and meet the Mirans man to man. None of Carpason's men were unprepared as a rush of natives threw themselves on them.

Stuck in the middle, Arnacin drew his own blade, blocking attacks when he had to. Charlin, however, kept most enemies from reaching the boy, likely on his master's command. The battle was too intense to feel much, even as bodies dropped like flies. All the same, it was to the islander's horror that arrows once again started raining into their midst, despite their closeness to the enemy. One native engaging Arnacin suddenly dropped with an arrow through his skull.

Ducking, the boy glanced to where he could see the movement of the enemy in the trees. As his glanced upward, he heard the rush of a swift-moving blade over his head and knew he could not move in time. Futilely, he dropped. As he turned to meet the attack, he saw that Charlin had already run the enemy through.

"Never take your eyes off your foe in a thick battle," Charlin warned with a slight grin as he turned his steed to face more approaching enemies.

Arnacin made no retort.

Giving the tree boughs one quick look, he plunged himself into the fray with one goal in mind. More through dodging and weaving than by direct contact with the natives, the islander slipped through the thick of the melee and flattened himself against the back of a tree. With another upward glance, he sheathed his sword and started climbing.

The sounds of battle raged all around. Still, the islander winced at every branch he snapped on his ascent, certain he would alert the archer perched at the top. Once on the other side of the trunk from his victim, Arnacin slowly leaned around until he saw the savage's shoulder. Then, pressed against the tree, the islander seized that shoulder, jerking the man into the trunk.

Yelping, the native twisted toward his attacker, only to be shoved off the branch to the ground below as Arnacin yanked the bow out of his enemy's hand. Turning to the branch where the archer had slung his quiver, the islander paused. One feathered fletching taunted him. Grabbing it, Arnacin took up the archer's position in the branches.

There, armed with only one arrow, he scanned the nearby trees for movement. Spotting a flash of shifting color from where another arrow shot into the mass below, the islander lined up his own projectile.

Loosing the bowstring, Arnacin was rewarded as his target plunged from the tree with hardly an audible cry—the islander's arrow through his throat.

His attack did not go unnoticed, however, and he felt the shaft tremble as an arrow narrowly missed scraping his neck. Angrily yanking the arrow out of the trunk, Arnacin shot it back at its owner, rewarded again with the sight of another native falling to the earth.

He ducked the next moment, seeing another arrow flying toward him as more of Mira's attackers noticed the islander. Now sitting on the branch, using his lower position as extra camouflage, Arnacin reached up, took the arrow out of the trunk behind him and returned it. To his aid, their fair skin and light hair made them a little more visible among the dark trees than he was.

A victory cry sounded above the shouts and screams from below, but Arnacin did not dare give it any of his attention, concentrating instead on the rustles in the other trees—not to mention the projectiles still flying in his direction.

Within seconds, however, the return volleys faltered and the trees' shaking increased as the natives began fleeing. Lowering his bow, Arnacin made no attempt to take down any stragglers, although it appeared that the natives striving to retreat below had to fight for every breath through the Mirans' continued attack.

Finally, only Mira's troop stood below, and Arnacin heard Charlin calling his name in worry.

"I'm up here," the islander called, soothing the anxious squire before starting down.

"Arnacin," Charlin sighed as the islander dropped the last few feet back to the ground, "what did you think you were doing?"

"What it looked like," Arnacin quipped. "I'm first and only an archer. Besides, someone had to draw their attack away, for their sake as much as ours."

For a minute, the squire simply appraised him, then whispered, "Thank you. They tip their arrows in poison, you know. Death is inevitable after only a scratch... Arnacin, tell me next time you are about to disappear."

Smiling, the islander promised, "I'll try."

Shaking his head, Charlin grinned back.

After the attack, Charlin pulled the islander up to ride behind him on his horse, causing Carpason to smile. That smile convinced Arnacin to ask his burning question despite the tense atmosphere. "Isn't there any remedy for the natives' poison?"

"No, there's no remedy," Lord Carpason replied. "Some men have lived after poisoning if the wound or scratch is in an arm or leg and we cut it off in time to prevent the spreading..." He halted at the horror-stricken look Arnacin knew had crossed his face.

Looking over his shoulder, Charlin grinned wryly. "It's war, Arnacin. Everyone here knows the loss of a limb is actually a gift in comparison. They no longer face death since they can no longer serve, and they live through the impossible."

Shaking his head, the islander insisted, "I'd sooner die."

"The day may come, if and when you are rescued from certain death, that you won't feel the same," Carpason stated. "Although we hope that day will never come."

"If you hope, I beg." Arnacin laughed. "I'm returning home as soon as I am able. I gave my word."

"Where is your home, Arnacin?" Charlin wondered, yet at his master's instant look, he dropped it. "Never mind."

"It was a perfectly innocent question." Arnacin shrugged. "I come from the west."

They were attacked once more that day. Still on horseback, Arnacin helped keep the enemy away from Charlin this time, as the squire kept many natives away from his master. Although a bloodier battle than the last, they escaped in the end, despite the many deaths.

As the troop continued their march, Arnacin sat behind Charlin, trembling as the extent of the slaughter became apparent. It was some time before he felt capable of supporting himself, and he was glad for once that he shared the squire's steed, for he knew he never would have been able to continue the march on his own legs.

After pitching tents when it became too dangerous to continue traveling in the dark, Charlin repaired such necessities as his master's shield and armor in Arnacin's tent. There, he sat opposite the silent boy. For some time neither spoke, staring out into the darkened woods and at the light of their campfires.

"So," Charlin finally ventured, dropping the tent flap. "After your second battle, what are your thoughts?"

"Your lord wasn't exaggerating," Arnacin joked to ignore his honest feelings. "Your food alone is enough to poison us. I haven't figured out what to do about it yet."

When the squire only smiled slightly in reply, the islander tried again with a sigh, "It seems to me, you're losing."

"That's the general opinion," the squire confessed. "We must fight anyway, and those real commanders among us, such as my lord, somehow lift their troops' spirits to continue without deceiving them."

"I'm not sure I know how that works," the islander muttered, pulling his blanket closer about him.

Laughing, Charlin stated, "Neither do I, and I'm Lord Carpason's squire. I should know, but I don't. It's a hope he gives just by standing–just by touching someone's arm or exchanging a few words, or even giving them a slight nod in passing. Somehow... Well, the best sense I can come to is that if he still stands, it means there is chance of survival, and his devotion to them creates a reciprocal devotion, thereby driving their wills even when they lack hope themselves."

Smiling slightly, Arnacin wondered, "How long have you served under him?"

An impishly secret look passed over the young man's face as he answered, "You could say, since the day I was born. I've never lived a day without him and, perhaps I'm partial, but I think he's the greatest man on these shores–not that he's without his own flaws."

"Strangely," the islander admitted, "I have yet to see any of those."

"And you're not likely to, either," Charlin chuckled, finally picking up the dented shield he had been working on. "He's a noble, and a good one. He knows his strengths and weaknesses. Part of commanding is that you remain a constant example. He buries all his flaws, except occasionally in private, where I'm his pillar."

Arnacin did not answer, glancing away as he slowly exhaled. Glancing back up, the squire asked, "You don't have a pillar, do you?"

"I was under the opinion I didn't need one," the islander half-joked.

"Youth tend to assume so," Charlin conceded. "And everyone else *pretends* they don't in public. It's all a lie, though."

Avoiding the subject, Arnacin returned to the prior topic, asking, "Would there not be hope if you simply allied yourself with your neighboring countries?"

"In a perfect world, perhaps. Yet it doesn't work that way. Those who allied would wait until the war was over, declare it as a debt we had to pay, and bleed us dry. The more aid we gained, the faster we would be ripped to shreds. Unless King Miro is extremely crafty in his politics, such as through marrying the princess off and thereby sharing this land's responsibility, we are forced to fight this alone. On the other hand, should he do that, he would basically sell Mira to whomever the princess wed once he died. I'm sure that's why she's not yet engaged."

Exhaling sharply in frustration, the islander started, "According to her–" Dropping quickly off, he shrugged. "I heard that she intended to rule alone, and that it is actually her father's wish that she do so. I mean, he trained her personally in both politics and Miran lore."

Piercing the islander with his stare, Charlin commented, "You're well informed, Arnacin, yet your informant forgot one thing: all of Mira will fall should she not marry. Should she produce no heir, this country will be fed to the dogs. Now, it might be the plan to trick our neighbors and have her only pretend she is interested in marriage until she can produce a forgery of a rightful heir, but that is playing on a dangerous edge."

"Would it matter if she just married a Miran?"

"There are very few noble men left."

"I meant a... 'Miran' Miran. Just a plain Miran without titles."

"Well, I suppose it would be no worse than if she ruled alone. But that depends, because if that Miran was not trained for politics, she would either have to create a puppet or his lack of knowledge would itself flatten us."

Sighing, Arnacin huffed, "The way you politically trained people talk, you might as well declare war on each other and stop the charades."

"Our mission is to remain free, alive and out of war. That takes a game," the squire said, nevertheless smiling without looking up from his work. "But I'm sure you can guess why someone like you is a breath of fresh air. We're actually lucky on Mira. Other lands' nobles plot against their siblings, yet every single noble under Miro's command is extremely devoted to each other and especially to him."

It seemed forever that Lord Carpason's troop continued pushing forward, despite the growing opposition. Killing was becoming an act of complete desperation.

Meanwhile, after the enemies' attacks had subsided into the darkness and the patrols had been posted, Arnacin's training rivaled the battle in its intensity. The swordmaster had somehow taken it into his head that the islander could now defend himself enough to increase the speed of attack to a natural pace. Or perhaps he simply decided they had no more time. His reasoning really did not matter, as Arnacin would spend every night feeling like he was simply replaying that day, narrowly avoiding death time and again.

Arnacin was always surprised that, when he failed to block the attack, the blow would halt an inch from striking. Then, before he could even draw another breath, the swordmaster would step back and start again. So it would continue until Arnacin could no longer stand. His legs would simply collapse under him and his trainer would haul him up and nearly carry him to bed. Too weak to protest, the islander would be given water and a complete massage before he was tucked beneath his covers for the rest of the night. Truth be told, if there were any attacks afterward, he would not likely have woken.

Finally, the troop succeeded in forcing through to the enemy encampment only to find that, although the marks of a camp remained, the natives had vanished. Uttering a few curses, Carpason turned his disheartened, famished and exhausted troop homeward. They all knew they had walked into a trap and the way out would be worse than the path there. As Arnacin was coming to expect, however, the noble's will seemed to inject energy back into the soldiers' bones and, as the next wave of furious attacks swept over them, no one would ever know the despair with which they had turned about only moments before.

Arnacin was not yet a soldier at heart, however, and he found himself moving slower than before—a pronouncement of doom. The time soon came when, engaged with one savage, he saw a shape lumbering toward him out of the corner of his eye. Hastily dispatching his current opponent, Arnacin whirled, just blocking the axe swinging for his head. With a vibration that shot up his arm, his sword went flying. The islander dared not even look to see which direction it went, instead dropping to the earth and rolling out of the way. Something ground into his thigh, trapping him. Twisting, he looked up to see the native—one foot pushing down on the islander's leg—swinging his axe back for the killing blow.

A slight ray of light glinted off the blade as it plummeted downward. Using his free leg, Arnacin kicked blindly upward causing the native to sink to the ground when his foot connected. The axe sank into the dirt at his shoulder.

Before he could regain his feet, however, he was seized by the throat. Fingers clawing into Arnacin's neck, the savage jerked his axe out of the ground and then promptly dropped on top of his victim, dead.

Carpason yanked his sword out of the native's back and, his breath returning, Arnacin wilted in weak relief. "Now, we're even," the islander gasped, trying to shove the body off himself.

Kneeling, Carpason asked, "He didn't nick you, did he?"

"I'm fine," Arnacin panted, stilling as the lord put a hand on his shoulder.

"Stay down, Arnacin. They'll miss you and, exhausted as you are, you can help no longer." Carpason did not wait for the reply, returning to the fray. It was all too easy for the islander to obey.

Pressing the heel of his hand over his eye, Carpason finally turned away from the Miran map and met Charlin's concerned gaze with a sigh. "They did it purposefully."

Smiling slightly, his squire shrugged. "They had to catch on to our plan sooner or later. It hasn't changed for ages. We wouldn't be giving them enough credit if we assumed they wouldn't eventually use it to their advantage."

Returning the smile, Carpason joked, "They're savages. They're not capable of such thought."

"And there lies the strategists' prob—" Charlin broke off as someone knocked on the wooden supports outside.

"Enter," the lord commanded, smiling when a thin dark form slipped through the tent flap.

"Arnacin, I'd expect you to still be training or asleep by now. You've been far too busy for us."

With a slight smile, the islander pulled his cloak closer, shrugging. "He told me it was sapping too much energy out of me and that we would resume once we reached relative safety."

"Let's hope we reach that," Charlin muttered.

Arnacin's gaze went to the open map. "Why not turn around?"

"Toward what?" Carpason wondered. "The only thing to turn toward is more enemy lines. If we're being cut down here, rest assured they'll cut us down should we turn back."

"I didn't mean to eavesdrop, but you said yourself that they laid a trap for you. It may not be the truth, but that could imply that they left their strongest opposition in front and that, should you turn around, you will take them by surprise. If you gain enough ground without strong opposition, you might be able to slip out of their trap and turn around somewhere else."

Studying him, Carpason nodded thoughtfully. "You have it well thought-out. Whether it will work outside of theory is another matter, and that decision is the 'commander's dilemma.'"

"What could happen should you try it?"

"We may not have enough supplies, for starters."

Nodding, the islander stated, "That's actually what I wanted to ask you."

Passing Arnacin a knowing look, Charlin smiled as his lord inquired, "What did you wish to ask?"

Grinning back at the squire, Arnacin commented, "I was wondering who hires the horrible chefs."

As Charlin choked in the background, Carpason said, "Did I not warn you before we began?"

"You did, but I was wondering why."

"Mostly because it has to be food that can last for some time. I'm surprised you ask, since shipboard food is said to be enough to cause vomiting."

"I'll ignore the slander," Arnacin joked. "But you're not at sea. Plants grow all around us. Doesn't anyone know anything about native botany?"

Carpason sighed. "When our original colonists arrived, a savage tribe helped them settle. Although they kept the ingredients secret, they made the meals until we had our own crops and trade was in place. Those days are over and some Mirans have dared to find the edible plants, but when so many died without the slightest bit of success, the research was banned, unless a native shared their secrets. Therefore, only the natives know anything about it and... You should understand how that goes."

"Yet, such knowledge could take care of the shortage of supplies and possibly lead to new field strategies. The natives obviously live off the trail."

"Are you volunteering your time? I don't know that they would tell a Miran."

Wearily, Arnacin nodded. "I'd be willing."

"Then I will contact Gagandep when we return. He is savage by birth, yet has lived in Mira almost all his life. More importantly, I trust him enough to ask him to teach you. He helps with the sick back home when all our surgeons are in the field. You may learn something yet, even if he won't teach me."

Even after the islander left, Carpason and his squire remained awake, contemplating the map and the lord's options. As the noble continued to stare at the parchment motionlessly, Charlin glanced at his master. Looking back at the map, he asked, "May I offer my thoughts?"

"Any time, Charlin," Carpason sighed, turning to the young man.

"I've been considering Arnacin's suggestion."

He shrugged, and his lord supplied, "And you've come to the same conclusion I have. We would be forced to travel too close to the mountain chain, which means that whether we lose our current attackers or not, our struggle would not decrease by any means. Only worse, we would be headed the wrong way."

"What if we didn't turn around," Charlin mused, "but slowly steered our course toward the sea? That wouldn't be as expected as our straight drive, and the natives grow less sure in the open."

"We would trap ourselves against the ocean unless a ship awaited us. For that, I would need to send a messenger, and the likelihood that one alone would slip through the mass swarming around us is extremely small."

"In other words, you think all our escapes are cut off. We either bully our way through or we die."

"I'm still thinking."

Quickly, the squire covered his mouth with his fist as a laugh escaped him, but at his master's glance, he spoke. "It's a good thing, then, that the savages are so confused about our alternating lineups and simply charge the group at large, or you'd be dead by weariness alone. Perhaps you should do the rest of your thinking tomorrow."

"In the thick of the fray?" Carpason nodded, sarcastically. "Yes, I'll be able to think so clearly then."

"It's so late, and I think we've beaten our choices enough for one night. No more are going to show themselves yet."

Studying his squire, the lord finally surrendered, "There are no more options. We'll angle toward the shore, there," he added pointing toward a spot on the map along the eastern shoreline of Mira. "And if there is no ship lying in wait, we will simply continue pushing ourselves through."

"Who do you wish to send as messenger?"

"Ride bareback and use a rope bit on your steed," Carpason said in reply. "Take one of the unshod ones. Silence is a necessity. Also, take Arnacin. At least you will have each other for protection, and he knows both woods and sea, not to mention quite a few of our captains and sailors."

"Will you have the backup you need?"

"I have the troop. If anyone is safe in these woods, it's those in large groups."

Nodding, Charlin bowed out and Carpason dropped his gaze to the floor.

Chapter 5

Sailors Assemble

"Arnacin," Charlin whispered, gently shaking the islander's shoulder. "We have to leave at once."

Moaning in tired protest, Arnacin pushed himself up. "Just us?"

"Just us. We have to reach Mira and find a captain who will take us around to the shore where Lord Carpason plans on leaving the woods."

Sighing, Arnacin kicked off his blankets and, grabbing his cloak, he followed the squire out to the horses. As Charlin adjusted the bridle, the islander softly inquired, "Why us?"

"I never ask, Arnacin. Remember, though, you are a sailor yourself and you know many of Mira's own sailors."

Hauling himself onto his mare's back, he helped pull Arnacin up behind him, asking, "Do you hear any movement?"

"From the woods? Everything before us is only too quiet."

"Then I guess we are forced to go around."

So saying, Charlin wheeled his steed around, causing his companion to swiftly renew his hold. Then the squire kicked the horse into a gallop, heading briefly toward the enemy's mountains.

To avoid as many of the natives as possible, they steered toward the coast before turning south once again. Dawn came. As they pounded through the tide-swept sands, a vengeful cry echoed through the woods running parallel to them and an arrow flashed through the sunlight toward them.

That projectile started a barrage and, as Charlin kicked the steed to greater speed, Arnacin reached forward, yanking the squire's arm to the left.

"Into the ocean!" the islander cried.

Charlin did not resist, nor did the horse. Swerving, it crashed into the waves, where Arnacin jumped off. The squire, however, hesitated until his companion insisted, "Into the water! You're still a target up there!"

"I can't swim!"

"Your horse can. Just hang onto it."

With a splash, Charlin landed in the water beside Arnacin and, surfacing, grabbed the horse's mane. Once they were far enough out, the barrage of arrows halted, although furious shouts followed them.

"Do you think they're angry?" Charlin joked through chattering teeth, evoking laughter from his companion.

Only once Charlin knew they could no longer survive the cold did they crawl up on a large rock protruding from the deep.

Coaxing the mare to lie down beside them, they waited for the cover of darkness and low tide. Stripping off his layers, Charlin laid his clothes over the rock to dry, whispering, "Good thing it's practically summer now."

Having fewer layers, Arnacin already lay on his back beside the squire. "The swim would have slowed us down," he mentioned, no louder than his companion.

Sighing, Charlin stated, "If we arrive too late, we arrive too late. Should we die, no one will ever arrive. I just hope there is no moon tonight or the darkness may not cover us as we expect, considering the water."

"Have you not been paying attention to the moon's cycle?" Arnacin's tone was muffled with drowsiness.

"No, I have not had time or thought to look at it."

A deeper inhale made Charlin glance over toward his companion. Arnacin lay fast asleep with the horse blocking the wind beside him and the sun-baked rock warming him, light glistening off his bronzed face.

Shaking his head, the squire lay there, forcing himself to remain awake throughout the hours. A bite of salt-ruined bread helped slightly, but he did not eat much, lest he choke on it.

Even the mare soon snored beside them, prompting the squire's glare.

As the sky turned deep red around them, Charlin nudged the islander awake and pulled his layers back on. Arnacin awoke silently, grabbing his own clothes–wind-stiff, yet dry.

Waking the mare, the squire passed his companion the remains of the bread, whispering, "Watch out. It's ruined, but it might return some energy yet."

Shrugging, the islander joked, "I should be used to it. Shipboard food is enough to cause vomiting."

Grinning, Charlin made no response, instead whispering the steed back to her feet.

In only those few minutes, the sky had turned dark gray and, using that dimness, they slid onto the mare, walking her back through the shallows to land. Only once on shore did Charlin again kick her into a gallop along the coast, although the light of the moon soon chased them into the cover of the woods.

Almost instantly, Charlin heard sharp rustles around them, yet the deep darkness of the trees relatively protected them from attack. Still, the enemies were smarter than Charlin imagined, as he was informed by Arnacin's sudden cry, "Halt! They're blocking us ahead."

With a jerk of the reins that practically pulled the mare onto her haunches, the squire sharply turned her to the right, but it was too late. The sound of swishing metal warned them of the savages' closeness, before and behind.

"Hang on!" Charlin snapped before charging the horse straight toward the shifting shapes before them. Then, reaching the enemy standing before a fallen tree, Charlin gathered the mare for the jump. In one mighty leap, she cleared both tree and savages.

Gasping, the squire felt the jerk behind him as Arnacin fell. There was no halting however, both because of the steed's momentum and because of the sound of the savages scrambling over the tree behind them. With nothing else to do, he kicked the mare into a full gallop and raced through the woods once again.

As the sounds grew slightly distant behind him, he skidded the horse around some ferns and brought her to a sharp stop. Panting, he waited–waited until feet pounded by and complete silence fell. Then he retraced the mare's steps slowly to the fallen tree, hoping Arnacin–and Arnacin only–remained there, alive.

Not a sound greeted him though, and he pulled the steed to a stop, listening. Seconds passed while he dared not speak. Then, to his delight, he heard a softly whispered, "*Charlin.*"

"Arnacin!" the squire gasped, seeing the shifting of shapes before him as Arnacin moved away from the tree. Hauling the islander back behind him, Charlin asked, "How did they miss you?"

"I rolled beneath the tree," Arnacin panted. "Go southwest. They'll soon realize they've lost us."

With one quick glance up at the stars peeking through the leaves overhead, Charlin heeled the mare back into action.

After another close encounter, thankfully in the daylight, the mare broke through the woods onto a dirt road by the darkness of the next night. Both riders exhaled in relief at the dim sight of the open low hills they still had to cross. As Charlin pushed the horse forward, Arnacin asked, "How long is it from here to Mira?"

"At a desperate pace, two more days. I don't think she'll make it, though. We'll have no choice but to stop somewhere to switch mounts."

"And if she collapses before then?" the islander wondered, noticing the choking sound the mare already made with each breath.

"Then there's nothing to do but to run on foot until we find a replacement."

That pronouncement in place, they pressed on in silence.

Once over the last hill, they increased their pace across the plains and, at an inn where another troop was staying for the night before returning to the capital, they procured a knight's mount. Providentially, the knight's charger was faster than many and they beat Charlin's assessment by half a day. Cantering into the city where the shops and inns grew along the docks, Charlin brought the steed to a halt, panting, "Go find a captain."

"Are you not going to come?" Arnacin asked, shakily sliding off the horse's back, weary and sore.

"It's not safe for anyone closely connected to the nobility to enter these places without a group."

Wickedly grinning, Arnacin said, "These men aren't that bad. You just need to speak their language–no political nonsense."

As Charlin snorted in sarcastic amusement, the islander slipped into the smoky main room of the nearest tavern.

The search was far from easy. Three different Miran captains told him sadly that the wind was blowing in the wrong direction. Another told him, after his question about the possibility of rowing, that the only ships with that potential were Ursan, and that the islander would not want to ask them if there were any in harbor–which there were not.

Finally, Arnacin found a merchant in another tavern who did own four ships capable of rowing. That merchant reluctantly agreed to instruct the captain of his only ship currently in harbor. Trailing the man, the islander met the captain, who at last agreed to set sail in order to rescue the assailed lord.

Smiling in relief and gratitude, Arnacin returned to Charlin while the captain assembled his crew.

Within another hour, they were aboard the ship, heading laboriously northward. "Can they not row faster?" Arnacin inquired, biting his lip.

"It's a heavy ship, Arnacin," Charlin commented from beside him at the starboard rail, where they stood watching the coast.

"And even the waves fight us," the islander admitted. "Without Supreme aid, your master and his men will all be dead when we arrive."

Inhaling slowly, the squire whispered, "My lord has always been a superb tactician..."

He trailed off, seemingly able to find no words for what he hoped to say. He finished instead by shaking his companion's shoulder slightly in wordless comfort.

All the same, Arnacin knew that the squire's heart, like his own, was beating a desperate tempo—faster than the swish of oars through water, pounding out the speed he wished they would move and counting every extra second.

Footsteps made them both turn to meet Captain Wilham, the vessel's master. "We should arrive by morning. We won't get there any faster by staring. Come, rest a little, and eat some. We have time—use it. My guess is that you could benefit from it."

Laughing, Charlin gently pulled his companion away from the rail. "Yes, come, Arnacin, let's be good commanders and not allow any agitation or concern to show. If we can eat and rest, let's do so in order to make sure we don't collapse in the time of need."

"I have no intention of being a commander, and the thought of food currently only makes my stomach heave with nausea."

"Time to retrain your system then," the squire said as the captain turned them toward the cabin. "You might pass your agitation onto everyone else, should you not, and then we may never arrive."

Motioning slightly in exasperated surrender, Arnacin made no comment.

Arnacin did drift off to sleep that night as Charlin sat with the captain discussing their plans for the morning, should they encounter any resistance from the shore. The islander was awakened by the squire, what seemed like only seconds later.

"We're nearing the shoreline where Lord Carpason intended to emerge," Charlin whispered. "Should there be anyone there, your archery skills will be needed. These sailors are only decent at best."

Unwrapping himself from his cloak, the islander rushed up to the deck behind the squire, where he was placed along the forecastle line of archers.

"You're in charge up here, Arnacin," Charlin said, patting his companion on the shoulder. "Our helpful captain has the main deck, I have the poop deck, and the first mate has the masts' nests."

Without waiting for a reply, the squire dashed off to his own post on the far side of the ship.

For a handful of heartbeats, everyone stood there, silent, immobile, watching the empty shoreline as they floated by. With a shout of victory, Miran men started pouring out of the woods.

Arnacin tensed however and true to his reckoning, a cry of furious understanding followed before there came the clash of metal ringing through the woods and the sharp hiss of arrows streaking after their fleeing targets.

The ship rocked as the rowers jerked them to a halt, and Arnacin commanded the sailors about him, "Fire into the treetops!"

True to Charlin's description of merely "decent" bowmen, a quarter of the volleys did not even make it to the shoreline–yet some vanished into the trees. Whether or not any arrow hit a mark could not be seen amid the flashing shapes beneath the edge of the woods and new screams would not have made any difference in the general cries of the dying.

Below them, jollyboats were lowered and Arnacin kept half his attention on their progress.

"Keep their archers occupied." The islander knew nothing more could be done to protect those boats.

As men started filling the gigs, the islander saw firelight blaze in the woods. Knowing the natives' plans, he drew in his breath and sent his own arrows toward its light, yet he knew it was too far a distance for any bow.

To the islander's amazement, the light disappeared within seconds, yet another one flared in a different location. Nothing altered in the ship's attack, for the land assault remained out of their hands, yet as each gig returned to the ship with the rescued men, the sailors would hand their tasks of archery over.

Against that tactic, the enemy's barrage on the fleeing men lessened as they turned to engage the attacking ship. Only the fire arrows continued to plague the escapers, as a jolly boat would suddenly light up from an arrow sinking into its side.

Somewhere inside the woods, someone was battling those fires with minimal success. But as the numbers of Mirans rushing the shoreline lessened, horses burst from the woods and Arnacin heard himself cheer as he recognized Lord Carpason's dappled charger in the lead. Alongside the last gigs pushing off from land, the steeds plunged into the water. Instantly, their riders dropped off, using their horses to stay afloat.

Despite the torrent of burning arrows still raining on them, the occasional man standing at the rail of the ship falling dead, and their continued attack on the woods' line, an eruption of whoops echoed along the ranks of Mirans as the horses swam for the other side of the ship. There, the vessel protected them while the riders climbed out of the water and hauled their steeds aboard.

With a voice capable of being heard above any fray, the captain shouted, "Drop sails! Keep those swine busy for another few minutes, men!"

Hooves pounded across the deck and the captain finally ordered, "Give it all you've got, boys. Now row!"

Keeping his own barrage up until he felt the ship dip freely beneath him, Arnacin heard laughter among the men and saw hats fly into the air. He turned just as Carpason and his squire embraced wholeheartedly in the center of the main deck.

Smiling, the islander threw the empty quiver he had been using over his shoulder and followed the sailors returning to the armory.

This was the Mirans' victory.

"We didn't think you would make it in time," Lord Carpason admitted as he, his squire and Arnacin sat at the captain's table over dinner.

"We didn't think *we* would make it in time," Charlin laughed. "Did you wait for us?"

"We didn't intend to, no," Carpason admitted. "When we arrived at the shore and no ship sat there, we once again attempted to break through by land. I had found it surprising after a day that the attacks had lessened somewhat, but I discounted it. I decided our battles were cutting them down as much as they were taking their toll on us. When we tried to turn around, I found out how wrong I was. We met an unbreakable wall of savages, striving to trap us against the sea. All those lesser attacks were only because they were regrouping. Somehow, we managed to hold our defense on the edge of the woods, with the aid of the trees. We wouldn't have lasted much longer, though.

"When the ship came into view, what I thought might be our last stand began, and I only kept men back to decrease the attack against us and yourself, Captain." The lord nodded his gratitude to Wilham, adding, "Thank you for endangering your ship and sailors at Charlin's request."

"Don't thank me," Wilham said. "My ship is owned by a merchant and I did it on his wishes. As far as I know, however, it was your dark-haired foreigner who did the requesting or... demanding." His lip quirked upward.

"I didn't demand," Arnacin protested. "I told your merchant that his heavy pockets might exist no longer if Mira fell and—short as she is of men and commanders—she could not afford to lose another." As laughter burst among the men, the islander muttered, "I don't see the humor in that."

Their hilarity increased and he purposefully exhaled slowly.

"I thought you said not to use political nonsense," Charlin commented. "I suppose arm-twisting is not part of politics?"

Pulling out a kerchief, the captain dabbed his eyes of their laughter-induced tears. "You're quite manipulative, young man."

"He wouldn't move for love of the country itself. He said his responsibility to his men had to be considered. Actually, he simply wanted a reward of some kind. When I told him it was all volunteer work, he then told me he couldn't ask his employees to break their backs or throw away their lives when they had little about which to worry."

Sighing, Carpason agreed, "It's true enough. Many of us fight for our own lives, but those who live at sea can simply leave forever, and death is not an easy thing to face. You, Arnacin, you are not made like most men in the world. A few young men in Mira think of glory and honor when they think of battle, until they're exposed to it and its cost. Then their mentality fades quickly enough."

"Speaking of young men..." Wilham coughed. "Do squires usually sit with their masters in Mira?"

"Only when no other nobles are present," Carpason replied. "Not that we do anything differently than every other noble or knight on Mira. We tend to be closer to those serving us, here."

Wilham nodded slowly and Arnacin barely caught the hardly noticeable look of amusement that the lord and squire shared. Sticking his tongue in his cheek, the islander glanced away.

Within a day of returning to the capital, Arnacin could not deny that something had changed. The swordmaster charged him to spend afternoons training, and he had volunteered to spend time with the adopted native, Gagandep, every day.

Yet, in the relative peace of the morning, it seemed a sheet of glass covered the world. Trying to squeeze the task of rebuilding his ship into the hours he still possessed for himself, he found the histories he attempted to read empty. His concentration was gone.

All the same, he spent his first morning back aimlessly wandering the library, running his finger along the shelves until finally one title broke through that haze—one book seemed meaningful, at least for the few moments remaining to him—*Savage Superstitions*.

Whatever that strange lack of feeling was, it thankfully disappeared when practicing his swordsmanship and left-handed archery. Neither did it return when walking with Gagandep in his little plot of backyard where he grew some wild plants.

Instantly, Arnacin had liked Gagandep, a man who looked to be in his early fifties, although his hair was already gray. With his easy smile, his round face and squarer shoulders, he reminded Arnacin of his village's fisherman, Lazarus.

It also helped the islander's instant comfort that the first thing the adopted native did was to introduce him to his family, including his Miran wife, Yarel, and his two daughters, eleven-year-old Renda and fifteen-year-old Kira. Gagandep said he also had a married daughter and a son, Firth, but he was on the field. Arnacin noticed that Gagandep hurriedly continued on to state that Yarel named all of her children, as if uncomfortable discussing the odd occurrence of his son serving in the Miran forces.

After the polite greeting, however, the ladies entered the house and Gagandep turned to Arnacin, his gaze suddenly appraising. "So Lord Carpason wants me to teach you about native plants?" His tone was suspicious, matching his eyes.

"Well..." Arnacin shifted uncomfortably beneath that gaze, unsure how to answer. Remembering how the suggestion came about, however, he smiled slightly, "Their food's disgusting and I wanted to learn how to make fresh meals while on the trail."

For a long moment, the adopted native's expression remained the same. Then he sighed. "Carpason said you are as different as your hair implies. Yet, I am wary. He is considerate enough not to push me, but I know, as a dedicated Miran lord, he wants knowledge of my secrets. I don't yet know who you are, Arnacin of Enchantress Island..."

In the pause, the islander felt his forehead crinkle. "Yet you agreed to teach me?"

"I was curious to meet you... Come. Walk with me among my flowers."

For awhile, they walked in silence. Occasionally, Gagandep would stop to pull a weed or prop up a drooping plant, but he did so without speaking. Butterflies rose from the flowers as they passed and some even alighted on the adopted native's back as he bent over his garden. Its peace, such a far cry from the sights and sounds of war, twisted Arnacin's heart and fueled his yearnings for home.

At last, Gagandep looked up, asking, "What did they give you for your help, and what benefit do they think to gain with you?"

"I don't know," the islander sighed. "I mean, I helped them because they asked me, because they need it, but I have no idea why they would ask. They somehow thought I could help." He shrugged hopelessly.

Standing, the adopted native leaned in so that their eyes were only an inch apart. "Do you think Mira is in the right?"

Warily, Arnacin countered, "Do you?" Gagandep said nothing and the islander wondered if it would betray Mira to tell the adopted native what he thought, yet he believed in the truth. "The natives fight for freedom and I would join them in a second, but for their fear and hatred, which murders without discretion."

A small smile passed the adopted native's face as he looked down at the weeds in his hand. Passing one with a fussy pink flower to the islander, he muttered, "This is trava. It grows only in the spring. Native parents hang it over their tent-flaps to give long life to their children. May it grant you the same."

It was not useful information, but an offer of friendship, and Arnacin accepted it with a smile.

Creeping into the library, Valoretta paused, smiling sadly at the sight before her. Arnacin slept with his head resting on his knuckles, *Savage Superstitions* lying on the floor where it had slipped from his loose fingers.

Softly approaching, the princess retrieved the book and straightened its pages. As she bent down, however, the islander stirred. Thoughtfully passing him the book, Valoretta whispered, "You're working yourself too hard, Arnacin. At this rate, you'll catch the winter curse long before winter."

"I never did sleep much," Arnacin softly admitted. "My family used the time of night as our time together and chores began early each day. I should be used to it."

"But you're not."

"It's not the amount of work. It's something..." He did not finish his thought, yet the princess nodded anyway.

"It's the war. I've noticed among some that they experience a period of not living, of losing all they once dreamed, when weariness is the only constant factor in their routine. I feared the same would happen to you when you left."

Running his finger down the words burned into the spine of the book, the islander breathed after a second, "I have too many goals to allow horror to dictate too many..." He shook his head slightly, finishing, "demands."

Gradually letting her breath out, Valoretta confessed, "I marked the page I thought might help you the most–" Grinning slightly, she added, "and you will not find it in *Savage Superstitions*."

Returning her smile, Arnacin stated, "Perhaps not, but since I intend to finish all my tasks by spring, at the latest..." His grin broadening at her sarcastic expression, he finished, "I thought it might come in handy."

"Arnacin, if someone can end our war in *three* years, I would consider him a son of gods, even though my father insists there are none. You are not going to bring about any type of closing by next spring, I assure you."

"Perhaps I am more of an optimist," Arnacin teased, his eyes reigniting in the challenge. Spotting the histories of Carta on the table beside them, Valoretta threw open the book to her marker and deposited it onto the islander's lap. "Finish your ship first, and then you can discuss our war. At least *start*. Now, read that."

Sighing, Arnacin picked up the book and read aloud haltingly. "'Just when... since,' no, 'as...' One of those. 'We thought we... ate? freedom–'"

"That's 'taste,'" Valoretta sighed, snatching the book from him as she did so. "The way you're struggling, you'll miss what you need to read.

> Just when we tasted freedom, a tragedy took place. Five men set sail and only the shells of what they were before they drowned washed back onto shore. Now, not only is our hope smashed, but should anyone find our dead companions, an investigation is sure to follow and our attempt at escape would be discovered.
>
> One of our members, bold beyond mortals, suggested that, under those circumstances, he would claim he murdered them in order to keep us undiscovered, yet I beg anyone who controls the motion of fate, that he should not have to do so.
>
> Regardless, our only guess is that, after all our work, there is still a flaw in our balance, something, as I have documented, we have learned is detrimental in every design, even more so on a raft or, as in our case, a ship with a raft for a bottom.

Finishing, Valoretta glanced back up to see Arnacin staring at her in expectation. When she said no more, he shrugged, "We already expected that."

Slowly letting her breath hiss out, the princess explained, "They worked it all out, 'documented it' as the writer wrote, and I hunted the references down. What I found is not their finished experiment, but with this one, the one that failed them, they made this..."

So saying, she pulled out a piece of parchment bearing her handwriting on it and a sketch she had made of a ship. "Look, they hypothesized that you could float two houses in midair, if what connected to the ground always remained on its axis. They also reasoned that its axis was not necessarily the center—as where your mast was in your ship—but wherever the weight is best supported by it. The length is as important as the mast and cabin..."

Very soon, she had covered the whole parchment in scribbles, yet as she continued, she noticed Arnacin's gaze shift, his bottom lip caught between his teeth. Smiling slightly, she knew she had given him what he needed and that his thoughts were far ahead of her.

Chapter 6

War's True Color

"Brackweed," Gagandep said, passing Arnacin a wildflower. "It absorbs vitamins from the earth like a fire burns grass. For this reason, the natives use the weed as their main food in times of trouble. That being said, it leaves you feeling as empty as before you ate and lacks quite a bit in flavor."

"In short, if someone wished to use them as a spice, it would never work."

"Not a spice, but an enrichment to any meal mixed with flavorful substances that lacks not the taste, but the strength. Silently, it adds the strength and, without ever knowing why, the troops fight like four thousand men in only one hundred."

Smiling at the way the native spoke, as if bestowing a deep magic, Arnacin asked what he had patiently waited to ask since their introduction–waiting while Gagandep grew ever more comfortable around him. "You remember all these things–would you know, or remember..." He paused, licking his lips as he glanced away. "Is there a remedy for their poison?"

For a long moment, Gagandep simply studied the boy, lacing his fingers together thoughtfully. Then, he whispered, "I will not say either way, Arnacin. Coming as a foreigner, perhaps you can understand my kind of loyalty. Our gods demand that we do not betray those who rescue us, or raise us, on the penalty of death. They demand that we take our rescuers' side in conflict and support them almost entirely. As far as it goes, Arnacin, I love my family, my parents who adopted me, my wife and children. I would slit my own throat before trouble came to them, but my kin—they are also my family, Arnacin. They are my aunts, uncles, fathers and mothers, and they hold that much of my heart. It cannot be released. Had they done something wrong, I would have no choice but to go against them, but they are fighting for justice, for a freedom they foresee others will someday try to rip away.

"This was our land and it was once beautiful and wild. To help a bunch of starving, desperate, slave-driven runaways, we surrendered part of it, but then they grew. They would not be satisfied. Now, Mira's army, its tactical superiority, its ability to study, would flatten my kin should they discover the largest equalizer in this war. If there was a remedy and I knew it, I would take the secret with me to the grave."

A question hung in the air as Arnacin gazed vaguely in the direction of the basket of native plants before them. Finally meeting that earnest gaze, the islander replied, "I don't know if I could feel the same. I do have a question, though. You said your gods demand loyalty on pain of death. Do you mean you aid Mira only through fear?"

"I do not understand how that confuses you, Arnacin. Have you no gods that dictate what you do? Even Mira does through its kings and nobles, though they all like to pretend they are each their own masters."

"I don't have gods, no," Arnacin admitted. "My land believes in one god."

"Then you fear someone."

"I hadn't ever really thought of it." The islander shrugged in contemplation. Eventually smiling, he laughed, "I admit that I've obeyed any given law for my own sake. Guilt breaks us after a while."

"Huh," Gagandep puffed, "Our gods kill those who only act for themselves. It's an insult to them, and they cannot abide insults."

"Tyrants," Arnacin muttered, hiding his comment by talking to the floor as he picked up leaves that had dropped.

Entering the great hall, the messenger bowed to the king and then, as if in afterthought, gave a crisp nod to his high councilor standing a few feet away. Smiling grimly, Miro asked for the messenger's report.

"The Earl of Garak has returned from Melmoor, Sire," the messenger said with a bow.

A jolt of hope shot through the king. "Send him in," Miro replied, maintaining his regality despite his eagerness.

The earl was a small man known for both his ability to escape notice and his tendency to stumble upon things. It was a joke in the capital to say whenever something was missing, 'Don't worry that it's missing. The Earl of Garak will find it eventually.'"

For that reason, Miro always felt more hopeful when the earl returned from combing Melmoor.

As expected, the earl had stumbled upon a camp located in the center of Melmoor. "If the troop moves carefully, the savages might not even realize an attack is coming. They were mainly busy just west of there."

"Thank you," Miro nodded, excusing the earl, and called for someone to bring Carpason.

Miro's high councilor (or as he called himself, the high councilor of all Mira), Memphis, clenched his teeth behind his closed lips as Lord Carpason entered, the doors closing on the corridor where the high councilor spotted Charlin waiting.

Those two were Memphis's least favorite people in all of Mira. While Carpason dared to consider the king a friend and was referred to as the king's closest friend and advisor, Charlin was loved by all. More importantly, Miro's greetings to the squire, on the occasion they passed each other, were much too sincere.

The squire was a potential threat to Memphis's position as the king's favorite, and as for Carpason... He was jeopardizing the entire councilor structure of Mira—the voice of the people, not of the nobility.

Keeping his face bland, however, Memphis watched, cursing Tarmlin's success as Miro asked Carpason to eliminate the discovered enemy encampment. As always, the lord bowed in complete submission. He never refused an order and he never challenged his monarch. It was this unwavering respect that increased their friendship and infuriated Memphis.

Once Carpason left, Miro turned to his high councilor. "Thank you, Memphis. There are some things I wish to discuss with you later. Meet me overlooking the bailey in another hour."

Bowing even lower than the lord, Memphis accepted the dismissal and exited through the doors on the lord's heels. He just heard Carpason ask his squire to find Arnacin before they turned down separate corridors.

Memphis snorted to himself. Let them find their precious sailor. The councilor was only troubled by their interest in the foreigner, and how secretive he remained. The foreigner's meeting with the king, in fact, and Miro's request for aid happened only when the high councilor was absent, perhaps unremarkable considering Carpason's involvement, but perhaps he should start paying more attention. Still, if ever anything concerning came to light, it would be a long while before it was out of hand, and Memphis knew how to read warnings.

He had not gone eight paces down the corridor, when he saw one of the lower councilors, Erlund, approaching. Erlund was unimaginative, gullible and constantly nervous about the future. Some said he might be one of the only councilors who took his job seriously, but his concerns aggravated all the rest.

"Oh, Memphis, I'm so glad I found you," Erlund gasped, and the high councilor turned to him, folding his hands to listen. "With the war going the way it's going, what if the knights are right and we're all going to be slaughtered in our beds?"

"Erlund," Memphis soothed. "That's the *nobility* speaking. They exaggerate due to the trauma they're facing. Go out into the city. You'll feel better."

"But–"

"Erlund, the savages are angry with the *government*. If the worst happens and our current monarchy falls, the people will elect a new monarch; one the savages trust. The war will end. Surely, you see that? Just do what you feel is right and don't worry about the rest. Good always triumphs."

Nodding in relief, Erlund allowed himself to be pushed outside by the shoulders. Stopping in the doorway while the lower councilor walked toward the city with a new spring in his step, Memphis nodded. The war was a necessary tool until the peasantry held the throne in the form of their esteemed high councilor. Yes, his wisdom and subservience would win the king's favor and the princess' hand in marriage. When that happened, the war would end. New government would make a whole new world...

If only those from Tarmlin would all die.

Smiling at the thought, Memphis brushed polished nails along the brocaded shoulder of his vest and turned back inside.

Arnacin was kneeling in Gagandep's garden, helping weed, when Charlin found him. Nodding to the adopted native, the squire turned to the islander. "We're returning to the field, Arnacin. Something's come up."

With a sigh, Arnacin brushed the dirt off his hands and knees. "How soon is your lord intending to start out?"

"The men were packing when I left to find you. You have some time, but only a little."

Nodding, the islander said, "Give me a few moments. I'll be there." As the squire left, Arnacin turned back to Gagandep, asking, "Would you like me to help you finish here?"

A note of sadness in his voice, the native shook his head, stating, "They will be awaiting you. I am quite able to burn the rest of these and scatter the ashes over the plants."

Offering his hand, the islander whispered in sincerity, "Thank you for your time."

"Thank you for your interest in things that truly matter," Gagandep returned. "May the gods spare you."

Touched by the gesture, but disbelieving that the native's gods would want to spare him if they even existed, Arnacin nodded, trying to hide his grin.

Entering the inner bailey, where men still prepared, Arnacin spotted the princess standing on one of the terraces beside her father and the high councilor, Memphis.

At the islander's glance, Valoretta covertly waved her farewell. With a slight dip of his chin, the islander turned away. Just as he reached the master swordsman's side, the call to line up came and, it seemed, the last week began over again, starting with a night of training.

"Eyes! Eyes!" the usual snap broke through Arnacin's concentration as his gaze slid, once again, to the flashing blade opposite him. Despite his original habit occasionally taking over, he had made quite a bit of progress, and even the master swordsman had noticed. "Watch the right thing and you will know, instinctively, where the next attack will be."

As the man glanced down toward the boy's unprotected leg, Arnacin swiftly blocked his attempted strike before exclaiming, "Now you're just making it easy."

"Then attack back," the swordmaster snapped. "Never let a moment of ease pass."

Waiting only a second, Arnacin swiftly moved his blade to the man's temporarily open chest, careful not to look where he struck. Without blinking, his trainer lazily blocked it, never breaking eye contact. At the stunned look on the boy's face, the man smiled.

"Now you should realize what I'm saying," he growled, sliding his own blade away to signal the end. "Watch the flickers in the eyes. Those tell you all intention. When you do that effortlessly, you notice other things from the corners of your perception that tell you the rest: a twitch of a muscle, a shift in stance. All these subtleties will eventually tell you everything, as long as you train yourself properly. You have grace and quick reflexes. Now learn to read. The smallest flicker in a shadow beneath a tree will have a clear meaning once you learn this task. There is nothing you won't know. You'll be able to read hearts, tell men their darkest secrets..."

"Really?" Arnacin smiled, skeptically. "Is that your belief? There's not a secret in the world once you train yourself?"

"Name an example," the swordmaster challenged.

"The endlessness of the heavens, the green of the trees–"

"Don't play with me, boy. Those things are not practical inquiries. Only women wonder over such whimsical things." Letting out an amused puff of air, Arnacin departed with a polite nod.

That night, Arnacin aided the chefs and, with his newfound knowledge, they created a large cauldron of soup. While everyone else praised it, the islander showed the chefs as much as he could with the limited resources around them. He did not tell them of the natives' beliefs themselves–somehow feeling that would be a betrayal–but he taught them all he did not feel would misuse Gagandep.

Two nights later, however, Carpason pulled the islander aside for a private word. "Will you share what Gagandep has confided in you?" Carpason asked.

"Honestly, my lord," Arnacin said. "Would that not be the same as telling everyone?"

"Arnacin, yes, to be honest, it would eventually make it around to all of Mira, but we need that information. You said it yourself. If we know how they use it, we may know how to turn this war around."

"Like what plants they use to make their poison?" Arnacin sarcastically replied.

"Has he told you that?" Carpason asked in shock.

"No, but even if he did, I wouldn't share it. You don't shake hands with a broad smile while concealing a knife in your other hand. No matter the gain, it can't be done."

"The end of this war would help him as much as it helps Mira."

"By lying to him?"

"Arnacin," Carpason sighed. "I'm not here to force you into spying for us, but answer this. The adopted natives lack any conviction as far as sides. They are on both sides or neither and, for that reason, they have never completely become Mirans. Yet they are outcasts and traitors to their own blood as well, alone in their own world, all because they can't make up their minds. Whose side are you on, Arnacin? You said you were on Mira's, yet you are unwilling to act thus."

Staring at the ground, the islander made no comment for some time while the lord waited. "I am on Mira's side as far as honor and righteousness permit," Arnacin finally voiced. "Gagandep spoke about his gods' demands. There is a higher law I must also follow. It must come before any allegiance, and deceit is against the most basic tenet of that law."

"Very well, Arnacin. Keep your secrets and his, but don't stop learning about them. Perhaps it may spare your life, if not save Mira's."

Bowing in assent, Arnacin excused himself.

They reached Melmoor much faster than they had the last time. Once inside, Carpason broke his men into groups, each one weaving through the woods in an attempt to lessen the risk of being noticed or of enemies learning the direction they were heading. Meanwhile, he sent a few scouts ahead.

After another two days, with suspiciously little resistance, the troop caught up with the scouts, who informed their lord, "It's there this time. Below, in the dell."

"Tell our men and position them as best you can in a perimeter around the camp," Carpason ordered before turning to the soldiers behind him. "Set up camp here, as quietly as you are able."

As the troop set about following their lord's wishes, Carpason took a few of his men, along with his squire and Arnacin, on foot, to view the native camp for themselves. To Arnacin's wonder, as they dropped onto their stomachs and peeked over the hill, laughter reached their ears.

A warm smell of food drifted near and the islander saw a mobile village. Dogs tumbled with half-dressed children, and women crisscrossed the camp on their apparently pressing business. The only thing alien to the islander's sight was the man hunched over the fire in the center of the camp, showering dirt particles in circles above it while he whispered words to the men sitting raptly around him.

"Why do you think they have guarded this place less, my lord?" Charlin whispered beside the islander. "It appears the same as their others."

"I have the feeling," Carpason breathed in reply, "that it's because their hordes are busy leading our troops away from these camps. For ages, their tightest defenses have led us to their camps, and they know it as well as we do."

"Yes, and while they change their tactics accordingly, we don't," the squire hissed in exasperation. "Well, we can thank the Earl of Garak that he didn't fall for it."

"I do, but I also know it was half accident." The lord fell silent as his marshal crawled up to them. "Is everyone stationed?" Carpason asked the soldier. At the nod, the lord sighed, "We'll attack at nightfall and hopefully, by dawn, no one will have escaped."

Looking up at him, Arnacin questioned, "It looks like any village. Even if the pillagers are taking refuge there, wouldn't it be better to–" He stopped as Carpason turned to him.

"To warn them of an attack so the women and children can flee?" At the islander's slight nod, the lord sighed, "This is war, Arnacin. Some morals cannot be upheld. Yes, we don't like it, and they know it. We often wonder if they take their villages with them into war to see if we will hesitate, to force us to make that grave mistake."

Pale now, Arnacin breathed, "But you can't."

"Arnacin, listen. They are not the innocents you would imagine. Their excuse for taking their village with them is that the women are their squires, of a type. The women take care of the weapons, make the bows, shine and paint the shields, sharpen blades and tips, and even brew their deadly poisons and coat the blades with them. Only after, are they their cooks, mothers and wives. Should we announce our attack, they would not run. No, they would take up their poisoned arrows and help shoot us down."

Arnacin made no answer, staring horror-stricken at where the little energetic dots of children ran about in the village below, so like home. It was only after a pause that he realized those nearby were all watching him, as if waiting for some type of response. Finally, he shook his head, croaking, "I can't... I can't help you in this."

"That's treas–" one knight started, yet as Carpason held up his hand, he fell silent.

"You are not Miran, Arnacin. No one will push you into this." Nodding gratefully, the islander quickly departed.

Blindly, he returned to the Mirans' hidden encampment and his tent. It did not matter what they said, he could not remove the image of his own village, of William playing with dogs in the street, and his mother carding wool with the village weaver. He envisioned Raymond and Charlotte sharpening stone for arrow tips, and then some army rushing at them from the woods with flaming brands.

With a gasp, he pulled his knees to him and tightly shut his eyes as if that could remove the terrible thoughts. If his mother was right and love was the only thing that stopped wars and ended killing, what was he doing?

It was some time later that Arnacin heard the tent flap open and felt Charlin slide down next to him against the canvas. He said nothing though, his forehead pressed into the heel of his palm. There was nothing to say.

After a moment, however, Charlin gently touched his knee. "Arnacin–" He sighed, falling silent.

Distantly, the islander breathed, "I'm already a murderer for the sake of your war, Charlin. Does Mira expect me to yield any more without breaking or going insane?"

"Is defending innocents with your life murder, Arnacin?"

Closing his eyes, the islander rested the back of his head against the tent. "What else do you call looking a living, breathing wonder in the eyes, and causing them to drop at your feet, motionless, eyes glassed over in pained horror, forever?"

"It's not forever–"

"No!" Arnacin snapped, finally turning to the squire. "It's worse than that. That look of horror is only what they leave behind! It's an echo of what they're feeling somewhere else."

Staring at his feet, the squire whispered, "So you believe in an afterworld? In truth, Arnacin, I can't understand why you would believe in something so disturbing."

With just the slightest ghost of a smile, Arnacin studied his companion's blue eyes. "Don't change the subject. I don't believe because I want to, and you know it."

"Arnacin, we've all felt this way. We all start by feeling sick when the first body falls before us, breathing one second and dead the next. As with Gagandep in the previous war, we have long rescued as many natives as we can, but we fight for a cause that can't be surrendered. We fight for the lives and freedom of hundreds who our enemy would simply cut through without thought, and should we just evacuate, others would murder our people. We can't just lie down and hope for peace and an end to the killing. No, we know what we must do and so we stand. The sickness and the trauma vanish after awhile. We grow used to it, I promise."

"What if I don't want to grow used to it?" Arnacin persisted. "What if I'd sooner die myself than become that cold?"

"None of us want to, Arnacin. Just like you say, you do not believe in an afterworld because you want to, so we don't choose to grow cold. But for those who need us, we simply must acknowledge that will be the outcome. We can't surrender, Arnacin. We can't betray

Mira. I've seen what they'll do. I saw it when they tore down and burned Tarmlin... killing my mother and three sisters along with everyone who didn't escape in the fight. I can't let the whole of Mira become like that city. "

An unvoiced question hung in the air, but it was Charlin's words about his family that reached the islander's heart. The natives would slaughter all villages and families even after winning. Mira would not. Sadly, Arnacin exhaled, "No, neither can I. I'll be there tonight when you burn the village."

"From you, Arnacin... those words mean everything to us."

It was as black as possible when Lord Carpason gathered his troops. When the lord knew his men stood ready, he lit the first torch, tossing it into the dell before them. Carpason's men echoed his action and a torrent of fire flew into the camp. Within the sudden roaring light, the troops tightened their circle. Instantly, natives leapt from those flames, hacking into the siege's living walls.

Once again, the sounds of battle and death rose about Arnacin where he stood as archer—a cacophony so common lately, he was coming to disregard it.

As something slipped beneath one of the Miran horses, he drew back and then froze, recognizing the shape of a child silhouetted against the blaze. Beside him, someone fired. With a twang, the arrow flew forward and Arnacin saw the slight figure drop.

Only the sight of a native lumbering toward him kept him from freezing, aghast at such action. The next few moments—or hours—were filled with nothing but senseless firing. Arnacin's mind was numb, frozen on the image of the dead child, yet his honed reflexes kept him moving, attacking each aggressor that escaped the soldiers' ruthless blades.

A horse suddenly screamed in pain, dropping only feet from the islander. Its rider, trapped beneath its body, strove as best he could to block his attacker's aim. It was no use, however. The knight screamed as the native's spear landed in his unpinned leg, and Arnacin loosed another arrow.

Leaving the rest of the killing to the other archers, the islander sprang to the aid of the knight, shoving the dead weight of the horse off enough to pull the man to his feet. Then, snapping the spear shaft in half and jerking the man's arm over his shoulder, he half-ran back toward the camp, where the surgeons' tents stood ready.

"Ignore me, boy," a familiar voice growled through gritted teeth and Arnacin noticed only then that it was the swordmaster he hauled beside him. "You can't be spared."

"I can for a few minutes," the islander stated flatly, "because if one man makes that much of a difference, you can't be spared to die, either."

Passing the swordmaster off to the surgeon who immediately hurried forward, the islander whirled to go, only to find that the injured man's hand had clamped tightly around his forearm.

"You might as well stay," the surgeon said briskly as he pulled a blade from a boiling pot of water. "We can use the extra hands for a few minutes. Amputation is the only chance to save a man after they've been poisoned."

Paling, Arnacin wondered, "What do I do?"

"Help hold him still," came the short answer, and the islander turned away as they prepared to remove the injured leg.

There was a scream and the muted crack of bone. Arnacin hissed in sympathetic pain as the master swordsman's hand tightened around his arm.

"Open that wine," one of the surgeons snapped at his companion.

Slowly, Arnacin turned back to the grisly sight as the swordmaster's fingers started trembling on his arm, and quickly glanced away again as the surgeon tossed the amputated leg into one of the fires.

While the surgeons worked on stopping the blood that soaked the blankets underneath him, the invalid breathed between gasps, "Never... Never..."

"Don't push yourself," one surgeon advised, as he plucked the cautery from the fire. Grimly, he soothed, "You won't need to worry about this hurting. With the amount of pain you're feeling right now, you won't feel it at all."

Yanking up what remained of the swordmaster's pant leg, they wrapped it with a soaked cloth and then set the cautery to the end of the stub of leg. Averting his gaze from their ministrations, Arnacin watched the man's eyes roll up into his head and turned to the surgeons in concern.

"He should be all right," the surgeon comforted him, "We've done this countless times and, for the most part, they live. I wish we were not forced to practically mutilate them first, but the pigs of savages give us no choice in order to prevent their poison from spreading too far." Arnacin made no comment and the surgeon added, "You should return to the battle now."

Nodding remotely, the islander exited in relief. Outside, he noticed the sunlight rising over the mountains ahead and the returning troops walking slowly over the ridge of the dell. Behind them, the black smoke of an extinguished fire rose into the air. The islander only watched them, all thoughts somehow deserting him. He just stood there, motionless, until one of the knights passed him, clapping him once on the back.

That touch only gradually sunk into the islander's consciousness. As it woke him, he asked, "Where's Lord Carpason?"

Nodding toward one of the medical tents, a knight answered, "He's likely in there. His squire was poisoned. It was only a scratch, but he was already rather feverish by the time I saw him."

The islander did not wait for another word before dashing toward the indicated tent.

Lord Carpason already stood beside his feverish, quivering squire when, white-faced, Arnacin stepped into the tent. As the islander drew near, the field-surgeon began preparing his blade for the intended amputation. "Don't," the squire's weak plea made them all pause. "It's too late," he panted. "I want to die with all my limbs, please."

Tightly squeezing Charlin's arm, Carpason licked his lips, yet he nodded his permission anyway. His squire said no more, closing his eyes, but as those gathered around him watched over the following minutes, his labored breathing cut off with a ragged sigh as the shivering halted, Arnacin knew, forever.

No one moved, although most gazes turned to their lord. Carpason was the first to stir, lightly pressing those limp fingers to his lips and then simply turning around and striding out of the tent. Slowly, those gathered also returned to the other things that called them. Arnacin, however, remained rooted in place, his gaze fixed on the body even after the surgeon covered it with a blanket.

It was a dispirited group that marched beneath the castle's portcullis almost a week later. No battles on the return trip had woken them. They had simply killed without thought, by pure reflex. Only Lord Carpason appeared unaffected, yet most there knew him enough to read his silence and emotionless commands. Although no one could describe his actions or words as harsh, his heart, which before had always been present for people to feel, had vanished overnight.

It was no less missing when the king ordered a ceremony to honor the fallen, although most of the bodies lay far away. Too numb to feel, Arnacin watched as mounds were raised over nothing, as was the custom there. On Mira, those mounds were the only markers for those who had passed. In what was once respect to the natives and now was simply tradition, no stones ever marred the ground.

Having watched Lord Carpason leave the castle alone the next morning, Arnacin followed on foot, guessing where he would find the noble. True to his expectation, the islander found Carpason standing on the rock that was the only marker of Mira's burial field, beside the newer clumps of dirt that grass had not yet covered.

Although the lord did not look over when Arnacin joined him, he apparently knew who had trailed him, as he softly exhaled, "There are occasions, Arnacin of Enchantress Island, when I could forget the fact that the savages are also humans, fighting for their own causes–times I could forget everything but that they are the enemy, the enemy of Mira, of..."

Finally turning his head toward his companion, he said, "But you have no need to hear grievances. You have enough of your own, I know."

"On the contrary, milord," Arnacin replied, still staring over the field himself, "I came for that purpose alone."

"You came to Mira for that purpose alone," Carpason sighed with a slight touch of humor. At the islander's sideways glance, he explained, "You keep many of us going, Arnacin. You listen to everyone's woes, throw yourself into a fight that is not yours... Did you just land here by accident? Some accident."

"You'd like more of them, I'm sure," Arnacin lightly joked. "I didn't come here to discuss me, however."

Finally turning to Arnacin, the lord inquired, "What do you want to hear?"

Dropping his gaze to the rock, the islander muttered, "Someone told me everyone needs a pillar. You lost yours, and its loss isn't easy."

Regarding the islander for a moment, Carpason asked, "And who is your pillar, Arnacin of Enchantress Island?"

"According to a certain lord, I came to be everyone else's. Perhaps I was crafted differently." At Arnacin's jest, the lord turned away.

For a brief moment, the only sound was the wind hissing by. After a few seconds, Carpason started, distantly, "It is Mira's custom, Arnacin, that the first-born son in any noble house takes the place of his father's servant until he inherits the family title himself. For a lesser noble family, they are the squires. For the higher ranks, they might be more. The princes move from squires to generals to high councilors, until such time as they ascend the throne."

He said no more, yet as his gaze moved back over the field, Arnacin whispered, "Charlin was your son."

"I'm almost surprised you missed the resemblance, except that almost everyone agreed he looked more like his mother. 'Son' is a small word, though, with little to no meaning. I never saw the deaths inside Tarmlin, but he did. I was on the outside with Tarmlin's troops when the attack came, but we were cut off. We tried everything to regain the castle when it went up in flames, but we never made it. Charlin broke through with those who had guarded the walls from the inside with the news that the savages had infiltrated, that everyone was dead. With no choice remaining except to face slaughter, we turned away. I would have given anything to remain and die, Arnacin, anything–but not my men's lives and trust.

"Despite all that, despite the fact that he had been the one to see... *them* cut down, it was Charlin who found his laughter again, in a way I have never felt since–who could still pick on all the men in an attempt to teasingly stir them to near frustration. He chose to live one day at a time, and to live that day fully. There was a time when I could tell that it was only a choice, but as he continued, that choice became part of him, and he little realized it, but I know who really kept hearts beating."

The howl of the wind was the only reply.

Chapter 7

Blood and Compassion

ARNACIN REMAINED BEHIND THE NEXT time Carpason left, this time to scout. Standing beside the lord's dappled charger as the noble mounted, the islander asked, "Who will guard your back now?"

Carpason smiled fondly. "I've made it before with only these men. Train hard, Arnacin. Perhaps you will be ready when next I leave."

Nodding, the islander stepped back as the troops marched out the gate. When the great doors had closed behind the last man, he turned back toward the library and the remaining calculations for his ship that awaited him.

Valoretta already stood there, leaning against one shelf, holding a thin book entitled *Sea Poetry* before her. Grinning slightly as his gaze took in the title, Arnacin wearily cleared the table they had been cluttering for the past two days with drawings, books and weights.

Straightening, the princess commented without lifting her head from the book. "This ending's for you, Arnacin." Then, the princess translated the ancient language, her voice rising and falling as if she lived to recite verse:

Black blow the waves, the crashing waves,
Yet faster than the storm,
Faster and darker than mortal ship be,
The Black Captain's Immortal.

Black blow the waves, the crashing waves,
Whenever is seen the Immortal,
For it rides on air, of its flat-bottomed hull.

Long and sleek, terrible and ruthless,
The Black Captain has stolen its secrets from gods.
Now, no justice can track it, no defender live.

For black grow the waves, the crashing waves,
Whenever is seen the Immortal,
Flat-bottomed, long and sleek, terrible and ruthless,
The Immortal.

Meeting her glance, Arnacin said, "Let's hope not."

"The Black Captain has stolen its secrets from gods," Valoretta repeated with a smile, "and our islander comes from the mists of the sea."

Fixing his gaze on one of the drawings, Arnacin mumbled, "Don't make that into poetry."

"Why not?" the princess teased, dropping into the chair opposite him. "You wrap yourself in so much mystery. It's perfect, but we should change it slightly, 'White foam of waves, those whispering waves.'"

"With that type of aid, you should leave me to work on this mess alone."

Laughing outright, Valoretta left her book on the edge of the table and they returned to the scales.

As his thoughts drifted in the following silence, however, Arnacin finally asked, "Valoretta? Why do Miran nobles hide their families as servants?"

After a glance of shock, the princess answered, "For protection. No one can target a person they have no knowledge of. There can be no hostages taken as bribes if the nobility have no family and, under cover, we can grow closer to each other without fear of politics interfering. Protection was what started it years ago, but we have found that it trains wisdom in our nobility as well."

"But you're not hidden."

"No," the princess whispered. For a minute, she remained silent before explaining, "It has always been a defect of our secrecy that heirs are considered by many kingdoms to be simply adopted from the lower classes. I've even heard some say that is the real reason our school for training peasant councilors exists–to train politics and warfare into peasantry for the nobles to pick successors. As long as it is a man that is adopted, Mira can hold its own regardless, but if a princess were adopted and there was no actual blood-right, that would give the kingdoms just another reason to think little of my reign."

"So Sara is...?" Arnacin prompted.

"I'd have to kill you if I told you," Valoretta teased.

Grinning back, the islander muttered, "I think I know anyway. If you even think to look for it, she shares a certain *sisterly* resemblance to the king."

"Arnacin, I think you know too much to ever be allowed to leave."

The islander continued to practice his Miran archery. He also continued spending much of his afternoons with Gagandep. In the early evenings, the master swordsman was carried into the courtyard to sit beneath a tree and oversee Arnacin's training against one of Mira's more skilled knights. The knights changed daily, however. Some of them, Arnacin caught off guard, while others backed him into walls, despite the master swordsman's snapped hints to regain the offensive.

Carpason had both returned from the field and left again before the master swordsman finally barked when Arnacin appeared, "You're done, boy. I've taught you all I can. The rest is up to your experience and use. So, go! Leave an old man to his miseries."

Studying the swordmaster, the islander whispered, "You'll grow tired of being left to your miseries, but as you think best, sir."

He bowed before turning away, yet the man halted him. "Arnacin."

The swordmaster's first use of his name whirled the islander back around. As the master's pale eyes again flicked over him, the man finished, "I thought our king had finally cracked when he asked me to train a boy on the actual field, but you have something, boy. That and your strange ways might make you great someday. Someday, mind you. Then I suspect they'll all want you as commander..."

Smiling in denial, the islander recited, "Never promise the garments before the sheep are sheared."

Grunting, the swordmaster huffed, "Now there's a shepherd's proverb for you."

"Actually, it's a weaver's."

"Whatever. Just remember this: never grow old, never let yourself slow down. It betrays you in the worst of positions."

Nodding, Arnacin confessed, "My father never did." More to himself, he added, "I almost wish he had."

Again, the islander turned to leave, pausing as the man finished softly, "And thank you. I'm too old to feel particularly grateful, but I'm forced to feel at least a little. Most of us are too well-trained to do as you did."

Only between periods of training did the islander return to his ship, finally ripping up his deck and extracting the old remains of his mast. Once he had that accomplished, a carpenter approached him, informing him that the king had already paid the estimated amount for the mast. It was only while meeting Valoretta later that Arnacin figured out how the king had known when he needed it.

Within another four days of almost constant work from sun up to sun down, the new mast rose into the air, firmly secured in the place that would faithfully balance his ship. That finished, Arnacin began replacing the deck boards.

Busy filling the cracks between the boards of his main deck with decayed rope, Arnacin looked up as a shadow fell across him. "Are you Arnacin of Enchantress Island?" a young man inquired.

Peering up at him, the islander responded, "Would you believe me if I said no?"

Glancing around, the newcomer said, "I see no one else with dark hair."

"I thought as much." Arnacin nodded, returning to his work. "Why do you ask?"

"The king has decided to send you out with Duke Cestmir, who should be passing Lord Carpason's troop at some point. Before you rejoin the Tarmlin troops, you may help somewhere else."

Sarcastically, the islander sighed, "Because working on my ship is not productive. Alright, I'll clean up and meet this duke in the bailey. I assume he's already preparing."

"He is," the man nodded, before turning away. "Good luck. He's not as forgiving of insolence as our lord."

"And how would you know that would mean anything to me?"

"Rumors spread like wildfire."

On that note, the man departed with a respectful half-bow. Closing his eyes, the islander shook his head.

Arnacin entered the inner ward a short time later to the hustle and bustle of war preparations. On the keep's steps, three dirty blond-headed boys, obviously of the nobility by their fine attire, stood by their father while he cinched a sword belt around his waist. The oldest of the boys, no older than nine, was in the process of passing his father a cloak.

With a sad smile, Arnacin looked back toward the troop. Yet he did not see the preparations.

Instead, he saw a distant shore and a village. Had William cried when Arnacin was not there that first morning after he left? Was his mother enraged? And now, a year later, would William still remember he had an older brother?

Those thoughts hurt too much to consider.

Charlotte was the only one he could picture for certain. He could see her at their favorite lookout on the mountain staring off to sea, still as the trees around her with her green dress and hair, darker than the shadows beneath the trees, blowing in the wind rising off the ocean.

"Arnacin of Enchantress Island."

The islander jumped as those words shattered his distant thoughts and returned his attention to his surroundings.

The boys had disappeared and the nobleman had stopped beside the islander. Hesitantly, Arnacin nodded in respect. "Duke Cestmir."

"In person," the duke commented off-handedly while he studied the islander. "I had pictured a man..." As Arnacin's chin rose a few inches, the noble finished, "...from all the things I've heard about you."

Arnacin remained silent.

Turning to the troops, the duke stated, "We shall see how much is made up."

"In other words, you doubt what has been said now that you see... a boy," the islander coolly voiced.

Simply nodding in parting, the duke called for his men to start out, and so began their relationship. During the marches, Arnacin remained vigilant at the duke's side, since his tactical layout of marching remained too consistent. Yet, by evening, Arnacin spent more of his time with the men and the chefs, naturally.

With a sack of dried herbs Gagandep had given him, he helped the camp's cooks the first night. The reception the food received was a delight, and the duke acknowledged Arnacin with a nod. The islander simply returned that nod with kingly pride.

From the men, Arnacin learned that another village had been spotted by Lord Carpason, who had sent a messenger ahead to inform a larger, fresher troop of its existence. Therefore, Duke Cestmir's men were off to destroy it before the natives could realize their danger.

The islander's response to that information was, "Had you told me that before we started off, I would have begged leave to stay behind for this one." Regardless, his support did not waver.

Then came the horrible battle itself. Arnacin had not been privy to any of Duke Cestmir's plans, but he assumed a more tactical plan had been made. Yet the natives were packing to leave when the Mirans arrived. Therefore, acting with urgency, the duke ordered the charge and the Mirans instantly swooped upon the savages. Refusing the task of shooting those taking flight, Arnacin joined the swordsmen.

When the battle ended in the evening, the duke sent men to scour the remains of the camp and take anything useful. The islander joined them. "If there are any weapons that are still intact, we better be careful," one knight warned. "They could very well be poisoned."

"None of their remaining weapons are poisoned, this time," Arnacin murmured beside the men. As they turned to him in surprise and suspicion, he informed them, "When they have poison on hand, they renew it after every battle, as long as they are intending to stay, but they were packing to leave. All their ladies would be busy with those preparations and the poison would be mostly forgotten, save by the men guarding the encampment."

"How do you know?" another of the knights pressed.

Unabashedly, Arnacin retorted, "You should know it yourself. If you know as much about your enemy as you can, then you can think how to gain the upper hand. Mira has been letting its opponents keep the high ground since the war began. Perhaps you should work to end that."

"*Where* did you learn it?"

"A few natives in the capital."

"Careful, Arnacin," another knight cautioned, "Those who have probed the adopted natives' knowledge die through their resear–"

He broke off as a clump of bushes shook. "Spread out," he commanded those around him, "See if it's just an animal in the bush."

As the men stepped forward, Arnacin dropped down, having spotted something else in the leaves. A small figurine lay there, made of white wood and oddly formed–oddly enough that it took the islander a second to realize that it was supposed to be a squirrel with its paws curled up to its chin. Odd as it was, however, it bore the signs of a child's love, worn and dirt-stained in places, chipped and only slightly painted. Yet it lay deserted.

Slowly exhaling, he brushed a leaf over it before turning back to the men. After whacking the brush a few times with no response and carefully pushing aside a few branches, one of the men sighed, "It had to have been an animal after all."

"It didn't sound like an animal," Arnacin commented, looking upward nervously. As he did, he noticed the slight figure in the tree above them and quickly looked away.

"No one is here. It had to be an animal," came the response.

"I guess so," the islander shrugged, although he thought otherwise.

"Wait," a knight called, grabbing the arm of the man closest to him. As the knight looked upward, Arnacin closed his eyes. "Someone's up there!"

Moving as one, the men surrounded the tree and one of them ordered, "Arnacin, your bow."

"You're not thinking of shooting him?" the islander protested, nevertheless sliding his bow off his shoulder.

As Arnacin strung an arrow to the weapon, the knight called, "Come down or we'll shoot!" No reply came and the knight nodded, "Shoot, Arnacin."

"He can't understand you. They speak another language."

"Listen, foreigner, for all your studying, you fail to realize that they only pretend not to understand. When they want to understand, they do, and our gestures should make it clear regardless."

"He's only a boy," Arnacin exclaimed.

"Is he, now?"

"Yes, can't you see him? Regardless of whether you can or can't, he doesn't necessarily know everything the adults understand."

"Arnacin," the knight sighed, "shoot. We have our orders and so do you."

Exhaling in frustration, the islander quickly switched the bow back to his left hand and released the tension. Its projectile skimmed only half an inch over the boy's head and, with a yelp, the native half-climbed, half-tumbled down the tree. As a knight seized the boy's arm, Arnacin stepped back, fairly sure he would have preferred to stay behind.

"Is any other savage hiding?" the knight asked the boy, who looked to be no more than ten, at most. When he received no reply, he shook the boy, demanding, "Well?"

"If there were, we would probably know about it by now," another knight sighed, earning Arnacin's nod of approval.

"Where are your other camps?" Still, they received no response from the boy, aside from trembling. Suddenly backhanding the captive, the knight tried again, "Answer!"

"If I did know, I wouldn't tell," the boy hysterically cried through a thick accent, "You're all dogs and the gods are enraged. You'll see! They'll rip your hair from your scalps and twist your gizzards into necklaces! You'll see!"

Only Arnacin started at this reaction. The rest simply nodded knowingly. "We'll take him to the duke," the knight holding the captive said with a sigh. "I don't think we alone can make any use of him."

Much of the troop watched that evening as Cestmir tried to glean information from the captive. When no promise, threat, or reasoning worked, the duke gave up, stating, "We'll take him back to the capitol."

"To hang?" one knight asked.

"That is the king's sentence," Cestmir nodded. "Those are the laws."

"You have laws to hang children?" Arnacin repeated in disbelief.

"We have laws for any and every situation. It is how order is kept. All captives go to the king. The king passes sentence and the sentence is carried out."

"So hanging innocents is part of those laws?"

"Never," the duke snapped, flushing red. "What type of barbarians do you think we are?"

"In that case, what is your excuse here?"

"That savage, if you speak about him, is a captive of war, an enemy, and therefore a threat! More importantly, he is as much a murderer as the rest of his kind. Is that clear?"

"He's too young to be a threat."

"So says the boy who thinks he's a man," Cestmir snapped before whirling away.

"You wiped out the rest of the camp!" Arnacin shouted after him. "He's only one, anyway. If you had any decency, you'd release him! You won't gain anything by killing him!"

"It would be an act of betrayal to Mira, and therefore punishable by death," the duke hollered from across the camp, before disappearing inside his own tent. Glaring at the spot where Cestmir had disappeared, Arnacin turned away himself.

In the following days, no more was said about the argument. Yet in Arnacin a war raged, ironically making his attacks on his assailants unusually brutal.

Yes, the native boy was savage enough when he did speak in their language, but the islander was sure, beyond doubt, that the captive knew no more of war than Arnacin had only a few months ago—except perhaps in the knowledge of hatred.

To kill him would be wrong, yet it was apparent that no one agreed with Arnacin or cared. But this time, the death of a child did not fall under the casualties of war, for the battle had been fought and the only survivor was the weaponless boy. Perhaps the Mirans were so cold they had grown blind, but that was the best excuse Arnacin could imagine. Otherwise, they were as bad as their opponents and he was guilty of assisting them.

After turning the matter over for two days, the islander stared up at the dark tent canvas above him, listening to the soft snores of the men around him. For a couple of hours, he had lain there, contemplating the risk, the consequences, the responsibility, and how much he truly did not wish to proceed with what he felt he must.

The boy was spiteful, of little worth to anyone–in short, a wretch. Moreover, should Arnacin act on his convictions, he knew, he would betray Carpason's trust, and then… there was home.

Home. To toss that away for a wretch of any kind was enough to drive anyone to the grave. Yet Arnacin's thoughts compelled him toward honor, justice and even his promise to Mira's king, for he knew–he *knew*–how they would harm themselves if they followed through with their laws.

Slowly, the islander pushed his blanket off and crept out of the crowded tent. By night, the captive was kept inside one isolated tent with men positioned at the entrance. Arnacin had no intention of trying that way, so he pulled his hood up and crept around the perimeter of the camp.

Footsteps crunched in the leaves nearby. Each one was punctured by a small clink of metal. A sentry was nearing. *Crunch. Clink. Crunch. Clink.*

His breath catching, Arnacin stilled. He reacted too late.

"Halt!" the sentry barked, his black form emerging from behind some trees as he neared. The islander heard the hiss of a sword being drawn.

For only a second, the islander's mind froze and then he sighed, "You always have the stupidity to think you can guard in complete darkness. It might hide your camp from a distance, but someday, you're going to run into your other patrols and all behead each other."

"That's a very thoughtful thing to say," the sentry grunted, nevertheless sheathing his blade. "What brings you out here, Arnacin?"

"Lack of sleep."

"Well, you might want to return to camp anyway, before you walk too far in the dark. As you just pointed out, it's not safe out here."

"I'm not Miran, either," Arnacin muttered, turning back into the camp all the same. He had been planning to do so before the sentry suggested it, yet there was no need to tell him that.

Approaching the back of the prison tent, Arnacin dropped to its base and, after looking around briefly, pushed himself beneath the canvas. Since the darkness inside was not very different from that outside, the islander could easily see the outline of the boy tied to the tent's center support.

A sharp inhale told Arnacin that his scuffling entrance had not gone unnoticed. Quickly, he crossed the space between them.

Barely speaking, the islander breathed, "We have only minutes. Follow without question and, if grace prevails, you'll make it to safety." Beneath the islander's hand, the boy nodded. Releasing him, Arnacin dropped his hand to his side where his blade hung.

As his fingers found the scabbard, he froze, feeling the carvings on its sides. An image of Carpason's reaction flashed sharply to mind and, slowly letting his breath out, Arnacin shoved the thought aside and drew his sword. As he had said only moments before, he was not Miran.

Seconds later, the twosome was creeping through the camp toward the horses, as quickly as silence allowed. Thankfully, the boy was native, with their seemingly innate level of stealth, and Arnacin had trained with his sister. A slight smile passed the islander's face at the knowledge of the superiority of his sister's stealth as he heard the soft sound of his companion's footsteps.

Arriving at the horses' picket line, Arnacin untied the first one. Shoving the lead through the horse's mouth, he tied the other end to the halter. "You know how to ride?" he whispered.

The boy nodded wordlessly and Arnacin shoved him onto the horse's back.

That second, a shout sounded throughout the camp. Without another word or glance, the islander slapped the horse into a run, while behind them, the camp's fires burst into life. With a clatter, men suddenly surrounded the picket line, some throwing saddles onto their horses before leaping on and others blocking Arnacin's escape, although he had no intention of running.

As the knight closest to the islander began to hoist himself onto his newly tacked steed, Arnacin reached out and yanked the girth loose. Yelping, the man landed on his back at the islander's feet, causing a slight grin of apology. Nothing more could be done to aid the fleeing native as sixteen horses bolted in pursuit. Likewise, nothing could alter what Arnacin feared was the end of his own life. Grace alone commanded both islander and native boy's future.

Only as the last horse disappeared from hearing did one man gasp, "Arnacin! What have you done?"

Although the islander's answer was only to flick his hair out of his face, his response to the duke's demand minutes later was required.

"What is the meaning of this?" Cestmir stormed.

"Did you expect less?" Arnacin challenged.

"Yes," the duke snapped. "Lord Carpason spoke much more of you."

"I never promised to obey your king for his sake, but for that of Mira."

"No, but you betrayed your word to help our cause, and thereby are still a traitor."

"Your cause was not aided in any way by that boy."

"No, but his escape aids their cause."

"You don't know that, do you?"

To the islander's tone of finality, the duke inhaled. "Then I have no choice."

Reaching the capitol, Lord Carpason heard that Duke Cestmir was on the field and that he wished to meet with the lord. With that information, Carpason turned back around with a fresh unit to join the duke and aid him if needed. He found the duke's camp three days later, on the edge of Mira's safe lands.

"Your Grace," Carpason greeted as the duke came out of his tent to welcome the troop. "It has been awhile."

"Well, you, my lord, are on the field far more than is good for you," Cestmir smiled, clasping the other noble's arm. "I was actually hoping to run into you, but it looks like you came back out to find us."

"Your sight is correct. I gather my messenger made it through?"

"He did," the duke said as he led the way back inside his tent. "And we succeeded in taking out another camp. We have been doing well recently."

"How great were your losses?" the lord asked, taking the seat offered him.

"Strangely, little. Our opposition on the way there and back was greatly reduced from the usual. I can only assume the savages were too occupied in chasing the hated Miran lord." He inclined his head in respect to Carpason, who smiled modestly.

"I admit we did *not* have less opposition than normal," the lord confessed.

For a moment, Cestmir did not make any comment as he gazed off into the distance. Finally, he stated, "We won a few provisions in the battle, nothing that will last for any amount of time, but every little bit helps." Softly, he stood, walking over to his cot. Then, picking something up and turning around, he whispered, "I believe this is yours."

Numbly, Carpason took the proffered weapon, feeling his heart still. In his hands lay the short sword he had handed to a foreigner, what felt like years ago. Forcing air through his lungs, he breathed, "What happened to him?"

Stepping into the tent that held Arnacin, Carpason studied the captive. The islander sat tied to the tent's center post by his wrists. His face was colorless, his lips cracked, his gaze averted from the lord's.

Sighing, Carpason let the tent flap close behind him. "If there was one thing I would never imagine, it would be to hear the word 'traitor' and your name mentioned in the same sentence, Arnacin."

Looking back up, the islander whispered hoarsely, "I'm not sorry."

Changing the subject, the lord inquired, "Have they not given you any water?"

"I won't let them," Arnacin confessed. "I won't allow someone to force-feed me as if I was incapable of doing it myself, particularly not when they're just going to kill me later."

Shaking his head, Carpason warned, "You may want your strength before we reach the city." Arnacin made no reply and the noble dropped beside him, sighing. "I gather you knew exactly what you were doing."

With a slight smile, the islander stated, "I'm not a hasty person by nature, although some might assume otherwise."

"Arnacin, listen. Even if the boy is not a threat now, his return to his own kind, with the story of the village's downfall, may only strengthen their wish for vengeance."

"They will find out regardless. Something as large as that cannot be hidden, whatever you do, and who knows what mercy may inspire."

Sighing in mild exasperation, Carpason insisted, "Arnacin, should you simply agree that his escape is a danger to our cause and say, that should you go back, you would not do the same thing, we can all pass this over as a mistake owing to your foreign roots. Should you not, I do not possess the jurisdiction to prevent you from hanging."

"Then you cannot prevent it. I knew most of your arguments before I acted, as I'm sure Duke Cestmir told you. If I did go back, I would do the same thing, as you assuredly know. To say otherwise just to avoid the consequences would simply be a lie, and that I won't do."

"Arnacin, this is war. Sometimes there are things that happen in the name of our cause that none of us like, but cannot avoid. You know that."

"Lord Carpason..." the islander persisted, "tell me, if a native woman squabbled with her people and then fled to the city, where you promised her sanctuary in exchange for information, and then her brethren arrived, swearing lifelong peace and the end of the war should you deliver her dead body to them, would you?"

The lord simply studied the islander's earnest face. The word "no" glued itself to his tongue, yet he knew the goal of the question and could not utter that desired answer. Still, it required contemplation. Was it even related?

After another second, Arnacin added, "It would end the war and save Mira. Why would you not?"

"There are some morals that simply cannot be compromised," Carpason finally replied. "But are we speaking of the same thing?"

"While he may eventually become one more for that side, it will be several years before he is old enough and he is just *one* more. The rest of that entire village was wiped out. There is no extra information he could give them that they do not already know. You would only compromise your own honor through murder, nothing more."

For a long moment, the noble remained silent, staring at the thin slit between the tent flaps, through which the waning sunlight pierced. "Then the duke spoke true. We can only leave the judgment to Miro, and although I love and trust him, I don't know if he'll be wise in this matter."

"What is wisdom in this matter, my lord?"

Again studying the islander, Carpason returned the question, "What is it to you, Arnacin? I have a feeling your opinion will be very different from mine."

"I'm almost..." Licking cracked lips, Arnacin breathed, "Wisdom would change that law yet still condemn me to hang."

Disbelievingly, the lord stated, "You are an alien, Arnacin. Why would that be wisdom?"

"I deceived to achieve what I did. That calls for justice..." He fell quiet, a slight tremble betraying his fear. Although he said nothing about that emotion, he changed his sentence's course. "But wisdom would also recognize the lack of justice that caused the original circumstances."

Shaking his head, Carpason surmised, "You are incredibly hard on yourself and everyone else, Arnacin. There will come a time when you will have to realize that life is not–cannot–function in a black-and-white manner. If it could, our role as leaders would be much simpler."

"And much less should be compromised than often is."

Laughing slightly, the lord moaned, "Oh, Arnacin, if you put your rulebook into writing, I don't know what people would do with it."

"Laugh at it or burn it," the islander guessed. "I have the feeling there's not a person in the world who would try to actually live up to it."

Exhaling, Carpason inquired, "If I temporarily release you, you won't try to escape?"

With a ghost of a grin, Arnacin reminded, "I have nowhere to go."

After untying the rope around the islander's wrists, Carpason pulled out the blade that had been returned to him, stating with a touch of lightness, "You might want this." When the islander hesitated, the lord insisted, "For as long as you live, Arnacin, this is yours. Even should you die, I will always consider it yours. I gave it to you with no intention of retrieving it."

Sadly smiling, Arnacin accepted the weapon once more.

Carpason found that informing Cestmir of his choice, however, was far more difficult than making it. "Do you doubt that I will take full responsibility for whatever happens?"

"Don't turn it into a matter of your honor." Cestmir pounded the table in frustration. "Your Arnacin is entirely unpredictable. It's nothing to do with your responsibility. I can't have something else happen."

"What could happen, outside of his potential escape, which I don't fear?"

"Anything! He's a ship in a storm! The wind could change any minute!"

"So he's unstable?"

"Not the usual unstable, no. He's said to assist Mira, but he has no notion of what that means and holds only to his own counsel, with no fear of the consequences!"

"Arnacin helps Mira to the best of his understanding, but–"

A shout of warning was followed by screams renting the air. The ensuing clash of metal and the natives' battle cries forced both men to action. Drawing their blades, they raced from the tent.

Natives engaged clumps of Mirans throughout the camp, over which the emblems of Cestmir and Carpason fluttered in the breeze, unhindered by the angry fray below. Thankfully, the skirmish was brief, despite its ferocity.

Once the enemy had retreated, Carpason scouted the perimeter before returning to the duke's tent. "They killed the patrol," he sighed.

"So I expected," Cestmir said, glancing up from studying the ground. "I should have expected their attack as well. With two of us here, the fact that we were on the edge of the woods meant little to them. What I still cannot fathom is the person who alerted us."

As the lord sat down opposite him raising his eyebrows politely, the duke explained, "The savages attacked before they were ready since they lost the element of surprise, and the person who told us, thereby ruining their surprise attack, was your islander."

Innocently, Carpason asked, "And why does that surprise you?"

With an ironic smirk, Cestmir replied, "It would be common sense for someone in his position to hope for the annihilation of this camp while he slipped away. With us gone, no one would know what he did. Yet does he do that? No, he does just the opposite, and secures his execution in the process."

Sadly, the lord nodded. "You do not yet know Arnacin. He wouldn't do otherwise. As I was about to say before, he does what he believes is right and lets the consequences come as they will. Every individual's life is sacred to him. He never kills lightly or allows another to be killed before him."

The combined troop arrived in Mira three-and-a-half days later and, much as the commanders had expected, the duke instantly received a verbal message from the chamberlain asking him to the king's presence for a report. As Cestmir left his horse with a stablehand, the messenger added, glancing at the lord, "And when all is reported, he would like to talk to you alone, my lord."

"I'll be there," Carpason promised, watching them leave before turning to find that Arnacin already stood beside him.

"Some people might find that summons unnerving," the islander whispered with a wavering grin.

"For five years, I have only received variations on that summons," the lord admitted, putting a hand on Arnacin's shoulder. "I wish I could say that we'll find a way through this, Arnacin, but the best I can say is that Duke Cestmir has promised not to speak of it himself. He'll simply alert the king that there is an issue for his judgment. Though you may doubt it, the duke is a fair, honorable man."

Smirking, the islander stated, "I'll be the judge of honor. Mira doesn't usually seem to understand the meaning of the word, present company mostly excepted."

Shaking his head, the lord gave no reply.

Chapter 8

Mediums and Savage Gods

"And what do you need to discuss with me that Cestmir could not?" Miro demanded almost as soon as Carpason entered the hall where the king stood with his high councilor.

"I assume he informed you of his success in wiping out that village." When the king nodded, his lord licked his lips, finishing, "A native boy survived the attack, and they took him captive... until he was released."

"What!" the king thundered, causing the lord to wince. "Who dared such treason?"

"I do believe he can tell you himself." Stepping sideways, Carpason called, "Arnacin."

For a second, it seemed as if the room itself held its breath before a quiet whisper sounded behind Carpason and he knew the islander had entered the room. As Miro's gaze darkened on a spot behind his lord, this was affirmed.

"Dare you defy your very word?" the king growled as the islander stopped beside Carpason, the lowness of his tone deadlier than his earlier outburst.

"No," Arnacin whispered after a pause. "My word could not atone for a lack of justice, nor did I promise to aid in injustice."

"And what, pray tell, is unjust about executing murderers?"

"Nothing, if it is indeed murderers you execute. In this instance, I do not believe it was."

"You are not here to believe in anything to do with this war, foreigner."

"Then why should I assist?" Arnacin demanded. As Carpason shifted beside him, he slowly exhaled, pressing, "The captive about whom we speak did not fight against us, and he was too old for you to truly trust if this city had attempted to treat him as they do others. Should they have brought him here, there would be only one course of action, and I could not be part of it."

"He was an enemy, with information we do not wish them to possess."

"Details or not, they own that information anyway. Do you think they come across those battlegrounds, see the signs of slaughter, of death, of birds feeding on the carcasses of their own people, and feel no rage at it–at least of some kind? They gave their land to Mira when it was in need, allowed permanent homes built when they scorn the tearing of the ground, and yet they never complained. When Carta later attacked Mira because of Cartian greed, the natives not only let Mira remain on their shore, they assisted with supplies and tactics.

"For years afterward, Mira remembered that and, with honor, they drew a map of the land they would need, handed it to their neighbors, and promised never to grow beyond those lines. Yet that promise and honor crumbled through Mira's wish for peace among foreign allies, and varying degrees of greed.

"Your Majesty, your neighbors, whom you war with now, expect you to lack honor. They declared war because of it, because they believed that should they not act, Mira's lack of honor would wipe them out. Whether they hear about it or not, you are capable of proving them right or wrong, and stories of honor, as well as the lack of it, have a way of traveling thousands of miles. Don't prove them right–don't prove them right by killing needlessly."

After a long moment of silence, during which both king and lord studied the islander incredulously, Miro inquired, "And for someone such as yourself, what would be your excuse for avoiding punishment?"

"I don't have one," Arnacin admitted softly. "Do as you wish."

Silence fell on the room as Miro contemplated the islander, whose skin shone unusually white against his black hair. What seemed a lifetime later, Miro sighed, turning to Carpason, "How much do you trust him, my lord?"

Unable to control a relieved, weary grin, Carpason admitted, "With everything, Sire—not just my life, but the kingdom."

A red flush colored the islander's face, and the king nodded.

"Very well, Arnacin of Enchantress Island," Miro growled reluctantly. "I cannot cast any swift judgment in this instance. Return tomorrow afternoon and I will have an answer—yet you must return." With that warning, the king dismissed them.

Once they were out of earshot, Carpason soothed, "I believe you need not fear any longer. Exactly what he decides, I cannot tell you, but I highly doubt death is an option."

Weakly, Arnacin breathed, "I hope so. I want to go home. I just want to sail home."

Smiling sadly, the lord whispered, "You have some gift of eloquence, Arnacin. I hardly imagined that most convincing speech, mixed with as much honesty and as much of our history as it was. Whether he discusses it with his councilors or not, I doubt they shall sway whatever his opinion is now."

Arnacin made no comment and Carpason wrapped an arm around the islander's shoulder in wordless comfort.

Heart racing, Arnacin responded alone to the king's summons the next afternoon. His worry deepened when he realized that the king was also alone. It was just the two of them in the room.

"Arnacin of Enchantress Island." Miro inclined his head as the islander entered.

Arnacin nodded nervously, and, looking down, the king confessed, "I cannot allow such treason to go unpunished. However," he paused, studying the foreigner before saying, "I admit that you are partially right. Mira cannot act as her enemies expect or this war will never end. In light of that, I have decided to allow you to live, on the understanding that your actions will not be repeated. That decision aside, your actions must still be punished. Since your return home means the most to you, I demand that you do not touch anything to do with your ship for a week's time. In its place, you will spend that time as a drudge in the kitchens."

Arnacin's eyes closed in relief, yet he said nothing and Miro finished, "Everyone present for that occurrence has been ordered to keep silent and, should word spread, the wagging tongue shall be found and executed. This will be kept between us. Yet, Arnacin, I expect in turn that should you ever find that you have a moral problem with anything, you will come to me with it, instead of acting on your own. Understood?"

Forcing a smile, Arnacin nodded and the king dismissed him.

Evening was settling over the city. The market was clearing on the wharf, yet the sun still shone. It was proof that summer was on the way and, standing on the battlements of the inner bailey, Lord Carpason sighed. Summer's heavier air meant Melmoor stank of death, and even the light armor the Mirans always wore to battle, enabling them freer movement, was too heavy beneath the heat of the day.

The natives themselves stripped for battle during the hotter months and, perhaps because they felt fiercer without their clothes, or because they sensed that the heat tired their enemy, their attacks often increased.

Somehow, every summer passed, however, and Tarmlin's army remained.

"Lord Carpason," someone called. The lord turned to see Gagandep throwing his sack over his shoulder as he strode forward.

"Gagandep," Carpason inclined with a smile. "How fare your patients?"

"Sick, sick and sick," the native stated, an impish grin curling the corners of his lips. "Nothing life-threatening, yet some are sick from boredom and others from all your diseases. If you Mirans would learn to stay healthy..."

He left the rest hanging and Carpason nodded. "I'm sure your kin are always in perfect health, friend."

"Hardly," Gagandep muttered. Self-consciously rubbing the back of his finger along the side of his nose, the native inquired, "How is Arnacin?"

"Have you not seen him lately?"

"Not since you returned, and I heard he's facing death charges after rescuing a savage."

Giving the native a look of wide-eyed surprise, Carpason inquired, "Really?"

"Your lack of knowledge is unconvincing, my lord," the native stated. "I wish to know if he has been harmed or not."

Sighing, the lord admitted, "That news is supposed to be secret, Gagandep, but since I know you will not aid the gossip, that rumor is old. Four days ago, Miro conceded our foreigner's view and ordered a minor punishment only. Currently, Arnacin is swamped with kitchen chores, which is why you have not seen him. He is ordered to continue practicing his swordsmanship, but other than that, I don't know if he has emerged from the kitchen at all in the last three days."

"You know, I thought from the start that there was something..." Gagandep shrugged, before restarting, "I would almost assume Arnacin is native himself, only..." He frowned in concentration and finished, "different."

"Don't encourage his actions," the lord warned.

"Encourage, my lord? I love him for them, yet for you, I won't dare." When Carpason made no reply, the native commented, "When you're all through trying to pervert him with Miran garbage, I'll simply have to kidnap him and show him what really matters in the world." Smiling, he ended, "I intend to."

Returning the grin, Carpason sighed, "Unfortunately, I don't think he'll be here long enough. As soon as temporary peace comes, he'll set sail for home. He waits only for the tide of life to change."

"I thought he was here to stay," Gagandep whispered with a sudden sadness. "That he had landed for the same reasons that had formed Mira."

"I'm afraid not."

"Well then," the native replied, brightening slightly. "We'll simply have to kidnap him as soon as he tries, you and I."

The lord sadly breathed, "I love him too much to forcibly withhold his greatest desire from him should he live through the war itself. All the same, I hope I never see the day."

Gagandep said nothing beside him.

Summer's heat struck the very next week and, although it did nothing to slow the battles or war, the heat often discouraged sleep. On one rare, exceptionally humid night, Arnacin joined Gagandep's family for dinner in the adopted native's garden. Even after the family had drifted away and the food had been removed, the islander stayed at the table, his chin on his folded arms, while he and Gagandep chatted.

"Gagandep," Arnacin asked, as night settled around them. "Do the natives' have their own name? What were they called before Carta arrived?"

"There isn't one name. The natives are broken into tribes, connected only by the gods we all share. My tribe was called the Ragoosh, then there was the Titiles—they are our horse masters, if they still exist."

"Why wouldn't they?"

"It's possible that even if Mira didn't wipe them out, the other natives did, as traitors."

"Why?" Arnacin asked, straightening on the bench in indignation.

"The Titiles loved the plains for their horses. This land all the way to the mountains was once considered especially theirs. They were the main tribe responsible for aiding Mira. It was through them we learned Mira's tongue, and they have always believed in peace, that the gods are pleased by their attempts to keep it.

"On the other side, many of the natives think the gods desire Mira's elimination for their continued disregard of the natives and gods. They think that anyone who doesn't join them in vouching for the gods' justice betrays the gods."

"How can they think both?"

"The chieftains don't commune with the gods on their own, Arnacin. Only the mediums are allowed–" He stopped abruptly, shrugging.

"What do you think?"

"As adopted natives, we're left in blackness. We have no communion with the gods at all and can only go with the rules they gave us, which can be very conditional. Some of us have tried to commune with the gods on our own, but those the gods destroy very quickly."

"How are they destroyed?"

For a moment, Gagandep was silent, then he leaned closer, whispering, "To hear the gods, one must go through a certain ceremony. No matter how secret it is kept, Mira always seems to know about it. They come in to arrest and hang those involved, but even when they don't miraculously know about the ceremonies, those who just performed it die in their sleep, without a mark or a sign of assassination on them–healthy and strong one second, dead the next. The gods alone pick their mediums and so we are left in blackness."

"Why not just switch gods?" Arnacin cheekily inquired.

Laughing slightly, Gagandep answered, "We would die trying." They were silent a moment. Then, punching the islander lightly in the shoulder, the adopted native sighed. "You should go back to the castle. You told me Carpason leaves early tomorrow."

Carpason was given the task of the search that time, to Arnacin's relief. He also noticed that everyone else seemed more relaxed as well, at least while they traversed Mira's plains along the western side of the Guardian Hills. In fact, Hadwin rode by the group of infantry Arnacin walked beside to heckle him about not learning to ride.

"Until everyone of your troop rides, I will continue to walk, thank you," Arnacin remarked and, laughing, Hadwin urged his steed farther up the line.

Although he wanted to talk to Carpason about the natives' mediums, the islander waited until darkness covered the camp to lightly knock on the front support of the lord's tent. A moment of silence followed before he heard the usual, "Enter."

The lord sat on the low cot pulling his boots on when Arnacin ducked inside. A sense of painful nostalgia seemed to fill the space and it took a moment for the islander to consider the oddness of Carpason's action.

"Were you going to rest?" he asked, settling on the grass by the side of the cot.

A brief smile passed the lord's face, edged with furtiveness. "No, I was considering the best place to enter Melmoor." He paused and then said, "And on the field, I keep my boots on."

Smirking, Arnacin stated, "You were cleaning them. You know you could use any squire you wanted. Your Sir Lindan has six squires."

Carpason laughed. "He can keep them. I don't want a squire. For things I can't do, I can borrow one, but I don't want an official one. Yet, I've found unless I have someone near, I think better while doing something." His gaze was distant and, after a moment, he whispered, "It didn't used to be a problem. I always had someone to keep my thoughts engaged." He shook his head. "But, what do you need?"

Holding out his hand for the boot, the islander nodded. "It so happens that I think better while doing something as well, and a half-done task is worse than a task not started at all."

Smiling, the lord pulled out the cloths he had quickly stuffed between the cot and its supports. Then, pulling off his boots, he handed one to Arnacin and resumed cleaning the one he had started.

Turning his own attention to cleaning, the islander bent to his task and asked, "I was wondering what you know about the native's ceremonies to become mediums."

Carpason stilled and Arnacin could feel the questioning gaze boring through the top of his head. "Why do you wish to know about such evil, Arnacin?"

The islander shrugged. Somehow, he felt it better to leave it as idle puzzlement for the time being.

"Gagandep said Mira would hang those performing the ceremonies. I thought that odd, considering that Mira doesn't believe in the supernatural. Why would you kill someone for something that will make no difference, unless they actually mean to use it against you? If it's just superstition..."

When Arnacin trailed off, the lord slowly exhaled. "Miro considers such ceremonies as a sign that they are aligning themselves with the enemy, that they no longer wish to be Mirans. Believe me, though, they are given a Miran's respect in their burial."

Considering that, a word made Arnacin pause. "Why did you call them evil?"

Rubbing the bridge of his nose, Carpason asked, "Can't you ask something else?"

When he received no reply, he surrendered. "Our spies tell us that the natives start their ceremonies by chanting. Then, those desiring to hear their gods walk across hot coals. Those that manage not to burn their feet, at least not terribly, have a mark of an eye burned into their foreheads. It's an eye I have seen many a time on foreheads of the dead, and I shudder every time I do. There's something about them. I think it's supposed to look insightful, but I see flames in them."

He shrugged. "I have no idea how they think they could hide those marks from us, but it doesn't matter, because I've never seen anyone in the city with such a mark, though I have been told that some are buried while the burn is fresh."

"Gagandep thinks his gods kill them for daring to communicate with them on their own," Arnacin whispered, shuddering.

"Well, he would."

Distantly, the islander admitted, "If anything, I think you do see flames. I think they're selling themselves."

"To whom?" Carpason's tone was quizzical, his brow furrowed when Arnacin looked up.

Shaking his head, Arnacin said no more. Just the thought turned the tent icy cold despite the heat, and his stomach twisted.

"You know, Arnacin. Sometimes I forget you believe in the supernatural yourself. You act so sane, and then you say the strangest things."

His eyes dancing, Arnacin smiled grimly, "You forget. I'm incapable of believing otherwise. I'm from Enchantress Island."

For a long moment, the lord studied him without reply. Then, he nodded. "Were they anything like the natives' mediums?"

Slowly, the islander shook his head. "If you're asking if they were as twisted as the mediums, then yes, dragon and enchanter alike, but there the similarities end."

"Why did you name your island after something evil?"

"Again, you forget. My island's not Enchanter Island. It's Enchantress Island–named after the enchantress, the only survivor of her kind, as well as named because of our history. There is no memory before the enchanters' reign, and the islanders' love for the enchantress made it desirable for them to name their home after her. She's gone now–I think I told you that–but the stories will last, I'm sure."

"Right," Carpason muttered, and that was the end of their conversation that night. Shortly after, Arnacin handed the boot he had finished back to its owner and returned to his own tent.

Carpason decided to cross the Guardian Hills, travel up the east coast, and enter Melmoor at the foot of the natives' mountains. There was a good chance that the enemy would not think to watch that entrance as carefully, and the troop could perhaps make more of their search. Taking this indirect route could potentially extend their time away from Mira, but it was worth a try.

Every night, the lord heard the light knock that he came to expect as Arnacin and after two nights he found himself listening for it hopefully. The conversations that followed where not always strategically helpful in Carpason's opinion and would often range from Mira's history with the natives to the supernatural, yet the islander seemed to consistently return to the natives' mediums.

On the fourth night, the first in Melmoor, the lord asked again about the interest as they leaned over a map of the woods. Trailing his finger over a river on the map, which flowed down from the mountains, Arnacin asked, "Does it not make sense to eliminate the leaders of an enemy as soon as possible—to charge as straight a line as possible to where a leader stands?"

"You know it does."

Arnacin's dark eyes fixed on the lord then, and he whispered, "I think the mediums are the leaders."

"Why? We know for a fact the chiefs make the plans, order the tribes' movements. They only ask a medium's presence to curse their enemies or bless their endeavors. They never do anything else."

"Who told you so? Do you know their language to hear what they say?"

"Mannerisms inform us."

For a long moment, Arnacin stared at the map, silent. Softly, he whispered, "Gagandep believes that they are blind without their gods, that their gods are calling them to war. I don't doubt that their hatred would carry on without that fact, but it would weaken their strength, and the war might fall apart in weakness."

Not considering the fact that he thought the mediums made the god nonsense up, it was logical, yet it posed a different problem. "Under those circumstances, we can't win by logic, Arnacin. We can't win by proving our strength and we can't win by mercy, as we've been trying both for years. Our strength we show by destroying their war camps here, and our mercy we show by leaving their home alone, but if these tactics can't reach them..."

Leaning over until his elbow reached the table, he buried his face in his hands. "Unfortunately, such thoughts are mere speculation, which means Miro will not make plans to incorporate such ideas. It's too risky to act on just a hunch."

"How would the plan change if he did?"

"If we knew there was real risk, we'd make some kind of evacuation plans. As it is, I don't know and, honestly, I can't answer any more of your questions about the mediums. I never gave them much thought, and even if I had, I'm not sure even the natives would know."

"What sort of thing in particular would you need to know?"

Rubbing his sweaty palms together in contemplation, the lord replied, "How many of them are there? Could they instantly regenerate? Do they have a code of what their gods want so that all mediums say the same things? And if they are goading on the war, how much do the chiefs rely on them? Would the chiefs continue on their own or not?"

Arnacin's gaze flicked from the map to Carpason and back. Then he shrugged, "Capture a medium, alive."

"Even should that work, I'm afraid that would end the adopted natives' loyalty to Mira. Their loyalty to their gods would make it impossible to force one of their prophets into giving information away. We would become the enemy even to those who only acknowledge their native heritage now."

After a pause in which Carpason knew they were both thinking of Gagandep, Arnacin sighed, "You have to try. You need those answers before it's too late."

Slowly, the lord nodded. "If we come across one in this search, we'll try. We may need to stay in Melmoor while we question him, which is in itself a risk, but the betrayal that would appear throughout Mira would be far worse."

They found nothing in their search, although they were attacked several times and, during one attack, the natives stole their supplies–food, water and extra weapons. Carpason forced them five miles to the south, closer to Mira, and then made them pitch camp as evening came on. Yet the lack of water after their struggle with the natives left them weaker and the lord called Hadwin to his tent. Although he noticed Arnacin following, he said nothing to stop the islander.

"Hadwin," he sighed when the tent flaps had settled behind them. "Tomorrow, we must change course, northwest to the closest waterway–"

"You'll walk into a trap," Arnacin spoke up. "If the natives think rationally at all, they will surround the nearest waterway, knowing you'll go there, and that you'll be weaker when you arrive."

"I'm well aware of that, Arnacin, but we don't have much choice. If we don't go there, they'll set upon us in a few days anyway, and we won't have the strength to fight them. Our only chance is to change our course now while we're strong and hopefully some of us will break through. They ripped holes in our water skins as well. We don't have a drop."

In the brief pause, Hadwin bowed. "I will let everyone know, my lord."

"Wait!" In Arnacin's haste, he had grabbed the knight's arm and Carpason smiled grimly. "Milord, I can help you steal some of the trees' water—enough to keep each man moving. I can also find some of the plants that will give the most energy and your cooks can make hard bread from it." Reddening, he released Hadwin, dropping his gaze to the floor. "Please."

Meeting Hadwin's expression of raised eyebrows, the lord nodded. "You've been trained by Gagandep, Arnacin, not us. If there is a way to cheat the enemy's tactics, we will take it."

A few hours later, the islander returned with some water held in a folded leaf. As he handed it to Carpason, he said, "I will be back by morning, but if by some reason I'm not, don't wait for me."

Carpason could not hold back his soft laugh. "That's not a request, Arnacin. It's a borderline order you lack the authority to give."

"I only mean—"

Placing his hand on the islander's shoulder, the lord nodded with a smile. "I know. Take at least ten men with you."

"It will be better if I go alone."

"Arnacin, if you take a light out there, you'll be ambushed in moments, and by yourself you'll have no chance of living."

A sly smile passed Arnacin's face. "I had no intention of taking a light."

Staring into those eyes, dancing with impishness, Carpason warily asked, "Don't tell me you can see in the dark?"

"Our island lived for hundreds of years without even the light of stars or moon, owing to the enchanters' power. I've heard it said that our eyes changed then and it has never altered back. As long as the slightest amount of light is in the sky, I can see outlines and shapes. I will be able to find different plants in the darkness. I can hear if someone approaches, and I will know the plants by their scent."

With a flip of his hood as he covered his head, he disappeared.

Arnacin's plan succeeded and, although they were attacked once more before they reached the safety of the plains, they survived. They did stop for the night in a village to purchase enough supplies to make it to the capital. Unfortunately, when they did, Carpason had nothing useful to the war to report, but when he told Miro of the savages' tactics and Arnacin's solution, the king turned away, rubbing his chin.

"Has he taught his knowledge to anyone of Tarmlin?" the king asked, turning back.

"Not entirely," Carpason whispered, his gaze fixed on the flagstones a few paces from Miro's feet.

"Why ever not? That seems to be extremely important information."

Bowing, the lord said, "I'll see what we can do." Straightening, he added, "What do you think the possibilities are that the savages' belief in gods are causing the war?"

For a second, Miro blustered without words. Then he exclaimed, "Preposterous! You might as well ask if a tree causes the war. It is absurd. Why would you ask?"

"I merely wished to know your thoughts."

"Then I have given them. Go rest."

Standing at the library windows, Valoretta trailed her fingers along its sill. Arnacin had not been there for weeks and the emptiness was starting to depress her. In the harbor, she could see the little dot that was the islander on his ship, kneeling on the deck. He had no need of the library's contents to fix his ship anymore, and there was never the time to return for other reasons.

Yet Valoretta lacked the freedom to join him instead. Or did she?

Her loneliness convinced her and, picking up her book, she slipped out. After asking a maid for a plain long shawl, she waited. The maid returned shortly with the requested shawl and though her curiosity was obvious by the tilt of her head, no questions were asked.

Wrapping herself in the shawl's folds, the princess slipped out of the castle and down to the wharf. Thankfully, her trips to the market with her nurse had familiarized her with the roads, and it was an easy matter finding Arnacin's little thing of a ship. Up close to it, she paused. It had never occurred to her how strange it was, with its long, sloping nose and a short, stubby cabin in the back.

Disregarding the oddity, she stepped up the ramp, asking softly, "May I join you?"

Arnacin jumped where he knelt, tarring the gaps between the deck boards. "Valoretta," he gasped, his gaze taking in the shawl she held tightly wrapped around her head and falling over her dress. "Are you alright?"

She nodded hastily and he stood, holding out his hand. "You'll have tar stains on your skirt." His own pant legs were rolled above his knees.

Accepting his supporting grip as she lifted her skirts, Valoretta sighed, "It's so much nicer out here. The library just felt like a black pit."

Guiding her to the rail to sit, Arnacin settled himself beside her, pulling his pant legs back down. His expression was merely thoughtful and, unsure of her reception, the princess slowly opened her book. She looked back up to see that he was also staring at the pages. "Valoretta," he finally whispered. "Do you believe you are right to read?"

The princess heaved a sigh of exasperation. "Don't go telling me what is proper and isn't! My mother and father believed it important! Why should I stop?"

Dark blue eyes regarded her without pride or condemnation. "I would never tell you what's proper, as you should know." A sad puff of amusement escaped him. "My family never knew the meaning of the word. I think you need to decide, though. If you believe you are right to read, read in the open, Valoretta. Only wrongs must be hidden. If you are right, reveal it, let the rumors spread. Don't ever let fear stop you. Your people deserve your conviction."

Valoretta simply stared at the islander while those words tumbled through her mind. After another moment, Arnacin returned to work and, still thinking about it, the princess' gaze traveled to the water, sea green and vast.

"But Sara," she finally said. "How could I just tell her I was going to read no matter what she thought?"

A smile passed the islander's face as he glanced up. "Is that a question of respect? I don't think acting behind her back is respect. Telling her why you feel it's right or stopping is respect. If she doesn't agree..." He shrugged, resuming his work.

It sounded easy, but as she slipped into her room sometime later and ran right into Sara, the easiness evaporated. Her nurse looked like a thundercloud, her arms akimbo. Hastily, the princess hid the shawl balled in her hand behind her back. "Look at your skirt!" Sara exclaimed. "Wood shavings, straw... Is that tar?"

Stammering, the princess pressed her back into the door, but as Arnacin's words again rang in her mind, she closed her eyes, and exhaled preparatorily. "I went to read outside, in the market."

Her nurse's face lost all color. "Valoretta, have you lost your mind?" she gasped. "Queen's aren't supposed to read, and what were you doing in the market?"

"I'm the heir of Mira, Sara, not simply destined to be queen."

"You will need a husband and he will need a queen, not a contester."

"No! Mira is my responsibility, can you not see? Her people must know they can trust me, that I'm wise..."

Softening, Sara sighed. "I know what your father wants, but I think he is being impractical. I don't ever want you to have the opposition such a path would take. Hopefully, you were not recognized, but even if you somehow avoided harm, never do it again."

"I think I need to, Sara," Valoretta said firmly, yet without heat. With a soft smile, she added, "Mira deserves my conviction, and I will give it to them. I have been taught to read by my father and I will continue reading to further my knowledge." She realized she had straightened while speaking. No longer resting against the door, she stood erect. "Even if I am ever shunted aside to become simply a queen, that knowledge will help the king and all of Mira. I must read, I will read, and I will do so without shame. Such is my right and my duty."

Sara's gaze was wide, even oddly afraid the princess thought. Yet in another moment, that expression vanished and the nurse stomped to the door. "Stay here! I will be back to change you into a clean dress."

As her nurse vanished, Valoretta collapsed against the wall with a satisfied exhale. At the moment, she felt she could face anything.

Instantly, Sara went to the king's private room, where he was settling for the evening. There, she told the king of what happened and her thoughts that the foreigner was behind it. Miro's reaction, however, left her speechless. He smiled distantly, as if he was picturing the change in his daughter. Looking up, he said, "I would call that wisdom, Sara."

"But, Sire," the nurse pleaded. "Think about this for a moment. She's a girl. She can never be a king, and if she holds more respect than her husband among the people, our allies are going to look at that as a sign of weakness and break their alliances."

Sighing, Miro stood, walking around the table to take her hand. "Sara," he whispered. "Why do you think I have deliberated so long in choosing a husband for her? At thirteen, she should at least be betrothed, but there are no easy answers with her. She needs to be ready for the worst, and the only way she can be ready is by making her own choices now. She's not a prince. I can't make her a page or send her onto the fields, and without being on the field, she would not make a very good high councilor. Reading and making her own choices are the only ways she can learn. You must let her do so."

Yanking her hand away, Sara dropped a curtsy, her gaze fixed on the floor. Somehow, she could not seem to make her fears understood. It was pointless.

Although true that most foreign kingdoms did not send ambassadors to Mira in the summer, some, such as Ursa, trickled in despite the war. It was while the Earl of Garak was conferring with the king that word came of an ambassador sailing under the emblem of the yellowed-eyed black bear on a crimson background.

"Ursa is on Mira? Let them wait," Miro growled, returning his attention to the earl. "Lord Carpason is overseeing repairs on the sea wall. Please send him to me, and then rest."

As the earl bowed and left, Memphis stepped near, bowing in the way he did when he had something to say, yet refused to open the conversation himself. Miro sighed, "Yes, Memphis?"

"Do you really want to keep Ursa waiting? They'll think something's wrong, and you know they're just looking for some weakness."

Drumming his fingers on his folded arm, Miro contemplated those words and then slowly nodded to the sea-gate messenger. "Tell the guards he may come after notifying the castle that the courtiers must come to the great hall. Ursa will never see us except in our finest. Sara is to keep Valoretta in her rooms, though."

Carpason entered a moment before the ambassador and Miro motioned for the lord to stand to the right of the throne in front of Memphis.

The Ursans' had sent their lordship, Catari, the son of their baron, Barrik, as the ambassador this time and, seeing him, Miro's fingers tightened on the arms of his throne. Catari was in his thirties, silver-tongued and smooth. Ladies would call him dashing if they were not Miran, for his physique was both strong and refined, and his short hair pure yellow. He had bested quite a few of the Mirans in tournaments and, with midsummer only two weeks away, the usual day of Mira's Summer Festival, the king did not doubt that the Ursans had sent Catari on purpose.

It was also common assumption, due to some of their similar names and rumors of their "magic," that the Ursans began as simply different tribes of the Miran savages. The Ursans might have adopted the common trading speech and customs, but underneath, they were as much at odds with Mira as the savages.

Ursan ambassadors stepped foot on Mira, or vice versa, and the real politics began—constant probing, ceaseless manipulation, pandering compliments, and veiled insults. This was no different.

"What makes his lordship come to Mira at this time of the year?" Miro asked as the ambassador bowed.

"We have been concerned, Sire. We have not been invited to one of your Summer Festivals in five years, and we were afraid it might be because you were too exhausted due to the war."

Keeping his temper controlled, Miro smiled without parting his lips. "Is that so?"

"Word has also come to us that your swordmaster, who trained all your magnificent men-at-arms, fell in the spring, and the thought came to us that perhaps you felt you no longer had the skill to waste in a tournament."

Purposely glancing at Carpason, who was one of the few Mirans who remained unrivaled by the Ursans, the king asked, "Do you feel exhausted, Lord Carpason?"

The lord's iron gaze never left the ambassador and his arms remained folded. "We would only rejoice at the prospect of a tournament, Sire. It would remove our boredom."

His smile overly bright in Miro's opinion, Catari laughed, "I'm so pleased to hear that. Ursa is graciously offering to give the rewards this year."

Miro heard Memphis click his tongue behind him. Smiling slightly, the king said, "Although a generous offer, I would not want to impoverish Ursa." The ambassador's blue eyes just barely flickered at the returned insult, yet there was no hint to Ursa's financial standing. Miro continued, however. "We were, of course, holding the festival as we do every year, but the invitations had become a death threat, at least that was how our allies took it. If, however, you have any men daring enough to accept this year, please do come."

Catari only bowed. "Then I will leave immediately and inform my king."

"Splendid!"

With that, Miro dismissed the court and, when the room was empty except for himself, Memphis and Carpason, he turned to the latter. From where he'd hidden it in his sleeve, Miro pulled out the map on which the location of the enemy encampment had been drawn.

"Deal with them, Carpason," he sighed in weariness. "But please, return in time for the festival. We don't have the money to allow any Ursans victory, or anyone else, despite the fact that their presence will increase our bathhouse's revenue and subsequently our treasury."

"I will do my best, Sire," the lord promised with a bow.

Chapter 9

The Islander's Troop

"We have a bit of a problem, Arnacin," Carpason said, walking his horse beside the islander in his men's formation. "We don't have time to draw out a battle to make sure a medium lives, if there is one, yet we need one. We also don't want the savages to know that we're after a medium. So how do we accomplish both?"

The lord was thinking aloud really. Yet he noticed Arnacin glance up at him, those dark blue eyes seeming to be waiting for something, serene as if the problem was only imagined by Carpason.

Coughing softly, the lord asked, "Alright, Arnacin. What are you thinking?"

A brief smirk of amusement lit the islander's face. Then it vanished as he shrugged. "What if you send half of your men around to make a blockade of fallen trees..."

"Trees they cut of course?"

"Yes, and then, when that's done, create a stampede of some kind that drives the natives toward that wall where your men will shoot them down from on top?"

"How is that supposed to accomplish both?" Carpason asked in complete bewilderment.

"It drives the enemy away from where they were and thereby leaves some behind." Arnacin was looking away from the lord, eastward, as he whispered that, his tone distant, and Carpason's free thumb tapped his thigh.

"You're not saying something you're thinking, Arnacin. It still doesn't make sense to me."

The islander sighed and abruptly stopped walking. Holding out his hand, he said, "Pull me up."

Once Arnacin sat behind him, Carpason whispered, "Is this about magic? You don't wish to be overheard?"

"Something like that, milord. 'Magic,' as you call it, has a connection to all of nature. Humans can train themselves to grow blind to it, but animals and plants, they never can. Therefore, it is my thought that, although a terrified, charging beast will trample anything in its path and run straight over cliffs at times, a medium can harness the power of that fear to stare them down, and even a charging herd of beasts will break around him like waves cut by a rock. That evil would become the source of their terror and nothing would make them go near it."

"Alright. We'll try it, as you have more experience in magic, Enchanter," Carpason muttered. "I think we'll have to stop in a village, though, for a herd of cattle. Horses charge, but they're not the same, and ours are war horses, which means they're trained to be very different indeed."

One man was willing to allow the troop to borrow a herd of his beef cattle after Carpason paid him in advance for any harm that might befall the cows and promised to return all still living. Driving the cattle before them, they approached the edge of Melmoor only a mile from the enemy encampment, which the lord's scouts had informed him was still there.

Leaving Hadwin to pitch camp there, still in relative safety, the lord took two-thirds of his men and Arnacin, skirting the enemy camp by a mile.

Just within the trees, however, Carpason pulled up, spotting a naked savage in the leaves, shivering with fever from an arrow in his arm.

"Circle," the lord whispered to his men as he dismounted. "And have a few of our archers climb the trees."

His men secured the place in moments and, untying the blanket that sat behind his steed's saddle, he approached the savage. "Do you want me to finish it for you?" he asked while lightly dropping the blanket over the suffering savage, again taking in the lack of clothes indicating that the savage had been in battle.

The savage just continued to tremble, his eyes scrunched up. Carpason had no idea if he was even aware that the Mirans were there. "Why did your own kind shoot you?" he asked all the same.

The savage's eyes flew open. "I refused to join the ground attack... in an arrow ambush." He twitched and, just by his movements and the color of his eyes, the lord knew the savage only said anything because his life was already over. In another second, his breath gurgled in his throat and the trembling stopped.

Pulling his blanket over the savage's face, Carpason remounted and ordered his men forward once again. They had to find a good place for a blockade, yet the savages' cruelty to each other dampened the air.

It was Arnacin who spotted the natural dip in the forest floor, almost on a straight run from the location of the enemy camp. If the savages were trying to flee a stampede, they would take the flat ground, which aided speed, and run straight into a blockade. With troops lined along both sides of the place the savages were to be directed, they could block off all escape routes.

To keep such a thing secret, they just had to build their blockade overnight.

The stampede caused what Arnacin had predicted. One native muttered unintelligible words in a deep voice, which caused the ground to tremble. High bellows of fear rose from the charging beasts as they swerved aside, but with only a grim smile, Arnacin bent his bow where he hid a few feet from where the Mirans chased the stampede through the enemy camp, scattering the natives before them.

As the islander's arrow pierced the medium's leg where he stood, he stumbled to the ground and the Mirans were upon him.

Knocking their captive senseless, they wrapped him in blankets and carried him to their own encampment.

There, Hadwin ordered fifty men to stand guard over the captive with Arnacin, while he took the rest to reinforce Carpason at the blockade.

Once the whole troop had returned, Carpason and Hadwin joined the islander by the tightly bound captive and they shook him awake. The medium's eyes instantly lit with hatred, matching something in the eye burned onto his forehead, a dark hatred quite unlike a human's, but then it disappeared just as quickly.

It was, however, a human who spoke, glancing as if afraid from Hadwin to Carpason with their drawn blades. "Please, I don't know anything. I don't join in the fighting. I would never think of it."

Carpason's cold expression remained unchanged as he snapped, "How many of you are there, and are you attached to individual tribes?"

Yet the medium's eyes had turned to Arnacin and the eyes glimmered, whirled into dizzying circles. Then, in a voice that sounded as if a million shrill beings were growling in unison, the medium spoke again, all trace of fear and pleading gone. "We are many, and one, as you already know. Come, do you truly wish to know more? We would be glad to show you. You are wise and don't ignore us. Come."

Sweetness had entered that sound, the drone of bees around a sweet fruit, and Arnacin felt exhaustion creep across him, yet he backed away, breaking his gaze with those swirling eyes to glance at the other two. They appeared quite still, however, as if they had heard nothing, or perhaps they heard something entirely different. Yet the voice coaxed on, "You want to do great things, Islander? You want to feel that you have helped the world? One small boy in all of this evil? Impossible. Your god plays with you, but we? We can give you the ability to do so. You can transform the world with our power, see people live in harmony, where flowers bloom and children sing. You can know that you gave everything for them, and feel that joy of purpose. *You* gave everything."

Those voices were so loud his ears rang, his head felt like it would split open, crack into quarters, and still those voices continued.

With great force, Arnacin jerked away. "Stop!" he cried. He dropped to the floor gasping, wrapping his arms around his pounding head. After a second, he whispered, "Just tell us what we want to know."

"Arnacin?" Carpason's concerned question snapped through the wailing in the islander's ears.

Looking up, he saw the medium laying on the ground, his eyes staring sightless at the ceiling with a trickle of blood running from his mouth and over his cheek. "What happened?" Arnacin gasped, quickly pushing himself back to his feet.

Carpason only shook his head in horror, and it was Hadwin who found his voice. "He was just shaking his head, pleading his innocence. Then suddenly he started convulsing, and he started... making sounds as if he had a million different voices he could use all together. It was high-pitched screams, laughter... squeals all at once. His face changed, skull-like, then he just stopped moving. His eyes glazed over..." He trailed off and, with a shaking hand, Carpason patted his shoulder.

"I don't think he could have said anything, perhaps," the lord whispered with a shudder. "But, Arnacin, what happened to you? We heard you scream something, but I don't think it was in our language and, after he died, you were shaking on the ground."

For a long moment, Arnacin was silent, unable to pull his eyes off the body only a few feet from them. Finally, he whispered, "I've never seen a sorcerer before. They're horrible."

"Come," Carpason ordered after a moment, and Arnacin flinched at the word. "We can't stay here. Burn the tent with him inside. I won't ever want to erect this thing again. And we have cows to return and a festival we're supposed to attend."

It seemed to Arnacin that the whole troop was subdued on the return trip, but perhaps he imagined it as those words from the medium tumbled through his mind. Why had he alone been so tortured? Was it because he did believe in the supernatural? Yet they had seen horrors that he had missed somehow, despite the fact that he had been staring at it until the very last moment.

Nothing seemed possible, but one fact remained. No one in Mira was any closer to figuring out what they had to know–the hints Gagandep had unintentionally dropped.

It was as he thought of Gagandep's loyalty to a people group that slaughtered each other without mercy, that he again thought of Carpason's reaction to the dying one in the forest and he looked up at the lord.

Arnacin had volunteered to work on the lord's armor that night and Carpason simply stood at the tent's entrance, staring out across the plain.

"Milord," the islander softly asked. Slowly, Carpason turned to him and Arnacin noticed the lines of weariness that had nothing to do with his physical condition. He did not comment on it, however. "Why do you not share Mira's view of the enemy? You'll actually call them 'natives.'"

Smoothing a wrinkle in the tent's flap, the lord sighed. Finally, he whispered, "I grew up around them, more or less. Tarmlin was our trading city with the mountains. When I was a boy, it was a swelling hub of natives and Mirans. Families would come into the market and, while the adults bartered, the children played. I had several I considered friends." His gaze was distant, his words slow in memory, and Arnacin did not interrupt. "I don't remember their names, but nationality meant nothing to us, except our skills when we competed in our games.

"There was one in particular that I liked. His thick build was cumbersome, yet he moved with the prowess of a cat. Nine times out of ten, he always bested me at whatever we played.

"Then those days passed. I moved to the capital to train under the swordmaster and, two years after moving back as my father's squire, war broke out. I was about your age when my father died in battle. All of a sudden, I was a commander, fighting alongside the prince, our Miro, *rescuing* him even. Our friendship grew in that time..."

For a long time, Carpason was quiet. Then he said, "He's a great man, Arnacin, despite his faults. I wish you knew that."

As the lord's eyes flicked to him, however, all Arnacin saw in his mind's eye was the despair of the knights and the massacre of natives. Dropping his gaze to his work, he said nothing, and Carpason sighed.

"As you know, the war ended when Prince Noblius ascended the throne twenty-two years ago to become King Miro. I went home to find it would never be the same again. Although we still had peaceful trade with the natives, they no longer flocked the streets. They came in silence for the things they wanted, and left in the same silence. As I was a noble, they avoided me and if they even glanced at me, it was with fear.

"I knew then that war might resume someday, yet I tried to stop that unease with a constant open friendliness. It did nothing. After ten years of this unsettled peace, the natives' tension grew until their young men would come to Tarmlin to wreck market stands and throw stones at Mirans. I didn't know what to do. I was afraid to fuel their anger by stopping them, but I couldn't let them continue.

"I asked Miro for his advice, telling him of my concerns. His response was to inform them that the attacks must stop or the market would close and they would no longer be allowed in Tarmlin. That warning only fueled their anger, and we were forced to carry out our verdict. Two months after they were removed, Tarmlin was attacked."

A long silence fell. Arnacin knew the lord was again feeling the loss of his family, but when Carpason spoke again, he chose not to relay the story of his loss. "For years, I thought of them as every other Miran does and was glad to destroy the monsters. Yet after eliminating one enemy encampment, we found an infant hidden in the forest. Considering his age, his mother must have hidden him–and likely died with the village." Carpason's voice broke. "I looked at those tiny fists, those scrunched eyes, and toothless mouth, screaming for a mother who was no more. In that moment, I remembered that they were people, whether or not they had started the current war. Underneath, they were people with their own hurts, their own reasoning..."

"What happened to the baby?"

"You must know, Arnacin, that adopting natives is now illegal. Their connection can easily make them enemies if they know. That aside, I gave the child to a new mother and father in one of our villages. They had a son about the same age as the infant, but I warned them never to let the child know he was native. As far as I know, he's still there. He's probably six or seven now. I hope the war will be over before he is too old for such a lie to deceive him."

Yet, without the answers the medium was incapable of giving, how could it? All those poor misled natives, all the despairing Mirans–they would destroy each other. The medium had spoken the truth–there was nothing Arnacin could do to stop the war except stumble along on the best course available and hope for a good outcome.

As if sensing the islander's pain, Carpason looked over, smiling. "Come on, Arnacin. We're not dead yet. There will be a way. Two days ago, the thought would have never occurred to us to enact the plan you devised. Even though it may not have turned out the way we'd hoped it would, it was a very good tactic and I'm sure you will come up with more of them."

Thankfully, Mira did immensely well against Ursa in the festival that year. Yet despite Carpason's insistence that they still had hope, no one could deny Mira was continuing to lose the war, slowly but steadily. After long thought, Carpason approached Miro on the subject in the autumn, four months after the spring in which Arnacin had arrived.

"Sire," Carpason inclined. "I assume you are well aware of our current position in this war." When Miro only exhaled in stressed acknowledgment, his lord continued, "I think we may do better if we have another troop on the field."

"Led by whom, pray tell? There are no nobles left fit for the task. They're all too young, too sick or immobilized. Unless you suggest allowing men to go without commanders–an outrageous idea–we cannot have another troop on the field."

"I think," Carpason began carefully, "Arnacin could lead." The look he received was pure incredulity. "Please hear me out, Sire. I know he's young and impetuous, but he has a mind for strategy and a way of thinking uniquely when problems arise. I think that if you give him the right men, who are able to coach him along, particularly in the area of mature caution, he can provide the insight even the better generals are lacking."

For a long moment, Miro contemplatively ran his fingers along his jaw, studying his lord. Finally, as if to himself, he commented, "He might need to learn those skills regardless, and perhaps the savages' knowledge of his honor can bring about some change if they know that Mira allows him such a position."

Smiling, Carpason asked, "Then you agree?"

"I will contemplate it," Miro promised. "Before I do, however, answer this: will all the commanders act as spies? If each troop gives ten of their most wise, most loyal men to this new troop under the islander, will they report everything back to their original commanders? Do not misunderstand me. It is not that I distrust Arnacin, but if he appears too rash, I wish to know of it before we lose control of the situation."

"I am sure we each have men who would be willing to do so," Carpason promised.

As autumn came on, the days were cooler, the dockside slightly quieter. On his ship's deck, making rope for ratlines, Arnacin barely had to pay attention to his work anymore, doing it entirely by rote. Above him, sitting on his rail, Valoretta sat in silence with a book in her lap. The shawl wrapped around her head did little to hide her identity should anyone really look, but neither of them cared much.

"Arnacin?" Valoretta asked, breaking the silence. When he looked up, dragging his thoughts away from the distant shores of his home, she continued, "What do you do at sea?"

"What do you expect?" Arnacin returned, completely perplexed.

"I mean, you're awfully young, and you don't even have someone to whom you can talk." She turned red as she said it and quickly muttered an apology, but the islander simply shrugged.

"It was a choice between going alone and not going at all. I–" He broke off as someone hailed him from shore. One of Carpason's men was approaching the ship. Reaching it, he glanced at the princess in surprise, hastily bowing low. Meeting Valoretta's gaze, Arnacin grinned, while she rolled her eyes in response. She quickly rearranged her features into composed dignity as the man looked back up.

"Your highness," the newcomer murmured. Then, he turned to the ship's proprietor. "King Miro requests your presence at once, Arnacin," he informed.

Glancing again toward the princess, this time in apology, the islander nodded, pushing himself to his feet.

"He can't be serious," Arnacin raved at Lord Carpason as they left the council room together thirty minutes later. "I'm trained in leadership as much as your cooks. All your knights know far more. Why does he not ask one of them? If you send out unknowledgeable men as leaders, you'll only reap dead men as a reward!"

"Arnacin," Carpason finally cut in, albeit gently. "If you are afraid of your lack of skill in weaponry..." Although the islander sighed, Carpason did not pause. "You need not worry. Most commanders only make up the brains behind their troops. Many of our nobles don't even step foot on the battlefield for that reason. They leave with their men, assess their target, and then stay safely surrounded while most of their troops do the actual fighting. Now, it was I who suggested you as someone to take command."

He smiled slightly at the islander's look. "You never try to hide your thoughts when you think things should be done differently than I am conducting them, my friend. More often than not, however, I find wisdom behind your words, a shrewdness and ability. I have complete faith in you. Your swordsmanship will continue to improve as well, never fear. None of us would expect you to be great after only four months, but you are improving. Whenever blades come into use, you have never failed to defend yourself, and you show promise that a third of the people I know never do." He comfortingly patted the boy on the shoulder and turned away, leaving Arnacin to glare at the wall instead.

Before Miro sent any armies out, he had each commander give ten men to the islander, amounting to a troop of almost two-hundred men. Carpason generously sent Sir Hadwin as one of his ten.

"My lord," Hadwin inquired, after Carpason informed him of the assignment, "I like Arnacin quite a bit, but isn't this madness? At his age, most nobility are not commanders and they're trained from birth for the mantle of leadership."

Sighing, Carpason gestured for his knight to follow him. Only once he was in the safety of his own rooms did the lord whisper, "I pushed for it, for reasons I will not tell the king. Tell no one, Hadwin, what I am about to confide in you."

Nodding in agreement, the knight nevertheless said, "If it is so secret, my lord, I need not be told."

"I am telling you because, as a man of your age and experience, I am hoping that if and when the need comes, you can counsel with a clear head. I want Arnacin to be a commander precisely because he is a foreigner. He has an unbiased view and also has the persuasive tongue to convince others of what he sees, as long as every part of his being fully believes in what he is saying. In short, Hadwin, I want him to realize that the only way to win this war is through infiltration of the natives' mountains, whether it must come to attack or not."

"My lord," Hadwin gasped, "what are you saying?"

"I have believed for some time that we cannot allow the savages to keep their sanctuary, but as many different ways as I try, I do not have the talent Arnacin does. I try reason—he comes from a view of absolute knowledge that his way is right." He smiled. "Whether he is or not is another matter. Therefore, it must be Arnacin to suggest this to the king and, for him to succeed, he must come to that answer by himself. I cannot tell him to go speak of this to the king, because if he does not believe in it, he will convince no one. Also, if he has to start infiltration before Miro gives permission, I know he will, but that is where I hope you can help. Should he need persuasion to speak to Miro when he does come to that conclusion, it is my wish that you push for it."

"My lord, this seems like a most dangerous game. What if he does speak to the king and Miro still, despite the winning passion and eloquence, refuses? Arnacin is not the type to sit by or submit."

"Then it will be one of those times I wish I believed in Arnacin's god. Nevertheless, it must be tried, for Mira."

Two days after receiving the command, Arnacin was personally requested by the king to gather his troop and scout for enemy camps. Slowly inhaling in preparation, the islander bowed out of the king's presence, knowing that in seconds, his command would end in uproar. No one would like his ideas for the troop, yet the king and Carpason had ordered him to command.

True to his expectations, a stunned silence followed when he directed his men to leave all their tents behind. If they could not carry something themselves, they could not bring it. Extra food, water and blankets would be packed on the warhorses' backs during marches, and every man would carry their own quiver, arrows, blades, a pack of food, blankets and a canteen of water.

When someone finally found their voice enough to ask about armor, Arnacin answered, "Pack only the most needed pieces on the horses."

They were too well-trained to question an order from someone the king had placed in control, but not long after the march had begun, taking up the rear in the cluster of men and horses, Arnacin felt their discontent flavoring the air like a burning pot over an open fire. "We'll all be frozen dead by tonight," someone close by muttered and Arnacin bit his tongue.

A few hours into their march, he halted the troop and, standing before them, began, "I did not explain things this morning, and I'm sorry. Being that you don't trust me yet and most of you have no reason to..." He glanced at Cestmir's troops. "I will explain myself. Should any of you disagree, now is the time to say why—after I've made my case.

"I'm a shepherd by birth and know much about moving in the woods. The less we bring, the less noticeable we are and the more quickly we can move. In addition, by using the woods' natural resources for shelter at night, we will lessen the attacks against us by dark. I am not that concerned about lacking food, since I both know how to use ours sparingly and replace it when we do run out, and I intend for each of you to learn yourselves, for your own sakes. Does any of that seem unwise to you?"

"What natural shelters do the woods offer?" one man inquired.

Before Arnacin could respond, another man, still young compared to many of the others there, answered, "Underbrush, piled leaves, things of that nature. By night, someone could walk right through us and never notice. Combined with blankets and each other's body heat, we'll be quite warm. The enemy does similar things with their patrols."

Regarding the man, Arnacin inquired, "How are you so learned?"

Grinning, the man repeated, "I mean no impudence when I ask, how are you? I'm Firth, son of Gagandep—and you, a foreign citizen of a land without wars. Father has not said anything of strategy, I know, yet I doubt you ever slept outside of a bed before coming here."

"Perhaps we do not make beds," the islander stated teasingly. "What do you know of shepherding?"

"I confess, nothing."

"Very well then. We will leave it at that. Any other doubts?"

"The enemies don't bring horses down their mountains. Do you expect them to hide as well?"

"I pray they are as well-trained as I've been told and will sleep beside you on the ground during the night. Is that possible?"

Several nods followed and, after waiting another few seconds for a complaint that did not come, the islander gently ordered, "Let's resume the march."

With that, he turned about, leading the way this time, and he felt the thoughtful silence with which the men followed.

As evening arrived after that first day of the march, Arnacin went around speaking to the men individually. His aim, outside of just establishing some knowledge of the men and their names, was to discover which ones considered themselves capable archers. He saved Firth for last.

Finally, stopping by Gagandep's son, the islander started with the usual question about skills, told Firth he was on first watch that night and, after a second's pause, asked, "If you don't mind my asking, how is it that Gagandep's son is in Mira's army?"

Glancing askance at Arnacin, Firth shrugged, "How is a foreigner?"

"I'm not killing ancestors and relations."

"I see. That's why you're asking." Firth sighed. "Three years ago, when Mira first started feeling the need for more troops, each troop sent men around the kingdom to find all able-bodied volunteers. Forced enlistment came only last year. Anyway, I was sixteen at the time, so I volunteered.

"Originally, they told me they couldn't take me, but I demanded to know why not when they needed men so much. I am Miran, I want to support the kingdom as much as they, and I view the savages not only as savages, but traitors also, who will murder their own kind without thought. I wanted–and still want–nothing more than to strike a blow for my father, my family, and my homeland. Would they not allow that?"

Firth shrugged, continuing, "I was allowed, but in many ways, they still don't accept me. No one will talk to me. I'm given marching orders and those are all the words I hear from commander or troops."

Sighing, Arnacin settled on the ground, wrapping his arms around his knees. "It must make you wonder if Mira is worth supporting."

"Actually, as much as it's lonely, I understand, most of the time. I mean, you know father's devotion to his gods, despite the fact that if the savages win, they'll slaughter him without a care for his loyalty. Some adopted natives don't even have his love for us. They see the whole war as our greed." The Miran was quiet a moment before saying, "When I told Father that I had been moved, he was pleased. He said I would not need to dishonor myself under you."

Slowly, Arnacin turned his head and looked at Firth standing above him. A question seemed to simmer in the air. Finally, dropping his gaze, the islander whispered, "Let's hope so."

"Are you afraid?" Firth asked in response to Arnacin's tone.

Laughing, the islander confessed, "Fear isn't something I readily confess to. Sometimes I feel that by confessing it, you allow yourself to fear—and that's something no one can afford, particularly not someone who is supposed to lead. However, I don't know that I *can* lead. Not that I don't possess the capability to invent, give instructions, and sound like I know what I'm talking about even when I don't." His smile met Firth's and he looked away. "No, I can't kill, Firth. I didn't realize what war would mean until I had already agreed. I knew it would be hard, but not what it is. I've never blinked once while killing an animal, not that I can remember anyway, and when I am protecting someone... when killing someone is the only hope in the moment, I can do that without thinking twice. But this? This is slaughter, and now I'm supposed to command it."

With an ironic smile, Arnacin lay back to look at the sky, lacing his fingers beneath his head. "I used to think I could lead in everything. If it had to be done, I was the boy for the job. If someone didn't do what was best for them, it was I who told them, who always knew what was best—as if I really knew anything."

As his thoughts traveled from the individuals of Enchantress Island, most of them leaders in their own right, to monarchs like Miro who spent the whole day worrying over reputation and how that affected their standing, Arnacin heard his voice drop to a growl as he added, "Leaders are only for those too stupid not to lead themselves, and those they choose as leaders should concentrate instead on teaching thinking skills and self-defense."

Realizing that he had just spoken in bitter exaggeration, he looked over at the Miran, who was studying him incredulously. As their gazes met, however, Firth joked, "Well, I have no problem killing savages, so if ever you want to step down, I'll be happy to fill in." When Arnacin laughed sardonically, he continued, "Savages are the same as animals. They're brutes, drunk on human blood. They're beyond mercy and compassion. No one in the world could think of them in any other light, unless they grew up with them."

Arnacin did not need to ask about such hatred. Had Gagandep been his father, whose very family threatened to murder him despite his undying love, the islander would likely feel the same. Yet, he knew better. "Thanks," he whispered, pushing himself to his feet. "I'll keep my command."

"Um..." Firth halted him as he started to leave. "What do we call you? We never call commanders by name."

"All your commanders possess titles *before* they become commanders," Arnacin reminded him. "I'm just Arnacin."

Within the following week, Arnacin had completely retrained his men on how to comb the woods. He kept them moving from before light even filtered through the trees until darkness enveloped them. They ate from their own sacks only before and after their long marches, never stopping between. When they ran out, they would refill their personal supplies with what was stored on the horses. Water was sipped while walking.

Although they were attacked throughout their journey, the islander had not been wrong when he said they would be missed during the night. Once darkness masked their movements, Arnacin would make them spread out within a certain perimeter, some against trees or under thick brush, and others in bushes. Horses vanished like deer into foliage, and the few archers the islander cycled through every night as guards reported that everything remained peaceful. In that way, although often stiff, the troop always woke mostly refreshed in the gray darkness to destroy any trace of their resting places.

Despite their success at overall protection, stealth and swiftness, they found nothing and eventually returned to the capitol, where Arnacin's report to the king consisted of a single sentence. They had found no enemy village.

Arnacin had barely entered the great hall after his third expedition when the monarch loudly exclaimed his name, "Arnacin!"

The islander jumped in surprise and Miro sighed, calming himself. "I must send you back out, my foreigner. It has been two weeks since Lord Carpason left on his own scouting mission, and there hasn't even been word from a messenger, nor a returning crippled army."

Arnacin paled in concern and the king nodded his understanding.

"Through your men..." Miro's lip quirked upward slightly as he said it, "I understand that you are able to traverse Melmoor as well as the enemy does. If Lord Carpason could not escape a trap, perhaps you can. Regardless, I must know what happened. Should you discover that the savages slaughtered every last one of his troop, as well as him..." The king paused before finishing, "You must bring that information to me as well."

"What if we also disappear?" Arnacin inquired.

His gaze hard in deadly seriousness, Miro ordered, "You will return with the conclusion that they are beyond the grave before that happens. Is that understood, son of Bozzic?"

Meeting that commanding gaze, the islander softly submitted, "I understand, Your Majesty."

"Then retrieve your men."

For two days, Arnacin attempted to find a way into the area the savages seemed to be circling, without success. However, even if the king had ordered the islander to return in defeat, Arnacin never could have. Yet the mere fact that he rose against such an impassable enemy blockade meant something. He reasoned that Carpason was a nemesis of the natives. If they had him in a corner, they would block off all opportunities for support or escape. This only caused the islander more nervousness with each passing minute.

"Should we return home, Arnacin?" Sir Hadwin inquired, joining the islander where he stood staring out into the overcast night, arms folded across his chest with his thumbnail resting against his upper lip. When Arnacin did not answer, only dropping his arm onto the other resting across his ribcage, the knight pressed, "What would you like?"

"Charlotte," Arnacin muttered.

Shaking his head, Hadwin asked, "Who?"

Arnacin finally looked at him and, pushing off the tree he leaned against, he asked, "Is there anyone in this party capable of moving with complete silence?"

The knight sighed in concentration. "I don't know if you'll like my suggestion, but there's Gagandep's son."

"Firth?"

"Aye, Firth. He is half-native after all, apparently without an inch of the loyalty or knowledge of their gods themselves. One can never know what type of influence his father had over him, though."

"I'll take him," Arnacin nodded. Remembering Firth's disgust of the natives, he smiled slightly. "I wouldn't take Gagandep with me tonight, but I trust his son's firmness all the same."

"Where do you intend to go?" Hadwin questioned. "And are we to wait for you?"

"Continue to guard the camp. I should be back long before morning."

"Where are you going?" the knight repeated.

"To do some secret scouting. If the sun rises and you have not seen us, return to the capital with the news that Lord Carpason is likely no more."

"And what would I tell them about you?"

"There will be no answer to that." Arnacin grinned. "At least not until another month passes without sight or sound of me." Before Hadwin could offer his concern, the islander ordered, "Send Firth to me. I'll be here."

Stealing through the woods, barefoot—as he had insisted they go—Arnacin found himself searching for Firth's arm from time to time in order to make sure the Miran was still there. Not a breath from Firth could be heard over the woodland noises, not even a rustle of feet over forest carpet. Whether or not Arnacin maintained the same level of silence, he could not tell with the sound of his own blood rushing in his ears, but it was to his slight assurance that he felt Firth's own searching hand brush his arm.

Progressing mostly by feel in that thorough blackness, the islander feared that the thick black shapes of the trees that sprang up suddenly before him would knock them off course. Yet there was nothing to do but pray and still wish for Charlotte, whose senses would have known where to head, in light or dark, in order to reach water.

A sudden scuffle in the trees above, followed by the soft whisper of the native tongue, caused the islander to freeze, grabbing Firth's arm to make sure he also stopped. Seconds ticked past while Arnacin's traitorous heart pounded in his ribs. Yet, as the fear of the hunted grew until he found it bearable no longer, the islander prodded Firth forward. Carefully, they inched beyond the trees.

Somehow, the arrows Arnacin expected never came and he breathed more easily as they left that spot behind. Not long afterward, however, the soft tramp of feet crossing their path not three yards before them drew the islander to an abrupt stop. Many other footsteps followed, and even a few whispers in the natives' language, while it seemed an entire army passed before the islander and the Miran. Finally, the sounds disappeared and the islander hurried them on as fast as silence permitted.

That pitch-black, stealthy journey through the woods seemed to last forever before Arnacin halted yet again, pointing to the large, flickering lights not too far to their left.

"Their current encampment," Arnacin whispered into his companion's ear. "We're not going any closer than this. It's too dangerous as it is."

Apparently too afraid to reply, the Miran turned in the direction the islander gently pushed him and they skirted the natives' perimeter. The sound of flowing water finally led them to a stream, where, setting his own sack in the mud, Arnacin slunk along the bank, searching for the objects of his mission. Finally locating a cluster of the precious brackweed, the islander retrieved his sack and pulled out a small spade, with the soft order for his companion to stand guard. Returning to the brackweed, he dug a small hole. Dipping his spade into the sack, he filled the hole he had created with what appeared to be moist dirt, yet smelled fouler. Once done, he carefully leveled the spot he had tampered with and then brushed leaves over it.

Seventeen times, he repeated this, under different clumps of the plant, and then, feeling his nervousness strengthening with each passing moment, he pulled his companion into the stream, where they covered any possible tracks.

Before returning to camp, however, Arnacin intended to discover if he could the exact predicament of the Tarmlin troops. Not much farther, sounds of clashing metal led them away from the stream. On a small rise, where one of Mira's old boundary markers lay smashed, Arnacin spotted fires burning. Drawing slightly nearer, he could see the camp, its figures locked together in combat, while cries of death filled the air. Above the skirmish, Tarmlin's emblem shone in the firelight.

It was Firth who broke the spell that had turned the islander into stone as he searched for any sign of Carpason himself. "Arnacin," the Miran whispered. "We can't help until you bring your own troop through. If we try, we'll likely also become stuck here."

Dropping his gaze, Arnacin led them stealthily back without a word. Tarmlin would need to wait for the islander's troop.

Arnacin kept camp for four days after he and Firth returned at dawn. Then, without a word of explanation, he ordered the attack—a straight drive toward the location of the native's encampment. No one questioned it until they arrived safely at the edge of the camp's perimeter without a single arrow shot in their direction. The islander only allowed the stunned gazes to turn in his direction for a moment as he took in the condition of the enemy.

None of the few natives the troop saw had noticed their presence yet, seeming to rave at the heavens or tear about without purpose. With one guilty glance downward, the islander ordered the mounted men to move in, reach safety on the other side of the camp, and burn all the tents on their way. No one was prepared for that attack. Some native men whipped out short blades only to be run through, but there was little struggle. The roar of flames and the screams of fear and pain, however, filled the air and ripped a hole through Arnacin's heart. Forcibly, he ignored it as the riders looped back to him and the other men who lacked steeds.

Silently, the Mirans watched, guarding the path of escape until the flames burned to nothing late that evening. There was no movement from the camp during that time and, dipping his chin in a silent salute to the fallen, the islander led his men forward once again.

"Arnacin!" Carpason exclaimed as the troop entered his besieged camp and he saw the islander riding behind Hadwin. "How are you here?"

Coolly, the islander replied, "Through dysentery and an ambush on their encampment."

"Dysentery?" the lord repeated.

"It's a water-borne lethal disease. How fast can your men return to the march? I don't wish a repeat of today."

Carpason said no more, ordering his men to prepare the disassembling of the camp. He easily recognized the look of hidden horror in the dark-haired boy and knew that only time would heal it. There were other things that had to be dealt with first, including the careful moving of ten injured men—a partial blessing and a rarity in Mira. All the same, he patted the islander's knee in silent comfort as he passed Arnacin, still seated on Hadwin's steed.

Chapter 10

Cestmir's Charge

When they returned to the capital, the king called a meeting of all present commanders. King Miro exhaled in relief as Carpason walked in. "Word came that you returned, but..." Controlling his expression of white-faced relief, he finished, "It's good to see you."

Turning to Arnacin, he thanked him profusely.

Glancing over, Carpason noticed how still the islander was in the midst of the group, his skin pale, his lips set in a hard line. To the king's gratitude, he only nodded, but someone else asked, "How did you accomplish it?"

As if his words stuck in his throat, Arnacin whispered, his mouth barely moving, "I poisoned the native camp."

Gales of delighted laughter burst around the room. "That's brilliant, Arnacin!"

"Ingenious!"

"Ha, those rats need such a lesson!"

At every word, the islander appeared to grow taller as he straightened every individual bone, his jaw locking, his eyes hardening like stone. Yet Carpason saw that no one else paid any heed. Everyone seemed too excited by the thought of the savages' reaction to such an attack.

"How did you sneak poison beneath their noses like that?"

"Oh, oh, we should just poison all the plant life in Melmoor and they will think it cursed!"

"The meeting," the lord reminded, but he was drowned in the general laughter. With another glance at the islander, Carpason suddenly imagined steam drifting from the islander's nose, such was the fire in his gaze. Before another word could be uttered, however, Arnacin nodded to the king and whirled toward the door.

Dead silence fell when Miro barked, "Arnacin!"

The islander halted abruptly in the doorway, his back facing them, but Carpason could see his hard angry breaths through the rise and fall of his shoulders. Sighing, however, Miro added, "I give the permission to go and come, Arnacin, and I alone."

Whirling back toward them, Arnacin declared in a voice as cold as the rest of him… "I told you I poisoned them!"

"A pure inspira–" One count started before Carpason stepped on his toe in warning. The damage, however, was already done.

"Oh yes, when has cheating meant anything to you? When has dishonor or even lives meant anything to you? So praise me as a brilliant hero, an ingenious strategist, but know this, I wouldn't repeat it if the same stakes were on the line." Finished, he nodded toward the king, inclining, "Your Majesty," and then toward the man he had said he would not rescue again, "Lord Carpason." Without another word, he vanished before the king recovered from his shock.

Regardless, it was the king who spoke first, "That boy will have to learn. I should have someone thrash him as a reminder."

Smiling slightly, Carpason nodded toward the door, "He is not one of your subjects, Sire, and you just unwittingly offended his honor. Perhaps you should regard him as an ambassador."

"Should I do that, I must inquire as to his kingdom so I may send a note of my displeasure to his king and demand some sort of repayment," Miro growled before excusing his nobles.

"There you are!" Carpason exclaimed as he found the islander leaning against his ship's rail, his hood shielding him from the lord's sight as he stared out to the vast expanses of the open water beyond the sea gate.

When no movement came as Carpason joined the still figure, he leaned out to look beneath the hood. "I understand the king has quite a few things he would like to discuss with you alone," he gently whispered, although those dark orbs continued to stare past him, as if unaware of his presence.

"And so he sent you," the islander finally said.

"When it comes to problems with his foreigner, he rarely relies on anyone else," Carpason shrugged.

"I had to leave," Arnacin breathed. "He wasn't allowing it."

"Tell me, Arnacin," the lord sighed. "Could you not simply take the compliments as they were meant?"

Shaking his head, the islander confessed, "I murdered them, my lord, pure and simple. I know I've said that before, but there is no excuse this time. They were already dying when we attacked and they didn't even understand how it happened. I saw them screaming to the heavens, as if betrayed with nowhere to turn." He paused for a second before pronouncing, "We cut down defenseless people and I should have been executed as a hypocrite, murderer and fiend. Yet instead, Mira heaps praise. I could have cut off all her nobles' heads."

Like usual, Arnacin's voice remained soft. It lowered into a growl but, at the moment, not one memory of the boy ever shouting rose to Carpason's mind. His words, however, grew consistently darker by the week.

Sadly wrapping an arm around the islander's shoulder, Carpason sighed, "I'm sorry."

"What have *you* done?" Pulling away, Arnacin finally looked at him.

"I never realized how quickly war could change one. Within five months, you are now discussing chopping men's heads off."

"My lord," the islander shakily began, "if I ask the king, will he allow me the freedom of stepping down from command? I'll help as one of the soldiers. I cannot lead."

"Until the day your commander asks you to 'murder' an enemy, in which case, you'll hang?"

Dropping his gaze, Arnacin commented, "You didn't ask me to take command to save my neck."

"No, I asked because we need you, Arnacin. We need the extra army and there is no one else who can lead like you, who has the talent needed. Learn to trust Miro, Arnacin. He'll learn to know what you need, but please don't ask him to bow before your command. He is king."

Raising his eyes, Arnacin breathed, "You said yourself, he's murdered Arnacin of Enchantress Island. He'll never know what I need."

"No, Arnacin. I murdered Arnacin of Enchantress Island through desperation. Punish me however you see fit, but don't punish Mira or her king, I beg you. Help while you are able, please."

Carpason's plea spurred Arnacin to action, and he permitted himself to work on his ship only when he deemed there was time. Of the books the islander now read, none of them had anything to do with ships, but of Mira's history, savage information, and any other material that might help him put an end to the war. He dug up every map he could find, tore through the section on medicines, and disappeared into the journals of well-known commanders.

Other times, Arnacin spent just as many hours with Gagandep, learning from him all he could not discover about medicine from his reading. He continued practicing his swordplay and archery and, of course, was constantly deployed with his troop at the king's command.

During this time, Hadwin became his second-in-command, Firth became his assistant slink, going with him on all scouting tasks, and one of Duke Cestmir's knights, the light-hearted and hot-headed Cornyo, became the troop's chief stress reliever.

In many ways, those three were all the men Arnacin required. Although he came to know and care for all the troops granted to him, those three were his companions and no one begrudged them the right.

Still, one fact plagued the islander, and every interaction with the natives drove its point ever further into his heart. After two weeks, he could come to no alternative than the plan he'd been formulating.

The troop often used the village, Winliy, as a resting place on their way back to the capital. It sat halfway between Melmoor and the city, and allowed the exhausted men hot food and solid sleep for one night, even if that sleep was caught in various places in the large village barn. Sitting in the hayloft door of the barn, Arnacin finally whispered to the knight standing against the door frame beside him. "There are many good things about your king, Hadwin. There are a few things I even respect."

He paused. Then chucking a handful of straw out the door, where the wind blew it into the fields, he finished, "But he's leading his kingdom to the grave. I can't kill just to lose. I didn't promise my help *to lose*. If those I'm trying to help save are already dead, I can't go on."

"Arnacin," Hadwin sighed. "You always had too much heart. No one will fault you if you back out. There are other men who have withdrawn due to such trauma."

"If I don't help..." Unable to finish that line of thought, Arnacin surmised, "It would destroy me, Hadwin. I gave my word. I can't let it mean nothing."

For a long moment, they remained silent and, even as Arnacin stared out at the last touches of red behind the rim of the natives' mountains, he knew the knight was studying him. Eventually, Hadwin asked, "What have you found in all your research?" He smiled. "At this point, you've done enough to compete with the knowledge of the ruling nobility."

"Nothing," the islander admitted in defeat. "Nothing useful to the war, outside of general tactics. Your natives guard their secrets jealously. *Savage Superstitions* has nothing but useless tidbits and myths, and still they murdered the chronicler for it. I've spent hours trying to find some way to use the information in it, but it's a pointless exercise." With an ironic, humorless smile, he asked, "How do you use the fact that they boil their furs before doing anything with them in order to prevent the animals' spirits from staying?"

Hadwin only shook his head in answer, and again, silence fell over them. "Perhaps I shouldn't say this," the knight eventually mentioned. "However, since I couldn't stand here and allow you to think Miro is the densest man in existence, I'll tell you this: quite a bit of political war takes place in the capitol. Our wonderful councilors know that our war increases fear and while they can pull on those strings, they hold quite a large amount of power–for they play on Miro's fears and, therefore, make even the throne submit to them. Though they also fear the natives, they will try to keep the war going for as long as possible."

"Is Miro that stupid, not to realize what they play at?"

"Just try to picture it, Arnacin. It's not that Miro's that stupid, but that, perhaps, he is too wise. He knows the wisdom and wiliness of his councilors. He knows they don't stand for him, but that in not standing for him, they speak for themselves and don't simply bow to his ideas. Therefore, he uses their views to test his own. He knows they play on his fears, yet he fears that they are right, and that to remove them would erase that counterbalance.

"My lord has long attempted to use reason, yes, even to use the councilors' own game against them when Mira needs it. Yet the councilors always have the first move, that first non-retractable strike–the power of words. There is only so much Miro and Carpason can do against it."

"Why did I need to know that?"

"Because you need to know."

"So that I'll know there's no hope, *ever*?"

"As far as hope goes, Arnacin, you must have some idea what to do to counter the natives. Your whole troop knows you glean information from more than just the library. I also know you were thinking something other than quitting on life. The Arnacin I know never does that, no matter how bleak the circumstances."

For a moment, Arnacin did not admit or deny it, resting his head against the doorframe. Then, he whispered, "To speak of what

I am thinking would be to ask you to commit treason. If I could convince your king to send me as a lone spy, it would be another matter, but otherwise..."

After a second of silence, Hadwin whispered, "Ask us, Arnacin. We're with you."

Turning to the knight in confusion, Arnacin studied him. "You know," he finally stated.

"You want to ask us if we'll go into the mountains with you." Hadwin nodded. "I've known it could come to this from the day you were given command, and I have only one request to make. Tell the king."

Turning away, Arnacin replied, "I will tell the king in my own time, Hadwin. One thing I cannot do is surrender this one chance to his whim. If I tell him and he refuses, I'll have only one option left to me..."

"Suicide," Hadwin finished. Arnacin said nothing.

Arnacin kept his thoughts secret until they were out of sight of Winliy, in the midst of the plains. Then, asking his troop to form a circle around him, he opened his mouth, yet no words would come. Biting his lip, he slowly paced in a small circle inside that ring and, after a moment, he started, "I can no longer lead."

"What?" he heard Cornyo exclaim.

"There are some things I cannot command."

"Arnacin," Hadwin sighed, "King Miro gave you command. Whatever it is, we obey."

With a grim smile, the islander glanced at the Tarmlin knight and gently replied, "No. If I told you to draw blades on each other this instant, would you do it?"

A stunned silence met him, and he saw Firth's head twitch. "No, you wouldn't, because of right and wrong. Above any ruler, no matter how great, there is a law, a law we know as infants. To a child, death is always terrible. A man's hatred is always a bad thing. No king could change that. They could make it the rule that murder is lawful, but that child would not agree until it was slowly schooled into that way of thinking.

"That law remains whether the king says 'yea' or 'nay,' and I at least must follow it even when the king says 'nay.' For that reason, I cannot lead."

"What has the king asked you to do?" Cornyo asked in confusion.

"Senseless murder until death."

Several cries of outrage filled the air. "He would never! What? We know Miro!"

It was Firth who said, "The savages are hardly..." Yet there he stopped and, as the outrage died down, Arnacin nodded.

"Your father is 'savage,' Firth. It is their betrayal of their own blood that makes the natives so horrible in your opinion. But, like your father, they are people, and I agreed to help protect Mirans and adopted natives alike. I never thought I agreed to the worthless slaughter this war has become, on both sides. There's no *end*, men—no victory. You kill until you drop, and for what?"

No one answered. Many of the Mirans were staring at their boots. It was Cornyo who whispered, "What alternatives do we have?"

"I don't know yet. I have a few suspicions, some of which even Lord Carpason knows, but our attempt to discover more failed. I know a place that will have those answers, though, yet the king has forbidden our infiltration, afraid that the natives will *never* trust Mirans if he doesn't keep this war inside Mira's borders."

Mutters were rising from the Mirans again. After a moment, one challenged Arnacin, "You think to order us into the mountains?"

"No," the islander breathed. "I can never order such a thing. I'm telling you, I can't lead anymore, and I am going back to tell Miro so."

"Arnacin," Hadwin muttered, his tone warning, yet Arnacin had no time to answer, for that moment, Cornyo stepped forward.

"I will never lose my loyalty to my king, but, Arnacin, you must know, if you think there's a possible way to help Mira survive, I will follow you to the gallows Miro erects for me."

Shaking his head, Arnacin licked his lips. "Cornyo, no. It would be deceit, betrayal against your homeland. I have thought about this all night. I can't ask it of you. If I tell Miro that I can no longer help in this war, I can sail off and slip into the mountains by my own decision, completely apart from Mira. The same absolution is not available to you."

"You'd die without support, Arnacin," Hadwin spoke up. "And if ever you found the real leaders, you would be incapable of eliminating them on your own. No, you must allow us to do this with you, or not at all."

Hadwin's harsh logic stilled the islander's heart. After a moment, he sighed in defeat. "Then each of you must choose your preferred course of action. If even one of you thinks we should not enter the mountains, we won't, but know that if you decide to defy your king to possibly save your homeland..." For a second he paused, and then with a slight smile, he shrugged. "Well, you wouldn't be able to continue as your lords' spies."

The whole group shifted, yet no one spoke, and Arnacin returned to seriousness. "In all honesty, if you choose the mountains and we are ever discovered, I will take full responsibility, but that doesn't guarantee that you won't be executed for it as well."

"My life belongs to my king and country, Arnacin," Cornyo vowed, sincerely. "If I die helping them, I will die willingly, and if I can succeed before I die, I will die with relief. I'll go into the mountains with you, for Mira."

Stepping forward to join Cornyo, Hadwin whispered, "For Mira." It took a few moments, but then the entire troop had shuffled around to join Cornyo as they all pledged their lives, "For Mira."

Submitting, Arnacin bowed in turn.

Soon after, Arnacin began secret missions into the natives' land with portions of his troop. Through his infiltration of the enemies' defenses, his way of traveling the woods without detection, the unique and completely devastating way he completed the king's orders for village attacks, and the knowledge that he never lost one man while on the field, Arnacin felt fear gather in the natives.

Those natives soon entitled Arnacin the "Black Phantom" and it became a terrified whisper or, when any of his men were spotted briefly, a cry. Even other Miran troops began talking of the Black Phantom as some sort of unknown ally. Slowly, the frightened enemy was forced out of Mira's borders and into the mountains.

Then, for just a few days toward the end of autumn, Mirans celebrated what they were sure was the end of the war, after the report that the last savage had retreated into the mountains. Boundary markers began to rise back in place and peaceful silence met the watchful troops along the mountains' edge.

Gagandep hosted a family celebration, including Arnacin, the night word came that Mira had won. Standing, the adopted native lifted his mug, saying, "To Arnacin's continued ship repairs..."

Feeling Firth's taunting elbow dig into his side, the islander smiled. Yet Gagandep continued without notice of the wordless remark, "...and to Mira's victory."

"Mira's victory" echoed around the table from the family, and the adopted native winked. "Perhaps I can already be peacefully in my grave before the next one erupts."

Arnacin only laughed sadly, unable to drink to victory himself, thanks to his misgivings.

Six days later, the easternmost point of the forest went up in flames.

When all his councilors had gathered in the great hall at his request, Miro slowly turned away from the view of the harbor. They stood there, nervously shifting, yet for a moment, the king thought of nothing to say. A king could never admit he was without an idea for future action, or even a hope. That was, unless he was speaking to Carpason.

As it was, however, he decided to say, "I would like suggestions on how to proceed, since the savages have clearly not conceded."

"If the choice was mine, Sire," Memphis said, "I would prove both Mira's strength and integrity through an action they couldn't ignore."

"Such as?"

"Attack the mountains."

"No," Miro refused, shaking his head as he turned away in thought. "Such action would prove their fears, despite any strength on our part."

"I don't mean for you to attack and keep it, Sire. I was thinking more that you gain a portion of the mountains, hold it for a day, and then return it to them. It would force them to realize that the reason you have not attacked them beyond your borders is not because you lack the ability, but because you care about your word."

Nodding slightly, the king was silent, rubbing his bearded chin. As his pacing turned him back toward the councilors, a bow from one of them caught his attention, however. "What are your thoughts, Councilor Krisno?"

"Perhaps the savages' lack of surrender is a sign that we should leave, Sire."

An instant murmur of anger rose from the councilors, but for just a moment, Miro considered the suggestion. His gaze traveled around the great hall with its familiar walls of blue lapis and opal, interspaced by gold pilasters; its eastern-facing wall lined with high windows. It was a beautiful, majestic great hall, and it was home. His father had ruled from the throne at the far end, and his father's father, and many more before them. Memories of them and of his own youth clung to the walls. He almost heard the laughter of simpler times.

Slowly, he voiced his thoughts. "We cannot leave Mira as Mirans. No one would give us land without a war we couldn't afford. We would need to disperse as the lowly into many different kingdoms, and subject ourselves to their rules and way of life."

"But if it would save lives, Sire?" It was clear from the glares of the other councilors that Krisno's opinion was highly unpopular, and Miro sympathized with the majority.

"Such a lack of hope, Krisno. I think you would have more love for your homeland," the king muttered.

"Memphis, your idea is a good one." His tone dismissed them and once they were gone, the king sent for Cestmir.

While waiting, the king wrote the order on paper, sealing it with Mira's crane. Not long after, the duke entered with a bow and Miro handed him the order, telling him of the plan, and that he wanted the duke to lead the massing of all Mira's armies. "Make the plans, Duke Cestmir. You know the area and the enemy far better than do I by now. These orders are so that no one questions your decisions."

Although his face had taken the pallor of a dead man, the duke muttered, "I'll only need such orders for the islander. Everyone else would take me at my word."

Smiling, Miro said, "Your men seem not to have any complaints."

"They love him, Sire, especially Cornyo."

"And you picked them for their loyalty to Mira of course."

"Of course."

"Then don't worry. We would all know if Arnacin did anything that would harm Mira. He has two-hundred zealous spies for men."

"Those savages are not deterred from attacking the boundaries we have just re-established," Cestmir informed the other commanders temporarily under his charge. "The fools force us to deny our pledge of leaving the mountains as the edge of their land." Emitting a sigh, he finished, "In short, we are to smash them for the next two months, until the year ends, in one large assault on their foothills."

He pointed ahead, toward the mountains looming in the distance, their tops covered by the tree line. "We are not to retreat before we have reached that ridge, and then, and only then, back off for them to return there, if they will. Our goal, set by the king and his council, is not to steal more of their land, but to make a point: that we can and will destroy them if we must–that by Mira's grace alone do they possess their land and that, should they not submit, they shall lose it."

Movement caught his attention, a silent shifting from one foot to the other in disagreement. Casting the owner of that movement a piercing look, he asked, "Yes, Master Arnacin? What is your problem with *this* order?"

For just a minute, the islander did not reply. Then he said, "If that is the goal, it will never succeed... Your Grace. They feel they are fighting for a cause that is just as desperate as yours. The only way to... *subdue* them is to take away every means they have of attack. Even then, each and every one of them would bite, kick and punch before they lost that cause."

"Are you suggesting retreat?"

The islander shrugged indifferently and the duke barked, "It doesn't matter! Whether the goal works in the long run is not the subject!" Beside him, Carpason covered his smile with his hand.

Yet Arnacin had not finished. "With all due respect, should the long-term mission not be considered, all smaller battles are not only in vain, they are a waste of lives."

"Master Arnacin, you are not on the council! The king gives his orders after hearing their suggestions and we are only here to see them through. We are attacking that ridge!"

"Very well," the islander sighed. "What plans have we been given for so doing?"

Passing him a resigned glare while many of the other nobles smiled, the duke returned to business. "Each commander is to take their troops to a marked position. We are to cover three miles of those foothills. At the first horn blast, the catapults will begin the battle, hopefully taking down enough of their foul archers to make our way forward slightly safer. Then, when my troop sounds its horn, the catapults are to stop and each troop's horn is to reply in order. When the seventh sounds, everyone starts forward. Amassed, we will charge those foothills tomorrow morning and take down all of their patrols once at close range. Is that understood?"

"No," Arnacin spoke up in the silence.

The duke grumbled under his breath before inquiring with gritted teeth, "What is not clear to you?"

"That is the entire plan?"

"Yes. There is no more."

"There is more. You are all planning to die in this, wipe out Mira once and for all. Isn't that in the plan?"

"We are making a char–"

"That–" Halting suddenly, Arnacin dipped his chin.

"We must push our message through," the duke sighed after a minute. "If we do not push for the hope that they will see the uselessness of their attempt, we might as well leave Mira now."

Although Arnacin said no more, bowing slightly in submission, Cestmir could see the wheels still turning behind his gaze. It was proven by the silence with which the islander departed back to his own troop.

"There is not a chance of them succeeding!" Arnacin exclaimed that evening around one of his troop's campfires, after angrily repeating the plan to Sir Hadwin. "It's not hope–it's despairing suicide and they'll take everyone with them!"

"We are at that point, Arnacin. We can only attack. If we are dead at this point, we are dead."

"If that is the case, make it work," Arnacin despondently whispered. "If it's time for a true last stand, then stand, don't throw yourself on spear ends."

"We must achieve those mountains."

"You know as well as I that their little encampments, hidden among slopes and trees–guarded by hundreds of archers with arrows that kill at the tiniest scratch, who own the advantage of height as well as position–will never be conquered in this charge."

"What do you plan to do?" the knight asked.

"I don't know yet. Danger, risks, narrow ledges, those can be navigated, but never suicide."

As night wore on, Arnacin remained, staring up at the mountain ridge from where he stood leaning against a tree. When told that he needed to rest, he simply shook his head and did not move. Then, before dawn, he woke his men. "Alright, there is only one thing to do. We must slip around the enemy lines as archers and take them down from the back."

"How are we to achieve that if the other troops can't break through?"

"By taking all the horses this troop owns, with only that many men, and entering by the coast. With all the king's men here, the natives won't guard that side as carefully. Those that remain here will join with Lord Carpason's troops."

"With the catapults, entering the foothills will be dangerous."

"By the time we arrive, they are not likely to still be going, but if they are, it will aid our cover."

Including supply horses, their troop owned a total of forty horses, a sizable amount, yet it took some time to divide the men into two groups, depending on their skills. While the chosen forty, who were to enter the mountains, tacked their steeds, Arnacin helped the rest of the men with packing up camp in preparation for joining Carpason's company. It was during that time that a knight rode up, glancing at the forty men purposely lacking armor.

"Master Arnacin!" the messenger barked after sputtering for a moment. "The duke commands that you ready your troops."

"And so am I doing," Arnacin growled with a trace of defiance.

Glancing at the men scattered about, the messenger scoffed, "Readying for what, I ask you—mutiny?"

"You may not ask."

"You are not given the choice," the messenger snapped, turning red. "You must ready your troops for the assault at once."

Coldly, Arnacin stated, "I will not order my men to commit suicide."

"You are not in highest command at this time."

"These men were placed under my command. You may take them away but as long as they remain under my command, I cannot order them to certain, pointless death."

Blustering, the messenger spluttered momentarily and then snapped at Firth, "You! Tell his lordship Carpason of this treachery."

When Firth remained where he stood, Arnacin gave him a slight nod of permission. As Gagandep's son hurried away using one of the prepared steeds, the islander pronounced, "Since we must wait, unless you wish to take this argument into actual battle, I will return to my preparations."

"You will stand right there, young man!"

"I dare not waste the time." So saying, Arnacin turned his back on the man, nodding for the watching troop to proceed with their tasks. The messenger could only sit there in seething frustration.

Moments later, two horses galloped up to them and, pulling his steed to a stop by the islander, Carpason gently commanded, "Arnacin, explain please."

"You should know where I stand, my lord," Arnacin softly replied with a respectful nod. "I cannot throw these men's lives away as long as they are my responsibility. Honor dictates that I be stoned first."

Quietly, the lord inquired, "Does honor not also dictate that you hold to your word of aiding Miro, and does that not mean submitting to his command?"

"I have never sworn to be his subject, my lord, and aiding Mira is the opposite of his current orders."

Sighing, Carpason submitted, "Very well, Arnacin. You may turn about and take your men back to Mira if you wish."

"What? My lord–" the messenger exclaimed.

"We are on the edge of battle, sir," the lord reminded. "There is no time to debate this and as Miro gave him command, only Miro can take it away."

"My lord–"

Holding up his hand, Carpason finished, "We are the king's servants, sir. Arnacin is servant of his own honor." As the islander blushed, the lord gave him a respectful nod and turned his horse away.

"My lord," Arnacin called. When the noble halted, the islander gestured to those of his men wearing armor. "They are under your command for the battle."

Casting the islander a shrewd glance, Carpason again nodded and, at his command, most of Arnacin's troop fell in behind the noble. As the host disappeared, taking the messenger with them, the islander turned to the forty left under his command. "Mount. Our race begins, but stay far beneath the cover of the trees until we reach the coast."

As Hadwin pulled the islander up behind him, the small force broke for the shore some distance away.

The last note of the horn sounded. Inhaling in preparation, Carpason led his command forward. Arrows rained down on them from the heights as soon as Mira's front line neared. Still, they pressed ahead, ignoring those who fell beside them.

As they ascended, the attack abruptly stopped and Carpason glanced upward. His eyes scanned the heights and, since he thought he spotted something, he quickly looked again. Arnacin stood on an outcropping above the lord's troop, an arrow nocked. Then, just as quickly as he had appeared, the islander slipped into the trees with a respectful nod.

"Enchanter," the lord muttered as he took another step upward. If it weren't for the enemy shafts that clattered onto the rock where the islander had stood a second before, he would have sworn that it was an apparition. Either way, the enemy's attention was diverted until Mira stood suddenly on their level. With a shout, the two sides clashed together in a flurry of steel, stone and muscle.

Several hours later, Mira's troops achieved the summit, continuing their advantage until the savages fled and the nobles again met after totaling their own losses. The Earl of Garak, it appeared, had fallen in battle, and his closest companion gave the report before disappearing.

Watching that knight leave, Duke Cestmir sighed, "Another noble house lost forever. By the time this blasted war ends, Miro won't have any nobles to his name at all."

"We don't know that," Carpason muttered. All gazes turned almost accusingly toward him as he spoke and bobbing on his toes slightly, he spoke for them, "Where's Arnacin?"

"Yes, my lord," Cestmir growled. "Where is our islander? I noticed the defense weakened against us halfway up. "

"Then your guess is as good as mine. I spotted him briefly behind the savages' line, but only once, and I don't know any more of his intentions than what I surmised in that glimpse. His men haven't said anything."

Huffing, the duke stated, "As likely they don't know anything either."

"Yes," Carpason muttered, "so Hadwin has told me in the past."

With an ironic grin, Cestmir mused, "I suppose he realized Miro was putting so many spies on him when we gave him that troop. That's why everything's failed as it has. All of a sudden, my loyal knights turn red and mumble reports as short as those Arnacin gives the king."

Carpason only nodded in agreement.

Sighing, the duke returned to business, deciding, "Very well, we'll hold this position until nightfall. Once dark comes, it will be too dangerous to remain. If he has not returned by then..." He broke off, looking over the hill they had just ascended through sweat and blood. "We will wait another day at the bottom before we return to inform the king of our victory—and of his two commanders' deaths."

Nodding, they each separated to their own troops to wait for Arnacin or the dark, whichever came first.

It was the afternoon. In the shorter autumn days, Arnacin had four hours to appear at the most. Pacing, Carpason rubbed his sweaty palms together, scanning the land briefly falling away from them before it rose again. Little copses dotted the mountainside, yet the savages had vanished to the eye.

Nothing moved. There was no sight of Hadwin or Arnacin. Neither friend nor enemy appeared while, around the alert Mirans, the shadows lengthened. Finding himself tapping the palms of his hands together, the lord quickly dropped them to his sides, only to find himself running a hand through his hair a moment later. Sighing, he finally folded both arms across his chest.

By then, the sun appeared to sit directly across from him, its light that garish shine of its last moments. Still, nothing moved in the trees. The mountain range remained uncannily peaceful, except for the scattering of crows feasting on the fallen.

"We should go." The sighed sentiment caused Carpason to jump, noticing for the first time that Cestmir had come to stand beside him.

"The sun's not down yet," the lord murmured.

"Those trees are likely crawling with savages just waiting for dark. Cornyo's out there as well, but we risk slaughter if we stay up here past dark, and they're likely dead, anyway."

Feeling suddenly exhausted, Carpason nodded. "I don't want to give up."

Patting the lord's shoulder, Cestmir agreed, "No, but we must face the facts. This is the savages' stronghold." He paused for a second, then sighed. "Alright, we'll wait until darkness."

"It would be insane—"

"We'll wait." With that, the duke turned away. Yet darkness fell without sign of anyone. In silence, Cestmir hurried their retreat down the mountain. Not even a savage stopped them.

As the duke wished, they waited another day in camps along the bottom with silence their only pursuer. Neither Arnacin nor any of the forty he had taken with him returned.

Sadly, they returned to the capital and, there, informed the king of all they knew.

Miro was quiet for a long time after he heard the report. Then, inclining his head, he congratulated them. "You have all done well.

Go rest. I will send some of you to watch the mountain when you are refreshed."

Nothing was said about those who had perished in the battle, but another mound was built on their memorial site in honor of those who had not returned.

Chapter 11

A Stirring of More

After any Miran's death, it was the task of the Miran recorders to make a list of each deceased's belongings and send the list to their next of kin. Those recorders left such list-makings for the dead of night.

Therefore, it was with surprise that Valoretta watched two of them—marked by their long brown robes and their tendency for plumpness—enter the library during the day. Even more oddly, they approached her with bows. "My lady, would you know the location of Enchantress Island?"

The princess merely stared at them in bewilderment, One of them—the slightly less round one—went on to explain, "Your father wishes to send the ship back as it is of no use to us and he deems the gold he has put into it the only gift he has for the islander's kindness toward Mira."

"What are you saying?" Valoretta felt oddly cold.

"Arnacin of Enchantress Island fell in the attack on the mountain."

"Oh," was all the princess could say for a moment. Suddenly, she was acutely aware of the large black expanse of the cavern around her. Only shelf upon shelf of dusty books and dustier scrolls crumbling in forlorn crannies filled that blackness.

The recorders continued to stand there and she quickly shook her head. "No, I don't know. Have you asked Lord Carpason?"

They bowed again. "Indeed, we have, My Lady. We would never disturb you if we could find the answers elsewhere. Yet, he has said the same as you."

Blinking at her, they remained standing there, waiting for her dismissal, and Valoretta realized that not only was the library lonely in Arnacin's passing, but never again would she meet anyone who saw her for herself and not for her crown.

Nodding, however, she said, "You may ask the king what he so desires."

They backed out of the library with more bows. With a sudden sigh of emotion, the princess locked the doors behind them and stood there, staring sightlessly at the paintings before her.

Slowly, however, her vision caught up with her thoughts. This side of the doors was painted like the rest of the walls. The story of Mira's beginnings and glory, told in the carvings on the outside, continued around the library's walls, with a new scene painted between each mahogany pilaster. Frescoes of mason's erecting the first stones of the capital, of the cranes in the natural cove on the first day the Mirans sailed into what was now their harbor (the reason for their emblem), of the crowning of the first Miro, and many other scenes lined the walls, disappearing into the blackness away from Valoretta before the doors. Again, however, she noted the lack of depictions of the savages.

Previously, she had always thought that fact ungracious of her people, but in that moment, as the slaughter was so vivid in her mind, she could not blame the artists for removing scenes of the savages' original aid to the Mirans.

Sadly, Valoretta ran her fingers along the arched neck of one of the cranes taking flight in the painting. Ironically, she had never seen a crane in their harbor, or anywhere for that matter. No, they were likely never to be seen by Mira again, just like their islander.

Turning away from the painted doors with a sigh, the princess returned to her book, yet the story's lightness could not capture her attention. After a few moments of trying, she happily exchanged it for a morose tale from an Ursan minstrel about a boy who disappeared into boglands and his parents' long search through the gray mists until they died without success.

Although she found the tale a bitter comfort, it could not keep her attention for long. Instead, she found herself resting her head against the window's glass, tracing the diamond patterns in it with her fingers.

What was Arnacin to her, but someone who was only passing through? Yet she realized she was a human in his presence, as he was the only human known to her. She stood as a goddess-statue among a palace of scurrying servants. Even the king was a distant, sometimes unconcerned father. No...

She lived only in Arnacin's presence. Without him, she realized, she was merely a lifeless, walking statue. He had given her life without her even being aware, until now, when he would return no more.

Such thoughts spun dizzy circles inside her for two days, while Sara herself could not drag the princess out of her library even to sleep. Life had stopped for Valoretta, and not even thirst, if she noticed any, could bring it back to her.

As morning came on the third day, a thunderous clamor rose from the city, rousing her dead curiosity. Slipping out, she stepped onto the closest balcony. The sight below caused her knees to give way beneath her and brought a smile to her face. Curled up against the rail, she inhaled the crisp morning air in delight.

Arnacin's troop returned to great applause in the castle and when the islander gave his report to the king, Miro simply sighed and dismissed him. It was Carpason who asked to see the islander as the lord again prepared to depart.

"Arnacin," he greeted as the islander entered the commanders' council room, empty save for the lord musing over the maps on the table. "We all owe you our lives and utmost gratitude."

Arnacin simply remained standing there, his own gaze on the maps, which ended with the edge of the mountains to the north and the marshes on the west. When the islander said nothing,

Carpason finished, "Take care, Arnacin. Should you push your lack of fealty too far, you will create discord and kill us all by that instead."

Looking up at the lord, Arnacin whispered, "Then ask the king to remove my command. I cannot be less or more than I am."

"Arnacin," Carpason sighed. "Can you not use all your skill within the areas assigned to you? I am not asking you to obey in times such as the last assault, but you *never* listen to the commands given you."

"Your king asked me to help you win this war, my lord. While, with good command, the council's plans might hold the enemy back, they will never win the war and instead will bleed Mira to death."

Smiling, the lord submitted, "One might as well never disagree with you, Arnacin. Leastways, I can never win a debate against you. Not that you convince me that you're right, I simply don't know how to refute it."

"Well," Arnacin teased. "They say back home that when such is the case, it is time to perhaps consider the other right."

Clapping the islander on the back, the lord stated, "Thankfully, we don't have such a proverb here. Now, my young cockerel–whose highest ambition is the gallows–will you do something for me?"

Giving a playful bow, the islander inquired, "What would my lord wish of me?"

"Are you any good at detailed drawings?"

"No," Arnacin admitted. "You might recognize what I've depicted, but my art is childlike."

"Could you then, depict the mountains? You and your men are the only humans outside of the enemy to set foot in them and live to tell the tale. I would like to start planning attacks based on their weak spots, yet if we know nothing of the land, that is impossible."

"You also doubt that Mira's last victory will settle the matter?"

Looking toward the ceiling, Carpason exhaled, "Let me say this: I assume our victory will instead enrage them and we may soon find ourselves fighting through the winter as well. Yes, we left our message as plain as if we carved it into the mountains' stone, but, unlike the council, I doubt they shall ever submit to such a warning."

"Those with freedom will sooner face death than lose it," Arnacin agreed, and Carpason looked at him knowingly.

"I dare say you would be knowledgeable in that. So tell me, is freedom worth the lives of all their children and wives? Does it hold that high a price?"

"For some, it alone is life."

"And you, Arnacin?" the lord pressed with a grin. "Would you, for instance, obey if freedom counted on it?"

Returning the smile, the islander quipped, "Honor is my freedom and I will die with it if I must and live with it despite all costs."

Playfully cuffing Arnacin, the lord repeated, "Will you draw my map while I am away?"

"I will draw it to the best of my knowledge, my lord," Arnacin promised. "How long are you planning to be away—so that I may know how long I can procrastinate?"

"I am to help the boundary camps watch for attack until winter settles. Perhaps all will be quiet, as is our deepest wish, yet I cannot trick myself into believing in such a peace if it existed. You will not likely be sent out again unless our stillness is broken, and I wish you much progress in your own projects."

Nodding sadly, Arnacin watched him leave, not without a certain heaviness of heart.

Winter finally came, allowing Mira the chance to breathe, as it had long desired. In that brief calm, Carpason returned to the capitol late one night, where the king met him.

"I fear this temporary foothold will not last, Carpason," Miro said, gesturing to the open seat across from himself.

Gratefully taking the offered seat by the fire, Carpason agreed, "It won't last and if we don't use it wisely, we will return to the near-total collapse we faced last spring."

"You are planning something."

"Sire," Carpason started, his words slow with caution. "It may be time to further investigate the enemy. We need more knowledge of their language and natural habits."

"The last man to try was murdered by his own friends, and you know why we do not touch anything beyond the mountains' wooded foothills."

"All for good reason, but sending a few of our spies into the mountains is not going to tarnish their land and, to win this war, we must know all that motivates them in their normal lives as well as on the field. It is their normal lives that motivate how they engage in war. Without knowledge of that, our foothold cannot remain and, if that doesn't remain, either they must be annihilated or we will be."

Contemplating in silence for a moment, Miro then conceded, "The last part may be true, yet the adopted savages should know much of their ways. Pull the information from them, if it is that necessary. You seem to hold some of them as friends. Tread carefully and you might avoid the last inquirer's fate."

Briefly compressing his lips, Carpason admitted, "Although I do have some sort of friendship with a few of them, they cannot forget that I am a lord of Mira and so they never discuss those things with me. When we talk, it is of trivial things only, such as their family's doings. They will not speak of anything else."

"Yet we know they speak to Arnacin of all sorts of things. He may assist in this, if they will not speak to you."

"Arnacin would view such a request as betrayal, Sire. They trust him because he is a foreigner. Please don't give cause to break that trust–his in you, or theirs in him."

"Break that trust? They themselves are Mirans. They should be offering the information."

"They support Mira as much as they feel able. Too many loyalties pull them in different directions."

"What loyalties?"

"Their tribal background is strong, no matter how much they love Mira. Those 'savages' are still their people. Then there are their gods–"

"Huh," Miro interrupted, sinking into his seat and folding his arms.

"Their gods... To them, their gods are very real. We know otherwise, but we must respect that loyalty."

"Apparently, *someone* must betray *something*, Carpason," Miro exclaimed in aggravation. "Mira will fall if they continue to cling to other obligations, and it will mean their deaths as well as ours."

Sighing, Carpason softly insisted, "Do not ask this of the adopted natives, nor of Arnacin. The natives would likely turn on you and Arnacin would simply break."

"And what other loyalties can possibly pull him away from aiding Mira? He has no connection to the savages."

"You know as well as I of his honor, which I believe stems from his own god–"

"His god," Miro moaned. "What god and its demands clouds his sight?"

"I'm not sure what his god dictates. On one hand, it appears that he dictates everything, on the other, nothing. He's about love and acceptance, yet there is no room for dishonor. There's something as different about him as there is about Arnacin and, I suppose, like Arnacin, I could never begin to explain or even know all he seems to be. Absolute loyalty seems to be the only constant thing I've observed in conversations about this god."

"I suppose mercy could be added to that list," Miro added. At the lord's pensive nod, the king sighed, "Is not Arnacin's desire to return home his strongest motivation for everything?"

Smiling slightly, Carpason asked instead, "Was it his desire to return home that caused him to agree to aiding us, or freeing the native captive when it meant his own death?"

"Yes, his honor," Miro mused. "The thing that causes all the natives, adopted or otherwise, to yield to him. And not just them, but all of Mira it seems would follow him to the grave."

"It will be the grave if we don't learn more."

"Then start listing ways to actually learn something, outside of crossing our borders."

Exhaling slowly, the lord inquired, "Have we not gained a foothold? Have you any conclusions as to why the war shifted in our favor?"

"What do you know?" Miro asked suspiciously. "Are you asking for the islander to start investigations in the mountains?"

"It was his idea," Carpason admitted. "He did not ask me to push for it."

"And has he told you anything about our suddenly untrustworthy knights and footmen?"

"They are not untrustworthy, Sire, yet you have asked them to tear their own loyalties apart. They now, I assume, share some of Arnacin's loyalties, as well as their loyalty to king and country. It must not be easy."

"Like everyone else," the king nodded. "The adopted natives have surrendered their hearts to him. The savages themselves appear to view him as some sort of god. Is not the reason he returns from the field without ever losing a man because the savages refuse to attack him, unless for defense? I believe they attempt to avoid him, and it is only his skill that allows him to find them."

"What causes you to believe such?"

"Have you not wondered how he returned from the mountains, unknown lands filled with the enemy after he took down their defenses, telling them he was there? There was no possible way, Carpason, unless they allowed him to escape." Carpason's gaze remained fixed on the fire, and the king confessed, "I fear when the war ends, they will not surrender to Mira, but to their Black Phantom and, if he leaves, that peace will end."

His gaze darting back to the king, his lord repeated, "*If* he leaves? You're not planning on letting him go!"

"What choice do I have?" Miro snapped. "If I am correct, the savages will yield only to him. For my duty to Mira, I will not be able to let him go, regardless of the following damage to my word. I hope only that if such is the case, it will not need to come down to force, that he will stay by his own choice. If not, I will force it. I will chain him in a cell if I must. All of Mira depends on it."

Regarding the lord for a moment more, the king added, his tone thick with warning, "Or don't you agree?"

Turning back to the fire, Carpason studied it in silence before softly whispering, "I trust, Sire, that when that day comes, you will know best."

The next night, Arnacin jumped as the library's door opened at midnight. As his gaze met Miro's, the islander shot to his feet, his face pale. Miro himself only paused for a moment before moving over to some of the scrolls on a lower shelf. "Isn't it a little late, Arnacin?" he asked, without looking again at the islander.

His gaze flicking briefly to the map he had been contemplating, Arnacin nervously inquired, "Is there anything I can do for you?"

"I'm just checking what Mira knows of a foreign kingdom's resources." The king's voice trailed off as he held up one scroll, his gaze traveling down it. Looking over at the islander, he commented, "I would think research on your ship is less pressing than rest. With winter, you can't apply anything, anyway."

"I... I was..." licking his lips, Arnacin admitted, "I was studying Mira's maps for any hint of the terrain of the mountains."

Snapping the scroll closed, Miro retorted, "There is no reason to look for that. Mira has never entered them before, and never will again."

"Your Majesty–" Arnacin began with a sigh, yet the king cut him off.

"Carpason did say you were discussing Miran spies with him. The answer is 'no.'"

"We were not discussing *Miran* spies."

"The answer is still 'no.' You of all people should understand why it cannot be otherwise. Did you not say yourself that the war started through lack of 'honor'? Should Mira encroach on their territory, it will confirm their accusations."

"With all due respect, Mira did just attack it." As Miro's eyes flashed, Arnacin dropped his gaze, whispering, "Your Majesty."

"The edge only–to demonstrate that Mira could take it, but chooses not to. Sending scouts throughout their land is entirely different."

"I am not Miran, Your Majesty. If I go, I doubt they will look on me as Mira."

"If I allow it, it will be Mira and, regardless, they know which side you support."

"I am for the lives of both. It is for that reason..." He paused, hoping for the least offensive way to phrase his next words, "that I cannot continue aiding Mira if the strategy remains the same as it is now."

Taking a furious step toward the islander, Miro hissed, "So you are capable of breaking your word. You have no choice but to continue aiding Mira according to your oath, and the current strategy is the only alternative to your stated 'dishonor.'"

"The current strategy is condemning one or the other side to death, whichever one out-brutes the other."

"Then so be it," Miro snapped. "Do you think their excited wrath will not condemn Mira should I listen to you and those you've convinced of your folly?"

"Then secretly send me up there alone and execute me after you win!" Arnacin snapped in sudden anger. "That way, no one can think you *condoned dishonor.*"

Miro had frozen, regarding the islander as if he had never seen him before. Softly, he muttered, "Perhaps I was wrong to suggest you would break your word. Regardless, such an act would be far worse than normal dishonor, Arnacin, despite your surprising allowance of it in order to assist Mira."

"Whatever you think best, Your Majesty," Arnacin pleaded. "You must agree to some such action. This war can't be allowed to continue until one side is annihilated, not for you or them. Currently, you are not even sure what drives them to persist in their hatred. Until that is known, the problem itself can't really be solved."

"Do not think I have not been contemplating that concern, Arnacin," Miro sighed, reaching out to touch the islander's shoulder.

Arnacin's backward step ended the gesture, and the king finished, dropping his arm back to his side, "But unless all the savages *were* eliminated, I doubt Mira would be any better off."

"Mira will not win this war if this continues, Your Majesty. They have more unknowns with more land and resources."

"I am hoping to fix that," Miro stated, looking back at the scroll still balled in one hand. "As to alternate plans..." It was the king's turn to pause contemplatively before he asked, "Have you tried asking the adopted natives for all they can tell you?"

"They have secrets they will bury with them in their graves, and I refuse to ask them to break their loyalty."

"Then what if they returned to their own kind as ambassadors?"

"The natives would kill them as traitors and leave the bodies for the carrion."

"Savages," Miro huffed before exclaiming, as his thoughts turned, "To what on Mira are the adopted natives loyal?"

"Their blood, Your Majesty, or can you not understand that?"

Miro only said as he turned to replace the scroll, "You should not stay awake any longer, Arnacin."

"Did you find what you wanted?"

"For now." Miro was already at the door when he turned suddenly. "Arnacin, I don't wish to ever hear again that you have been in the mountains."

"Unless things change, I doubt you'll hear of any such thing," the islander whispered.

Miro started to open the door and then shut it, pressing, "And, Arnacin, I trust you have not betrayed Mira with such action already?"

"I would never consciously betray Mira, Your Majesty. It was *Mira* I gave my word to aid."

"Very good," Miro said with a nod. "Now, go to sleep."

With that, the king left. Sighing, Arnacin snuffed out the candle. Yet there he stood, staring out the windows which the stars now shone through. His only movement was to approach that window and, with a sigh, drop his weight against its frame, where he stayed for hours more, watching the night pass.

For some time, Arnacin continued pushing himself so hard that he came down with the winter curse on its first sweep of the city. It kept him confined to his quarters for the better part of a week, and he recovered just in time to hear that he might wish to stay in his room. Not only was winter the common time for ambassadors to converge on Mira, but Miro had also chosen a new queen to give them more troops after losing so many over the year. The intended bride, Princess Rosa of Vemose, had herself arrived that very morning. Therefore, Arnacin holed up in the library to avoid all of the additional commotion this event caused.

Once all the ambassadors had arrived, the hustle to prepare for the wedding truly began, as Arnacin knew from sitting in the kitchens. Usually, the chefs were constantly placing food in front of him for as long as he remained there, but now they often forgot his very existence while he would watch them running hither and thither, on this assignment or that one. It often seemed to him, during that time that he had flown off the world unbeknownst to himself while it still continued to turn without him, spinning without pause.

In the shadows of the upper corridor surrounding the ballroom, Arnacin and Valoretta had a perfect, undercover view of the guests coming down the stairs opposite them, and those in the noisy ballroom below. Uninvited, and largely uninterested, the islander was nevertheless drawn to his current observation point against one of the columns, along which the railings of the opened corridor ran. Shortly after his arrival, the princess had joined him and proceeded with a running commentary on all the guests.

As a thickset, bewigged man walked stately down the stairs, the princess remarked, "Lord Fruea from Comsta." She shook her head. "They practically stuff themselves there, according to their fashion. As far as those absurd false curls, though—there are worse. Vanderoo men braid their hair and that's not even the worst country out there. There is a country that occasionally sends ambassadors, Garamitx, where the females cut their hair short and the men let it grow–which is completely backwards."

She met her companion's incredulous glance and shrugged. "It is their belief that long hair is noble and cropped hair is a show of meekness and servitude. Therefore, they scoff at us as a kingdom where our females are the 'masters.'" Arnacin smiled at her wicked grin before turning back to watching the guests.

"Oh, and to add to that land's strangeness," Valoretta added, her previous thought gone from her face and tone, "I believe you can appreciate this one... If you were to tell them you were a shepherd, they would take it that you are a layabout–useless, lazy and good-for-nothing–unless you said it while guarding sheep. That word has two meanings, you see." The answer she received was an amused puff of air.

For a couple of seconds, they stood in silence until another man passed, fluffing the ruffles at his throat. Unable to control his laughter at the absurdity, Arnacin mockingly imitated his stiff stance and flapping hand gestures until Valoretta's elbow made sharp contact with his ribs. "It's not funny," she breathed. "That's the Baron Daequan and he very much wishes to impress me."

The islander's reply was to raise his eyebrows. Smiling primly, she answered the unvoiced question, "He has much to learn about impressing me. Personally, I think his only intention is to attain equal or better status than his king."

Both turned quickly as someone stopped behind them. There stood Miro, his crown gleaming on his brow, dressed in his own finery. As Arnacin paled, shrinking against the banister's pillar with an apologetic bow, the king passed him a brief smile of comfort before offering his arm to his daughter. "My Lady, it is time. We can no longer avoid the festivities."

Sighing, the princess slipped her arm into her father's and together–suddenly both looking coldly regal–they descended the stairs with the honorable guests, Princess Rosa and her brother, falling in step behind.

Arnacin remained leaning against the pillar, while below the music and dancing began. It was with contemplation that he noticed the many shifts in Valoretta's character, depending on with whom she was dancing. With those she felt safer around, she remained quiet, almost expressionless in all her stateliness and, with those she disliked, a petty, childish smile would cross her face while she prattled non-stop—to her partners' clear annoyance—all for the sake of quickly removing herself from them without fear of insulting anyone.

As was the custom in Mira, Valoretta performed the first dance with her father and was then passed off to the new bride's escort, the second prince of Vemose. For a moment, the Miran princess remained quiet until her wish for information overcame her nervousness and, smiling coyly, she asked, "Now, why would your father be interested in agreeing to Mira's proposal?"

"Why?" the prince repeated, before turning the question around. "Why would Mira make the proposal?"

Laughing in false gaiety, Valoretta stated, "Honestly, you ask the wrong person. I'm a princess. I never know what passes in the world of politics."

"Is that so? Your father never tells you anything, even if only to inform you how to act?"

"Of course not. He would never approve," Valoretta continued in her light, air-headed tone. "But perhaps you would tell me. And then, I'll know anyway."

Her ploy worked and, laughing almost victoriously, the prince's fingers tightened possessively around the princess' waist. "I will tell you everything after we're married," he stated in a secretive murmur.

It took all of Valoretta's political training not to pale and twist away. Instead, she fluttered, "Married? We're not going to marry."

"But we are. You asked before why Vemose agreed—such a connection might gain more as time went on. In the mass of your suitors, we will stand in higher regard."

"Your connection won't sway Father's mind. He may have someone picked."

Valoretta's words were too much of a challenge—she knew it—yet the words had freed themselves even as she tortured her mind for an excuse to escape his clutches without arousing his suspicion or hostility. Her dance partner, however, grinned. "My sister is marrying your father for this reason. She will have his ear for our cause, I'm sure. If you know otherwise, I can call off the marriage."

She did know otherwise, or she hoped she did, but giggling pettishly, she crooned, "I'm marrying someone more handsome and rich than you. Father promised."

All suspicion died in the prince's eyes and, smiling as if he knew far more than her, he finished the dance with her and passed her along to the next arms that presented themselves. Trembling, Valoretta did not even look up, only knowing she danced with a Miran by the style of boots moving before her swaying skirts.

"Don't worry," the soft words made her jump slightly and she looked up into Lord Carpason's tender eyes. "The new queen will have no sway over the king."

"How can you know?" the princess breathed.

"In the first place, this marriage is only taking place to further the war's needs, as I'm sure you know. Therefore, the king has no love for the poor thing and will never begin to give her his ear. In the second place, she was chosen partly for her lack of character. Naturally, her family believes she will push for them since she has always done exactly as they tell her in everything. They forget that once she is Mira's queen, those with the highest authority will be Mirans, not her siblings and father. And, lastly, I know the king has already picked his future king."

Paling, the princess gasped, "Who?"

Her searching gaze received no more answers than her ears, as the lord shrugged. "I wish I knew. The fact that I know you are engaged at all comes only through observation. For instance, his disregard whenever the subject of your marriage arises and his stubborn refusal to begin examining some of your suitors."

As the princess lowered her gaze in sudden hopelessness, the lord added lightly, "If that does not lighten your fears, I know a princess who knows how to achieve exactly what she wants."

"What do you mean? I am not disobedient."

"Except with your nurse?" Valoretta could not quite maintain her bland expression of innocence and a fond laugh escaped the lord. "It would not be hard at all for said princess to suddenly grow dangerously ill on the day she was to meet her future husband and remain on the edge of death long enough to call off the marriage. In fact, under certain circumstances, Sara would even aid in the lie, I am sure."

Smiling in mock offence, the princess quipped, "I see you are so eager to give me suggestions on how to avoid foreign marriage. To whom, then–closest friend of the king–do you wish to see me wed?"

"I had no one in mind, but I would agree with your nurse on this one. I would pray for a Miran."

"Yes, that way I will become engaged to a grandfather and, on our wedding day, it may be him on his deathbed."

"Or," the lord stated mischievously, "the king may pick a child for you, and no question will be in anyone's mind as to who rules, since there will be ten years between you and the king."

Smiling at the joke, the princess curtsied at the close of the dance and twirled around to the next man awaiting her partnership.

When the meal came, Arnacin finally turned away from his observation point, rolling his eyes at Valoretta's game, but at that moment, as extreme cold washed over him, a sharp cry rang from below and the lights appeared to dim.

It was with pure instinct that he whirled back around, his hand shooting to his side where the Tarmlin blade hung–yet nothing existed to cause such fright that he could see. Still, everyone in the room below had become like statues, their gazes all fixed on the same, empty spot. While Arnacin's gaze bored into that spot, he thought he heard, as if from far away, the low hissing of evil words, their menace clear even without understanding what was said.

Just as suddenly as the sensation had come, the room lights reignited and warmth crept back as, around the islander, doors slammed and dozens of castle inhabitants swarmed into the corridors above the room. The sound of frantic conversation erupted, thousands of questions and concerns crashed like a wave on the shaking nobles.

A trembling touch on his arm caused Arnacin to glance over to where Sara suddenly stood beside him. “Did you see it?” she nearly squeaked in an attempt to control her own voice.

“What happened?” Arnacin inquired, suddenly realizing that his knuckles were turning white around his sword hilt. Dropping his arm to his side, he looked back up to see Sara staring at him in wonder.

“Did you not even hear it?” the nurse pressed.

“What exactly did you hear?”

“Don’t lie to me, boy...”

“I never lie. Now, what happened?”

“The whole castle saw it, heard it or, at least, something like it...” Through her fluster, her eyes looked at Arnacin as if he was a spirit himself. “Look, whoever you are, a mist rose and through it I saw the gnarled bones of one of those horrible savage priests. Before I could scream, the eyes lit...” She trembled, steadying only as Arnacin grabbed her shoulder. “I can’t explain it. It told me that all of Mira should leave this land by tomorrow or death will sweep over us.”

“Don’t listen to it,” the islander advised after a moment of horror. “If they did have the power to do so, don’t think you’d be standing here now.”

“So you say,” Sara scoffed. “What do you know of their intentions?”

Arnacin did not reply, watching the king command silence below. As the panicked voices came to order, Miro stated, “We will ignore the pathetic threat. It has no power behind it, save for scaring those who allow it to scare them. Their charlatan sorcerers cannot even heal the sick through their magic. If this is what they have resorted to, it is only a sure sign that our victory is near..."

Calm settled over the crowd. Yet, despite such logic, Arnacin continued to feel uneasy until the sun broke over the far mountains in the east, dispelling the night's ominous shadows and hidden evils.

Chapter 12

The Savage Trap

"Arnacin," Valoretta finally spoke up as they sat in the library that afternoon. Looking up from a journal written by one of the most skilled generals in Mira's past, the islander waited. "Do you think we shall be wiped out for not leaving–that the savages can call on their gods to do so?"

"I highly doubt it," Arnacin comforted her, while returning to his book. So far, the mediums only seemed capable of scaring people. "I don't think much of their gods in general, much less that they could just wipe you out on the natives' request."

"You don't believe they exist, do you?"

"I don't know if it matters whether I do or not," the islander contemplated. "I haven't given it much thought, but I know one thing–if they were gods, they could not simply be told what to do, which would mean your leaving or not leaving would not be in the natives' jurisdiction."

"Yet what if they became increasingly angry and finally decided they had had enough? What then?"

For a long moment, Arnacin was silent and still, pondering those words. Eventually, he shrugged. "They don't have the power."

"Your island believes in only one god, yet you don't believe other gods can have power? Where one god exists, can't others also exist?"

"I really can't answer that." The honest truth was, Arnacin would not consider it for long. One fact remained regardless of the potentially unnerving answer. "But I know that other gods are powerless in comparison."

Looking away, the princess sighed. "Father doesn't believe that anything higher than a human exists, period, but I disagree. There's an evil intent thrown against us, far more powerful than us. I can feel it. There are things out there—things beyond our sight. I can't ignore them, and I'm scared, Arnacin. Terribly."

Gently, Arnacin reached across the table and squeezed her hand, whispering, "You needn't be, Valoretta, when you know where to turn."

As the day of the wedding drew near, Valoretta grew increasingly apprehensive. Finally, the night before the wedding, she asked Sara to see if the king would speak privately with his daughter.

After the king agreed to see her, Valoretta wasted no time in coming to her point. "Vemose only wishes to rob Mira of its wealth. Prince Harman practically said it himself."

"Yes, I know." Miro simply shrugged, putting aside his work to meet her distressed gaze. Before she could make any exclamation, he explained, "It's the fact that they think to gain so much from this, that it's at all possible."

"So, you've lied about the arrangements?" the princess asked disgustedly.

"No—rather, they have. The proposal suggested that the marriage would give troops for gold with no fear of debt to one kingdom or the other. Our spies tell us they are struggling financially. We struggle with population, particularly young men.

"What made them agree so readily, however, is that they think they can completely claim Mira and its vast riches as part of Vemose, come your marriage. Moreover, our agreement is so perfect because they also do not want Rosa to bear children, particularly not any sons. If so, your marriage is obsolete. The next king will be Miran. Therefore, there will be no outrage if they overhear that I have no intention of *bonding* with the girl."

"What happens when they realize I will never marry their prince and your lack of *bonding* means she won't convince you of anything, either? Could they not demand war for the outrage to their princess?"

"Anyone *can* declare war, Valoretta, but since they never set that as part of their agreement and they don't want to interfere with their own plans for you to remain the heir, there is no actual obligation that we do otherwise. They would simply break their alliance and former peace treaty by so doing."

Nodding slowly, Valoretta compressed her lips. Yet as her father continued to watch her, she swallowed her disappointment, asking as if she completely agreed, "Was all this manipulation your idea or must I thank someone else?"

"I have the strange feeling you want to know for other reasons than to thank everyone involved."

With an innocent smile, the princess stated off-handedly, "Only to make sure which councilors I should exile for being dangerously clever."

Smiling slightly, the king nodded. "I suppose I'll need to guarantee I outlive Carpason."

"Indeed, if it wasn't for the fact that I trust him."

"Then we have that settled. You must remember, Valoretta, that your duty to your kingdom comes first in everything. This had to be done, for Mira. There were no other options."

"I understand," Valoretta truthfully replied.

Throughout the day, visiting ships had dropped anchor in Mira's harbor after braving the winter storms, all in the name of alliances. All the castle's rooms were full to the point that Arnacin offered his room to be used for guests while he happily took blankets and a pillow to his ship. That night's activities started early, first with the wedding ceremony and then, Arnacin supposed, with whatever usually happened after such an event. The islander himself, however, did not even watch the rite and, when the corridors became too busy with the hustling traffic of servants, he slipped into the empty, snow-lit courtyard.

It was around midnight when he heard the soft swish of skirts over snow carpeting and turned to see Valoretta approaching him. Noticing her bare shoulders and white forearms, the islander shook his head, stating, "Valoretta, you'll freeze out here."

"I couldn't take any more of Prince Harman's company and Sara would realize what I was up to if I tried to fetch my cloak, so I simply feigned dizziness and retired... to the courtyard."

As Arnacin began to loosen his cloak with a sigh, the princess shook her head. "I'm quite warm from all that dancing, at the moment."

Together, they turned between the branches of two large rose hedges, now barren except for the snow draping their many limbs.

"So what have you been doing out here, Arnacin?"

"Avoiding the general mayhem," the islander shrugged. "I probably would be out on my ship, but the sailors of all those ships are having their own party on the pier and, well... it's best to stay far away from that one."

Laughing, Valoretta joked, "You mean you haven't ever joined them? From a sailor himself! My, my, how noble... You should have joined us instead, then."

Returning her grin, Arnacin said, "Only if I wished to make a fool of your kingdom by tripping over myself and everyone else."

"Don't you know how to dance, Arnacin?" the princess asked in surprise.

"Not your dances. I've watched them. They're unlike any dance I know. Furthermore, I don't know how well I could do the island's either, by now."

"I'm sure the knowledge is still in there somewhere." When the islander did not reply, Valoretta wondered, "What are your dances? Are they very different, or only slightly?"

Giving her a sly grin, Arnacin teased, "Oh, you know how it is with a dance. One can never explain them. If you don't know, you don't know and you leave it there."

"Is that so?" Valoretta asked coyly, holding out her hands. "Then you shall simply teach me."

"I shall?" the islander repeated, teasingly stressing the order.

"I command it." The princess nodded, a laugh escaping her mock regality.

"Then I refuse," Arnacin flatly replied, turning away impishly.

Continuing with the game, the princess caught his hand, imploring, "Then I humbly beg you, as a meek friend, to teach me something beyond stiff court dances."

Arnacin's eyes glinted merrily as he nodded. "Ah, if it is for the sake of rejecting political games, I shall oblige you, My Lady."

With that, he took her hands, starting their dance at arm's length as they concentrated on the steps. Princess Valoretta, trained in grace, lightness and dance, learned quickly—as fast as Arnacin's memory supplied. Then, when he could remember nothing more of his own dances, they moved to the Miran common dances, whirling through the snow-dusted paths, seemingly forever.

Unexpected laughter emitting from the frozen courtyard roused Miro's attention as he made his escape from his new bride. Opening one of the doors to the courtyard's upper walkways, the king paused. It was easy in the relatively dead courtyard to make out Valoretta, her hair falling out from its elaborate coiffure, strands hanging over Arnacin's arm about her waist, and a broad uncommon smile brightening her face. Smiling himself, Miro shut the door behind him and leaned against one of the pillars, unseen by either as he watched them dance.

They continued to host ambassadors throughout the winter, which demanded most of Miro's and his daughter's time. Although winter was always busy with the other kingdoms' business, this year was particularly bad, considering all the treaties with Mira's new allies.

This also meant that large dances were held almost every other night, during which Valoretta never was given a pause from one dance to the next. Too many foreign men wished her as their partner and the only slight break she received was when a Miran guessed her hidden distress and took a turn with her. As the heir, unlike earlier Miran princesses, her presence was required for the treaties, as it was for trials.

When Sara would wake her every morning—extra early to make sure she was correctly dressed in the appropriate exquisite manner—Valoretta never felt refreshed and would slide out of bed as if ancient. To make matters worse, that long process of clothing and hairdressing, which could take over an hour, would often need repeating before dinner. Sara simply ignored Valoretta's threats that she would cut her own hair off if the nurse did not leave her alone in the evenings, and also ignored the occasional hysterical wrath that arose from the princess' exhaustion.

It was rare to be able to retreat to the library, cool and quiet, and settle down by the islander who spent most of his time there. It was on one of those occasions that the princess fell asleep on her book while Arnacin was painstakingly drawing a map on parchment—a map of *what* he would not say.

When Valoretta woke, it was to Sara's frustrated shaking. Arnacin, and any trace that he had been there, had long disappeared, other than a blanket now tucked around her shoulders. Not that the nurse would see the islander in that sign. Sighing as though she had not really heard Sara's complaints, the princess followed her nurse to change once again for the evening.

Finally, spring came, but before all the ambassadors had departed, word came to the capital that the savages had come, before the first real thaw, to pillage and burn some of the towns and farms closest to the woods. Because they had been spotted in the plains beforehand, no one had died, yet this was the best that could be said about the savages' refusal to let the Mirans rest.

With the first thaw, Miro sent six of his armies out to engage the enemy. Arnacin was not sent, for reasons many guessed, considering his disobedience on his last mission. He was there to see Carpason off, however, and to pass the lord a rolled parchment, its contents unknown by most. Without looking at it, the lord simply stowed it in his saddle bags.

Without any regard for the whispers against him, the islander returned to working on his ship, where Valoretta happily joined him, free once again from the demands of entertaining ambassadors.

"My Lady." The soft call halted the princess on her way to the library one day. Seeing the queen, in truth a girl hardly any older than Valoretta herself, the princess nodded politely, though inwardly she groaned.

A closer look at the fear in the girl's eyes softened the princess' heart, though, and relenting, she asked, "What may I do for you?"

"I wished to know..." The new queen paused. Glancing down, she admitted, "I'm very lonely, My Lady. I had hoped, being a noble lady yourself, you would understand my need."

"I?" Valoretta repeated in pride, turning away, "I whom you apparently came to force into marriage to your glitter-eyed brother. I should think not."

"Wait, My Lady," the queen pleaded. "That is only one of their wishes, but the other... the other they would feel it suicidal to admit. To be honest, My Lady, Vemose is on the edge of financial collapse. When Mira asked for a union, Vemose agreed in exchange for gold. The agreed-upon amount would seem as nothing to a kingdom of such riches as yours, though. They, of course, need more if they are to continue prospering, but I must tell you I did not marry even for those reasons."

Valoretta had frozen, still turned away, yet at the pause that followed, she looked back over her shoulder.

The queen's cheeks were bright pink, her delicate lashes lowered, yet, as if hearing the princess turn, her blue eyes flicked upward. Shy determination shone there. "Call me a complete romantic idealist if you will, but all my life, I've wanted what I see our commoners possess. Their ladies are not just pawns to be bartered away for money or power and, when they wed, something magical exists in those unions. I love my family, and I'm sure they love me—but I'm nothing. And here, despite all my absurd ideas of how a husband and wife would always learn to cherish each other eventually, I am unloved instead. Therefore, I pass from nothing to a lonely nothing, with the ridiculous title of 'queen.' I've seen it, My Lady. Mira only has one queen—the title will not be robbed from her, and you are she."

As the princess turned all the way around in surprise, the queen whispered, "The king married me for the men I would bring. Now, as far as he is concerned, I can be disregarded, for he will not even take the chance that a battle could ensue over your sovereignty. Am I Queen Rosa of Mira? The title only serves to mock me."

Shaking her head slightly, Valoretta stated, "I'm sorry, but if you feel sold, you sold yourself."

"Father would have made me if I refused."

"But you didn't—you said so—and if he truly loved you, I hardly think he would actually have asked that you be dragged here, now would he?"

"For the sake of his kingdom? Love must sometimes be sacrificed."

"Not slavery, Your Majesty..."

"Rosa. I said the other name is a slander to me."

"As you wish. 'Your Majesty' or 'Rosa,' my point remains. Was it not your choice, for whatever reason, to marry? You already said it was."

Rosa looked down, twining her fingers in her skirt. "You are a queen fit to rule, Princess Valoretta, yet you do not fool me. If you had no like fears and thirsts, I should wonder at your open friendship with that sailor, a nobody your father apparently deems a temporary plaything given to keep you content. If it wasn't for that, I would wonder that he didn't object to it. "

Lifting her head, Valoretta retorted, "Arnacin is a friend of Mira. He is no mere sailor, and even were he..." She paused, pondering the truth of the charge, despite herself. "I, unlike you," she finally compromised, "refuse to be dragged about on a chain. Arnacin is a friend. Nothing would make me act otherwise and I would only be a liar and coward to try hiding it."

Studying the princess, Rosa breathed, "So you will not sympathize with my plight? I thought we might possess something in common."

Once again softening slightly at the look of complete desolation, Valoretta admitted, "We might, yet I have nothing in common with weakness." With that, she whirled around, practically striding away in anger due to her lack of answers to Rosa's charges.

Later that day, Arnacin and Hadwin stood in a less frequently used circular stairwell of a tower. The location allowed them more privacy and alerted them when someone approached, for the sound of feet echoed on the stairs. Although their low voices also echoed, they knew from previous testing that only tones could be made out.

Therefore, they kept their conversation going even when the stairwell clomped with footsteps, swiftly switching topics without altering or breaking their tones to hide their true discussion.

"If Miro doesn't send us back out, we'll have to think of some way to convince him to abandon Mira," Arnacin said, tapping his palms against the stone behind him. The slit of a window beside them looked out on the southern mists rising from the kitchen vents.

"Or we could just tell him every–" Light footsteps sounded on the stairs above them and, smoothly, Hadwin changed topics. "I never was a very good conversation starter. Girls just made my tongue stick to the top of my mouth."

Despite Arnacin's growing smile, the knight continued as a page continued down the stairs. "Before I knew it, I was quite settled as a bachelor, and that's tha–Arnacin, stop laughing."

"That's what you thought of in a split second?" the islander exclaimed, covering his mouth to hide his laughter.

"Stop wasting time. I have no intention of hiding in this stairwell all day."

Sighing, Arnacin remarked, "Hiding? If we were hiding, I know of better places. And no, I tried to talk to your king about the mountains. Your lord told me he also has spoken to Miro about it. I even told him I would be forced to resign. Nothing worked.

"If we tell him all: that mediums are encouraging the hatred, that they don't belong to any tribe but wander throughout the continent, and that it takes twenty years to apprentice new ones, I think the only thing–"

Clomp, clomp, clomp. More feet sounded on the stairs.

"I often wonder if those kitchen vents are actually safe," Arnacin continued, looking out the window. "I mean, poison can just as easily go in."

"Good luck finding the vents if you walk through that mist. They're many and small. I recall hearing that there are over a million ant-sized vents in that kitchen to stop exactly that sort of attack. That was while studying siege warfare."

The footsteps left the tower and Arnacin finished, "Miro will just be furious that we've spied for so long. We have to find some way to dangle Mira's potential victory before him or I fear speaking about it."

"Yet if we don't speak and we're not sent out," Hadwin muttered, "How are we to convince them of anything?"

Covering his face in his hands, the islander sighed. "I don't know." Then, thrusting his hands back to his sides, he admitted, "With or without our further action on the field, I think Miro needs to evacuate. I know why he will do almost anything not to, but it's senseless."

"Even if we could convince him to turn this war strictly against the mediums?"

"We'd have to kill them all at once or it would never work. Once they realized they were the target, they would vanish, and yes, peace would come, but in five years or so they would return, perhaps with greater hatred and strength. I don't think Mira would have a chance, then."

Hadwin's own gaze followed Arnacin's out the window. With the strength of the sun, the mist took on a hard appearance, shooting the light back toward the coast.

Slowly, the knight let his breath out. “Perhaps the mediums hold meetings, during which we could fall on them all at once. It's our only hope, Arnacin.”

Saying nothing, the islander nevertheless felt his eyebrows rise and Hadwin meet his questioning gaze with an apologetic shrug. “This is also my home, Arnacin. The prospect of leaving our nationality, friends and extended family, as well as our homes, is one that none of us desire.”

“I understand that, but–”

“Yes, you've left your own home, but I know how desolate you would feel if you knew you could never return.” It was an argument that caused Arnacin to shudder.

The next few days passed and still Miro only sent out other troops. Arnacin paced. On the evening of the second day, Cornyo pulled the islander to a room with the rest of their company. There a small table sat in the midst of the men, a game board atop its polished surface.

“The basic rules to Molshunting are fairly straightforward,” Cornyo explained after convincing his restless commander to learn the game. “The object is to move all forty of your mols”–he held up the wooden playing piece–“around the board and into their home. The opponent moves in the opposite direction to his home. Your strategy is to block your opponent from moving and hopefully send him back to the start when you can. If you can land on him when he only has one mol in that spot, you send him home.”

Pulling out an eight-sided cube engraved on each side with what looked like a different animal, the knight proceeded to explain the game. After he finished the basic rules, saying that there were complications best learned while doing, they started.

Very quickly, however, Arnacin began to suspect that either no complications actually existed or they were being added to, since those watching would try to hide smiles or break out laughing as “complications” were encountered.

Cornyo proceeded to keep Arnacin completely trapped with detailed rules like, "Only six mols can fit in a space at a time. If I can fill in the rest of a space, I can knock all of yours sitting there back to start. I can choose to move backwards if I wish to land on you."

Raising his eyebrows at one point, Arnacin moved one of his pieces backwards to where Cornyo had one lonesome mol. Yet as he picked the knight's piece off the board, Cornyo exclaimed, "That's only a move that can be done as the last ray of sun shines in a day."

Laughter erupted around them and, sliding down in his seat, Arnacin kicked his opponent's chair over. In the following crash, he proceeded to move all forty of his own pieces. By the time Cornyo looked again, Arnacin's pieces resided contentedly at home.

"Hey," the knight interjected. "That's not in the rules."

"It is."

"How?"

"Because I said so." Ignoring the new eruption of mirth, the islander stated, "And there's this convenient law that says troops listen to their commanders without question."

As the laughter only grew in strength, Cornyo grinned. "All right, all right... I'll stop inventing rules and show you the right way to play. So..." His smile turned impish. "The basic rules to Molshunting are fairly straightforward. The object of the game..."

Groans echoed around them as he proceeded to replay the beginning, his eyes glinting in acknowledgment of the implication. Implication aside, however, he stopped taking advantage of Arnacin's lack of knowledge of the game and only barely scratched out a win in the end.

"All right," Arnacin sighed after they cleaned up. "To bed with the lot of you. We don't know when we'll be moved back to the field and if we make a habit of staying up 'til midnight, it won't go well." With muttered "good nights," they all split up, more or less retiring for the night.

Although Arnacin refused to feel concerned about his lack of field orders, he found himself closely listening to the rumors regarding the king's councils–knowing he was frequently mentioned. He also impatiently awaited word from the troops engaging the enemy.

Finally, they began trickling in, with the terrified whispers that "the eagles have been released." To Arnacin's inquiry, they would only shudder, or some would shrug, and the islander gleaned nothing more until Carpason's troop returned from the field.

Carpason had barely entered the city with his men when he noticed Gagandep watching them with the air of a man waiting for a private word. As their gazes met, the lord also saw the adopted native's eyes were rimmed with terror.

"Continue to the castle," Carpason ordered his men. "I will be there shortly."

With that, he turned his steed onto the street that would take him to Gagandep's. The midst of the city was no place to talk.

As Carpason looped his horse's reins about a lower tree limb, the native met him there, rubbing his head as if wearied or stressed.

"What is it, Gagandep?"

"Are the natives actually using eagles?" The native's voice was shaky.

Taking his friend's arm, Carpason seated him on the garden well. "Yes, an eagle killed one of my men." As the adopted native swayed, the lord caught him from falling into the well. "Gagandep, what is it?"

Had he not feared letting go, he would have drawn some water for himself, but he continued to hold on and, after a moment, Gagandep shook his head. "They've cursed everyone. Who knows how long we have before this entire continent bursts into flame."

The adopted native must have taken leave of his senses. Kneeling in front of him to make eye contact, Carpason shook him slightly. "What are you talking about?"

Gagandep gulped, yet finally looking at the lord, he whispered, "The eagles..."

Miro's reply to the news was to ask Carpason to inform the other field commanders of his information. It took impressively little time for all of them to assemble in their council chamber.

"They train their eagles to hunt man—not track and kill, mind you, hunt," the lord informed those gathered.

"You mean they...?" Yet no one seemed to be able to say it. Most of the nobles had paled, their eyes widening. Others, like Cestmir, crossed their arms, their disgust written across their glowering faces.

"Whatever the birds kill is the enemy's dinner. In a war, this feeds their men. As of yet, we've been fortunately exempt from that attack, since they consider it a lack of honor to eat a worthy opponent. Yet we're beginning to see the return of eagles on the field. Something's changed. We don't know what, but they no longer honor us as worthy opponents. For this reason, it is particularly imperative now that no one strays from their assigned position."

The lord's gaze flicked briefly to Arnacin before he finished, "They have grown in ferocity and, should no one know where to reach you, you are beyond our aid and at their mercy. Are we agreed?" A low murmur of scared consent followed, except from the islander against the wall, whose dark eyes simply hardened unyieldingly. "Arnacin?" Carpason pressed.

For a long moment, the islander made no reply. Then, dipping his chin in acknowledgment, he stated, "I understand." Another second of silence passed while the lord looked at him reprovingly, but then Carpason dismissed the field-commanders, until only Arnacin remained.

Together, they exited the room. Only then did the lord comment, "So, you only understand, do you?"

"I can't agree," Arnacin admitted.

Carpason sighed, adding to his earlier warning, "Those birds can see at least sixty miles away, and we'll receive no allowance from them, whether because we crossed some line or..." He glanced once again at the islander walking beside him.

"We're simply badgering them too much." Arnacin shrugged. "This is not a war they're willing to lose, with or without other influences. It's for their home. If we take away their hope of winning, they'll throw all they can at us and end allowances in the light of the cause. Under their circumstances, I'd do the same." Meeting the lord's half-exasperated look, he shrugged, "I didn't mean the cannibalism part."

"Then why are you on our side?" Carpason joked.

"Their actions are far from upright, and only slaughter will come of their winning."

After a pause, the lord pressed again, "Arnacin, what has made us harm their hope lately? What's changed to make them react so? Only at great peril would they risk the honor of their god of war, for it is his rules they follow at such times." When the islander did not answer, he finished, "I didn't say this in front of the others, but I think they're after you personally–that their eagles are meant to bring you down, one way or another. You have forced them to retreat once too often, and they're scared. Should you continue to pursue your current activities, I am afraid they shall succeed in their mission."

"And they will have succeeded in their mission if I don't continue," Arnacin flatly remarked. "It is only through my 'current activities' that they have been forced back."

"Arnacin, the war strategies are not ours to plan. It creates discord–"

"And harmony creates a standstill, at best," the islander snapped back.

"An entire council should be trusted to plan wisely–"

"A council of fools," the islander scoffed.

"Arnacin," Lord Carpason groaned. "You are not in a place to change that, even if it is true–particularly when you have men under you. Moreover, you're an alien, a young alien to add to that. We have no right to allow you to put yourself at such risk–"

"You have no right to force me to do otherwise."

"We do have every right to take command from you."

For just a minute, lord and islander faced each other, opposition and challenge simmering in the air between them. Then, Carpason slowly exhaled, "Should they kill you, your help will have ended, and what good will that have done?"

"They'll have already won–"

"You gave your word to aid the king–"

"Therefore, I will keep it to the death if need be, and retreating would do the opposite. My aid was not my allegiance to his every command, but to Mira."

Rubbing his forehead with a sigh, Carpason surrendered. "I have said all I can, Arnacin. If reason will not bring submission from you, I know you too well to continue."

"I can't," Arnacin softly repeated.

"Well then, for friendship's sake, I won't tell the king, as perhaps I should." The reply was a small heartfelt smile.

Arnacin was still not sent on the field, but he began taking his troop into the open, outside the city, to practice their archery in a new way. Some passing by looked on in bewilderment as men would fire an arrow into the sky and another archer would attempt to shoot it down. Others more familiar with the islander simply shook their heads.

Even Arnacin failed miserably at it at first, whether he aimed with his left or right, but as his troop sagged with despair, the islander persisted. When the sun set without anyone's success, the troop slept outside on their commander's orders so they could resume with the first rays of light. Firth scored the first shot, to Arnacin's frustrated glare as he lowered his own bow.

"I'll best you later," the islander promised.

The Miran grinned in reply.

All the same, it took the whole afternoon for the promise to be fulfilled, with few breaks except for a meal. With that victory finally won, Arnacin allowed the troop rest, and they gratefully returned to the city.

"You better keep practicing, Arnacin," Firth commented before they went their separate ways, "or I'll beat you again."

The islander was too exhausted to rise to the bait, though, and he disappeared with a weary smile.

Since his dance and conversation with Valoretta that winter about the future king, Carpason frequently found himself contemplating the destined leadership of their kingdom. The fact that bothered him the most was that Miro pretended he had no one in mind, nor was he announcing any weddings.

As that thought again fixed itself in the lord's mind, his gaze wandered to the night sky out his window.

There were several solutions of course. Miro might have picked a foreign husband for his daughter and wanted to protect the other kingdom's noble from jealous assassination. But, no... Even if both kingdoms had agreed to keep it secret for a time, there was no reason to hold off such a wedding, and every reason to bind two strong kingdoms together, even if just to give the Mirans a home to which they could retreat.

Was it pride? Was Miro so intent on holding his throne that he would not make his announcement until he was on his deathbed?

Yet that hardly sounded like Miro. Under those circumstances, Mirans would at least still retain their standing, even if it merged into another. The nobility might become lesser nobles, but they would avoid becoming mere peasantry.

In short, Mira would be preserved by such a choice. So Miro's reluctance must mean he saw some other solution. Therefore, Miro's successor could not be part of another kingdom. But if he was Miran, what reason could the king have for keeping it secret...

Carpason's quandary was fathomless, so he forced his attention back to the map he was determined to learn by heart. As he looked down, however, the answer came... The secret must be because of the intended king's reaction as much as everyone else's. Miro had to keep it secret until he could force it on the man he had chosen.

Gasping, Carpason shoved the map of the mountains back into the chest, locked it and asked the first passing servant if anyone knew whether the king had already retired for the night and if he was alone. The answer was that he was alone in the council chamber. Thanking his good fortune, Carpason turned toward the indicated room.

"You intend for Arnacin to be king," Carpason gasped as soon as the king's guards had announced him and shut the door. Miro practically ignored him, busy with the many parchments before him. "I'm asking, Sire, don't go through with this."

"Why do you think I wished him to be commander?" Miro asked, finally looking up. "Lord Carpason, you already know I do not intend to allow him to leave. How is this so much worse?"

"He's a shepherd, not a noble!" When the king only raised his eyebrows knowingly, Carpason insisted, "This will imprison him for life! He'll never even have time to visit his home and let them know why he cannot stay. I had hoped that the natives would see something different in Valoretta, and Arnacin would at least be able to return home then."

If Miro noticed the unintended insult, he did not take offense. Sighing, he nodded to the chair next to him. "Come, sit."

Once the lord had joined him, he lowered his voice. "You seem to forget that there are hundreds of kingdoms all straining for this throne–that until someone claims the title of king, they will continue trying to force Valoretta into marriage, through war if they must, once she is queen. Peace between Mira and her natives may come, but the war will not end until her right to rule is secure.

"Furthermore, it is *her* right to rule. She alone must sit on that throne. Mira has only ever had one ruler with their consort, who is in the best of circumstances their right hand. Valoretta will be Queen Mira, not Queen Valoretta. Therefore, her king must be someone who will allow her to rule, a partner and not a master, someone who can lead in the battles, but not take over.

"And lastly," he paused, his gaze growing distant, "Arnacin has the unyielding virtue Mira needs for peace between her people and her neighbors. He is someone who will not surrender what he views as right for what many label as the greater good. This was my queen's one wish for the next king." Only thoughts of Valoretta's mother could cause such sadness in Miro's voice. "I think she was and is right. I am incapable of such, but for Mira's peace, it is needed." He smiled slightly, "I expect there to be frequent arguments between Mira's future monarchs, but I know they will strengthen each other."

Carpason nodded in understanding, yet still asked, "But if you break Arnacin in so doing?"

"He does not appear such a defeatist. Rough as it might be for a little while, I think he will realize how much this continent needs him."

The lord simply dipped his chin in submission.

"Arnacin." Miro nodded as the islander stepped into the throne room. "The savages have finally been pushed back as far as our borders, yet not back into their mountains. To Mira's frustration, they have returned to their foxholes in the woods. I must ask you to take your men out to help with the searches, for one week, mind you."

"Your Majesty," the islander inquired, "may I ask why you did not send me out before, if you are willing to send me out now?"

"I think you know the answer. You are sent out now, because there is a reason to place trust in you once again. In these searches, no one can be spared."

Bowing out, the islander whispered before leaving, "I'm sorry Mira ever caused need to doubt." Before the king could process those words, Arnacin was gone.

Four hours later, the troop marched out—on foot, as only Arnacin's troop went, with horses in tow. "He should not have gone out," Memphis sighed beside the king while they watched the troop fade into the distance. "He has yet to agree to change, and there are suspicions about what he does on the search."

"He has never lied to me," Miro whispered. "In what manner he searches, no one knows, but he searches and that is what is required."

Whatever argument Memphis brought up, the king repeated those words, yet he wondered inwardly if he was wrong.

Slowly, a week passed. Not one of Arnacin's troop returned the seventh day, nor a few days after. After two weeks, he made Carpason return to the field to search for the islander or any of his men. When the lord did not return after another three days, Miro sent out more of his armies to join the hunt for the vanished troop.

By then, he was forced to confess to himself that part of him did not trust Arnacin, as his mind invented all the least likely possibilities as to how an entire troop could vanish.

A horse's clarion call made Arnacin glance up from the impaled native just falling at his feet. Through the fray around them, he saw horses swarming into the melee. For just a second, his blood froze at the thought that the natives had finally brought their cavalry in to guarantee their enemy's demise. That fear quickly died as a cry of alarm rose from the attacking natives and they began a desperate retreat, though not without throwing all they could against Arnacin in their flight.

Somehow, the islander–and Hadwin beside him–kept time with those attacks until horses surrounded them, preventing the attackers from escaping through them. With no strength left to stand, the islander used the excuse of cleaning his sword to sink to his knees and rest.

"Arnacin," Carpason's alarmed voice informed him who rode one of the horses above him. "Your arm's bleeding."

As Hadwin helped him back to his feet, Arnacin nodded. "That's not new. It just reopens with every attack."

"What happened to it?" the lord inquired, now more interested than concerned.

"My encounter with one of the five eagles we killed."

"Firth killed," Hadwin muttered.

Arnacin ignored him, adding, "This one came the closest, as you can see."

Smiling slightly, Carpason dipped his chin. "Maybe next time you will take my warnings more seriously, then."

"I took them seriously," the islander protested, sliding his sword away. "We spent days practicing our marksmanship on plummeting targets. You saw us doing it, too."

Laughing, Carpason informed him, "Well, we arrived to see what happened to you and to make sure you return safely."

"We can use that," Arnacin wearily gasped, before slipping by to check on his men. Only later, now riding behind Lord Carpason, did he confess, "Our search was fruitful, if there is still time to alert Miro."

"I'm surprised, Arnacin," the lord said. "I surmised that you had been bottled up on the native's boundaries, and that was the reason none of your troop had been seen."

To the gentle reproach, the islander remained silent.

Arnacin had wished for a private meeting with the king. However, as soon as Arnacin and his troops returned, Miro called together all his generals so that each could know what the rest were doing, as he did on rare occasion. Despite that, what the islander had to say could not wait. Therefore, when his turn came to report on his latest mission, he licked his lips, starting, "All of their tribal leaders and all forty-nine of their mediums have gathered in a camp just on the other side of the mountain."

For a second, the room filled with the silence of a tomb as every eye studied him with one emotion or another. "And pray tell, how does that mean anything to us?" Miro finally demanded, his own voice cracking in wonder. "All their gods themselves could gather on that side of the mountain, and it would make no difference to us since we still cannot reach them."

"You can," Arnacin whispered. "I've been up there almost every time I've been out on the field–my men with me."

Sharp inhales met that piece of information and the islander saw Carpason close his eyes on the other side of the room.

"You've been where?" Miro demanded, his brows suddenly knit together as his eyes glinted beneath.

"Gathering information," Arnacin breathed, fully knowing what his words meant to those around him. Not giving any of the Mirans time to react, however, he pushed forward explaining, "I know all the paths up there, all the ones less watched, and if we ambush that encampment, you can end the war now, at least for several generations. Those remaining will be lost without the communications of their gods, and forced to surrender."

He had nothing else to say, but he knew without looking that most of the nobles were stuck between admiration, hope and disgust.

After another pause, however, the king snapped, "We will wait until such an opportunity presents itself on our land! Everyone is dismissed. I shall send for you when I decide where to send you. Islander, you will stay here."

After all the nobles had filed out—Carpason casting a backward glance toward where the king and Arnacin stood, glaring at each other—Miro barked, "How long have you been disregarding my orders?"

"What orders, Your Majesty?" the islander challenged. "Your loosely defined 'searches' hardly have any boundaries whatsoever. As to the other missions, I take down your villages for you, when they are found."

Red-faced, the king retorted, "It is a rule—by common consent—that no one steps foot into those mountains unless under very special orders. You, boy, who cares so much about not murdering, appear to care very little about your own men."

Several heated words rose to the tip of the islander's tongue, but taking a moment to force them back down—an effort that felt close to strangulation—he whispered, "I was simply trying to aid Mira, Your Majesty. The troop, after all, has already sworn their lives to that cause and they felt that information gathering was less of a waste of their lives than…" There were no ways to say it without it insulting, and Arnacin finished lamely, "usual."

Sighing, Miro paused himself. "I little realized how impulsive you were, Arnacin of Enchantress Island. When you return, I may need to do something about it, but currently, every troop is needed. You have made me aware of one thing: they could be gathering to start a large-scale march into Mira and every troop has to be stationed along our borders to stop them, should they try. Succeed diligently in this task, and you may yet retain your command."

It was a clear dismissal. Bowing, the islander began to leave, until the king commanded in parting, "Before you leave, send Lord Carpason to me. There are a few things I should say to him as well."

Halting, Arnacin insisted, "He wasn't fully aware of what…" At Miro's sharp glance, he broke off.

"I have said nothing of thinking him involved in a conspiracy with a foreign islander, have I?" Arnacin shook his head slightly and the king nodded him off. "Send him to me."

As they marched away from the capitol, on foot as usual, Arnacin softly addressed his troop, "Hadwin has already said we need to, but for this I must ask all of you. Do you really want to attack the mountain camp? I don't see any outcome where you live. I'm–"

"Arnacin, stop," Cornyo whispered. "Did we not tell you where we stood when you first asked us?"

"But the real treason has finally come."

"It makes no difference." Firth shrugged. "But now that treason has come, what about you? This isn't your home, Arnacin. Are you really ready to stand with us in our lone defense?"

"I'm expecting to be thrown off of Mira at best, but I can't do otherwise. Should we succeed, your war will end. Should we fail, at least we will have tried–something your king is apparently not willing to do. If I can help I will."

"He would hesitate until we were all wiped off the map," Firth mumbled, before commenting to his commander, "Yet, you're not surrendering much. You want to be kicked off Mira anyway."

Laughing, the islander confessed, “I'd prefer a dignified farewell, but if exile is what it takes, and it's half my fault anyway, I'll take it. I promised to return home and I hope to keep that promise. I doubt it will happen, though.”

“Well, we're with you, Arnacin,” Cornyo promised, his grin clear even from his back. “If we're alive and Miro decides to hang you, we won't let you die alone.”

“That's very comforting, I'm sure,” the islander laughed, pushing the knight forward a few steps in play.

Arnacin pushed himself and his troop to greater speed for four days, allowing them to rest only once they reached the foothills of the mountains. There, he gave them an entire day to regain their strength, while they remained hidden to all passing eyes.

Once refreshed, they started up the most treacherous part of the mountain. The trail Arnacin liked best was not a trail at all. It was a way he had found to ascend the mountain undercover. By scrambling under, over and around large protruding boulders and up dirt-slicked sides, sometimes at almost a ninety degree angle, they avoided enemy eyes—hidden by hanging brush. It was particularly useful for bringing all of his men, as the islander had to that time.

Somehow, as with every other time they took that route, Arnacin guided them to the top, where they disappeared two at a time, into the woods hanging over the cliff edge. For another day, they threaded through the mountain range like shades, stepping carefully in their commander's footsteps, occasionally crawling along an exposed ridge, until they felt the ground slowly starting to slope more often downward. During the second day, the brush beside the troop suddenly trembled slightly against the wind.

Arnacin jerked to a halt, whispering, “Go back,” and then more insistently, “Back.”

It was too late, however. Natives jumped out all around them.

Reacting to a shape springing before him, the islander's bow was instantly in his hand. Yet before he was able to loose the shaft, before he was able to move at all except by reflex, something slammed into his back thrusting him forward by his shoulder–right before pain burst into a million stars about him. Struggling through them for reasons only his training would know, he briefly distinguished running shapes and heard the echoing sounds of battle above his head.

Then, the stars won.

Chapter 13

For Love of an Islander

After his escape from Miran captivity with the help of the Black Phantom, Shashidha, originally of the Wa-tennie tribe, had joined the first tribe he came upon. There, in the Gootika tribe, a medium currently traveling with them asked the boy his story. That medium's reaction was shock and meditation. The next day, he declared that the gods had rescued Shashidha in order to serve them and so the boy had begun his training.

Now, the once unimportant boy watched as his mentor ground steaming herbs together under a pestle, while continuing to mumble under his breath in prayer.

Since only the gods had the right to heal, it was an insult and risk not to defer to them when administering to the sick. For that reason, only the gods' mediums worked with the sick and injured.

Looking back down at the captive shivering in fever beside him, the boy tentatively ran his fingers through the black hair whence came their captive's title. The fire in the tent cast everything in an orange glow, yet still the Black Phantom's skin was the pasty color of the dead.

Shashidha looked up again as the medium slid back into place beside him, finished making the drug.

Knowing he could speak now, the boy inquired, "Are you going to leave the wound as it is?"

"There's no healing that," the medium muttered. "Not only did it pass all the way through his shoulder, but he fell on the tip, causing it to mutilate anything remaining. If he even lives long enough for the barter, the gods will have performed a miracle on our behalf. After that, he is meant to die anyway. Mira cannot be allowed to keep its dangerous tool."

Passing the cup to his protégé, the medium instructed, "Give him this. It will slow the blood flow, which should decrease how much of it he loses and keep him fully unconscious for the trip." He left the tent then without any explanation for his departure. The gods' mediums never explained anything, Shashidha knew.

Regardless, the boy slipped his arm beneath the Black Phantom's head, as instructed. That movement, however, half-roused the captive who then attempted to jerk away, his dark eyes snapping open. Through the haze in them, Shashidha did not know if the captive could actually see or not, but switching to Mira's language, the boy lied, "You will be fine. Just drink this."

He had not really expected an answer, but a low denial emitted from the Black Phantom as he stubbornly turned his head away from his captor's reach. It was with surprising pain that Shashidha heard Mira's accent blending with what he remembered as the captive's own. Softly, he asked, "They've destroyed you, haven't they?"

For a minute, he wondered if the invalid had again lost all consciousness. That thought left as the boy again attempted to obey his instructions and felt a weak pull against the arm cradling the captive. "You don't trust me, do you?"

He wondered why his entire being pleaded for the opposite of the feeble "No" he heard, yet he could not say he had anticipated anything else. Regardless of the pain, Shashidha knew the drug had to be consumed, yet he also knew that a struggle would probably kill the captive. Gazing at the side of the invalid's head, the boy contemplated his options.

It was believed among his people that names were sacred–and therefore a powerful weapon in the hands of the gods' mediums. Those not in communication with the gods could safely use their companions' names, as long as they did not swear on or by them. But the mediums–those granted a touch of the gods' power–dared not speak any true name, lest they bless those they would rather curse, or worse destroy those they served. It depended on the medium's deepest, often subconscious, yearnings toward the person of whom they spoke.

In the case of the Black Phantom, Shashidha knew his yearnings, confused as they were, and he also knew he alone held that power over the captive, since he alone knew the Black Phantom's true name–a secret he would take to his grave. Under the circumstances, he knew not what else to do.

Running the tips of his fingers along the captive's arm, he breathed back in his own tongue, "Arnacin, trust me." Within his arms, the Black Phantom suddenly grew limp and, for a split second, Shashidha wondered if he had done something terribly wrong. Then he noticed the gradual rise and fall of the captive's sides and felt warm air against his fingers from the captive's mouth and nose.

Breathing again in relief, the boy gently tipped the drug into the captive's mouth and slid his arm from beneath him. No matter what anyone said, he knew that since the gods had granted his intent, they would send Arnacin home and leave Mira to her natives without more war. He knew it. He had known it as he breathed the captive's name in both fear and love.

Miro had sent all of his generals out to watch the mountains, except for Carpason, from whom the king demanded suggestions regarding what to do with the islander when he returned. The responsibility for the islander's conduct, Miro said, was only due to the lord's previous advice. He further proceeded to remind his noble of all the things the lord had said to gain the islander a command position, only halting to allow Carpason to make any suggestions when out of words.

"Sire," Carpason wearily soothed. "Did we not all know, almost from the beginning, that Arnacin follows his own rules? You knew as well as I that you could never buy his obedience, that he agreed to all you asked only because he felt it was right. Whenever he felt otherwise, he disobeyed as swiftly as he agreed. Can any of us deny that we knew that about him?"

Turning away, Miro huffed, "Politics are certainly not his strong point."

Forcing his smile under control, Carpason shook his head. He remained silent however until the king turned back, reminding him, "We have discussed other possibilities. I wonder if they are still an option in light of his recent activities."

"As usual, Sire," Carpason sighed, "he had a point and..."

"And should I have acted on it, the war with the savages would likely be over," Miro finished the unspoken thought with a resigned sigh. "Yet he fails to understand politics."

"Or chooses to fail," the lord muttered.

He broke off as the door opened and one of the guards standing there announced, "Councilor Darien has urgent information, Sire."

"Send him in," the king sighed, echoing his lord's resigned irritation. It could hardly be anywhere near as urgent as the councilor apparently thought.

Carpason could not have been more wrong, as, after the normal courtesies, the councilor said, "Two of your nobles were talking as they left, about our current place in this war and how we only have the *foreigner* to thank for our respite."

His face quickly darkening as Carpason's paled, Miro demanded, "And?"

"They wonder if they would already have seen the end of the war had they all likewise disregarded the council's... your orders, Sire." When the king remained silent, Darien persisted, "Sire, if the boy is allowed to continue as he is, no one will listen to you anymore. Arnacin of Enchantress Island must leave the field."

Sighing, Miro admitted, "Yes, he must."

Seeing the thin-lipped smirk that began to creep across the councilor's face, Carpason narrowed his eyes.

"There's only one thing for me to do," the king continued. "Make him my war councilor."

Darien's smile vanished in horror. Sputtering on the words, he choked, "What? Sire, that would reward treason!"

"No, it would bring an end to treason. He thinks only he has the mind for strategy, so if he creates the plans himself, he certainly cannot undermine my final decision and his clear talent can still aid Mira in her need."

Now it was Carpason who was smiling as the king commanded one of the guards at the door to send a messenger to drag the islander back to the capitol. In the humor of discovery, Miro laughed, "And if he protests, arrest him."

Indeed, it seemed an enchanted sleep had befallen the Black Phantom. Although he breathed, nothing caused him to stir–not as the Ragoosh chieftain lifted him from the tent, nor as he was tied onto a horse. Had he truly been dead, he could not have moved less.

"The gods have said you must go the sacred way," Shashidha's master instructed the chieftain. "There, you will move swiftly without attack. The gods have promised their protection while you cross their lands."

"Can I go?" Shashidha asked as the chieftain bowed.

"Only as far as the edge of the sacred way. There, you must turn back and meet me at the praying fields. The gods' servants must not enter the plains of the enemy."

Bowing, Shashidha mounted with the nine tribesmen and they set off with their captive between them. When they reached the edge of the marshy land that was the beginning of the sacred way, Shashidha nodded to the tribesmen. "Here, we part."

Before leaving, however, he touched the Black Phantom's uninjured shoulder. "We will not meet again," he told that still form in the Miran tongue. "But I do not doubt the gods will go with you."

Then, raising his arm in farewell, he turned his steed north, toward the other side of the mountains where the praying fields lay covered in the most blessed of plants.

Not five days after a group of knights went to the mountains to bring back Arnacin, a messenger came flying into the capital, with a panted cry to speak with the king.

"What now?" Miro growled as the messenger entered the hall where he stood with Carpason and Memphis.

"The islander's dead, Sire."

"What!" the king exclaimed, leaping to his feet. In his horror, Carpason only glimpsed the smile of relief that passed Memphis's face.

"The savages ambushed his troop. He was the first one hit, or so his men told me after I found them scurrying out of the mountains."

If Carpason had thought the king's face red before, he had not truly known the color, as it intensified ten times over. For just a moment, no one breathed, fearing the reaction that such wrath would create.

Slowly exhaling, however, Miro hissed, "How much of the troop was lost?"

"Surprisingly little, Your Majesty," the messenger quaked. "Apparently no more than eight or nine. The savages did not seem all that interested after they had felled the islander. Most of those that did perish died from the poison during their flight."

After another moment, Miro excused the messenger, sending his high councilor out with him. Carpason waited, forcing his own breath through his lungs in the ensuing stillness.

Sighing, Miro dropped back onto his throne and growled, "I hate him and love him, Carpason. You tell me how that works."

"Only with Arnacin," Carpason painfully surmised. "Not that it matters now."

Once again, silence fell while the king seemed to study the floor beneath his feet, and his lord sadly watched. After a long time, in which the shadows all but disappeared due to the height of the sun, Miro stood with a sigh. "Well, I find I am glad, for the second time, Arnacin was not an ambassador, or I would certainly be writing a rather infuriated letter to his king with the news that he no longer lives."

His lips twitching in a slight smile, the lord whispered, "You would be writing a book of complaints, Sire."

"Mira has no choice, Carpason," the king breathed as they walked out of the throne room. "It shall simply return to how it made its plans before that..." The king's voice trailed off. In the pause that followed, the lord could well image the words, "swine," "antagonist," "genius," "hope" and "beast" pass through the king's mind. He finally decided on, "...that *phantom* ever arrived. For now, however, his death will not be told."

"You are hoping he'll return somehow," Carpason surmised, at which Miro cast him an almost guilty glance and stepped out through the doors.

It was in a dream that some shape-shifter appeared to Mira's king, mutating in rotation from a being of light to a twisted, mummified corpse. In its lighter form, it stated, "Dare you to wish for the Phantom's life? He is not dead."

"You again," the king scoffed. "Why should I believe a thing you say since you are sent by those charlatans hidden behind their mountain? Specter or not, you would say whatever they wished you to say."

Now the cackling corpse withdrew something from where a human's organs would have been and held it out for inspection. "Vision only, it may be. Take it as you will, yet here is his heart. See how it thumps still. Far away, it is beating in fever."

Aghast, Miro drew back, yet his gaze remained transfixed by that morbid sight–a beating, brown heart in the browner talons of its captor. Some distant thought speculated that the color likely had something to do with the lighting of the entire vision, yet it was a small, conscious thing in the otherwise unconscious unreality.

Cruel hisses of what might be laughter emitted from the being and it extended the thumping heart out farther. "Take it, if you will," it sneered, but as the king's hand twitched indecisively toward the still-beating organ, the talons snapped shut about it as the creature rasped, "Only if you leave your land to her natives. Else..."

Miro felt a scream rip itself from his throat, thousands of miles away, as the talons continued to crush the heart through them and a dark, thick liquid seeped down the creature's appendages. "Await us. In two days, we will arrive for your answer."

It would be understating Miro's relief to say that he welcomed the darkness of his room the next second as one would welcome sunlight after crawling through lightless tunnels.

The dream was too real to be forgotten and, despite all fears of reacting to it, Miro sent for Carpason while it was still dark on the morning of the second day. "Lord Carpason, gather your men and position them in a hidden perimeter around the gate, in the trees, around the first buildings in the city, and behind the bushes. Savages are coming today to parley. I will convince them to leave their hostage a few feet before them, but you must act then. If they have not seen the trap, perhaps all will go well."

Carpason merely nodded at the strange orders, asking, "Do you want us to kill the savages?"

"No, arrest them. I will decide what to do with them once I know what type of offer they bring."

Although the lord said nothing, as the daylight grew and the shadows dissipated, the king felt his rising fear that the savages intended to make him appear insane. He could already guess what Carpason's men were thinking, crouched in various hiding places for hours, painfully stiff and afraid to shift. Miro could curse his own gullibility.

Then, a guard came to tell him that savages were right outside the city and they wished to parley from the outside. "Come," Miro hurriedly ordered, dashing to the outer ramparts.

"Sire," the guard protested, puffing behind. "They have clear aim at you–"

"They wish to parley. Very well, I will hear it." Arriving on the wall, the king saw nine savage riders arranged below, their horses stamping their feet. Over one of the horse's back, the king saw black hair protruding from a rolled bundle.

"Have you come to offer peace?" he demanded of the savages, looking to their leader, marked by the number of feathers at his shoulder.

"We have come to offer life and the return of your Black Phantom. Should you leave in the next week, we will harm no one."

"What Black Phantom?"

Carefully, the chieftain pulled off the furs around that bundle before him, revealing Arnacin within. Yet, no movement came from the islander.

"Ha," Miro scoffed, swiftly looking along the wall to make sure none of his archers were present. "You seek to bargain with a corpse. Even should he live, you would stab him with poison the minute we agreed to your wishes."

"We will not come inside your walls. You must trust us."

The king drummed his fingers on the parapet. "Put him between us, where we have an open view of him and perhaps we will discuss things with you. Naturally, if the gate starts opening, you will be able to reach the body first."

As the king watched the savages glance at each other and then nod, he was glad Arnacin could not know what was happening. The islander would only condemn Miro's deceit.

Below, the natives carefully unbound their captive, carried him just beyond a line of trees, and then retreated. Except for how terribly death-like the islander looked, Miro might have smiled grimly. All Carpason had to do was act. In the meantime, however, the charade had to be continued.

As the savages remounted, Miro called, "Now, what action would you accept as proof that we intend to leave Mira for good?"

"Your immediate act–" But men were leaping out of the trees, dashing from around bushes, and charging from the city. With a cry of rage, the savages leapt toward the men now surrounding the islander's body–proof that they at least thought he still lived.

Carpason's men were too many for the nine savages, however, and they were quickly overpowered.

The royal accommodations consisted of the whole top quarter of the keep, including the roof, although the roof was only ever opened during a royal wedding for the newlyweds to have a private ball under the stars. Poor Rosa never received that honor, but she was unaware of its significance.

Beneath the roof, the royal family–including those who had remained servants all their lives–had what might have been an entirely different castle in the same building. The only type of rooms they lacked were cellars and kitchens, and the largest population in the accommodations *was* the servants–great aunts and uncles. Though the cousins moved out once they married, the number of men and women living there was still a fair number.

Their bedrooms started one floor above the library's level, and most of them faced the courtyard. Valoretta's room, however, looked northward toward the gates and the distant bluish mountains beyond. Although she had not picked her room–Sara had when she was an infant–the princess liked its less tame view. These days, however, the sight was a reminder of the war.

Stifling a sigh, Valoretta sat on her window bench while her nurse did her hair. A small commotion near the gates drew her attention. It was with a nervous flutter that she recognized the figure of her father standing on the ramparts beside the guards. Only some horrible situation would put him in the line of fire, the princess knew.

"My Lady," Sara hissed in exasperation as Valoretta pulled away to lean closer to the window. The princess paid no attention, however, as below a group of horses burst through the gates, which slammed shut behind them. Most of the knights dismounted, handing their horses off to the boys who stood ready, but the horse that had been in the lead simply stopped in the yard, where men rushed around it. Valoretta briefly saw that something or someone was slung in front of the rider before the converging men blocked her sight.

Even at a distance, however, she could tell that they were lifting the horse's burden. Seeing a flash of what appeared to be black, she felt her stomach clench. As she shot to her feet, she felt some of her hair part with her scalp.

"Valoretta!" her nurse exclaimed. "What are you doing?"

The princess did not reply but simply lifted her skirts and dashed from the room. Whatever her nurse shouted behind her was lost to the pounding of the princess' heart. Down the steps she raced and out the keep's entrance, only slowing as she reached the group of men huddled around a figure.

"Father, what's happening?" she gasped, pressing her hand to her aching ribs as she stopped beside the king. He did not have time to answer as the huddle parted to allow a physician to approach them from the middle. In that moment, all her worst fears were realized. Through that gap, she saw Arnacin stretched on a blanket, his features colorless, blood covering his right side, where, through the bubbling mass of his flesh, his collar-bone showed.

"He's still alive, Your Majesty... Majesties," the physician informed them, stopping before the king and his daughter. "I highly doubt he will remain so..."

"Do everything you are capable of," Miro barked, wrapping an arm around his pale daughter. When the physician sighed, the king inquired, "So the weapon was not poisoned?"

"No, they wanted him alive, at least for the time. Their weapon went straight through his shoulder, however, and the wound is past the area where we could amputate, anyway. If you want me to try to save him, he'll live or die with his arm."

"Is it possible to move him?" the king pressed.

"We'll have to chance it. On your orders, Sire, I'll see what burning the wound will do, but I'm telling you, we might as well save him the pain and let him die in peace."

As Valoretta choked back a despairing sob, Miro ordered, "Take him inside. And let it be known that if anyone breathes a word of his condition outside the castle, the punishment will be death. If Arnacin survives, he will need his wound kept secret."

Bowing, the physician turned to relay the orders.

The princess had not cried since she was a small child, not even when her mother died, but watching the men carrying the broken islander inside the keep, she felt very near to surrendering. Somehow, for sake of her faked strength–for her royalty–she again resisted, feeling her father's arm tighten lovingly about her shoulders.

Beside them, only Lord Carpason remained, still holding his horse's reins as he and the king shared sorrowful glances. "All we can do is hope," the lord finally whispered before turning away with a bow to take care of his steed.

After assuring his daughter that the islander was in the best of hands, and that was all they could do, Miro retreated to the great hall, where he soon began to pace. Only Carpason had followed him and, finally shaking his head, the lord asked, "What do you wish to do about the prisoners?"

Miro halted abruptly, looked up, shook his head and then continued his pace. With a slight smile, the lord tried again, "Sire, you can't just let them rot. The abuse they'll receive while doing so will be worse than execution. And if you tell the jailers they are to be considerate, they'll think you're mad and possibly disobey anyway. Such is the extent of their hatred."

"Carpason," the king sighed, "you must realize that if I have them executed, word will reach the savages that we murder our enemies even under a white flag, and if I send them back, they'll tell everyone of the trap... under a white flag."

"Is that why you're pacing?"

Again halting, Miro turned to his lord. "Would such a choice not make you pace?"

"Perhaps, Sire, the only thing you can do is release them. Hopefully, the act of mercy will soften their anger."

"Huh." With that snort, the king circled back to his throne, collapsed into it, and ran his hand over his face. "Carpason," he moaned, "should I have just told them to finish the islander? He's dead anyway. If he breathes a few more hours, I'll think he's cursed."

A laugh escaped the lord before he could cut it off. The question was too serious for humor. "All I can say, Sire, is that I wouldn't have been able to permit such a thing and, since it is a past decision, your only possible action is to decide what's to be done now."

The king's eyes flicked up to Carpason's gaze. After a moment, he sighed. "Do you know of anyone other than an adopted native who can take a sample of the poison off one of those blades and discover its compounds?"

"I will try to find someone, Sire." Bowing, the lord left. His search was futile, but in that time, Miro made his decision. He chose to release the captives. Sadly, only Carpason seemed to think it the right choice.

Mirans grumbled against the decision and the natives only scoffed. In fact, the chieftain taunted before they rode off, "Ha, your king means to trick us. No one can lie to the gods."

The councilors' reaction was to blame Arnacin for all of the natives' actions.

Carpason found them all clustered in the corridor outside the islander's room, whispering angrily. "And how has Arnacin changed the savages' view of Mirans?" he demanded.

Councilor Erlund shrugged. "He's been the only one to disregard the right of their boundaries."

"Of course, he is just a boy," Darien said, his glinting eyes fixing themselves on Carpason. "He was schooled in his tactics. Perhaps, Lord Carpason, his death is your fault. You caused this. You were stupid and unfeeling enough to suggest the aid of a foreigner. First, you twist an innocent boy into a disrespectful killing machine, and now he lies dying... at such a young age, thanks to you."

"I don't see *your* tears." Carpason snapped, shoving past them into the invalid's room.

No matter what anyone said, however, no one held out much hope for Arnacin's survival.

Cornering Hadwin as soon as Arnacin's troop returned, Carpason snapped, "What were you thinking? Did you not caution him at all?"

Dropping his gaze, Hadwin guiltily whispered, “There was no other way, my lord. As long as the natives have people and the mediums call on their gods, man and woman, boy and girl, down to the youngest child capable of holding a weapon, all will fight to the death. We had to silence their gods. We’re ruined, my lord, as much as I loathe saying it.”

For a long moment, Carpason was silent, staring at the floor. Finally, he whispered, “This is what you found out, in all those months?”

“Yes, to our loss.”

“How do you silence their gods?”

“The only way is to silence every single one of their mediums, or at least all the ones pushing for war, and that is an impossibility. We had one opening and it failed.” Closing his eyes, the knight breathed, “Now, even Arnacin’s dead somewhere in those mountains.”

“Indeed,” Carpason distantly replied, too deep in thought to register the knight’s last comment. Instead, he asked, “Are there any still in that encampment?”

“I don’t know,” Hadwin answered, his brow furrowed.

“I intend to find out.”

“What?”

“The king will send us this time and we’ll see what we can do.”

“Why would he ever agree to such a request?” the knight nearly squeaked in shock.

“Because his hope is also dashed and it is then that you jump at any possibility of hope handed to you, as long as it is approached in the right fashion.”

Blackness filled the room, aside from the physicians’ candles scattered about. In their flickering light, Carpason sat next to Arnacin’s bed. Although the lord had relieved the doctors of their careful watch, one still slept in the room to tend to any change in the islander’s condition. Studying those ashen features as if staring into a void, Carpason placed his hand against Arnacin's brow, pitying the clammy pallor.

The soft sound of the door closing made him look up in surprise to see Miro enter, seemingly having escaped there without the knowledge of his constant retinue.

"Sire!" the lord gasped, causing the physician to stir in his sleep.

Staring down at Arnacin for a moment, the king sighed. "He did one favor for Mira. He proved what happens when one defies her king."

When the king again dropped silent, his lord replied, "A few days ago all your councilors were condemning him for ripping Mira to shreds simply by existing. When he dies, you'll no longer have that issue."

Snorting, Miro stated, "Should he perish... I fear Mira loses all her hope." The king finished his thought in a whisper, as if worried about being overheard.

Once again looking down at the islander, Carpason inquired, "Then you agree with me? Arnacin–Arnacin and his peculiar ways alone–can save us."

"You know I agreed with you in my own way, until now," the king sighed. "Now, however, he has lost all face, even to most of the nobles who held him in awe only a short while ago. Yes, even Mira was beginning to wonder if the savages' scared whisperings about the gods sending a phantom to end the war were true. That question is no more. Now he is simply a failed–if once talented–foreigner."

"Had he succeeded, Your Majesty," Carpason whispered, grinding a few of those black hairs between his fingers in frustration, "I think we would have won. I realize, under the circumstances, that politics dictated your disregard of his strategy, yet... I still believe that politics has therefore destroyed us."

Turning to his lord in scrutiny, Miro pressed, "You are thinking something. What is it?"

"Sire, now that Arnacin has paid the price for his foolishness, would you allow me to prove that his war trail was the one to take and do what he could not?"

"He could not because it was impossible, Carpason."

"No, Sire, it was because it had been made precisely for his death. I think they knew all that he was discovering. They knew better than we did how often he trespassed on their land, and they knew what would bring him up there at a time of their choosing, within range of their killing shafts."

"And what makes you think they will remain as they were now that they have succeeded in their mission, pray tell?"

"It was a large gathering behind their own lines, and the threat to them–they believe–has been destroyed. Perhaps not all of them will linger, but I hope a good quantity has remained for the present."

Sighing, the king whispered, "Very well, Lord Carpason, if you will fight to restore his honor and return any hope remaining to us, I pray you do so, and may you return unharmed."

Inclining his head, Carpason whispered, "I will do so, my King, for you, for Arnacin, and for all of Mira."

Chapter 14

Shifting Sands

In the dead of that night, Carpason asked messengers to gather all the knights and infantry in the inner bailey. There, he told them of the need to attack the native camp in the mountains.

"This is not something I can order anyone to do. Although Mira needs a sizable number, those who fight in her hour of need must come by their own choosing."

Naturally, the men of Tarmlin and Arnacin's men instantly pledged their services. Many more also volunteered and, in total, a host of five thousand swore to follow the lord into the mountains that same night.

For the sake of speed, each man had to have his own mount. Those who did not volunteer still helped by lending steeds for the horseless infantry.

While the five-thousand hurriedly prepared, Carpason took Hadwin aside, pulling out the map of the natives' mountains. Compressing his lips, Hadwin looked at it. "Arnacin's talented in many ways, but he can't yet write in Miran."

The knight was speaking of course about the way Mira's marks were so carefully applied. Each line had its own starting point and the space between each mark was calculated in order to avoid making one letter look like another. Arnacin, of course, had not trained for hours on the perfect mathematics of their script. Although he wrote their letters as precisely as possible, it was occasionally hard to decipher one letter from another, and it looked nothing like a Miran's handwriting.

"Never mind that, Hadwin," Carpason sighed, hastily dismissing the thoughts of Arnacin's lifeless body in the keep. "You know these mountains. Where's the camp, and what's the best way of infiltration?"

Hadwin pointed to a wide blank space marked only as "Witilin Valley." Drawings of cliffs rose on either side, with thin passes to the east and west. "It's a large valley, where they can see an attack coming long before it reaches them. Arnacin was just going to cut off their escape and burn the valley from all sides."

Nodding, Carpason commented, "Yes. Unfortunately, we will need to be able to identify exactly how many mediums we kill, so that we know how many of the forty-nine remain."

The closest place to scale the mountains was a stair marked on the east coast. "Are the Windy Stairs well-guarded?" the lord asked, looking up.

"They shouldn't be. The natives know our commanders don't swim and those stairs are more or less a natural formation that leads directly into the ocean."

"Very well," Carpason decided. "We'll ride the horses as swiftly as we can there and, at the foot of the stairs, we'll leave a few men to take them back to the capitol. We'll go through the mountains on foot, which will hide our passing at least a little."

Unsurprisingly, yet unfortunately, word of the troops' movements reached the enemy encampment and when the five thousand Mirans arrived, the natives were packing hurriedly. Quickly, Carpason positioned his men in a wide arc in an attempt to trap the enemy in the center. Once they were on all sides of the encampment, he ordered the attack. If a native was spotted with an eye burned into his forehead, the Miran strike honed onto him and he was swiftly cut down.

Even with five thousand men, however, the Mirans were outnumbered and with the desperation of both sides, the fight was fierce. In the sweat and heat of battle, a single scratch went unnoticed, until the fevers came.

As the world swayed before Carpason, he knew even before he noted the red slash down his sword-arm in his peripheral vision, he only had moments left. In that moment, he knew he had no wish other than to spend even his dying breath living for Mira.

Incessantly, he parried each native attack as his muscles began to burn in fever, his head pound, and his eyes lose sight of the colors around him. His vision turned the world red and gray, yet despite the fact that he knew he had become an easy target, he felt no weapon pierce his flesh.

His elbow bumped one of the Mirans and he heard Hadwin's alarmed voice. "My Lord!" Shaking his head, and wincing as the movement caused his nauseous stomach to protest, Carpason ordered with a moan, "Keep going."

The world, however, was shaking the lord, spinning around him in flashes of random color. He could no longer see or hear an attack, nor could he keep his legs under him. As the insidious poison at last managed to bring him down, he heard a shout all around, and it seemed the sounds of battle ended. Then, the darkness of unconsciousness swept in, leaving pain behind.

The moment Carpason collapsed, the natives had all backed away, refusing to fight, and the Mirans had warily mirrored the movement, glad for a chance to breathe themselves.

Panting, Hadwin slowly lowered his blade as the chieftain across from him, marked by the three feathers he wore at his elbow, gave him a half bow. "Return to your home," the chieftain said in Mira's tongue, thickly accented as it was.

"What?" Hadwin asked.

"Go, in honor of your noble."

"But… the bodies…" It was impossible to say that for the Mirans, retreat was forbidden.

The chief, however, nodded. "Yes, you fought well. We will both gather our own dead together." Several snorts of disbelief and distrust sounded among the Mirans nearby. A smile crossed the chieftain's face. "We will both all leave our weapons with men outside the valley."

Looking down at Carpason who was still shivering with the last moments of life, although beyond consciousness, Hadwin felt his resolve shake. The likelihood of winning through destroying the mediums was not a practicality anymore, for many had probably left after they had packed. Mira could likely gain as much by accepting the honor granted Carpason as by wiping out the remaining mediums.

Submitting, he nodded, and as orders were sounded on both sides, Hadwin crouched down by Carpason. The wary shuffling of many feet sounded around him, but the chieftain joined him placing a hand on the lord's hot shoulder.

Although Hadwin twitched in a second of disgust, he allowed it. Arnacin's benevolence toward the enemy had effected the knight too much to look on the chieftain's act as anything other than what it was–remorseful compassion.

In his own tongue, the native said something and then, looking up at Hadwin, he repeated it in Mira's language. "May the gods pardon your..." He stumbled in his translation, then finished, "wrong loyalty and give you happiness in your new life."

Then, standing the chieftain said, "We offer horseless carts for your bodies."

At the moment, Hadwin could not laugh at the peculiar phrasing, but he nodded. The chieftain turned away with that and the knight remained there, wishing he could soothe the ache of his lord's passing.

Around them, Mirans and natives alike were departing to discard their weapons. Oddly enough, the natives seemed unperturbed by the temporary arrangement of peace. Only many of the Mirans looked disgusted.

An abrupt change in Carpason's breathing caused Hadwin to look down. The fever's chills had stopped, yet the lord still breathed, no longer in broken gasps, but evenly, as if he simply slept.

That seeming health was only momentary, however, and then Lord Carpason of Tarmlin breathed his last.

"A god accepted him." The awed voice caused Hadwin to turn. Only a few paces away, a younger man, one of the savages, stood staring wide-eyed at Carpason's body.

"What do you mean?" the knight asked.

"The fevers continue until death," the native explained, "unless they are accepted into the richness of the afterlife, in which their pain here ceases to be a moment before they die. I have never seen it happen, although we share stories of it."

The native nodded at Carpason. "It happening to him..." He shook his head in awe. "The high god must treasure him."

Before Hadwin could ask about the natives' high god, the young man hurried away.

There could not have been a queerer day in all of Mira's history, Hadwin was sure. Mirans walked alongside savages, their very enemy that day, without fighting and mostly without resentful glances, picking up the dead. The savages piled their dead in a heap and provided carts for the Mirans. Only Firth seemed to remember why they were there as he whispered to Hadwin in passing, "We eliminated twenty-eight."

The knight only nodded and the thought fleetingly crossed his mind that if Arnacin's research was correct, there were still twenty-one mediums left–twenty-one who would, if they were smart, instantly begin training more. The Mirans had lost.

His despair came in force as he placed Carpason's body in one of the native carts, made of whole logs, with wheels of the same logs, rounded in the imperfections and cut to a width of five inches. As he gently arranged his lord's limbs, he felt the tears running down his cheeks.

"Here," a thick female voice said and, swiping the tears from his eyes, the knight looked up to see a native woman holding out a bouquet of pearly flowers. "These seuteeja will bring him well in the afterworld."

"You may place them." Hadwin nodded to the cart and, hesitantly, the native accepted. As she finished, she drew back, whispering, "If all Mirans were Carpasons, we would not war."

"Yet you started your war in Tarmlin itself!" The angry words came out before Hadwin could think about them and he hastily bowed his head in apology. There was no need to begin the fighting again in that moment.

"Those were... men... angry, very angry... very temper. The gods tell us, though, that Mira's time must end. There are few Carpasons, if not no more. Yet today, we honor a worthy opponent. The gods kill him for his service to Mira, but not for else. Tomorrow, we war, but today, we peace."

"Thank you." It was all Hadwin could say.

As the woman turned away, however, she said, "Tell your king this."

"What?"

"All I said and all we do today."

As the Mirans lined up around the carts, the chieftain who had ordered the temporary peace again approached Hadwin. "The gods order your safety back to Mira. No one will attack. Do not flinch if you see something thrown. If anything, it is seuteeja for the fallen."

"Thank you." The knight bowed.

"Do not enter the mountains again. The gods will not favor you twice." With that warning, the chieftain also bowed and the Mirans started off, many wary, some simply defeated.

It was to afternoon sun that Arnacin weakly awoke with someone's fingers pressed against the side of his neck. One of the castle's physicians sat beside the bed, his brow furrowed as his head bobbed in time to his slow count.

"If that isn't the slowest pulse of a conscious person, I've ever felt," the man finally grumbled. As Arnacin tried to push himself up, the physician snapped, "Don't move. Not an inch, boy." Only when Arnacin relented did the man continue in a softer tone, "It's a miracle you still draw breath. Push your luck this early and you're not likely to continue doing so. As long as you are awake, however..." He carefully lifted the islander's right hand in a gentle, practiced grip. "We'll give it a slight test. Can you move your fingers–just your fingers, mind?"

It was harder than he first imagined and the islander did not know whether he had succeeded or not as sharp pain burst just beneath the right side of his collarbone. Instantly, sweat broke out on his forehead and a cry escaped him, drowning out the man's following words.

He lay there for a minute, unaware of anything beyond his own pain, until an arm slipped beneath his head, and he looked up into the physician's comforting smile.

"It all still works, boy. With time, you might be able to use it again. Drink now. We'll worry about putting you back on your feet when your heart rate is normal."

Taking a sip, darkness swooped in and Arnacin did not try to fight it.

"Arnacin." The clipped tones caused the islander to jerk awake, finding his left arm under his head and the pillow discarded unceremoniously on the floor. One of the castle's older squires stood nearby, his hair graying, frown lines in his weathered skin. He held out a thin, rolled parchment. "You are deemed ready to be about soon, and so the king wishes to give this to you."

Wincing, Arnacin slid his arm back out from under his head and slowly pushed himself up. "Kings," he muttered in exasperation at Miro's impatience, not even allowing him a full recovery before issuing orders. His remark caused the squire to shove the paper onto his chest.

"Whatever you intended by that, young man, you may skip it. Read it as soon as you feel ready..."

"What if that's never?"

"Then let me remind you, you are in this war of your own choosing. We all know about your argumentative side and most of us don't care to hear it. Lord Carpason would likely have been given the duty of telling you in person, but we buried him last week." To disbelieving silence from the islander, the squire made his exit with a crisp, "We'll see you tomorrow, when the physicians release you."

As the door closed with a click, Arnacin forced his mind out of its current blankness, glancing down at the parchment in his lap. Slowly, wincing as he used his right hand to help, he unrolled the orders, flattening them against the covers. A glance at a few of the words caused him to angrily wad it into a tight ball, his temper causing him to disregard the pricks in his shoulder, and chuck it across the room with his left hand. How much did Miro expect from him, as if he were Miran, not a visitor from the sea?

And yet, there it was. He hadn't been forced into it. He had, as the squire said, chosen it. So if the king wished him to serve the war on the political front, his honor dictated it. Hopefully, it would lead—as the islander knew the king hoped—to a quicker end to the endlessly dragging war.

Slipping quietly out of the library and easing the door shut behind her, Valoretta started back along the corridor to where she knew Sara would be awaiting her with a lecture about how she should not be disappearing. Glancing out the window, she paused, however. As a smile brushed over her face, she quickly changed direction. Arnacin was trailing along the terrace's rail below.

Joining him, she remarked, "I heard you were awake last week. Has it taken all this time to escape the physicians?"

"All this time," Arnacin repeated with a slight smile, though his tone was preoccupied. "A week sounds like a very short time to me."

Valoretta smiled and her gaze traveled to his shoulder. There, she noticed what she reprimanded herself for not seeing instantly—Arnacin was now dressed in Miran attire beneath the cloak he had pushed off his right shoulder. Although the cloak looked like his old one, it also showed signs of having just come off the loom. The detail showing in the shirt's embroidery declared how much love had gone into its crafting and, with a fond smile, the princess looked back up. Arnacin had not noticed her quiet appraisal, looking out toward the hills.

"That fits you better," Valoretta softly commented, dragging her companion back to where she stood.

For just a minute, he simply stared at her, before comprehension lit his eyes and he teased, "Yes, the thieves. They just couldn't wait to filch Matalaide's craft."

"Matalaide?" Valoretta repeated.

"Our village weaver. She's always grousing about usurpers. Actually, she fakes it all, and some of the boys love testing how far she can go without cracking a smile or tanning their hides. She once told a friend of mine, Tevin, that she would stop making any clothes for him if he didn't change his behavior, and let him struggle with all the work."

Watching the islander's smile, the princess prompted, "What did he say to that?"

Almost laughing, Arnacin admitted, "He started off about how he would make sure to steal her position as best weaver around. I thought for sure she was cornered. She has said she drowns thieves, but she simply scowled and yanked him in, telling him it was about time he learned something useful. Five minutes later, Raymond and I saw him running for the safety of the woods."

His twinkling eyes furnished her with an image of a bunch of boys howling in hilarity at another boy's flight. Finding herself laughing, Valoretta choked it back, asking, "Did you learn from her?"

"No, I like to say my family knew the craft before Matalaide came into existence. My grandfather knew it, my father, and naturally my mother knew it. I was... four or five when I started learning." Arnacin nodded toward the harbor where his ship bobbed on the gentle waves. "We made our sails from scratch. I remember sitting outside, working on one, and Matalaide telling us she would need to poison us or her entire job would be at stake."

"Nice lady, Matalaide," Valoretta commented.

"She's simply an old humbug. We can take almost nothing she says as truth, until she's harping on someone about something they're not doing to her standards."

"The harping sounds like a distinguishing trait of your village," the princess could not help but tease. Whether he caught on to her jibe about him, she couldn't tell, as slowly his smile slipped away while he continued to stare at his ship. Sadly, she whispered knowingly, "You miss them, don't you?" Obstinately, Arnacin turned his gaze back to the hills in the distance, but she knew anyway.

"What is on your mind, Arnacin?" she softly pressed.

Sighing, the islander turned back inside. Companionably, the princess stayed by his side listening to the soft sound of their feet over the flagstone corridor.

"Is Carpason dead?" Arnacin finally inquired.

"They brought back his body slightly over a week ago," Valoretta confessed, dropping her gaze to the floor. "He doesn't speak about it, but I can tell our lord's loss has devastated Father. It's how he listens to his councilors without cutting them off halfway through and how slow he is to make any decisions. He has also seemed twice as impatient for your recovery since then."

Arnacin simply snorted and, for a moment, they continued in silence. "It feels strange when I think about it," the islander again broke the stillness with a whisper. "I guess most of my disbelief is because I wasn't there to see it happen, but he didn't deserve it. He was the most honorable man here."

Studying her friend, the princess reminded, "You told me we all deserve death."

"Some more than others, I think," the islander shrugged, glancing at her.

"Someone agreed that you didn't deserve it, at least," Valoretta commented, slipping her hand in his. "For now, anyway," she added with a small, teasing laugh.

Returning her smile, he gently squeezed her hand back.

When Valoretta returned to her room, she took no notice of her nurse's hysterical reproaches. Instead, she settled herself against the wall, smiling out the window toward nothing. She felt blessed and pleasantly devoid of thought or care. In fact, it took her a second to realize that Sara had moved over to the window and begun squinting through it, as if searching for something, before glancing from the princess to the window and back again.

"Is something wrong, Sara?" Valoretta wondered–solely out of politeness, since she had long been of the opinion that anything that troubled her nurse was not troublesome in the slightest.

"What do you find so interesting, My Lady?" Sara asked, suspicion dripping from her tone.

Shifting more comfortably against the wall, Valoretta choked back her laugh. "Nothing, Sara," she whispered in distant joy. "Can I not just feel happy and completely at peace? It's a beautiful spring day and the birds are singing out there–if you would just leave the keep every once in a while–and the flowers are so fragrant." Drifting off into a reverie, she added, "And it's such a soothing relief to know that Arnacin is better."

Sara jumped like someone had slapped her, but her eyes narrowed as she pressed, "Did you see him today?"

"Why, yes," the princess replied bemusedly.

"And was he... handsome?" The tone was one of disgust.

"Sara," Valoretta laughed, "only you would ask that, as if good looks are a crime. I haven't even thought of it..." Her tone shifted once again as she did think about it. "But, yes, he is–very, isn't he? It isn't something that's changed, though. He always has been."

"Your father take heed, child! Do you even realize what you are doing?" It was a charge–a scream of fury–and yet Valoretta felt entirely immune to it.

"I know. Standing here, doing nothing, and I shirked my duties this morning. I detest all those lady-like qualities, though. I needed a break from being a dutiful beauty all week. Can't I learn something useful, Sara? I'm not even supposed to use my skill of sewing, so what's the point? Am I just something to look at?"

Sara simply stood, her face a furious white. "You are supposed to be a lady! As he is supposed to be leaving! What type of nonsense has he put in your head?"

"Nothing," Valoretta snapped after she stood for a second in stunned silence. "I should ask what nobles have stuffed in everyone else's heads. If you are speaking about Arnacin, I resent that completely. Why is it that he alone treats me as a person, not some moving statue? Let me tell you something, Sara, so that from now on we understand each other–if I were not the heir to this kingdom, if I were simply a princess or a king's bride, I would commit suicide sooner than live that meaningless life. Do you understand?"

For a minute, Sara was stunned speechless before she spluttered, "It is you who needs to learn something, Valoretta, because someday you are going to be a king's wife. There is purpose and a gift in such. For now, we'll start over. I hear you like reading. Then I challenge you, for your own sake, to study proper political behavior and the work that goes with it. It takes more than you give it credit."

As the nurse started to leave, Valoretta dropped angrily onto the window bench. Sara wheeled back. "Ease down, My Lady!" With that, the door snapped shut behind her.

Ordered to remain off his ship for another week on pain of being drugged for another *three* weeks and having nothing to do until such time as the king called for him, Arnacin slipped off to the dockside taverns.

A view of Mira from the sea was of cheery cream-plastered buildings with brick-red colored shingles and lots of tiny chimneys rising up the hill to the castle at the top. The first buildings seen, however, were the taverns. These were marked in the plaster with their names above the doorways, and often with boasts of their finest foods and drinks inscribed where they might otherwise have windows.

The shadows that caught in those recesses often made it look like they did have windows from a distance, but the taverns on

Mira were always without, at least on the first floor. Some of the taverns farther back into the city possessed two, or sometimes three, floors and once above the noise and smell of the streets, they cut windows into their walls.

The dockside taverns, however, seemed quite proud without.

"For now, I haven't been moved any..." The islander looked up at the familiar voice and, as he did, the knight who had been conversing quietly with a comrade outside a tavern dropped silent as he spotted the islander. "Arnacin," Sir Hadwin inclined, little warmth in his beaten tone. "It's a blessing to see you alive and about. How's your shoulder?"

Refusing to discuss it, the islander simply gave a half-nod of acknowledgment before stating, "I'm actually surprised to find you living yourself. I figured that if you had escaped our attack, you would have rejoined Lord Carpason's troop."

"Oh, I was there," the Tarmlin knight sighed. "The savages simply watched us walk away after..."

"They allowed you to leave without attack afterward?" Hadwin's knight companion exclaimed. "They've only ever attacked harder whenever we achieve a victory."

"It was out of respect, I'm sure," Hadwin whispered, as if the words were wrenched out of him. "I saw their nods as we passed, their eyes straying to where we had... to my lord's body."

An uncomfortable silence fell. Arnacin turned his gaze back from his ship, asking, "Was it another search party or a village raid?"

"Oh, Arnacin, you know as well as I those routine things could never fell my lord. We demolished your village, the one you were after."

Paling, the islander demanded in stunned disbelief, "In the mountains?" Choking on his wine, Hadwin's companion excused himself, chortling as he left.

His expression that of strained patience as he watched the other knight's retreating back, Hadwin admitted, "Yes, in the mountains. Between the map you made for him last winter and a few of us who have been up there repeatedly with you, we attacked everyone who remained in that camp. We still were able to dispatch twenty-eight of the mediums."

"It was suicide," Arnacin stated coldly, feeling the wrath of an overprotective friend. "He knew that. What would make him drag a whole troop up to a camp on high alert, a snare from the start, simply to... die?"

Looking at the islander with pity, the knight breathed, "None of us were dragged, Arnacin. Each and every one of us volunteered to be there. He clearly stated that he would take no one unless they wished to go."

"Wh..." Arnacin ran through all the five questions, and still found no words to finish his utterance of incredulity.

"Do you not understand, Arnacin? We did it for Mira, for you and your honor, and half of us, for Lord Carpason. Tarmlin would never allow him to go without his troops behind him, and the rest... knights and soldiers like Firth, Duke Cestmir's troops that he once gave you, and so on–they, like my lord, could not live while your honor and wisdom were in question. Whatever flaws you have, Arnacin..."

Shaking his head, the knight bit back whatever words he was about to express and slipped back into the tavern. Paralyzed, Arnacin continued to stand there.

By late afternoon, the king had still not called for the islander and a restless, bored and irate Arnacin decided to start retraining his shoulder to its earlier strength. He knew better than to instantly push his shoulder for all it was worth, and so he used his own bow since he had found that his island's bows had an easier draw than the Mirans'. He had grown up believing that, once treated, wood bent almost as easily as softened metal from the fire. On Mira, he had often found the opposite, depending on the range of the bow.

Even with his own bow, he dared not actually use his right arm to draw back, and so continued practicing as a Miran. As he pulled his string toward his left shoulder, however, it was as if a new sun burst into life inside his right one. The world reeled onto its side and as the ground rammed into Arnacin's shoulder, he heard a scream of pain. If it was his own, he could not tell, and some distant part of him, the part that was still conscious, was glad of that.

When full consciousness returned to him, he found himself in his own bed, Gagandep leaning over him, holding ice to the exposed shoulder. The sound of rustling cloth told him without needing to look that a large audience stood against the walls. "Gagandep," Arnacin breathed in surprise.

Smiling fondly, the native explained, "Once wounds are largely internal, I know more than most and so am called on frequently. Under the circumstances, the swelling in your shoulder is hiding all its information, so we shall simply need to wait. In the meantime, you should rest."

"No. Wait," Arnacin protested, throwing his left arm up to stop the native from uncorking a flask. When the healer paused, he asked without taking his gaze off the potential threat, "Will I be any use to you as I am, Your Majesty?"

A couple of heartbeats passed in which the room appeared to buzz with silent surprise at his knowledge that Miro was among the audience.

It was not the king who answered, however, as a well-known voice growled, "Our king can find uses for a man with one leg in sword fights. He can find uses for you if you're bedridden for the rest of your life."

Despite his slight smile, the islander persisted, "I thought it wasn't protocol for anyone to answer for a king."

"Unless he's not present."

Finally turning to the audience and meeting Miro's wary gaze with a sly grin, Arnacin quipped, "Every inhale, exhale, movement and rustle sounds too much like you for me to be fooled." Arnacin did not admit that he was surprised to see Sara among the many physicians and the king's high councilor, Memphis, against the door with arms folded.

"Unless you become mute, son of Bozzic," Miro answered, "you need not fear tarnishing your honor."

Still grinning at the display of the islander's savage-like senses, Gagandep gently requested, "Sire, there will be a better time to discuss this. Currently, I cannot think there is anything you can discover by remaining."

Nodding, the king commanded everyone except the native out, yet he did not move until Gagandep promised, as if repeating himself, "I would not harm Arnacin if all of Mira depended on it. Nor will I speak of his injuries to anyone outside this keep."

It was both a commitment of loyalty and a lack of it. All the same, the king accepted it and left.

Trembling as he turned back to the unavoidable drugs, Arnacin admitted, "I'm afraid it may never work, Gagandep. If it is as painful as this at the slightest strain..."

"Shh..." the native soothed, gripping the islander's left arm in comfort. "You have no patience, Arnacin. A wound like yours will take months to heal before we can even know if you can return to work, yet you try within the first day you are allowed on your legs. Wait six months and then we'll try again."

"Gagandep," Arnacin persisted, as if his life depended on it, "I can't not know for six months–"

Again the native hushed him, holding the flask to the islander's lips. "Drink now. When I can figure out if you did any real harm to yourself, you may wake." With little choice but to submit, the last thing Arnacin heard was Gagandep's low chuckle, "To think Miro trusts me with every other man, but when it comes to his foreigner, he commands a roomful of witnesses to be present. And he can't even trust *them* without his own presence."

Chapter 15

The Councilor's War

After three days of waiting, the king finally called for Arnacin and the islander found himself closeted with the king and his high councilor. There, Memphis was given the responsibility of updating Arnacin on all the generals' reports, those who were present in the capital and who remained in the field.

In that report, the islander also learned what happened to his troop. Firth was discharged from service and moved back with his family, and the Tarmlin troop had been given to Hadwin. The rest of Arnacin's men had dispersed back to their original commanders. When Memphis was finished, the islander remained silent until the king softly asked him, "Do you have any comments, Arnacin?"

"Only one, Your Majesty, and you may do with it as you see fit." Glancing at Memphis, he seemed to brace himself before stating, "With all due respect, I cannot understand why anyone has never thought to suggest that you organize your armies to scour certain areas, one in one place and another in another, and thereby cover your boundaries from one end to the other."

He ignored Memphis's glare as he continued, still looking at the map on the table, "Your generals have long tried doing it themselves, yet they never know where anyone is and therefore can only organize their own troops, often guaranteeing that they are simply searching a place just combed."

"Indeed," Miro muttered, himself glancing toward Memphis, who turned a furious shade of red at the look. "If that is all, Arnacin, you may leave."

Bowing, the islander departed, meeting the high councilor's glare in challenge before disappearing.

When it was time for Arnacin to once again fall under the swordmaster's training, the first thing the older man did was take him to Mira's bathhouse. "I thought Mirans didn't know how to swim," the islander commented when told where they were going.

"Most of the ruling nobilities don't. There is nowhere they deem safe enough to learn. The bathhouse is open to anyone with the coin, which goes straight into the royal treasury, and even with the private section only for Mirans, too many others–ambassadors, richer merchants, and sailors alike–use the place.

"For that reason, we must not say anything of importance while there. The chance for spies is too great."

Arnacin nodded in solemn understanding. Yanking the islander's hood over his black head, the swordmaster led the way.

Situated in the center of the city, the marble bathhouse rose across the street from Mira's university. The steps of these buildings were the second most popular spot for meeting, outside of the market on the pier itself. Arnacin had only passed the bathhouse once or twice, however, in his year and a half of dwelling there. Despite the rare marble, he had never taken any interest in it while passing. Stepping inside behind the swordmaster, however, he nearly froze in wonder.

The outside stone both hid and supported crystal walls that danced with the light and flickered in various ethereal colors from the moving reflections of people and water inside. Light pouring through the uncovered roof of the same material flickered across faces, softening them almost to an angel-like appearance.

"Observe the wealth of Mira, but do not stop moving," the swordmaster hissed from beside him. "This is still public grounds."

After paying the keeper on duty, the swordmaster clunked his way across the dancing, blue marble floor to a physically identical room. This place, however, was quieter, with only a few Mirans using their break time to either swim or soothe aching muscles in the hot water.

In his crisp, no-nonsense manner, the swordmaster quickly outlined his rehabilitation plan. They spent the rest of the evening beneath that otherworldly light, which danced across the long shirt Arnacin wore in the water to hide the massive scar over his shoulder.

Weeks went by without Valoretta seeing the islander and then, crossing one aisle in the library, she spotted him sitting on the floor, his back pressed against a shelf as he wrote on the paper supported by his knees. As she approached however, Arnacin threw the quill feather, hissing in sudden pain as he did so. Sinking down beside him, Valoretta retrieved the quill, placing it back in his hand and gently wrapping his fingers around it, before looking up into her friend's simmering gaze. Those dark eyes reminded her of liquid in a pot under full boil, bubbling and swirling without ceasing.

"Arnacin," she sighed. Attempting to lighten the mood, she half-joked, "Surrounded by books and so much information no one could ever learn it all if they ate, slept and breathed in here... Where else would you wish to be?"

"Anyone within this city could tell you that," Arnacin quipped, resigned to scribbling out paragraphs in frustration. As she placed her hand over his, he sighed, whispering, "I'm afraid, Valoretta, terribly so. I can't even move my right arm with any swiftness without seconds of intense pain–"

"You have six months, I'm told," the princess explained patiently. "And you needn't even fear never being able to use a weapon again, since Father has no intention of returning you to the field."

Shaking his head, Arnacin turned his face away, but Valoretta easily recognized the cold stiffening in his pose. For a moment, she studied him, pondering his reaction before she tried a guess. "Will it impede your return to your home?"

It was with the softest breath that he replied, "I won't be going home." During her sympathetic silence, he turned back to her, adding, "If it doesn't heal, I will have no strength to do all that is necessary aboard a ship and there is no one who could do it for me."

Feeling guilty at the stirring of hope she felt deep inside, Valoretta whispered, unable in that moment to meet his gaze, "If I wasn't chained here, I would volunteer to be your sailor."

After a moment of silence, the islander exhaled. "Partial use is hardly better than no use at all. It's simply a ruse meant to taunt you." He slammed his left fist into his knee, but with that movement, it appeared all his energy vanished as he rested the back of his head against the books behind him. "Valoretta, what am I going to do?"

The princess had no answer to that helpless, lost question, but slipping her fingers into his, she carefully rested her head on his shoulder. It was not an answer or anything resembling a solution, but it was a gesture of understanding and sympathy, and comfort lay in that movement of love. Clearly recognizing it, Arnacin squeezed her hand in return.

Several days later, the princess again found the islander on the floor in some corner in the library, thinner and more tired-looking than before. Lifting her skirts slightly so as not to trap them beneath her, she knelt beside him, whispering, "Arnacin, you can only take one day at a time."

As he looked over at her, she pressed, "You have not been eating lately, have you?"

Studying her almost warily, the islander challenged her, "Perhaps I am simply too sick due to injury for eating to do anything."

With a smile, Valoretta admitted, "I had Sara ask the kitchens if you had been down there lately."

Rolling his eyes, Arnacin muttered, "Spy."

Slowly, the princess' smile faded in the ensuing silence. "The future is the future, Arnacin. Worrying about things that are out of our hands only kills us. I should know since I have found that leaving it is the only way I may live."

He turned to her questioningly and she admitted, "My life has been written out for me, beginning to end. I've never even been outside these walls, except for when I sneak off through the city or Sara takes me to the market now that she deems me old enough. I have no choice in the matter, and you could say I'm afraid of everything, Arnacin, if I allow myself to be so. I'm afraid of the war continuing, that the longer it continues, the more likely the savages will bleed us dry. I dread rulership, in reality. I could drop dead at the thought of Father choosing a king for me to wed, and I'm even afraid of the day peace ends the war."

"How could you be afraid of the end of this stupid war?" Arnacin demanded.

"I've lived practically all my life in this war, Arnacin. It's become fairly comfortable to me and, when it ends, everything I know and anticipate about every day will disappear. Father will be able to concentrate on finding a king, the war will no longer keep ambassadors out of Mira during the seasons when the fighting is more aggressive, which will mean more stately dinners and grand balls. And..." She could not speak her worst fear, the thing she dreaded to think about more than all the rest–Arnacin's return home.

Realizing she had to finish her thought somehow, she tried to make it sound less important, shrugging, "And then of course, you'll go home."

"I hope so," the islander whispered, fiddling with the fingers of his right hand in contemplation. For a minute, they sat in thoughtful silence before Arnacin glanced up at his companion, asking, "Do you really want freedom from your cell, My Lady?"

Grinning as if she thought it was a joke, the princess inquired, "Oh, did you steal the keys from the only person who holds that right?"

"You already have them," the islander said. "Live like the natives. When you become queen, demolish everything more permanent, and wander under the stars and leaves like them. The natives would no longer resent your presence. They would hardly realize you were any different from themselves."

"How would we defend ourselves against our neighboring kingdoms, who would want the riches of this city?"

"The natives would defend you and their land themselves. They'd attack every ship in harbor, burn it, poison everyone struck by the shafts until all learned to fear this place as it should be feared. They would soon realize Mira, as a kingdom, was nothing more than a nightmare, a hellhole, believe me."

Valoretta jabbed him in the ribs, but otherwise remained silent until he added, "At which point, I don't even think you would need to stay, at all."

"Yes, I would," the princess whispered. "We could not accept their gods as our own, and therefore would need someone to judge, to hold people to the law. A queen, or king, would still be imperative. No matter what I do, I'm still chained here."

"Chained, Valoretta? Only if you make it so. Queen or not, you'd have free range of this entire continent without fear of attack, you'd be able to run through woods, splash in the rivers, dance and sleep in the grass. No one can dictate all of your life, Valoretta. Do with it as you please."

Although Arnacin left then and Valoretta did not see him the next day, she found, on the lower library shelf against which they had sat, a roughly carved wooden key with a string looped through it. Smiling, she picked it up, running it through her fingers. No words or patterns decorated it, yet she knew all the same that it was a reminder of her sovereignty, not just over her kingdom, but over her own life and, lovingly, she slid it up her sleeve. Her islander had stolen her a key indeed.

It had been while contemplating Valoretta's advice that Arnacin busied himself with aimlessly shaving wood off a block. Sitting on his ship's rail, too restless to return to the work that still remained before the ship's reloading could start, he had simply dug holes into the small piece of wood he was holding.

Only as he looked at the three crude holes his left-handed carving had achieved did the princess' question about a key echo in his thoughts. With a sigh, he reworked his carving. Slowly, it began to take shape, even as he conceded the princess' point. He could only live one day at a time. Had not Carpason said the same once in regard to how Charlin lived? One could not control the future, and only very little of the present.

Therefore, leaving the finished key in the library as a gift, he slipped off to talk to Gagandep about actions to which the natives would agree. Looking up at the islander sitting on the edge of his table while the family worked on grinding wheat, Mira's adopted native smiled hopelessly. "Their trust was broken, Arnacin. Sometimes, I think a celestial messenger would need to threaten them with the gods' desertion before they forgave enough to agree to peace."

"That can't be the only answer," Arnacin insisted, not looking up from his task of taking the heads off the sheaves. "Outside of near-annihilation, there must be something they would look on as either useless to resist or something that would stop Mira from being able to expand."

Laughing, Gagandep joked, "Well, no one will stop you if you want to cause lightening to strike the mountain boundaries, and cause Mira to split into two separate continents with an ocean between them."

Rolling his eyes, the islander muttered, "I'm serious." He met Firth's fond smile and looked away, reading the thought that agreed with the healer's view.

"I am also serious, Arnacin. I know of no course that will lead to peace," Gagandep whispered, putting aside the bowl of wheat he was sifting to give his full attention to their phantom. "But I know that if you put your heart to it, you will think of something."

Shaking his head, Arnacin contradicted, "I'm not a deity, Gagandep. If there is nothing, I can't make it something."

"I'm not even going to wonder what you are, Arnacin, but don't try to tell us that you can't work the impossible. You still draw breath, you know."

The islander did not comment as his shoulder burned, seemingly in protest against that statement.

The king continued to call for Arnacin from then on, asking the islander's advice on army operations, even which group to send forth in search. No encampment had been seen and there had been little native movement in Mira since Lord Carpason annihilated their large gathering—yet they attacked in small bunches here or there to remind Mira of their refusal to surrender.

Apart from those audiences, Arnacin spent much of his time staring toward the mountains from some vantage point or another, with his own words and Carpason's questions echoing scornfully back.

This is not a war they're willing to lose—it's for their home.

Tell me, is freedom worth the lives of all their children and wives? Does it hold that high a price?

For some, it alone is life.

Mira would bleed itself to death with the natives' poison, he knew, unless it found a way to restore its honor. Along that line of thought, he had copied and hung the original map of Mira's borders and the oath that had accompanied it on the south-facing wall in his room. Mira was too large to return to that promise and with it died the easiest answer.

He knew that no promise to make a new sworn boundary would satisfy the natives. They would see it only as a cunning way to gain peace until Mira wished for more land once again. The tired, sarcastic side of him wondered if they would agree on wars only at specified times, to thin Mira's population.

And with that thought, he sat in the library, staring at the map of Mira's borders, old and new, when the door opened.

"No," the sigh of exasperation jerked Arnacin out of his reverie to see Valoretta attempting to toe a fox-like creature back out the library's doors. It persevered however and, with a hiss, the princess left it to wander the room as it pleased, while she shut the door with a snap. Then, striding over to the table, she said, "I am not sitting."

Grinning, Arnacin turned back to the map of Mira's oldest borders, muttering, "As is your prerogative. Don't let me deter you from standing on ceremony." Hazy along the edge of his vision, he saw Valoretta's fingers clench and he wickedly glanced up to meet her simmering gaze.

"That thing, Arnacin, that thing! I would gladly strangle it with my bare hands if it wasn't one of the queen's *precious* companions. You have no idea the agony it puts me through, simply because it has decided I am likable. Oh, why she even needs their company is far beyond me."

Inwardly laughing at the extent of her wrath, Arnacin pulled his sword out, laying it on the table. Pushing it toward her, he suggested, "Well, if you are sure you would like to dispose of it, you may do it more swiftly and be certain of its demise, should it appease you."

Looking at the blade, a smile finally graced her features and she broke into laughter. "The moment I sit, Arnacin, it thinks it must warm my lap. It decides at every opportunity that I hardly look a lady without its fur adorning the bottom of my skirt, where it catches its abominable hair at the slightest touch. It's not that I would particularly mind, but that its taste vies so completely with Sara's. In contrast, she is of the opinion that one single strand is a blemish that must be eradicated on sight and therefore has me stripped down without further delay, to repeat the four-hour process she must do every morning to dress her *goddess*. And for some reason, the minute my gown is altered, my hair must be similarly altered because, in her mind, one hairstyle is only fit for one color, or something." Pausing in her long rant, she finished, "Furthermore, the dog always makes me think Rosa is spying on us through its gaze."

Glancing at the creature nosing through a bottom shelf of scrolls, the islander conceded, "She probably is."

"I suppose the dog is capable of speech," Valoretta teased.

Arnacin shrugged. "If you call that a dog."

"Oh, what is a dog in your mind?"

"An adult dog..." For a minute, the islander trailed off, but as his companion waited, he ended, "Their backs rise to your waist, or at least did when I was shorter."

"Were they not dangerous?" the princess breathed, receiving a shake of his head.

"Most of them would never even show their teeth to a human... unless one caused another harm."

"You say most of them?"

"Well," Arnacin grinned, "never ask about Tevin's family. His father's dog thought it was his sole responsibility to keep, shall I say, his pups in line. No, he never bit any of them, but it was not rare to see the dog and Tevin wrestling with each other, whether in play or reprimand. That dog died shortly before I left, though."

"Were you not at all scared of their dog?"

"Him? If his master's boys were not afraid of him, none of the rest of us could possibly be either. He used to walk through anyone's doorway as if he owned the world, and if you happened to be on your stomach–playing with a little child for instance–he would drop his fifty-plus-some weight directly on your back and proceed to doze there. Therefore, you would be stuck for so long as he decided to sleep and yip and snore and whatever else he felt like doing in his dreams." His smile distant, Arnacin breathed, "It caused a toddler I knew to roll on the floor in hysterics."

"Your brother?"

Softly, the islander confessed, "Charlotte and I sometimes split the shepherding responsibilities in order to help Mother and Father once William was born, depending on how tired they were. Will was so easily satisfied, so ready to laugh at any and everything. He fed off our small frustrations and we intensified it for him."

Arnacin's voice drifted off and the image of home burned ever more fiercely. Little William would be near five, and hopefully he was as happily energetic as he had been at one, when he had been a round little child laughing in the sun that bounced off his black hair.

Watching him, Valoretta asked, “He didn’t lose any of that laughter when his father died?”

Dragging himself back to the library, both metaphorically and in reality dim, Arnacin whispered, “He never fully realized what happened. About three days after Father’s death, it finally seemed to register that he was no longer there, and he cried for a whole day, asking in his wordless way... He only wanted to be held by... that missing person. Charlotte and I fled the village, cowards as we were.” Bitterly, he whispered, “We both pretended that nothing could bother us, that if tears had been shed, we were beyond that by then.”

Valoretta dropped her gaze to the desk beneath her fingers. Understandingly, she remained silent, letting his thoughts take the conversation where he allowed it, whenever he allowed it. As the dog pushed himself against her skirts, however, she dropped down to pick it up with a sigh.

Watching the princess as she rose, Arnacin opened some of his thoughts to her. “My father would have put all the nobles in the world to shame.”

Glancing back at the map occupying the desk, Valoretta asked, “How so?”

Coldly, the islander whispered, “Standing next to them, he would make them all look like spoiled youths trying to pretend to be men, to be human.”

“Your father looked noble?” the princess asked lightly.

“To the day he died,” Arnacin insisted. “His hair might have been gray. I never remember a time when it was otherwise, but instead of making him seem old, it had a way of making him seem...” He paused, staring far away in a search for the right word. “Wise and ageless,” he finally whispered. “Certainly he never acted old.” Meeting Valoretta’s gaze, he added, “Laughter fell like moonlight from his eyes and his smile was insight itself.”

Laughing, the princess corrected, “Don’t you mean that insight lit his eyes and laughter warmed his smile.” At Arnacin’s serious, slow shake of his head, her laughter cut off.

"No, he smiled and you would swear that he knew every dark secret you and the world possessed, and acknowledged them with fearless grace and love. I never even considered that he could be wrong, never pondered whether it was right to do as he asked. He only ever asked what was right and true. He spoke and we did..." Arnacin smiled slightly, "Or at least, we made an effort to obey. Certain things, such as 'pardon your sister's obstinate pride,' were harder to carry through."

"I'm sure she was asked the same regarding you," Valoretta chuckled. Slowly, Arnacin's smile faded and with a sigh, he returned to the map.

Yet his thoughts were no longer on the war or even on Mira and, after a long time, Arnacin again whispered, "Why is it that nothing ever happens to one without them being a fool first? Why is it they always choose their own disaster in reality? In the stories you are so fond of, people land in adventures because some person simply walked by and handed them some hunted article. It then leads to a lost treasure trove or the rescue of some great noble. What happens in real life? Some idiot sells his home to search for diamonds or they run away from their families because life was too boring, and then they're arrested in some foreign land for possessing no money to pay the taxes, or for hunting the king's deer." His voice cracked and he again fell silent. Softly Valoretta slid around the desk to place her hand on his arm.

It took a whole day to force his mind back to the problem at hand, but the next morning as he was sitting with the master mason while the old man described the castle's defense constructions and the holes in the battlements above the portcullis's long tunnel, the islander froze. Quickly, he changed topics, inquiring about the soundness of the walls and how best to make them impenetrable. As night fell, he remained in the library drawing his own construction plans.

He had just finished drawing his plans that evening when word came to him that Miro wanted him in the council room. Sir Hadwin had arrived with a report, and both the king and Memphis awaited the islander before they would hear the report from the field.

Or more likely, Miro waited and Memphis merely stood there pretending to be everything he was supposed to be.

Hadwin's report, however, was simply that Melmoor was quiet, as if the very air awaited something that was coming, but not yet there. He had found nothing and the king dismissed him.

Once Miro looked to his councilors, however, the islander held out the plans he had brought.

"Will you consent to see this, Your Majesty?" he asked, unrolling the parchment on the table. As Miro bent over it, the islander explained, "Should you build a wall on the borders, I think the natives might agree to terms of peace."

Regarding the islander, the king wondered, "And how should you even manage to build a wall while they continue to rain fire and poison on the workers?"

"Mira tells them ahead of time," Arnacin stated. "Even if they do not believe that Mira would keep within its wall, there are two walls depicted wherever your land touches theirs, with a space down the center. One wall is theirs, the other is yours, and should anyone ever try to pass their own boundaries, they would become trapped between those walls without cover for either side to easily slaughter at will."

"Who would tell them?"

"May I speak, Sire?" Memphis interjected, raising his own eyes from the plans. When Miro turned to him in permission, he said, "They will likely only see it as a weakness, which would instead encourage them to attack harder. Why would we raise the question of a wall if we had the strength to defeat them? Moreover, since from such action, they would understand that Mira was on the verge of collapse, they would make every effort to take their land back once and for all, now and forever. Savages never forgive."

The king did not answer, but he noted the fire burning in the islander's eyes as he glared at the high councilor. Miro then asked,

"I will not judge that in the current light. The main point is that I do not think they would listen to anyone Mira could send."

Looking back up at the king, Arnacin breathed, "I think they would trust my word."

The high councilor huffed sarcastically.

Overlooking the fact that the islander unintentionally slandered his own honor, Miro reminded him, "They fear no one more than you at this time, Arnacin. Before you could speak, before you could breathe, they would see an arrow through your heart, should you step within range. They have heard too much about your prowess."

The fire in Arnacin's eyes vanished as he turned to the king. "I think they also wish for a way to be certain of peace. They should be willing to at least hear what you have to say if it comes from someone... about whom they have heard certain things."

"And how is it, we may ask, that the savages even know about his deeds?" Memphis inquired when Miro remained silent, causing the islander to raise his head at the implied charge. "If not for the fact that he lets enemies live to bring word back to their own as messengers to his 'greatness,' they wouldn't. He may think that the fear he instills will prevent their attack, but we of more experience know that it only strengthens their fury and revenge. Sire, good intent our foreigner may have, but for Mira's safety, consider his rash council before acting on it."

Silence met his words. Instead of answering, the king turned to Arnacin inviting the islander's own defense. Dipping his chin in gratitude, the islander said, "Some natives were allowed past my ambushes when they fled in earnest. My attacks are meant to extinguish their threat, not to execute unjust murder."

"We are at war!" Memphis exclaimed.

"A side that falls to murder to achieve their end is not worth the strugg–" Arnacin cut his burning retort off as Miro raised his hands to silence the two.

"Thank you, Memphis, for your wisdom, as always," Miro sighed. Recognizing the unspoken dismissal, the high councilor bowed out. As the door closed behind him, the king turned to Arnacin, placing a hand on the islander's shoulder. "He is right, Arnacin. You are full of good intentions, but you must gain experience before you can expect your suggestions to be taken. In troop movement, I would ask no one else to advise me, but your long-term goals lack understanding."

Lifting his gaze from the floor, Arnacin inquired, "Your Majesty, you have tried the same plan for ten years. It's not taking you anywhere. They continue to pick the battleground, which according to some means they are still the masters of this war. Can you not think of some new, long-term plan to best them?"

"There may not be one, Arnacin," the king said before concluding, "You may go."

Obeying, the islander instantly strode out toward his ship, pausing only when he heard his name called by the princess' voice. Turning, he allowed her to catch up with him before they entered the city's harbor.

"I gather whatever you suggested was not agreed upon," Valoretta sadly noted.

Glancing down at her, the islander exclaimed, "Mira is losing, slowly but surely. If they don't alter their long-term plans, I will be of no help."

"And?"

"And, according to them, I'm simply inexperienced, rash, proud..." She choked beside him, causing him to turn once more to her.

"They're right in that, Arnacin. You are proud."

Smiling himself, the islander confessed, "All right, I'm proud, but I hope not in the way they are saying."

Turning to him, the princess suggested, "Well, what is your long-term plan? If I like it, perhaps I can help you find a way to convince them and, if not, to help you fix its flaws."

Reaching his ship's port rail, facing the sea, Arnacin ran his hand along it thoughtfully. Then slowly he nodded and, like so often before, Valoretta fell into role of adviser.

Chapter 16

The War on Two Fronts

Despite Valoretta's aid, the king did not change his mind and Arnacin's frustration grew. All the same, the war continued and he aided where the king permitted his council. In fact, it was only a week after the first argument about the wall that word arrived, in the form of Sir Hadwin, that the natives were again massing in the border woods, particularly on the east side.

Slowly, as it became increasingly apparent how much of the natives' forces swarmed along the east coast, Arnacin counseled a closer watch on the western side. Meanwhile, theories of why they were gathering in the east were tossed back and forth. The speculations traveled from Mira's generals, to the men themselves, to the three-way discussions among the king, his high councilor and the islander, and–Arnacin assumed–to the other meetings Miro called with his official councilors.

After five days, Arnacin and Valoretta estimated that half the castle thought the natives were hoping to claim that portion completely as theirs, therefore preventing anyone from going around the land to enter the mountains. The other half thought that their enemies were simply engaging them far away from whatever it was that the enemy really wanted.

"What do you find more likely?" Valoretta asked, sitting on the islander's ship rail.

Arnacin thought for a moment, sealing the last medicine jar with wax. "I find the latter less wild, but I fear we're missing the real issue. The natives don't strike me as the types to continue pushing that tactic. They use it often enough. It works often enough—but they must realize by now that we are somewhat aware of it."

"Yet we know there is nothing to gain from blocking the ocean there. If we were to decide we really wished to go around, we'd take a ship, and they won't be cutting us off from any of our trade—" Valoretta stopped abruptly as the islander's head jerked upward, his gaze flying over her shoulder to the Guardian Hills, the eastern mountain range ending at Mira's harbor. Before she could ask anything, he glanced quickly toward the open seawall itself and then shot to his feet.

"Come," he commanded, before jumping onto the dock. The swift rustle of silk a second later told him Valoretta had dashed after him.

"What is it?" she inquired as she caught him.

"They're taking the shoreline to this end of the mountains, where they'll disappear, slowly trickling more men into the hills, before attacking the sea wall," the islander hastily explained. "Once they hold that, they can stop any ship from entering or exiting, and it's not just about supplies, Valoretta."

"They could deny ambassadors entrance," the princess gasped in realization. "Other kingdoms would think we had become hostile and attack. We might find ourselves at war on every front until the savages could simply slip away and watch us annihilate each other. "

"I suspect such are their very thoughts," Arnacin whispered as they strode into the castle's keep, headed to warn the king.

Although the king instantly ordered a watch and extra guard on the sea walls, one day passed into another and another without any sign of trouble. Perhaps, this could be credited to the fact that troops had also been sent to engage the native cluster on the eastern shore. What Miro feared, however, was that they were falling for some trap, pouring their strength into the very thing the enemy wished. It did not help that Arnacin himself voiced that doubt.

Around the capital, the same doubts echoed in forms such as the messenger from the sea wall asking for the reprieve of men weary from their exhausted tenseness. As the king maintained the men's new routines, Arnacin mentioned, "You must tread carefully, Your Majesty. No one can continue waiting for long, and if their watchfulness ends when an attack is forming, you will surely lose."

"Tread carefully, you say," Miro huffed, ignoring the look of strained patience on Memphis's face. "How exactly would you go about keeping them tense? Randomly ordering attacks on them yourself?"

Smiling, the islander whispered, "No, I leave the decision to you." His smile growing slightly, he added, "But if that is all you can think of, why not?" Shaking his head, Miro excused the islander and soon retired to the royal chambers to muse alone before a fireplace.

Knowing no other course of action, Miro sent his swordmaster down to create drilling practices for the men waiting, while others watched. They would then trade off. Five days after the drills had started, the sea wall was attacked, forcing the swordmaster's instant retreat. As the able-bodied men were all needed in defense of the wall, the swordmaster was the one to slip away and alert the king to the skirmish taking place at the wall.

Standing on the highest east-facing parapet, beside his master swordsman and Arnacin, Miro viewed the battle with the aid of a telescope. Natives poured down from the hills under the cover of their archers and the Mirans' archers could not fire a single shaft in the midst the natives' furious torrent of arrows. Their sole defense lay in the slow, blind launch of their catapults' projectiles.

"Send a messenger down there," Miro ordered his master swordsman. "Let the troop know that if the savages gain the wall, they are to burn it to the bottom of the sea." Bowing, the man hobbled away, and the king growled to himself, "They dare to enter our capitol. Very well, they will pay the price."

At his side, Arnacin glanced toward him yet remained silent. Recognizing the locked jaw, however, Miro asked, "Have you any suggestions?"

"If you are willing to burn the wall down at all, Your Majesty, I think you should let them have it, come around to block their escape, and then burn it. Make it look like you could not stand up to their attack and were forced to retreat. I assume they won't suspect, and they wish to keep the wall themselves in order to trap you inside. On that note, I also guess that whatever army they snuck into those hills is a sizable one, one you would not want to escape alive."

Arnacin had finished without once looking away from their view. Studying him, the king nodded. There were times he wondered if he knew the islander at all—but as that was currently unimportant, he made no comment, instead ordering another messenger sent to the wall's captain with the newest strategy.

As the Mirans then began their retreat, the king sent another messenger to order all the ships in the harbor to load small catapults onto their decks, set sail, and bombard the hills once at sea. Although Arnacin winced as Miro relayed his strategy, the islander again remained silent. This time, Miro did not ask why, yet he started to guess when those ships headed for the open sea, very low in the water, swaying back and forth far more than they should have. "As long as they arrive within firing distance," the king soothed, "it will not matter. The water is shallow enough." He received no answer and, expecting little more for the islander to do, Miro excused him.

It was late that night when Arnacin received the news that the battle was over and the Mirans had won. Of the wall, only stones remained, but amid the flames, the last savages risked suicide by jumping from the fiery walls in their final attempt to escape. As to the ships, they were gradually limping back as they were freed from the shore. Upon hearing this, Arnacin slipped off to bed, hoping, if not expecting, that to be the last of the natives' drive.

As if to validate that hope, the days continued in relative peace. Cestmir reported that the savages massing on the east coast had retreated once again into their lands and resumed their normal attacks. On the king's orders, men began rebuilding the sea wall. Meanwhile, the councilors continued their own backstabbing.

This Arnacin would only hear of after the councilors had already hissed their poison and his response was often to escape to the wharf. There, among the honest and carefree play of the sailors and commoners, the islander's frustration could temporarily fade into the background.

Focused on resupplying his ship, Arnacin was waiting for the market's barrel maker when the sound of his name caught his attention.

Sitting around the dockside's tavern, Samundro and five other sailors were watching him. Nodding toward the men, all of whom had helped him rebuild his ship, the islander turned back to his own business—yet it was now impossible not to listen to their hearty conversation.

"How much ransom do you think he'd earn us exactly?"

"I'm not sure, but I know one thing, it must be pretty high considering that he's acted against the king's commands several times and is still here, alive and unharmed. He's a nobody who's the king's war councilor, and Lord Carpason died in order to clear his honor. Someone values him quite a bit."

"That's not even all, if you've heard the gossip..."

"Yes, the princess. From their talk, she would give her own skin in return for him, if she had to."

"Aye, but that part, I can't guarantee. What I can guarantee is that he'd be worth a fortune in gold, and there he goes, a treasure chest walking about on the pier by itself." The speaker paused while they roared with laughter. "The six of us could easily take him while no one's watching. Gag him, bind him, and drag him aboard a ship, where we set sail before sending someone back to retrieve the ransom."

By that point, they were pounding the table with their hands in laughter. Glancing at them, Arnacin could not help but shake his head with a small smile. Apparently spotting his look, Samundro called out, "Arnacin, join us, mate!"

"I'll wait until the temptation's weaker," the islander replied to even greater hilarity. An hour later, however, after paying the barrel maker and taking the new barrels to his ship, Arnacin headed over to the sailors still sitting with their tankards.

"So how's the beer here in comparison to your own ports?" he asked with a smile.

Some said that it was the best they knew of and others that it was comparable. Grinning, the islander quipped, "Well, you won't want to lose the ability of drinking the best beer in these seas just for a dusty trunk of gold that would disappear sooner than you reckoned."

Bursting out with more laughter, Samundro commented, "Snake. That's how you wriggle out of capture, is it? Using our weaknesses against us, are you? I'd take you captive just for that alone, matey, 'cause I don't put up with them games."

Laughing with them, Arnacin excused himself and returned to the castle.

Time appeared to drag in those days. Summer passed, filled with too few projects, too many frustrations, and the growing ache for Mira's peace and his home. Each time the king sent troops out, Arnacin would watch, feeling his resolve to convince the king to build a wall rekindle. It would only intensify when the beaten troops returned, limping back beneath the portcullis, carrying their wounded or dead. As if in sympathy, he would find himself pushing his hand beneath his shirt collar as his shoulder burned yet again.

In disregard of the islander's sentiments, the king was swayed constantly by Memphis's arguments against said wall and, after a month or so, Miro ordered it not to be discussed again. With that, Arnacin left the castle for his ship.

There, he angrily yanked on the knot he had just finished applying to the ratline's rope. Valoretta's voice was simply another sound in the background as she read aloud about the great horned whale and its healing powers. Her voice was no different than the splash of sea against his ship, the hiss of wind, the cry of sea birds, and the barking men in the dock's market.

"What is that?" Valoretta's sudden question made him glance up, realizing only as he did that she had stopped reading long before. She now slipped beside him, cautiously running her fingers along his gradually elongating ratlines. "It's silky," she mused. "Most rope is brown, is it not made out of hemp?"

Shrugging while he returned to his work, the islander stated, "I use what I have. It's slightly cheaper, and I really don't have any other use for this stuff. There's hemp between this, but this spares some and works just as well as the tougher strands. I've tested it."

"But what is it?" When Arnacin simply grinned, otherwise ignoring her, she ripped it away from him, running it through her fingers. His teasing grin broadening, Arnacin simply pulled more of the shining dark strands from a pouch and started on another length that he could attach later. "Arnacin," she gasped "is that your hair?" A brief smirk told her all and, shaking her head, the princess wondered, "Do you find use for all things?"

"No, but I am a shepherd," the islander shrugged, retrieving the rope to continue working on it. "We tend to know a bit about fabrics, yarns, ropes and their materials."

Sitting back on her heels, Valoretta contemplated, "That is the first time you have used that term with any kind of satisfaction in it."

"I think I've learned at least a few things here," he admitted, striving to hide his teasing grin. "Such as, there is so much more pride in being called a shepherd than a councilor-that-nobody-listens-to."

As the princess laughed, his grin won, spreading across his face and, with a glance at her golden cheeks, he once again returned to work.

"Is it better than court jester or comedian, or how about tease?"

"Oh, no. 'Tease' is the best you mentioned. I hate looking foolish," Arnacin replied with some success at a serious air.

Pursing her lips, Valoretta leaned forward, whispering, "But what if I were a tease? Would that be better than princess?"

"Were?" Arnacin repeated, managing to look convincingly surprised. "The word I think, m'lady, is *am*, and you are."

For just a second, the smile slipped off the princess' face as she regarded him carefully, as if trying to decide if he was serious or not. Shaking his head fondly, Arnacin once again returned to his work. "Is that a compliment or an insult?" she finally asked.

Done with his current knot, Arnacin again met her gaze, toying with her. "I would love to say insult. Nobles hate them so..." As her smile wavered, he finished, honestly, "...but I can't. I don't think I was really thinking of either."

It was Valoretta's turn to shake her head in fond hopelessness. Leaning closer again, she whispered seriously, "That I may be then, but you beat me by far, Arnacin of Enchantress Island."

His dark blue eyes flicked up to meet hers in wicked laughter.

Blushing suddenly, the princess hastily climbed to her feet, turning her back on him to lean against his rail. "I hope, Arnacin, that I at least soothed your temper and frustration."

Though she said it in a bare whisper, he glanced up at her, admitting in consideration and gratitude, "You did, actually."

Valoretta may have provided a temporary break from the anger and even fear, yet as night settled in, Arnacin did not move from the window he had finally, restlessly, settled in to think. How long had he and–little to their knowledge–Valoretta fought for the wall, simply to be ordered silent in the end? Miro pretended he wanted peace and yet...

A soft whisper of movement along the dark corridor made him turn away from the moon shining above the castle and, softly sliding one foot onto the floor, his hand dropped to his side. The sound did not repeat itself in the next few seconds, however, and his gaze turned to the double doors of the hallway that led to the king's wing of the castle. He was just about to pass it off as one of the guards shifting on the other side of those doors when he suddenly noticed a black shape out of the corner of his eye. Silver flashed in the moonlight as the Tarmlin blade whipped out and the islander pivoted around to face the creeping figure.

"Arnacin," the shape gasped, and the dim outline of a bow dropped beneath a cloak.

The voice, the islander knew well, and he felt his muscles lose some of its tenseness. "You're hardly anyone I would expect here yourself, Firth," he breathed. "What are you doing here?"

"I was instructed to guard... the corridors." A tremor of unease sounded in the last words and, warily studying what he could make out of Gagandep's son in the dark, Arnacin glanced toward the double doors only a few feet away from them.

"Why would they ask that?" the islander inquired, forcing himself to believe such an odd statement. There was no reason not to, considering its trusted source.

"I... I..." Firth stuttered, shifting slightly. "I don't ask those things, Arnacin. I'm just a man in one of the king's armies. If there is any trouble though, I'm probably being distracted."

His heart pounding with thoughts he wished did not exist, Arnacin slid his sword away and started toward the double doors. "Then I'll leave you to it after making sure Miro's guardians won't mistake the sound of your watch for intruders."

"Arnacin. Don't take another step," Firth warned, his tone still quavering, yet deadly all the same.

With a partial turn, the islander noticed the bent bow, its projectile pointed directly toward his heart. Forcing air back into his lungs, he slid one foot back toward the royal door. "It's poisoned, Arnacin," the half-native informed him, causing his target to freeze completely for the moment. "If it scrapes so much as skin, you'll never return home."

"You can't make it," Arnacin breathed in stubborn horror.

"I figured it out over the summer. I intended to tell you... Please, Arnacin, go to bed."

Casting a look over his shoulder to where the doors stood, asleep to the drama outside them, Arnacin felt a flash of resentment that Miro would so unwittingly rob him of his life. Looking back at Firth, however, he whispered, "I won't let you kill the king, Firth, should you be telling the truth or not."

"Arnacin," the intended assassin breathed in an obvious entreaty as he bent the bow back farther.

Taking another step backwards, the islander asked, "Why?" His question was without plea, and he saw the bow tremble.

"You know why, Arnacin. You know why. Miro condemns us to death. If it is to be a battle until extinction, we will assuredly be the extinct. Yet we know you have the ear of the heir."

Arnacin had halted without realizing it. Regarding the young man he considered a friend, he pressed, "I can't if you kill me. Therefore, what's your second plan?"

Now trembling mightily, Firth falsely affirmed, "I'll take care of her as well, if I must."

Shaking his head, Arnacin took another step toward the doors. The air stood still. The bow tautened and the islander's hand fell silently on the door handle. As Arnacin glanced down to push the door open, a gasp sounded followed by the soft thump and clatter of the dropping weapon.

With a sigh, Arnacin looked back to what was now a crumpled ball on the floor, quiet sobs emitting from it. Sliding the weapon out of reach, the islander knelt beside the culprit, waiting. "Why did you have to be here, Arnacin? There were a million places to think, why here?"

As the muffled sound reached him, the islander shrugged. "The view looked nicer." He did not mention his wish to continue his debate with Miro about building a wall once councilors no longer swamped the area, or how he had continued to gainsay that urge, coolly watching as Miro had disappeared inside those doors for the night.

Groaning, Firth begged, "I can't kill you, Arnacin. Execute me however you like, but please don't tell the king."

"Execute you," the islander sarcastically repeated. "You ask the wrong person for your judgment. I'm not even Miran."

Pushing himself up, Firth insisted, "Please, Arnacin. I won't take death from anyone else."

"Leave, Firth," Arnacin sighed. "Tell your family what you almost did, board a ship, and never return. If I don't see you again, I'll have no cause to mention it to Miro."

Those words seemed to take a moment to register, as if the half-native could not believe life would be granted to him. Yet after a moment, Firth opened his arms for an embrace.

Finally breaking away, Firth pulled something from beneath his cloak. Arnacin tensed, yet the would-be assassin only pulled out a small pouch pushing it into the islander's hand. "If ever you are poisoned, Arnacin, turn this into a paste using alcohol and spread it over the wound. It is not a foolproof remedy. Father told me that if they make a cut above the poisoned wound to let the blood escape, it has a stronger effect. However, even doing so, only five natives in the entire course of their history survived the poison. 'You need the gods' favor, first and foremost,' he told me. I cannot say what its ingredients are, but take it, please."

When Arnacin nodded, Firth implored him, "Take care of them, Arnacin, however you feel best." Then, retrieving his bow, he slipped away.

Still on the floor, Arnacin watched him disappear forever.

Chapter 17

The Princess and Her Lord

With autumn in the air, the master swordsman again began teaching Arnacin sword fighting–this time, however, left-handed. He also changed how he wanted the islander to learn.

"With the state of your shoulder, you need to avoid contact with an opponent as much as possible. Naturally, you should just learn to use your left for everything, but you never want to be in a situation where your left is injured and you can't switch to your right."

As if to encourage Arnacin, the swordmaster engaged in the exercises himself, despite his peg-leg. For two hours, they practiced. The first hour, the islander was ordered to stand, blade toward the ground, while the swordmaster lunged. Before the lunge could finish, he was to pivot away at the last second and jab the swordmaster in the side with the wooden sword.

If the swordmaster could read his turn, the attack was blocked. After the first hour, Arnacin still had not succeeded and they turned to the basics, left-handed.

When they stopped, even the swordmaster groaned, rubbing the stump of his leg. Straightening, he nodded to Arnacin. "How's your shoulder?"

The islander could have pretended he thought the question was about his left, but he knew better. Grudgingly, he admitted, "It hurts."

"Huh. I bet it keeps you awake at night as well."

Arnacin did not bother to admit it did, but he had no need as the swordmaster continued, "Ripped muscles heal the worst. You..." he sighed, "you are hyperactive in your own way and youth is on your side, but it won't save you from pain, boy."

The islander said nothing, thinking again of his ship and how much he needed his shoulder. That fear was something he could never admit, except to Valoretta.

In his silence, the swordmaster watched him. Then, with a sigh of pain, the older man turned toward the keep, beckoning for his pupil to follow. "Have you considered training at our school? It is a small fee, which the king will likely be happy to pay. It may help you in your arguments. It will also keep your patience better and your mind busy."

"I've been studying politics," Arnacin scoffed. "The only thing attending the school would teach me is how to mire myself more deeply in the mud of politics. I don't care to learn any more than I have already."

"Honesty is a blessing and a curse in government, boy," the swordmaster growled. "You can hope you have the right balance of truth and discretion."

Perhaps even more than his ship, Arnacin found the pier a huge relief from the frustration of politics. There, amid all the laughter, commotion and joking put-downs from traders, sailors and whatnots, lay a simple peace. Of course, as far as put-downs went, Arnacin was their favorite victim either because of his connection to the nobles or because of his ship.

Passing one stout vendor, Arnacin heard, "Do that thing even seel? I bet it don't even have the proper instruments, boy." As Arnacin raised his eyebrows in reply, the sailor passed the back of his hand over his table welcomingly. "Do you ship possess such fine instrumentses as feese?"

Curiosity slightly aroused, Arnacin stepped over. Lovingly, the sailor flicked away a large wood shaving from the perfection of his display.

After examining the craftsmanship, Arnacin teased, "All these instruments, sir, are just tools for what already exists."

Roaring good-naturedly, the sailor quipped, "So, you mix insult wif flattery, m'boy. *Sir*, iendeed."

"Well, if you prefer sea-rat, I don't mind obliging," the islander returned with wicked delight as the man laughed heartily.

"Well, boy, you've seen nofink yet," the sailor jabbed, pulling a crate from under his table. He proceeded to carefully place a multitude of compasses on the table, each inset into frames of finished wood carefully carved with various shapes. Within seconds, whales, sharks, dolphins, a man holding a compass inside a fish, an octopus, and a helm on a string covered the table.

Laughing with delight at the islander's incredulous look, the man challenged, "Now what do you say?"

Finally ripping his eyes from the beautiful, detailed work, the islander remarked, "The real tools are called stars."

"Oh-ho, but every good seelor knows fere be days wifout sight of 'em stars." At Arnacin's slow smile, he added, "Unless fis be you confirmation fat you never been out fere."

"You're simply trying to sell your wares," the islander remarked in a flat tone.

Grinning, the man's gaze flicked to the compasses that had held Arnacin's view longer. Slowly, he ran his finger over the man-eating fish and then picked up the helm, spinning it around where it dangled from his fingers. With a knowing smile, Arnacin rolled his eyes.

"Have you ever seen anyfink like it?" the man whispered, as if mesmerized by the glinting helm, yet Arnacin took note of the sly, quick glance thrown his way.

"No," the islander admitted with a laugh. "Nor this obstinate of a vendor either. Fine, since you'll die if I don't ask, what do you want for one of them?"

"Ah, tradesmen know how to battle, but for someone leek youself, I'll be generous and settle at... two gold coins. Very cheap considering..."

"Cheap?" Arnacin smirked. "No, that's my ship."

"Oh, you have a point about you ship," the man laughed, causing the islander to flush a dull pink. "But come, come, from a boy we all know the king favors so richly, two gold coins is leekly only an eighf of what you earn ien a day..."

"Really?" Arnacin asked. "Now why do you suppose that?"

"Don't try fat one on me, boy. We all know even the knights are paid, small crumbs from the table, mayhaps, but come, come, you hold a higher position fan fat, we hear. We need no furfur proof fan fat you weer the coveted embroidery of Meera. If nofink else, you have lots to trade."

"You are so knowle–"

"Arnacin." The princess' chiding voice made him whirl around to see her standing behind him with amusement across her face. "Stop torturing the poor man." She turned to the sailor stating, "I'll give you three gold coins for the compass he likes best. That's in repayment for his lack of manners."

Despite the teasing jibe, Arnacin stared at her in disbelief. Looking back at the sailor, he realized he was being eagerly watched. Not wanting to be seen contradicting the princess–and quite liking the craftsmanship–he relented with a sigh, "The helm."

Happily, the vendor agreed to the trade and the princess snatched the compass out of reach as the man held it out. Quickly, she stuffed it behind her back as Arnacin held out his hand.

"Oh, no," she said with a laugh. "I purchased it. I hold the right to choose how to present it." At his silent frustration, she smiled, lifting her chin in regal grace. "Kneel, good sir," she ordered in a voice bursting with cheer.

"I thought you hated custom," Arnacin persisted, inclined more to leave her with the compass than to obey.

"I do," she stated brightly. "But I don't consider this among the normal customs. I insist upon this honor." He did not budge, and she dipped her chin, beseechingly, "Please."

Noticing suddenly that all noise had quieted around the twosome and that every eye was trained on them, Arnacin studied the crowd, almost looking for someone to give their advice. Some were nodding encouragingly. Sara was frowning deeply in the background, her face white as if turned to stone. Still others just watched, excitement in their gazes. Looking again at Sara's scowl, it came to the islander that the princess would ask for this "honor" simply to make her nurse scream for yet another breach of decorum.

Again meeting Valoretta's teasing and yet pleading countenance, Arnacin slowly complied, feeling her slip the black cord over his head. Tucking the compass down his shirt, he looked back up to see that all color had left the princess' face.

"There," she whispered as he rose, studying her with concern. "I just... I mean... I... presented it."

She would never pale so just for angering Sara in public. Something apparently both so wonderful and so terrible had just taken place. It was clear it was of such unfathomable importance to her, but Arnacin could not discern its meaning.

Yet as Valoretta bit her lower lip, Arnacin felt duty-bound to reassure her about whatever had suddenly troubled her. In that strange moment, he felt her unknown fear turn into his own and no reassurances came to him. Instead, he nodded slightly, whispering, "Thank you."

Again meeting his gaze, the princess smiled gently, although her color did not return.

The silence, in which the ocean seemed to roar instead of talk softly to itself, was broken as someone seized Valoretta by the arm. Only Sara's furious tones prevented the islander from reacting to the unexpected move. Low murmurs broke forth all along the pier as everyone watched in confusion while the nurse practically marched the princess back to the castle by her upper arm, carrying on a heated debate from which Arnacin could not make out any actual words.

Just as she entered the city's main street, however, Valoretta ripped herself from her nurse's grasp and, yanking her skirts up, fled to the castle on her own. Once both ladies were out of sight, eyes began turning once again to Arnacin, who stood at a complete loss. Feeling the crowd's gazes upon him, however, he glanced at them with an uncomfortable smile and quickly slipped away to the safety of his ship.

Storming through the double doors of the great hall, Sara just remembered to bob a crisp curtsy before she spat, “So you take no concern in it, do you? Do you realize what your numbskull daughter just did?” Although Miro barked her name, her fury drove her onward and she screamed, “She claimed that worthless rag from the sea! With a *compass*! In the custom of a lady choosing her lord!”

The hall fell silent. Briefly, the king’s eyes bore the same expression as when they were children and she had caught her younger brother repeatedly jumping off the throne. In that second, she saw his thoughts whirling. Then, surprisingly, he dismissed it. “Really, Sara,” he sighed. “Is that necessary? Do not forget you speak to your king.”

Behind him, Memphis’s face had lost all color. “What are you going on about?” The councilor’s tone was one of complete bewilderment.

“Valoretta claimed him, Sire,” Sara exclaimed, now choking on tears. “Worse than that, she fully realizes it and says it’s the best thing she’s ever done. Sire, I beg you, send him away before this grows any worse. He’s nothing, not even from the same country. What do you know about him, really?”

“Sara,” the king said, with little patience in his tone. “At least I know that he is a man of his word–”

“Boy,” the nurse mumbled, causing Miro to turn red in fury.

“Don’t you *ever* contradict me!”

“Please,” Sara gasped, sinking low as he stepped angrily toward her. “Your forgiveness, Sire.”

Taking a controlling breath, the king stated, “Yes, he is a boy. All the more reason for your fears to be senseless! He is still too naive and honest to even think of harm. Do I make myself clear?”

“Yes, Your Majesty,” Sara whispered. Behind Miro, a deep frown had appeared on his councilor’s face.

"You are dismissed." Bowing, Sara obediently departed, her shoulders slumped in defeat.

Rain pummeled the ocean in the distance and streaked down the library's only glass windows. Staring out at the storm, Arnacin rested his head against the windows' wooden frame. Beyond the castle's city, lying out in the harbor, was his small craft still moored to the dock. There it writhed in the tossing waves. Late autumn had once again sent all sailors to their home berths–all but that last little vessel bobbing in the bay. How Arnacin wished that it too was on its way to its own berthing place.

Yet it was not, and although the recent renewal of training with the swordmaster's patient–if gruff–instruction had restored some hope that his shoulder would eventually heal enough to allow him freedom, Arnacin was beginning to believe that the war would never permit him such peace. While the arrival of heavy snow had produced a few breaks in the bloodshed, the war itself had not halted.

Hearing light footsteps approaching, Arnacin quickly straightened and, turning, he saw Valoretta with book in hand, coming to join him. She stared out of the window for a minute before mentioning, "Winter gives us a break from the wars, as you know–desolate as it may seem. You can be thankful for that much."

"Yes," the islander exhaled, dropping his shoulder back against the wall. "At least it gives us that much."

"Arnacin," the princess breathed sadly. "What troubles you, beside the fact that the season stops your work on your ship?"

For just a minute, Arnacin studied her, contemplating emptying all his frustrations, fears and burdens on her. Once again, however, he bit back the words and temper screaming to be loosed, venting it instead into wicked teasing. "Very well, My Lady. King Miro..."

"Never mind," Valoretta cut off, quickly clamping her hand over his mouth as she did. Even with the band of her signet ring pressing into his lips, Arnacin could not suppress his grin. "I understand the aggravation," she continued, "but should I allow you to joke on that subject, I shall be a very disloyal daughter indeed."

As she released him, Arnacin shrugged innocently. "You asked what troubled me."

Shoving her book into his chest, Valoretta pierced him with a knowing look and stomped off to fetch another volume. Arnacin watched her go, his victorious grin firmly in place.

The princess returned shortly thereafter. Instead of opening the new volume she held, however, she said, "I think the king needs a friend. Carpason's dead. There are no others. In his desperation, he's looking to you."

When Arnacin only snorted softly in contempt, Valoretta joined him, placing her hand on his arm. "Please, Arnacin. Try to be a friend and overlook your disagreements. He needs it so, yet I have no audience with him. I'm not his war councilor, an attendant or even one of his generals. There's only you. Don't let the politics divide you."

For a long moment, Arnacin stared into her face—at her earnest, sky-colored eyes, compressed lips, and locked jaw. Finally, he nodded and she smiled in gratitude.

Arnacin did not have a chance to act on his promise until late one night, when he noticed the great hall's doors still guarded and knew what it meant. Approaching the nearest guard, Arnacin asked to be announced.

Inside, Miro stared out the far window into the blackness beyond. "Your Majesty?" Arnacin inquired with a slight bow. "It's rather late. Is there anything I may do for you?"

A slight smile flickered across the king's worry-laden features, yet other than beckoning the islander closer, he did nothing else at first. Finally, he looked over, softly demanding, "End this war, Arnacin."

His shoulders stiffening, Arnacin reminded him after a pause to gather self-control, "With all due respect, Your Majesty, I'm not a god. I can't clap my hands and restore peace." It appeared that

Miro was no longer listening. Urgently persistent, Arnacin continued, "If you wish to end it, there must be some..." He faltered, yet he had already gone too far and in a whisper, cursing himself for his lack of tact, he finished, "...cooperation."

Regal coldness abruptly returned to Miro's countenance as he turned back to his throne, and Arnacin knew only providence would keep the king from seeing the islander's whole reason for entering as manipulation. "Thank you, Arnacin of Enchantress Island, for your concern. Yet you need your own rest." His tone was coldly polite. Of course, providence would overlook them.

Bowing in response to the dismissal, the islander tried once more. "Is there anything else I may do for you before I go?"

With a small sigh, some of the remoteness left the king. "No, Arnacin," he whispered, "You need your rest."

Thunder cracked across the bay and rain poured in heavy sheets from the sky. Slamming the keep's door on the storm, Arnacin sighed, slowly pulling his soaked hood off his head.

"You were out in that?" The stunned voice caused him to quickly straighten as he searched for the speaker and met Councilor Darien's gaze.

"I was making sure my ship was alright," Arnacin replied, starting coldly past.

"I have a warm fire in the other room," Darien mentioned, gesturing to the nearby doorway. "Dry off there and talk with me."

Pausing suspiciously, Arnacin inquired, "What do you really want? You couldn't care less for me."

"Are you that unforgiving?" the councilor questioned softly.

Pulling his dripping cloak closer about himself, Arnacin drew back.

"I wish to come to an agreement–that is all. Will you refuse to give me a chance?"

Too cold to argue, Arnacin followed the councilor into the side room and allowed the man to take his cloak before he slipped wearily into a chair by the fire.

"It must be nasty out there," Darien commented, hanging the drenched cloak nearby and then joining Arnacin in a chair across from him. "I admire your staunchness to keep at that..." He paused, a faint sneer apparent even as he tried to hide his disgust by serving hot cider and offering some to the islander. Then he regained control of his expression and finished, "...ship, but you waste your time and energy, my boy."

"How is that?" the islander demanded, declining the offered cup.

"You have an obligation to Mira, which does not seem likely to end, Arnacin."

"Now we understand each other," Arnacin stated coolly. "You wish to convince me that I had better leave, if I have any real intention of doing so."

"Do not try to misunderstand me," Darien warned, with the first trace of temper. "I was merely venting my frustration about the fact that we are fighting a losing battle."

"If you felt so deeply about peace, I would expect you to start suggesting things to your king."

"My king, Arnacin?" the councilor pressed, lifting an eyebrow. "Do you not also serve him?"

"I am an independent. Never have I claimed anything else."

"So you think this is not your war?" Turning away from that piercing gaze, the islander said nothing. "If I told you I have pondered the means of gaining peace, what would you say?" Darien pressed.

"Then say it."

Slowly leaning back in his chair, the councilor drawled, "The savages hate and distrust Miro–he will never appease them. But if someone new were to take control, someone they revered and who promised peace, the whole thing may be at an end." He paused, waiting for the islander's reply. When none came, he commented, "Although your plan is well thought out, it is naive, as anyone should expect from someone your age. A wall will only serve to give the appearance of fear, which will encourage boldness on the other side. We must never falter in our show of fearlessness and strength. It is the only thing that upholds a kingdom. Think about that before you speak again, lest everyone's high opinion of you is shattered."

Leaping to his feet, Arnacin snapped, "I'll have you know, I don't care what they think of me, and however seemingly appropriate all your plans are, they're sixty times as weak! I would sooner be deemed weak and prove more unbreakable than your hidden, spineless backbones!"

Chuckling softly, the man inclined his head. "Exactly, but there is only one way for you to succeed in that goal." He let the words hang in the air for a moment before he concluded, "A revolution."

Arnacin turned coldly away at that, yanking his cloak off its hook. As he reached the door, the councilor seized his right arm, whispering, "You possess the skill and the mythical image–I possess the brains. Mira can be saved from the war and her current monarchy. Does that mean nothing to you? Does this land's safety and peaceful tranquility with all nationalities mean nothing to you?"

"If it did, I would do it honestly–"

"I see. It's protection of the princess that holds you back."

"You prove to me by the second that you, in fact, lack the brains needed," Arnacin hissed, struggling to yank away from the fingers digging into his arm. Strangely, Darien's hands bore all the strength his character lacked, or else Arnacin's shoulder was even weaker than he had admitted to himself. "I gave my word to Miro to aid him."

Arnacin gasped as Darien slammed him into the wall. "Every man here knows you barely gave any such thing," the traitorous councilor hissed. "You refused to give your word, as a matter of fact. You simply nodded. Now you have seen Miro's stupidity. Your very honor *demands* you help everyone live better than they do under him. He's killed thousands of men in his quest for supposed peace, kept us all ducking our heads in fear of attack, weaseled taxes out of all he can. Is that who you support?"

"Should I support you instead?" the islander growled, struggling to pull himself away. "You and your mass of high-thinking snakes, who worm about the king's feet with all their acclaimed wisdom and intelligence? If you complain at his actions, you complain twice as much about yourself. Miro is weak–there is no argument there–too prone to listen to the hissing of imbeciles like you who only really want one thing–your own glory. When did you start concerning yourself with peace? Was it when a spark of fear entered that perhaps you'll lose, or when this mad idea entered that you could see even your savages worship your goodness and wisdom? If ever you succeed, I will still know you for who you are."

Backhanding Arnacin across the face, Darien warned, "Be that way, *cockspur*, but if you breathe word of this conversation, it will be your neck in the noose. You yourself have said the snakes could accomplish it."

"I wouldn't think of saying anything, only because you are all true-blooded chickens, far too cowardly to be any type of threat. I'm sure anyone with intelligence already knows you'd stab the king in the back if ever you felt you could gain from it."

Darien's grip loosened and Arnacin yanked himself away, storming out.

Chapter 18

Cornyo

Although storms remained frequent that winter, heavy snows only came for a few weeks in the middle of the season. Those weeks paused the war only that long and, due to the continued battles, the ambassadors who normally filtered in during those months never appeared. Any ambassadors who did arrive quickly left as soon as their business was completed.

Regardless of the political respite, tensions remained high. Despite the howling wind and blowing precipitation that kept Mirans at home, towns would frequently burst into flames along their borders.

Meanwhile, Arnacin continued training under the swordmaster, inside on the bad days and out on the better ones. As the last month of winter came and he became better at moving at the last second, the islander was ordered to switch to his right hand.

When the swordmaster thought it time to test Arnacin with other knights, however, his shoulder was not up to it.

"You pivoted too soon!" the swordmaster snapped, halting what had become an actual bout between Arnacin and Hadwin. As Arnacin stepped back, panting, his palm pushed into his right shoulder, the swordmaster shook his head. "Your turn must be sudden, boy. It must be quick, seemingly unplanned, completely smooth, as if you are not moving at all, or the better swordsmen will engage. You cannot allow that sort of pounding on your shoulder.

You must have no contact with their weapon at all. You'll not have a shoulder left, and very likely no life either."

Arnacin did not reply, striving not to cry out from the unrelenting pain running through his shoulder. "I'm sorry," Hadwin spoke up. "I should have stopped."

Meeting the knight's deeply concerned gaze, the islander shook his head dismissing the need for apology, yet the swordmaster spoke for him. "If you don't block when you see it coming, he won't learn." Turning back to Arnacin, he ordered, "Have one of the physicians run cold water over your shoulder and then come back. We can't waste Sir Hadwin's time."

Nodding, the islander stumbled away, passing the remains of the Tarmlin troop packing for their leave early the next morning. Hadwin had left them to it, having agreed to assist the swordmaster for the day he was there.

When Arnacin returned, the swordmaster ordered him to use his left arm and they continued until nightfall.

Before the swordmaster, the knight lunged at the islander. Time and again, Arnacin either stepped back or slipped to the right or left and, if Hadwin turned, he dodged again, striving to slip a blow in with the practice blade or, at the least, avoid engagement without being hit. By the time they quit, the swordmaster was rubbing his forehead with his fingers and Arnacin was swaying in pain. Despite not using his right hand after that first bout, it burned.

"Enough," the swordmaster sighed. "We've worked too hard. You have the grace, boy. Use it! Yes, he knows what you're going to do, but not to which side!"

Calming, he commanded, "Don't use your right shoulder at all tomorrow and wash it regularly in cold water. As a matter of fact, don't leave your bed unless called by Miro. I'll have the physicians hold you to it. The day following that, we're going back to the bathhouse."

Without possible argument, Arnacin merely sighed as he bowed his begrudging submission. Hadwin voiced it best as they turned away together, "I know. If only sailing didn't count so much on your arm's strength."

"Something like that," the islander whispered.

That night, fevers attacked Arnacin, and it was both easy and hard to stay in bed as per his orders once the sun rose. He had been the one to push his training this time. He could not complain that the swordmaster was too harsh.

All the same, there were occasions where his shoulder reaped its revenge, and when the physicians came in later that morning to find him shivering with sweat running down his face, they informed the king that he had come down with a minor bout of the winter curse due to overexertion. Whether they knew what they were talking about or not, it hardly mattered.

They told their patient to stay in bed and perhaps the sickness would be gone in two days. Between the fever and his throbbing shoulder, the islander had no will to argue. With their help, he slept through most of the day.

He woke intermittently, however, from various dreams where his own stupidity left him stranded on Mira. For it was his own stupidity. The swordmaster had been very careful with Arnacin's training considering his nature.

The truth was that the islander was slowly healing and growing even better at controlling his pain. He knew many would call him foolish, but fear forced him to continue. He was fearful that his shoulder would never heal and, if he let it sit, he would never learn to control the pain, never learn to fight well through it. Also, he feared that he did not have the time the physicians had mandated. A small persistent whisper in the back of his mind said that he needed to appear completely hale and whole before the spring.

There were times, he wondered if the swordmaster suspected what he was really doing, but if so, it was still allowed to a small extent, watched and guided, forced only when most necessary. For that, Arnacin was grateful.

Naturally, Arnacin was not called for meetings, although Miro himself slipped in that evening to discuss the natives and how they appeared to have no goal in mind. Neither the islander nor the king believed that. What Arnacin suspected, however, he kept to himself, lacking evidence to support it. He also knew his silence looked like a result of his fever and, thankfully, Miro left without pressing him for his thoughts.

It was Gagandep who noticed the islander standing by the terrace's balustrade two days later, his thumbnail between his front teeth while he stared northward. Inhaling sadly, the adopted native put down his medic sack to join the young war councilor. "What brings you out here on such a day?" Gagandep wondered.

Looking over at the native, Arnacin merely nodded politely.

Sighing, Gagandep said, "I heard that the king and the swordmaster had a large disagreement about how to re-train your shoulder. The swordmaster won apparently." When he still received no reply, he said, "You haven't been to see me since you asked if I thought of a way to satisfy the natives. Did I say something wrong?"

Folding his arms, the islander shrugged. "After Firth... I couldn't..."

Slowly, the adopted native nodded. "I miss seeing you, Arnacin. As for Firth..." For a long time, he was quiet. Then, sadly, he shrugged. "I can't hold you accountable. When he was a boy, I worried about his hatred. After he came to know you, it seemed to settle somewhat. He no longer hated my kind. Little did I realize he had just changed the direction of his hatred.

"I know you were only trying to keep him safe when you told him to leave. Now, at least, he is free of the fate of Mira. Should we fall, he can still live."

"If his hatred doesn't kill him somewhere else," Arnacin muttered and Gagandep pushed his shoulder.

"Have faith, Arnacin. It will ease your stress. Now, what troubles bring you out here on a day like this?"

Slowly, the islander asked, "Is it a trait among your kind to... lead everyone by the nose?"

"What do you mean?"

"They're attacking all but the northwest towns and villages. In fact, their attacks have led constantly more eastward. Miro—or *his councilors*—assume they are running out of border homes to attack and are simply trying to scare us without endangering themselves by penetrating Mira more than they need. I'm not sure I agree."

Turning fully toward Gagandep, the islander continued, "What's in the west that they would want? The maps end over there."

"Nothing's over there." The native shrugged.

"Nothing?"

"Marshes, muddy waterways... in short, nothing."

Giving him a look of exasperation, Arnacin repeated, "In short, nothing. I read that marshes are disastrous."

"They are to any wandering travelers, yet there is no way to use them for a weapon. Marshes can't be picked up and thrown."

Laughing slightly at the image, the islander surmised, "So, unless they are planning on surrendering their land to Mira in order to make sure they have a holding that can never be crossed, you don't think they could have any use for the west."

"To my knowledge, Arnacin," Gagandep affirmed, turning back to the interior. "They know no more of those lands than Mira does. I grew up fearing them. My whole tribe considered them holy land—'the Sacred Way,' we called it. Only one with a god's supreme favor could enter and live, or the land would open at his feet and fire would burst into the sky from the fissure while it ate the intruder alive. Smoke does wisp in tendrils from those lands, and the natives watch from the mountain posts."

He whirled back as an impish voice replied, "Then I could, of course, enter without fear." Seeing the wicked amusement in Arnacin's deep blue eyes, the native laughed before he left, shaking his head.

No sooner had the adopted native departed than feet stopped in the archway and a voice shuddering with fear called, "Arnacin, the king requests your presence."

Closing his eyes, the islander collected his patience before promising, "I will be there in a minute."

With one last sweep of the view, Arnacin turned away and headed to the great hall where the king and Memphis met with Duke Cestmir, who had just returned from the field. While his men and others like them kept Gagandep busy with the rampant annoyance of frostbite, as well as various sicknesses arising from the constant cold and dampness, the duke had taken Cornyo with him to report.

As Arnacin slipped to the side of the throne's dais without notice, Cestmir was saying, "We continued the pursuit to Norton, occasionally rescuing the towns, sometimes arriving too late. In every place, however, the savages made off with some of the women and children. At first, we thought we would free them when we caught up to the monsters, but they weren't ever present. I can only think that they were swapping their raiding parties after every attack, but…" Glancing at Arnacin, the duke finished, "No one in my army knew how to look for proof of that."

Doubtless, no one missed the duke's envy of the islander's ability to track in that glance. Arnacin could spend all day insisting his skill was actually very small indeed, but none of the Mirans believed him. Charlotte bested him by far, although he never mentioned her to anyone but Valoretta anymore. Regardless, the Mirans considered the islander's skill at least equal to that of the natives.

Noticing Memphis's glare fixed on him, Arnacin looked away.

"What we do know," Cestmir continued, "is that no bodies were ever left on the trail, and the captured victims were never left with a village's dead either—at least, so one of my men tells me, since he knows one of the captured families.

"When the natives finally turned back toward the mountains, we retreated for home ourselves. What do you wish to do about the hostages, Sire?"

His fingers tapping on the throne's arm, the king sighed. A moment later, he whispered, "Nothing. Regard them as dead."

Behind the duke, Cornyo gasped, exclaiming, "Sire, they're your own people. As long as they draw breath, should you not–?" A glance from his lord cut off the rest of his words.

With a fleeting look between Arnacin–who stood staring at his feet–and the knight, Miro replied, "Yes, they are my people but so are all the rest. If we can assume anything, it is that they have taken them over the mountains. It is beyond our lands, and the trespass shall only bring a greater intensity of war. Although some have succeeded without causing more wrath," he again glanced at Arnacin, "a full-scale search in their lands, and then an attack on a likely peaceful village to regain our people will not be overlooked. In fact, it may be exactly why they were taken if some of the savages are playing at their own politics."

"They're not smart enough," Arnacin muttered. Naturally, no one heard him but Memphis, whose glare sharpened.

"Sire," Cestmir inquired, "may I point out one thing?" Miro nodded resignedly and the duke stated, "Not only, therefore, are we condemning the women to either physical abuse or forced marriage, regardless of previous husbands, and the young men likely to torture and death, but the children who are young enough might even be turned against us as spies and more in later years. Given that, do you still wish for no action?"

Defeat resounded in the king's tone as he announced, "I cannot change my answer, but let us hope the war ends before our own kin starts betraying us to the enemy."

As the duke and his knight bowed out, the latter with a last pleading look toward the islander, the king sighed, dismissing them, "I'm sorry, Memphis, Arnacin. There is indeed nothing to discuss."

The look the high councilor passed Arnacin dared him to disagree, yet the islander only glared right back. Both gazes vanished as the king turned to them. With their own inclinations to the king, they left, swiftly separating once out of the great hall.

Not more than five steps away from the hall, though, Arnacin halted, spotting Cornyo standing by the wall, obviously awaiting the islander. Reading the knight's thoughts in the desperate lines of his face, Arnacin sighed. "Cornyo, I have no more say in there than a fly to a mule. It constantly swarms around biting, and the only response is a twitch of skin. Besides, this is not something I could disagree with if I held any sway."

"Arnacin," Cornyo sighed. "Please, talk to him—without the presence of His High Puppet Master, if you must."

Slowly exhaling, the islander asked, "Why, Cornyo? Under the circumstances, 'His High Puppet Master' said nothing. Miro made the choice himself." Dropping his gaze, Arnacin admitted, "And I'm forced to admit he's right... this time."

"I can't let it rest, Arnacin. Could he not even allow one person to try, just to try, for the country... for its people? If only one man went, for personal reasons, whatever 'politics' they intend would be disregarded."

"What personal reasons? We don't know any of them more than in passing."

Smiling slightly, the knight corrected, "You mean, *you* don't know any of them in more than passing. I'm often surprised you even know them that much, as foreign as you are, yet you have a way with low folk.

"There was a time, however, when a few of Cestmir's troops had to stay behind due to injury. The duke forced us as far as the nearest town and then found people to take care of us until we could return home." Looking down, he whispered, "I came to know a lady while I was there. She was wonderful, Arnacin. I had hoped..." He dropped off. Then, clearing his throat, he shrugged. "They took her, and there is my personal excuse."

Sadly, Arnacin whispered, "Also the reason you're letting your heart rule your senses. You couldn't track them, Cornyo. You admitted as much. No one knows the entire land beyond those mountains, and they could have taken them anywhere. Lastly, how are you supposed to raid a whole village for its captives single-handedly, and retrace your steps—with escapees in tow—without men to protect them?"

His gaze darkening, the knight stated, "I bet you could think of something, if you actually tried."

Looking away in frustration, the islander admitted, "Maybe, if I were going..." Dropping his own gaze, he admitted, "But I am incapable of returning to the field. The natives made sure of it."

Pity mixed with temper in the knight's eyes. Exhaling, the knight whispered, "I'm sorry, Arnacin. I hope you will find a way to rise again, our hero."

With that verbal slap, he whirled away, while the light in the islander's gaze continued to darken as those words ignited his own frustrations.

"Arnacin!" The urgent call echoing down the corridor leading to the library the next morning made the islander turn to see Duke Cestmir striding toward him with the urgency of someone trying to retain a royal demeanor.

"Duke Cestmir." Arnacin inclined his head. "I figured you would be preparing to leave again."

"The men are doing so." Lowering his voice as he neared enough to do so, the duke whispered, "Cornyo is absent."

Shifting his eyes away from the duke, Arnacin sadly breathed, "Is he?"

"Arnacin, if you persuaded him..." Cestmir did not finish the horrifying ending.

"Your Grace," the islander sighed. "What do you suspect Cornyo's done?"

"I think you know. I had hoped that Miro's wisdom would sway him, which is why I brought him yesterday, yet it apparently has not. Please tell me what you know about it."

"No more than you, and perhaps less, Your Grace," Arnacin admitted, meeting the noble's gaze in earnestness. "He did ask me to... convince the king for him and, when I refused, he left."

"When was that? Would there be time to catch him before it's too late?"

"I don't know. He would likely expect pursuit though. So, even if he left Mira late, there is not much chance of catching him—even were he on foot, which I doubt he is."

"Arnacin, this is serious. If word of what he's attempting makes its way to the king, you know what I'll be forced to do if he returns, whether victorious or not."

Sighing, the islander nodded. "As does he. He went despite the fact that it means his death one way or the other, not heedless of that fact. They, and Mira, I suppose, mean that much to him."

Studying the islander, the noble shook his head. "You have an almost nasty way of making others think like you. My question is, what will you do if he returns?"

"He will never return, I suspect. He certainly won't return without the captives, and it is too much to expect him to succeed."

"Stop avoiding the question," the duke growled. "As impossible as it is that he will return, what will you do should he?"

"Why is it so important to you that I answer?"

Taking a step closer to the islander, the duke softly breathed, "I love my men, Arnacin of Enchantress Island. That is why, and you have just destroyed one of them. I want some sort of satisfaction, at least the knowledge that you are horrified by your actions."

Studying the noble, Arnacin noticed the tears in his eyes. After a moment, just as softly as the other, the islander said, "You ask the impossible, Your Grace. I care very much for your knight and I even feel humbled by him, by his loyalty to his country and friends, even without support–but I can never be horrified by those actions. I am far more horrified that I ever agreed to help with this war, that I ever agreed to become the... war-hardened wreck you see before you."

Cestmir's eyes hardened. Whirling away from the islander, he said, his voice ringing, "There are times, Arnacin, I wish the same. I wish I had never lain eyes on such a character as you, a weaseling, snake-tongued, selfish, impudent *commoner* as yourself."

Once again at his maps, poring over uncharted edges as if he could see through the parchment to the land it knew nothing about, Arnacin finally glanced toward where the princess sat beside him, attempting to please her nurse somewhat by working on her much-neglected embroidery. Of course, that was only after she quit studying the map herself while they discussed alternate ways to convince the king to build a wall of peace.

If Miro continued to refuse to build a wall and if it was Mira's only escape outside of evacuation, could the people build it themselves? Would they even consider building it without the king's consent?

"Valoretta," the islander at last asked aloud. "What would happen to someone who forged the king's command?"

Yelping as she stabbed herself in the finger in shock, the princess gasped, "Arnacin, you can't be thinking of doing that, not even for possible peace."

Smiling slightly at her reaction, Arnacin admitted, "I'm not, really. I don't think my honor would allow it, but the wall brought the question to mind. What is the punishment for that?"

Sighing, Valoretta said, "There are many crimes that result in hanging on Mira. Stealing, after a certain amount, mistreatment of another person, and so forth. Should a man ever be fool enough to pretend Miro ordered what he did not, they would be tarred before their hanging."

"Tarred?" the islander repeated.

"Have you never heard of it?" When Arnacin shook his head, the princess shuddered, explaining, "They'll boil the pitch and then throw the person into it while it's still bubbling. Not that I've ever burned myself, other than my tongue on a piece of food or drink, but I understand that if you ever have been burned by boiling water, it is nothing to compare with boiling pitch, which is not so easily removed. There... I..."

Unable to finish whatever image raced through her mind, she concluded, "Undermining the king in such way is considered the highest degree of treason imaginable, and so no one is light with the justice."

"The highest? Yet people do it all the time through manipulation."

Whacking him with her arm, Valoretta warned, "Don't dare suggest such a thing, or you imply that Miro is weak. The king is not brainless, Arnacin, whatever our private frustrations."

Arnacin's sole reply was a long sigh.

The month passed and then another. Whenever Memphis mentioned Valoretta's claim on Arnacin, Miro simply said it was nothing and dismissed the high councilor. With that, Memphis turned to watching the islander very closely. Finally, he ran out of patience.

"This must go nowhere," Memphis growled, after having secretly assembled all the councilors except Arnacin, of course. As all around him nodded solemnly, he whispered, "I know who the king has chosen as the princess' consort. He has chosen none other than Arnacin of Enchantress Island as the next king."

Gasps of disbelief echoed off the walls. Hushing them, the high councilor explained, "You must have heard it in the streets. Princess Valoretta claimed Arnacin as her lord. When Miro heard about this outrage, he made up excuses as to why it means nothing. Even now, so long after the occurrence, he has done nothing, not even to order their separation to ensure that it never *can* mean anything."

A frozen silence had entered the room. After some of the shock dissipated, one brazen councilor voiced, "Why is that so bad? Arnacin's annoying, but not horrible."

Twenty glares bored into the culprit.

"He's a foreigner, dunce," Darien finally hissed. "Not only does he not care for our way of life, he completely hates councilors. What do you think will happen to us if he acquires the throne? What will happen to *Mira*?"

A fearful silence fell, driven by each one's imaginings of Mira's end. "How do we convince Miro of the looming disaster?" someone finally asked.

"You can't," Memphis intoned. "He has not offered it for debate and he would deny all such accusations. Mira will fall to an islander unless someone is brave enough to risk everything to save her. I don't know how they'd do it, short of eliminating the brat, but I wish there was such a hero."

With a large sigh of defeat, the high councilor trudged out.

Pulling his hood closer about his face, Darien slipped into the most likely tavern. Li'l Smokey was, as its name would imply, windowless and filled with black smoke from a badly vented chimney that no one had ever bothered to repair. Perhaps, the tavern's owners just never had the money, but regardless of the reason, it dissuaded a richer crowd and concealed petty crime.

Not all the Mirans there were of disrepute, but they were poorer, simpler, more often drunk, and willing to obey a single command of the king without question, as long as it gave them some extra food for their table.

It had taken little trouble to rip off the wax bearing the royal seal from one letter and melt it with its imprinted crane onto forged orders. Showing it to the right people and whispering into the right ears, Darien knew it would be done. As he slipped the supposed orders into a reliable man's hand, his work was completed. The threat would soon be no more.

As night descended over Arnacin, leaning on his ship's prow, he sighed, straightening. It was still too cold to be out at night as the sharp wind, steadily growing more frigid, reminded him.

The usual hubbub of the inns greeted him as he started up the streets toward the castle. Drunkards stumbled from one inn to the next, followed by the rowdy ruckus that would emit from the door they had exited, only to be picked up by the new entrance. There was even the occasional wretch who would suddenly fly out into the street as the proprietor felt the need to eject him. It was one such incident that bowled the islander over as a man was flung into the street.

As he was passing a tavern, the door flew open. He saw a flurry of movement in the doorway. Then, before he could step out of the way, a man smashed into Arnacin's right side. With a cry, the islander collapsed, the man's concentrated weight on top of him. He reeked of alcohol.

"Sorry, mister, sorry," the man's mumble was slurred as he shot to his feet. Grabbing Arnacin's right arm, he hauled upward.

The tug on his shoulder caused a sharp burst of pain that leapt straight into his head. Almost pleading in gasping agony, Arnacin tried to gain his feet on his own. "Let go. Just let go."

To the islander's complete shock, the man suddenly yanked him within both arms. A strong-smelling cloth was shoved over his mouth and nose. His throbbing shoulder allowed no chance to halt his quick breaths, forced out between his teeth, and within seconds, he knew no more.

"Those are the King's orders?"

"From what I've been told, yes."

Slowly, the voices filtered into Arnacin's consciousness. "Why would he order us to kill the boy? He could execute him any time he wished."

Full awareness jerked back to the islander to find that his wrists and ankles were bound tight and a thick cloth had been shoved into his mouth. Tall barrels blocked his vision, yet it was plain from the nearness of the sounds of movement that men stood close by, whispering.

"I was just told what you are to do, but from what I heard, the king fears he's instigating treason. Yet he fears killing him where everyone knows about it. Arnacin's too popular to discard safely. So, when you're done with him, make sure there is no sign–none whatsoever."

Footsteps receded and, still suffering under the drug, Arnacin urgently struggled with the rope pinning his arms behind his back.

"Easy now," the soft sigh caused the islander to look up as a small man climbed over the barrels, a flask in his hand.

He pulled Arnacin into his arms, taking out the gag, and the islander weakly gasped, "It's a lie. The king's not that much of a coward."

"Shh, that's more than I can say. I can't take that chance." Arnacin did not dare reply–the hand on the back of his neck restricted his head's movement while the waiting flask pressed against his sealed lips. Gradually, his attacker forced the flask's contents through, however, and as pain and darkness swooped in, Arnacin heard the distant apology, "I'm sorry. This is all I can do."

As word spread that Arnacin had deserted by taking passage aboard some ship and the search for him showed no promise, Sir Hadwin asked for an audience with the king.

"Sire?" Hadwin bowed as he was allowed entrance to the great hall. Miro did not even turn to him, staring out the dark windows. "About the reports of the islan–"

"He was *seen* leaving," Miro growled, cutting the debate off there, or at least trying.

"Has anyone you personally trust said as much?"

"Trust," the king scoffed. "Trust is not for kings. Occasionally, a king will have a friend or two they trust, but those friends soon die or are killed through various means. I currently have none. Only reason can be trusted."

"Sire, you know that is only defeat speaking," Hadwin sighed. "You know in your heart you have many around you whom you can trust, including Arnacin."

"Is that so? I know in my heart, you say?" Those words were a sarcastic snort. When the knight only waited, the king abruptly erupted. "Stop standing there making wise comments like a philosopher or an oracle of old! Had I wanted those, I would pull that walking corpse, our oracle, out of his tower! Reason itself says Arnacin did exactly as the people say he did!"

If he expected Hadwin to bow out at that, he was wrong. Without even a preparatory breath, the knight exclaimed, "Sire, I don't believe it. Arnacin would never just abandon us."

Miro simply stood there, his back still turned to the knight while he stared out the great hall windows. Finally, a sigh escaped him. "There is a very good reason he would."

"Do you know him at all, Sire? He would sooner commit suicide than desert. What reason do you think higher than his commitment to honor?"

Whirling, Miro snapped, "Then explain why there has been no sign of him! This is Arnacin of Enchantress Island, a person the entire city knows by sight! They would set up an instant cry if they saw anyone attack him! So why do they only say they saw him board a ship—*saw*?"

Studying the floor, Hadwin confessed, "I don't know, Sire." Seconds passed before he spoke again, asking, "Sire, give me the order to search his ship. Perhaps I may find something."

Chuckling sardonically, the king said, "Don't think he'll have left so much as an outline to hint at his home's location. That ship will be stripped clean of anything that could be used against him."

"He has a bow, Sire. A beautiful bow. I've seen him use it. It's so light that he can use it even now, despite the state of his shoulder. You would never think he has an injury when he uses it, and I know he kept it on his ship. I highly doubt he would leave it behind, not only because it is such a fine weapon and a sentimental one for him, but because in his condition, it may be his only defense. If I don't find it, it will give credence to the rumors, but if I find it, believe me, his remains, at least, have not left Mira."

Sighing, Miro nodded, "Take a small force and search the ship."

Taking ten of Tarmlin's men, Hadwin boarded Arnacin's ship. Dusk was already upon them as they stood on deck, looking at the lack of places to hide anything. With only the hold—a hold barely tall enough to walk through bent double—and the cabin, Hadwin sent three men down into the hold and took the cabin himself with one other, leaving the rest of the men to keep watch.

Upon lighting the lantern hanging in the cabin, Hadwin quickly realized there were no potential hiding places there either. A bed and a dresser alone decorated it. The drawers would not fit the bow, but since it did not appear to be anywhere else, he decided he might as well see what the cabin *did* hold.

The first drawer kept only what he might expect in a medicine drawer–but in the second one down, he discovered a small book beside a few ink jars and writing utensils. One lone book, its leather ruined and rumpled with dried seawater, its pages crackly as Hadwin carefully pulled it out and opened it. Toward the middle, after the complete ruin of ink and paper, careful script bumped along wrinkles in the pages. It was written in an unfamiliar language, but as the mental images of Arnacin writing it swam before Hadwin, he felt his eyes moisten in the knowledge that the islander might be gone forever. A dull clunk interrupted his thoughts.

Meeting his companion's gaze, who had come to stand at his elbow to look at the book himself, Hadwin raised a questioning eyebrow. The knight in turn nodded toward the bed. One careful look caused Hadwin's grimace of disgust with himself. The bed did not rest on a solid wood frame as he had first thought. A thin line down the center revealed that there were sliding doors over a compartment.

Dropping onto his knees, he pried his fingers into the crack, pushing one side open. A thick wad of green wool blocked the opening, yet tugging impatiently at it proved futile. It remained jammed. He stopped suddenly, however... for in touching it, he had revealed a foot the folds had previously hidden.

"Arnacin," he gasped, shoving open the other side to reveal the rest of a green cloak that someone had carefully positioned over the opening. Shoving both hands in, the knight found shoulders and gently pulled the captive out. Arnacin barely stirred beneath his hands, yet he breathed, his ribs rising and falling.

Quickly unbinding the islander, Hadwin commanded the other knight, standing there in shock, "Bring some water. Hurry!"

In the ensuing silence, he examined the islander as best as his limited medical knowledge allowed. Whoever had bound their captive had kept the ropes loose enough to prevent any harm to feet or hands, but other than that, the slightly stale scent of alcohol, and the perspiration that was likely due to the tight space, Hadwin could tell nothing more about Arnacin's health.

A scuffle broke out at the door suddenly. Looking up, Hadwin saw three of the knights enter with a small, struggling man in their midst. "He started to board until he saw us," a knight explained. "We felt it odd enough to give chase."

"What do you know?" Hadwin barked, still cradling Arnacin.

"Nothing, nothing!" the man protested.

"What's Arnacin doing here?"

With a sudden breakdown, the man exclaimed, "I couldn't do it! I couldn't!"

"Do what?"

Taken aback, the man fumbled for words. "Kill him, like the king ordered."

"What!"

"The k–"

"Never mind. What did you do to him?"

"He'll wake any moment now, Sir. I was coming to give him his nightly dose. Don't harm me! I'm loyal to the king, I swear!"

Feeling Arnacin shift in his arms, Hadwin looked down to see unfocused eyes opening. Without needing to be asked, the knight who had left to retrieve water passed over a flask, yet the islander jerked away. "Arnacin, it's alright."

"Hadwin?" the islander moaned. Then, as his eyes focused, "Why are we on my ship?"

"You were reported to have deserted. The king asked me to search your ship for evidence."

Arnacin's gaze flicked to the open drawer and the book still sitting atop it. Instantly, all color washed from his face and, shakily pushing himself to his feet, he breathed, "Out. Take your men, yourself, and everyone else off my ship."

Shocked, Hadwin protested, "Arnacin! I promise, we only did it out of worry for you. "

"I know. Now leave."

"We'll leave," Hadwin sighed, pushing himself to his feet. "Just come with us." Turning to the knights as Arnacin shut his drawer–the book simply disappeared–Hadwin gestured them out. "We'll take the suspect to the king. He can figure this mess out."

Once at the bottom of the ramp, he looked back to see that Arnacin was leaning on the rail panting, his face flushed. "Are you alright?"

With a slight smile, the islander gasped, "It's just dehydration."

"It has been five days since anyone last saw you," Hadwin said, pulling the islander's arm over his shoulders. Arnacin did not comment and he softly asked, "What are you protecting, if I may ask?"

"Our freedom, Hadwin. My worst nightmare is that my home will know the natives' pain. No kingdom must ever know where Enchantress Island lies."

Hadwin only nodded.

"So you just believe anyone who forges the king's command?" Miro said after the story had unfolded.

Before him, the culprit quivered. "Please, Sire... He showed me the royal seal."

"What!" Miro exclaimed as everyone else in the room—Memphis, Arnacin, Hadwin and the rest of Tarmlin's knights—stiffened.

Shakily, the culprit pulled out a piece of parchment bearing Mira's royal seal.

Miro's face turned white in fury. "Who gave that to you?"

"M-Mulch, the vineyard owner."

"Bring him here now!"

"He didn't forge it!" Arnacin interjected, glancing toward Memphis. "He can't have. It was an inside job. The kidnappers knew too much about my injury for it not to be."

"I don't care who it was! I will discover who dares if I must search the whole city and castle combined!"

"Your Majesty," Arnacin pleaded, still watching Memphis. "Don't follow the trail given. The culprit obviously has good contacts who will warn him if you start closing in and your trail will end with witnesses' murders."

"If I must hang the entire city, I will find the culprit. This outrage won't be ignored."

"Your Majesty, please," Arnacin protested. Knights and culprit alike paled at the king's threat. Memphis, however, remained impassive. "Do you not know how that will harm your kingdom? Your people need to feel safe under you. The natives don't, which is why you're at war. Don't lose face with your own people."

For a moment, silence hung in the air like an executioner's axe and it seemed that the room had emptied, save for those two actors. Then, the king sighed, "I can't let the forging of my command stand, Arnacin. It must be dealt with or it will happen again."

"I know. So allow me to do it my way. I might find more direct ways." He saw Memphis's eyes narrow and continued, "You'll never find the culprit by arresting the general populace."

"And how would you accomplish that?"

"I'll find a way–I promise."

Finally, Miro dipped his chin. To the culprit standing there, he said, "You may go home once you hand over that seal. Say nothing of what's happened."

Nodding hastily in relief, the man slapped the parchment into Hadwin's hand and bolted from the room.

"If you could learn some wisdom, Arnacin, you might make some progress, as this has proved," Hadwin commented as they left the great hall together.

"Wisdom, you say," Arnacin snorted. "Your king could do with learning a little selflessness. He's sure everything that happens is due to him and that everything that could happen will affect him."

Smiling, Hadwin shrugged, "Somewhat, that is the truth of kingship." He laughed as Arnacin emitted a growling sigh.

"You know exactly what I meant."

"That he's a little more pigheaded than he needs to be? Perhaps, but you are not easy to put up with as soon as you hold opposing beliefs. You have to admit that."

"Little more pigheaded," the islander repeated in sarcastic resignation. "Little Pighead could go on his door."

"It should go on yours," Hadwin returned, to both their laughter. "I'm glad we found you," he admitted.

Despite his earnest search for the forger, Arnacin met dead ends. Suspecting that one or more of the councilors had commanded the crime, he discovered nothing to prove which one, if any. The only information that Valoretta could provide was that Memphis had pushed the most in support of the theory of Arnacin's desertion, but as they both knew, he would have done so anyway.

Meanwhile, no sign of Cornyo surfaced and Cestmir mostly kept further native attacks away from inhabited areas. Arnacin wondered if the enemy was allowing the duke's success.

Then, on a rainy day two months after his disappearance, Arnacin slipped out onto a balcony despite the damp cold that seeped through his skin. The wind was so fierce of late it pummeled water droplets into everyone's faces, hoods or no. After yet another debate with the unyielding king, his brewing temper delighted in the harshness of the wind and rain that beat his cloak into his face and legs.

His brooding changed to numbness as he spotted Cestmir's troops pouring through the gates—surrounding a captive. Quickly, the islander stepped back beneath the archway, hoping no one had seen him, while his heart suddenly burned. Somehow, Cornyo had returned.

Sliding down against the wall, Arnacin closed his eyes.

After a few hours, the islander pushed himself to his feet, and turned down the corridor to the stairs that would take him to the lower floor, the guardroom of the dungeons below ground. He had always avoided it, trying to forget its existence, knowing that it was all too likely that he would be hauled there himself any moment. For Cornyo, however, he would risk it.

The guards in the room, however, halted him before he could even finish descending the steps. "Arnacin of Enchantress Island," one guard called. "We know why you're here, and we've been given strict orders that you are not allowed. We have also been told to arrest you as well if you don't turn back up those stairs."

For a long moment, the islander stayed in place, halfway between one step and the next, glaring at the guards. Yet they did not back down from their position, waiting for his decision, their weapons pointed toward him, and their expressions void of compassion.

At last, Arnacin pulled his cloak around him like some dark bat, around the cold that had seeped up his spine, and returned back up the stairs until he was out of sight. Once the door had been lost to view around a curve, he charged up the steps three at a time until he reached windowed corridors.

There, he let his body sag against the wall as his heart rate settled, both his anger and fear dissipating.

Yes, he knew who had given the orders to keep Cornyo and himself apart—Duke Cestmir. Duke Cestmir who thought Arnacin would fuel Cornyo's rebellion, if not help him escape. Little did he know that nothing would shake the knight's loyalty to Mira, nor add to his stubbornness. Helping him escape was equally impossible. Even without guards, Cornyo would never run.

No, the only thing the duke had denied was Arnacin's earnest apology. Little good it would have done anyway.

Sighing, he pushed himself off the wall, heading toward the steps that would take him to his room. Before he had gone five paces, he heard the light footsteps of a child approaching.

"Arnacin." The soft call made him turn. Duke Cestmir's oldest son walked toward him, a plea written in his young eyes. "The duke… You know Cornyo, you must know what… Talk to His Grace, please. He hasn't moved since his discussion with Miro and, Arnacin…" His voice trembled, "I have never seen tears on his cheeks before. I'm afraid…"

Sighing, the islander said, "Show me where he is." He doubted he could be any help at all considering how badly his last meeting with Cestmir had ended, but he could not bear to say so while held by that gaze.

The duke stood alone in a passage off the great hall, staring out of the blackened windows, even though nothing but the rain still streaming down them could be seen by then. After waving the boy away, Arnacin whispered, "Your Grace."

The only answer at first was the lowering of the duke's head in anger. Without turning around to meet the islander, he whispered, voice cracking with grief, "You have forced us all to be traitors, boy. Cornyo chose to betray his king, and I was forced to betray my men, to ask them to attack, arrest and drag a friend to the capitol. I am forced to see him hanged, to testify against him, else I also betray my king and country. Is that the reward he is given for victory? For rescuing our own, he must perish at his own people's hands." Whirling, Cestmir growled, "And who do we have to thank for this betrayal that tears us to shreds by our own hands?"

Arnacin said nothing, his own gaze locked on the windows. The rain pouring down them gave the illusion of them crying, but their distress was less painful than sight of the tears streaming down the noble's cheeks.

He knew there was nothing he could say to soothe Cestmir's pain. He *had* betrayed Cornyo, and they both knew it.

"What good have you ever brought us, Arnacin of Enchantress Island? Are we any closer to the end of this hell-driven war? Not since the day you arrived. You have achieved rather the opposite." The duke was making no effort to retain his usual placidity.

Finally meeting the pain etched into Cestmir's face, the islander whispered, "Those are perhaps the most honest words a noble has ever spoken."

Fury turned the duke's face red and his hand flew to the sword at his side as he snapped, "Go! Go before I take your head off."

With a lamenting bow, Arnacin turned away. Yet as he left, those words burning in his heart, the duke added, "And I hope never to see your horrible black head again!"

That was not to be the end of the islander's misery. Around midnight, he still sat on the edge of his bed, staring blindly at the floor while the candle burned to nothing on the bedside table. Only the knock on his door roused him and, fully dressed as he remained, he simply pattered softly across the floor.

"Sara," he gasped upon opening the door. Valoretta's nurse stood there, nervous agitation on her face. Pressing her finger to her lips, she gestured for him to follow. Choosing to trust her, the islander obeyed.

She led him straight to the door leading to the royal accommodations of the castle. There, Arnacin froze. Pushing him forward, Sara breathed, "The king requests your presence. Come, we cannot be seen here."

Still, Arnacin remained where he was. "It's pain of death past these doors for–"

"Yes, hush. That is why we cannot be seen. Hurry." Hoping the nurse did not actually plan his death, the islander followed her, cringing as the doors slammed shut behind him. Instantly, the corridors changed. The floors were covered down the middle by a long carpet, the edges tiled with something shiny, now glittering in the low firelight from the hidden torch bowls cut along the corridor's walls.

Noticing that the islander had again halted in fear as he looked around, the nurse sighed, stepping back toward him to pluck impatiently at his sleeve. When he finally moved, she strode off toward the withdrawing room, where Miro stood staring into the fire blazing in its hearth. Nodding to the king, the nurse moved into the shadows where Valoretta sat, the only other occupant of the room.

"Close the door, Arnacin," Miro commanded without turning from the fire. When the soft click of the latch sounded, he asked, "Is this what you wished, Arnacin? The complete disregard of Mira? It was admitted that you told your troop to ignore orders. Is that true?"

"You ask as if I have betrayed Mira," Arnacin whispered.

Whirling, Miro stormed, "You have betrayed Mira! You've charged her king with incompetence, convinced all you could of that lie, stolen the imaginations of the people, and used Mira's mercy to do so! Is that not a traitor?"

Dropping his gaze to the polished wood under his feet, Arnacin agreed, "I would consider that a traitor, if it were true."

"If? I say there is no *if*, Arnacin, son of Bozzic. Did you or did you not tell your troop to disobey orders?"

Feeling as if it was pried out of his throat, the islander confessed, "I told them there is no such thing as a god-king, that there is a right and wrong, an honor and, sometimes, any man's commands can fail, can go against that justice, righteousness or honor. I said that, even more important than any king's law, is righteousness, and that *all* things must be tested against it–that they must think for themselves and ask themselves what is important to them. That is what I said... allowing them to decide for themselves what was right before I took them into the mountains."

Darkly, Miro demanded, "Do you not even feel sorry?"

"Sorry, Your Majesty?" Arnacin softly repeated. "Yes, I am sorry–sorry I ever had to ask myself what was right or not–sorry that to accomplish what I felt was ultimately right, I committed other wrongs. Should I have done differently, however, I would've murdered the natives without cause, and if I couldn't do that and withdrew my agreement to Mira, I would have betrayed its people. I still deem the actions I took as those with the least evil, but I *am* sorry." Looking down as his voice cracked, he added, "Sorry that lives ever weighed so heavily on my choices. And I don't know why–since you find me so destructive–I don't know why you ever asked it of me."

Fire popped in the silence, but as he looked back up to meet the king's eyes, Miro hastily turned away.

"Why?" the islander breathed, pleadingly.

Clearing his throat, the king asked, "Whatever I decide for the knight, you realize you must witness it, and that whatever sentence he is given, you are responsible for all of it."

"If I ever thought otherwise, I have been firmly corrected many times in these past months," Arnacin whispered dully.

Nodding, the king dismissed him. However, the islander did not return to his room that night. Despite the dark and the rain and howling wind lurching the vessel about, Arnacin left for his ship.

Although Valoretta kept silent for some time the next day, she watched Arnacin's restlessness with concern as he walked slowly up and down their library row from one end of the shelves to another.

Finally, however, the princess sighed. "Is this to be your new habit, Arnacin? For months, I've concerned myself over how such an active person as yourself would stand frozen still for hours at a time, staring out some window or over some view, and now you've been pacing since I entered."

Halting, the islander drew in a shaky breath. "I can't avoid the truth and I was tired of staying still."

"What truth are you avoiding?"

"I must take whatever punishment Miro intends for Cornyo," Arnacin stated, as if merely a fact.

For a long moment, the princess remained dumbstruck while, from a distant past, the islander's words rang in her memory: *That's shifting responsibility, and it's cowardice, pure cowardice. If someone under your charge does something wrong, you must pay the penalty, and you alone.*

Eventually, she breathed, "I thought you wished to go home."

Kneeling before her in earnestness, Arnacin softly admitted, "Valoretta, surely you know there is nothing I want more. If I could..." He hesitated, his gaze lowering, yet she did not dare interrupt, yearning for his heart to stay open.

After a moment, he spoke, visibly pained. "I want nothing more than to sit among sheep, talking and, yes, competing with Charlotte again. I want to be there when she lets go of her bitterness and marries. I want to be at her wedding. I want to be there when... when she wickedly announces a first child. I want to play with William, to be there to teach him how to craft, care for, and use a bow when he is old enough. I even want to be there as Mother grows old. I want to go home."

Slowly taking the princess' hand in his to arrest her gaze, Arnacin finished, "But no matter how much I yearn for all that... no matter how strong that wish is, I cannot betray Cornyo. They're all correct, whether the knight is under my command or no. I am responsible, for in this, he is my knight. If he must perish, so must I."

Running her finger along the hand in hers, Valoretta whispered, "I once grew upset because I thought a boy was insisting another should have done what he himself would never do. I almost wish my anger then was justified, but as I knew long ago, there is no other Arnacin–Arnacin of Enchantress Island."

He simply bowed his head under the intense burden only he could fully know and, leaning forward, the princess planted a kiss on top of those black curls. For the sake of all honor, she could not stop him.

Chapter 19

Darien

For some reason, Miro waited another day before calling together all those needed for a Miran trial. Since it was to be in the morning, Sara woke her charge extra early for her customary yanking of the princess' hair. For once, the nurse had a very still, quiet and cooperative subject and, pausing in concern, she asked, "Are you well, Valoretta?"

She had to repeat the name in growing alarm before the princess sighed, "Yes, I'm well, although perhaps I shall never be again."

"Tsk, child," Sara chided, resuming her work on the auburn stands. "How could this trial ever affect your future health? Stay still," she commanded as Valoretta's head turned to cast the nurse a sarcastic gaze.

"In the first place, Sara–as you well know–this is a trial of a beloved Miran knight. In the second place, he is charged for treason simply because he loved those innocents more than..." She could not finish with the "we" that wished to come forth.

Instead, as she dropped off, Sara nodded as if knowing her thoughts, and accusingly supplied, "More than his king."

Yanking her hair away from the nurse's grasp, Valoretta snapped, "I'll do that myself, thank you very much."

Sighing, the nurse repeated, as she had so often before, "You can't be expected to do your own hair with any decency. You'll look like a street rat before you're done."

And so, the oft-reiterated debate began, ending of course with Sara victorious and Valoretta shipped out to her father in all her sternest regalia.

Not long after that, the princess followed her father into the throne room in the long, official procession dictated by the trial. Valoretta, Arnacin and Memphis took their places directly behind Miro, the queen after them, and then the other councilors and Sara.

The accused, Cestmir and others of the duke's men already stood present in the great hall. None of them looked happy. Cestmir glared outright, his gaze directed toward Arnacin, while Sir Cornyo himself simply looked as one resigned to his own death.

For his own part, Arnacin looked at none of them, his gaze fixed on the floor. Only Valoretta could guess why, as she glanced at him in shared pain.

For a long moment, Miro only sat on his throne, his laced fingers resting on his chin as he contemplated the culprit. Then, softly he asked, "Sir Cornyo, what have you done?"

Running his fingers along the chain connecting his manacled wrists together, the knight did not look up as he whispered, "I rescued the Miran captives, Sire."

"How did you accomplish this?"

Slowly, Cornyo looked up to face his king. A second passed in silence and then he cleared his throat. "I apologize, if I do not answer all your questions, Sire. I refuse to lie to you, but there are some things of which I cannot speak."

Miro's thumbs tapped briefly together and Valoretta stole a glance at Arnacin. He was still studying the floor beneath his feet.

"If it's the difference between your life and death, would you speak?" the king asked.

Cornyo miserably shook his head.

"The captives had been taken into the mountains?" A nod. "Areas of which you already knew?" No response.

After another moment of silent contemplation, Miro asked, "Did you speak to anyone here before you left, hinting at your plans?"

"Arnacin, Sire."

The islander did not flinch at the inclusion of his name. If he had been guilty, it was a good show of a clear conscience, except that he was still not watching.

"And what did he say?"

Cornyo's gaze flicked briefly toward the islander as he whispered, "He told me my heart was ruling my head, and that you were right. The captives were lost."

Even sitting with only a partial view of the king's face, Valoretta caught his lips' brief twitch of amusement.

"Did you suggest to him, or anyone else, your actual plans?" It was obvious Miro wanted to know if he could wring the information out of someone else.

"No, Sire. I made them as I went."

"As ever, impulsive," someone muttered in the group of Cestmir's men.

As if knowing he would receive nothing more from the culprit, the king looked to Cestmir. "Where did you find him, Duke?"

"Winliy, Sire, halfway to the capital already."

"Was there anyone with him?"

"Only the Mirans that had been taken captive."

"Did you ask them if they had more than one rescuer?"

"They all said Cornyo was alone. Of course, they also seemed unable to remember much of the journey back."

Cornyo's gaze had fallen back to the floor, revealing nothing.

"Did you have trouble arresting him?"

"No, Sire." Cestmir's words were a sigh then, as if that truth added to his sense of betrayal. "He surrendered to us willingly, and there were no escape attempts on the way here."

"Very well," Miro said with a nod. "Would any of your men like to add anything?"

Soft whispers from the councilors carried in the long following silence to where Valoretta stood nearby. The condemnation they uttered made her chest tighten with agony, and she again glanced at Arnacin wondering when he would act, knowing he would, and wishing he would quail.

Finally, it seemed the king had made his decision. Nodding to himself, he stated, "Sir Cornyo, I would give you the chance to admit your transgressions and swear again your utmost loyalty, but I know enough of the source of your choices to know that you will instead choose death rather than to consider your actions wrong. So be it–"

"Your Majesty." The soft, yet not whispered, voice cut into the king's words, triggering an audible gasp around the room.

Leaning back in his throne, Miro acknowledged the voice, with a sigh. "Arnacin."

Valoretta paled as the islander stepped around the throne to face the king. "You know the source, you say. Is not that source the truly guilty one? Why speak to the foam lying on the shore after the ocean has withdrawn? I cannot be the one to say Cornyo is innocent–he would testify against himself if you asked that question of him–yet the crime he has committed is no worse than mine. It is far less, in fact. If you are to execute anyone, Your Majesty, I ask..." Slowly, as if fighting some part of himself, the islander bowed to one knee, finishing, "I beg that it be me. I am the instigator and, in this, the commander of his recent action. Should you still think his action worthy of death, at least make me share it, for my honor."

As he spoke, a spell of silence had fallen over the hall, but when he finished, Cornyo gasped, "Arnacin, you can't. You're guiltless. Sire, he tried to dissuade m–"

He fell silent as Cestmir grabbed his arm in wordless warning, yet Miro did not even appear to have heard, staring at the islander without movement.

In the ensuing silence, Memphis whispered, "He is right, Sire. You judge the snake's coils for strangling someone, not the serpent himself."

Valoretta, close enough to hear, could have run him through, but she dared not say anything. This was a battle the king had to fight alone, yet she feared that its end would result in Arnacin's as well.

A moment passed and then Miro's fingers twitched, as if he would have reached out to run them down the islander's cheek, but restrained himself. Instead, he stated, "I must be the judge of that, Arnacin. You, unlike Sir Cornyo, are not Miran. Be that as it may, I am fully aware of your part in it." Looking up toward Cornyo, he declared, "Sir Knight, you are no longer a knight of Mira. That title and property are hereby taken from you. I also banish you from Mira forever. You have until dawn tomorrow to find passage, bid farewell to all you would, and leave. Take any family willing to go, but it is for life and those who accompany you must know they also share your exile. Should you ever return, you will not see another day. So I have decided. As for you, Arnacin," he added, looking back down at the islander, "I will content myself knowing that you are fully aware of your responsibility, that it was Arnacin of Enchantress Island who drove Cornyo from his home forever. That I deem punishment enough."

Breath returned to Valoretta and she was glad in that moment that Arnacin did not look up, for she was sure that her love was cascading from her eyes like a waterfall.

As if it had been prearranged, Arnacin met Cornyo and the duke in the same corridor where the islander had met the knight two months before. There, islander and former knight embraced, neither able to find the words to express themselves.

It was Cestmir who ended the silence as the two broke apart. "I apologize, Arnacin. It was most unfair to so judge you."

"No," the islander whispered. "You were right. I've only brought ruin to Mira." Raising his gaze to the exiled knight once again, Arnacin added, "I'm sorry, Cornyo."

Shaking his head in denial, the former knight stated, "Don't feel guilty, Arnacin. I've been handed wings. The war is no longer any concern of mine. I can start a real life... and you've given it to me, Arnacin. You've shown me what it means to live in the first place."

"Know this, Arnacin," Cestmir added as he turned away, leaving them to their farewells. "You proved you are a man, today. A real one." He did not give the islander a chance to reply to that statement, but his gratitude and the greater shame it brought left no words anyway.

Turning back to the former knight, Arnacin simply whispered, "Go on, Cornyo. You have much to do before you leave, I know."

Clasping the islander once more, Cornyo whispered, "Good-bye, Arnacin of Enchantress Island. I hope we will meet on some other shore, when your mission is done here, although I do not expect it. Sadly, the world is very vast indeed and, if I know you, you'll make a beeline for Enchantress Island when given your freedom."

Arnacin did not bother to deny it, but as the former knight turned to leave, the islander stopped him. "Cornyo, how did you do it? You never answered Miro."

Grinning slightly, Cornyo teased, "Oh, over a game of Molshunting, I'll tell you some day."

"I'm not going to ever play Molshunting with you, and you know it."

Laughing, the former knight conceded, "I wouldn't say because I had help. You trained us well, Arnacin, even when you intended no such thing. I hired one of our adopted natives. He had distant family among those captives, and so he was honor-bound to rescue them. He also spoke his native language and was wise in the ways of tracking. Of course, he will never share his knowledge since that would be a betrayal of his people, but he considered this more a matter of protecting their honor. As soon as we reached a settlement safely, I told him to escape. Mira knows nothing of his mutiny and I promised him that they never shall."

"They never shall," Arnacin promised.

While the islander and Cornyo conversed thus, Darien paced back and forth before his fellow councilor, fuming, "*For his honor.* The nerve of that wretch from the sea! As if anyone as insane as he is, is capable of possessing honor."

"Insane?" the councilor's closest companion, Erlund, inquired.

"Yes, insane! Take note of how he fights battles. While anyone with any mind at all goes off to bring peace through killing mortal beings, Arnacin of Enchantress Island goes to kill gods." Growling, Darien exclaimed, "As far as the enemies themselves, oh no, he *protects* them, *sides* with them even. If Miro possessed any sense, he would have hanged that traitor long ago."

"No one has any sense in regard to him," Erlund hissed. "He's taken over everything." Lowering his voice, Erlund stated, "It's high time we did something about him."

"That was never in question," the older councilor snapped. "It's what we do. I already offered him the kingdom." Huffing, he sighed in pleased imaginings, "How Miro would have murdered him had he agreed–'for loyalty and honor,' of course."

"Do you think he saw through you?"

"Ha, he thought I was making a play for the throne myself. He never dreamed of what I truly intended."

Sighing, Erlund concluded, "Well, there's no use crying over dry wells."

"Cornyo," Darien suddenly growled, causing his companion to pause. "That knight should be dead. Very well, the islander can convince the king to sway as he wishes. So can I."

"What are you thinking?"

"He and his family will be found dead in the streets tomorrow."

"How are you going to achieve that?"

"Armed villagers will do the deed." Darien smiled malevolently.

"They'll never do that."

"They will obey their king's orders."

"What?" Erlund exclaimed. "If you are intending to forge the king's command–"

"The king will never know. Random men–who disappear. All Miro will know is that the exiled are dead, that men are angry at his lack of authority. During the time of mourning, we can convince him of how easily he was manipulated in the first place. At the least, if we can't see the wretch of an islander executed, we can bring an end to all his successes."

A scattering of soot into the cold fireplace caused them both to freeze. "Who's there?" Erlund squeaked. No answer followed, but he panicked. "What if that was one of the chimney sweeps? What if he overheard you?"

Hissing, Darien stated, "No lowly servant can accuse any of the king's councilors. He would look like a conspirator himself."

Quaking, the younger councilor persisted, "All the same, I'm not helping. I'm not being tarred and hanged, thank you."

"Fine, remain a coward. Something must be done and, if I'm the only one with enough backbone to do it, then so be it."

Had someone asked what made Arnacin so miserable in that moment, even he could have found no real answer, and if they asked if he had actually wished to hang, he knew he might have said "yes" in the end. For indeed, there was a part of him that wished to quit, to forever end the fear that the war would drag on indefinitely, that all his plans and moves were and would remain futile. Miro's wisdom, or the islander's honor, had narrowly avoided splitting the kingdom internally. Should the fighting continue, what else might happen?

Practicality, usable arm or no, told the islander that he would never see home again, not unless he first betrayed all he knew of himself and life. It was that part which simply wished for death, which begged for it. And so, beginning to feel horribly caged, he took a walk beyond the city's grounds, where his only companions were the blades of grass protruding out of the muddy puddles that blanketed the ground. There, he let his thoughts seep into the blankness of the squelching and splashing of his booted feet. Beyond his sight, the ocean roared and the crash of waves battling rock felt pleasurably catastrophic to his tormented heart.

He had not gone far, however, when hurried splashing footsteps sounded behind him. Yanking his blade out, he whirled. Running toward him came a boy, every inch of him smeared in what Arnacin took to be charcoal.

"Arnacin of Enchantress Island," the boy panted, causing the islander to take a wary step backward.

"You apparently know who I am."

"Never mind that," the stranger gasped, halting before Arnacin and placing his hands on his knees as he fought to regain his breath. "I was sweeping a chimney..."

Looking again at the black streaks covering the boy, the islander nodded, "That much is certain."

"Listen," the boy snapped. "They're plotting against you!"

"They've been doing that since I arrived," Arnacin said, immediately turning away in bitterness.

"Not like this. I was up the chimney and heard mutinous-sounding whispers, so I stopped and listened. They said this and that, always with you as the subject of their disgust, but then one says that they can't let you win, and they'll forge an order of the king's to murder those leaving tonight."

His attention captured, Arnacin demanded, "Who would be fool enough again?"

"For ambition, almost anyone, I suppose, but I can't remember that they said anyone's name."

"*Anything* that would tell me who purposes such a crime."

"Um... The main person pushing for it said he offered you kingship and that you refused. He said it like he had been planning to turn you in as an assassin the minute you agreed."

It took Arnacin not a minute to drag the memory forth. Hissing softly, he pushed past the boy.

"Are you going to tell the king?"

Whirling back, the islander asked, "Tell him what? Without any evidence, it's too high a charge for anyone to believe."

"I told you because I thought you would believe me, no matter what my position. Doesn't the king trust you enough?"

"In what, Chimney Sweep? Against his councilors? They rule, and I have too much to gain by accusing them."

"What do you plan on doing, then?"

Although he was tempted to say, "Kill those given such orders," he knew it was a futile move. Despite the careful hours the swordmaster had spent training strength back into the islander's arm, he still could not keep up with an ambush.

After a moment, he whispered, "I don't know."

"May I suggest something?"

"Anything you like."

"Speak to the king. Find some way he cannot doubt you."

Arnacin bowed in answer, causing a red hue to shine even under the boy's blackened skin. Smiling slightly, the islander strode back to the castle.

After the king had dismissed everyone but Memphis, he sat there, watching the men file out. Long after they were gone, he still sat there, contemplating his decision.

Cornyo, one of Mira's most steadfastly loyal knights had rebelled against his country. Yes, he had admitted to doing it because of a lady, and for love of Mira itself, but the fact remained that before Arnacin appeared, not even those things could have made him.

As wrath bubbled inside Miro, he shot to his feet and stormed over to the windows. It was obvious, no matter what anyone said, that Cornyo had help in his rescue, and it was not the islander. While Cornyo himself swore that was not the case, if it was, Arnacin himself would have admitted it.

No, there had been someone else–someone Cornyo had carefully kept secret even from those he was rescuing. Miro doubted even torture would pull it from the man. Considering how white he had been during his interrogation in the cells, he had expected it, but the king was convinced that torture would yield nothing, and would be a poor reward indeed for their hero.

"Sire," Memphis finally commented from behind the king, "I fear how Cornyo will inspire the next hothead. He did not seem to take his punishment as he should have and that is almost as bad as receiving none."

Without even turning away from his view by the window, Miro muttered, "Are you daring to question my judgment, Memphis?"

"By no means, Sire," the councilor puffed, yet just as he was about to finish his assurances, one of the door guards announced, "Arnacin of Enchantress Island, Your Majesty."

Considering how the islander entered before the guard finished announcing him, the king pictured the herald spotting the islander's determined stride and quickly blurting his words out before Arnacin could fully pass him.

Smiling slightly, Miro inquired, "And did you also come to question my judgment, Arnacin, son of Bozzic?"

Only a sharp gaze would have spotted the brief glance Arnacin threw in Memphis's direction, as if confirming the question's origins. Then he replied, "In such circumstance, I can hardly question them. No, Your Majesty. There is a rumor..."

This time, no one could have missed the look toward Memphis in the hesitant pause that followed.

"What type of rumor, Arnacin? There are many for me to choose from should you not finish."

Turning back to the king, the islander dipped his chin. "A rumor for your ears alone, Your Majesty."

"And what ears are you concerned about?" Miro pressed.

Something hostile flashed in the islander's gaze as it again flicked in Memphis's direction.

Guessing some of the unsaid words, the king sighed, "If this rumor is of such importance, Arnacin, it is likely that Memphis shall hear of it before long."

A long silence followed, in which the king felt entirely forgotten as an invisible duel appeared to transpire between his high councilor and his war councilor. To Miro's surprise, it was the islander who backed down, whispering, "It is my understanding that someone will forge your command to gain their means. Should word of the rumor leak outside your hearing, I fear that any possibility of truth in said rumor will end, and the culprit will therefore hide until another chance for evil."

Suspiciously, Miro warned, "I will not have you suggesting that Memphis is plotting against Mira, and should that not be the aim of your hints, I see no reason to fear his ears and mouth."

For a long moment, Arnacin stood there, and then bowing, he whispered, "Your Majesty."

With that, he departed, leaving Miro with the unsettled feeling that he was ignoring a warning of imminent danger.

After another five minutes of silence, the king excused his high councilor while he remained in the great hall to mull over his own fears and the many pitfalls that awaited him should he make the wrong choices. Hardly had the councilor left, however, before a dark shape slid soundlessly into the room from a side door, causing the king to whirl in alarm.

Coming face-to-face with Arnacin, Miro breathed, "What happened to the guard?"

"He let me in," the islander whispered, shortening the space between them. "Your Majesty," he added in deadly seriousness, "I do not suspect Memphis of anything at this time, yet I do believe he and the other councilors... are close, that it is common for them to share their complaints, if nothing else."

"Your persistence, Arnacin," Miro huffed, "is tiring. Very well, what rumor have you heard?"

"Someone attempts to order Cornyo's assassination before his departure, along with anyone going with him. I don't know for certain if it's true or not, but if it is true, I wish not only to stop it, but also to catch the culprit. Will you give me the authority to command a detachment of guards tonight in secret to protect the exiles?"

Trying not to humiliate the islander by glancing at his shoulder, Miro asked, "You anticipate an attack and hope to find the culprit thereby?" At the slight nod, he demanded, "What would any fool gain by forging my command in this, outside of death? It is an absurd rumor, whatever the case."

"It is," Arnacin agreed, looking past the king's shoulder to the sky outside. "But I'm not willing to risk Cornyo's life by ignoring it."

Asking himself the question the islander had left unspoken, the king sized the islander up.

"There are times, Arnacin," he whispered, "that I wonder why I feel certain of your honesty." As the islander's gaze flew to meet his, he continued, "Do you wish to know what I am thinking? As you wish. I am wondering what you could achieve by making the whole thing up and then saying tomorrow that, unfortunately, no attack came. That is what I am thinking."

Pride flashed in Arnacin's dark eyes, yet he made no comment.

Submitting, the king exhaled, "Take your command, Arnacin. I cannot think of anything you could gain."

Coolly inclining his head, the islander strode back out. Watching him, Miro called forth the guard responsible for allowing Arnacin entrance in the first place. The islander had indeed stolen Mira's heart and mind, but there was a limit.

Through inconspicuous messengers, Arnacin warned Cornyo of the impending danger and asked him if he had yet found a ship willing to take him. The answer returned that one captain had agreed–albeit with some complaint–to set sail just before dawn, leaving the former knight with as much time as possible.

The islander's greatest fear was that an attack would push them beyond the rising of the sun, and he could not predict Miro's decision if Cornyo pushed such a line.

With no control over that matter, however, the islander spent the day gathering any of his old command currently in the capitol, passing word from one to the next to meet him outside Gagandep's home as the moon conquered the sun. While they continued to inform each other, the islander sat with the master swordsman to consult him regarding the state of his shoulder.

"Leave it to them, boy," the master swordsman advocated. "You are not capable of handling the force of anything striking your blade. If you have any desire to go home, you'll give your men your orders and leave the rest to them. That is my advice."

After a moment of staring at the tufts of grass peeping up from between the courtyard's flagstones, Arnacin sighed. "If not for the fact that it is so necessary for them to remain out of sight and hearing, I would listen. As it is, I feel I cannot, and you know it. I asked you for advice about ways I could avoid the actual conflict while still being present. Please be so kind as to provide it."

Meeting him full in the face, the master swordsman growled, "I have answered you, boy. You are known too well on Mira. Should you be there at all, there will be no avoiding the fray and you will forever ruin what little chance your muscles still have of any sort of recovery. It's too much for them."

"We've been working all winter," Arnacin exclaimed in frustration.

"Impatient boy," the swordmaster warned. "What type of war veteran are you?"

"I hardly consider eight months of waiting a lack of patience," the islander reminded him, "and under current circumstances, someone's life is in peril."

Sighing, the master swordsman pushed himself to his foot. "They can easily protect him from death, boy. Let your vengeance rest this once." So saying, he hobbled away on his peg leg.

Watching him leave, Arnacin remained sitting in thought... Was it vengeance to wish Darien brought to justice? Indeed, could it be worse than vengeance? Could it be a manipulative drive to best an opponent in any way possible?

There were no answers forthcoming.

Gagandep's house was a likely place for them to meet without suspicion, due to many of the men's friendship with the family through Firth. Most on Mira did not even realize Firth was no longer on Mira, and the men trickled there without alerting anyone.

Shortly before the ship's scheduled departure in the wee hours of the morning, Arnacin led his men from Gagandep's house. The troop walked along a road parallel to the one Cornyo and his lady had taken, tracking the pair by sound alone.

It was a strain for Arnacin to listen for an ambush above the soft scuffle of his men's cloth-muffled feet and the noise of his own pounding heart. Regardless, he somehow heard it—the hurried sound of feet on the adjoining street, the hiss of Cornyo's blade as it was drawn, and the cry from the former knight's new betrothed.

Staying behind, however much he hated so doing, Arnacin silently ordered his troop to engage the attackers. Pulling his hood closer about his face, the islander slipped into the shadows next to one house, where he could watch the desperate skirmish ensuing in the street. From where he stood, he could not tell one man from the next and knew only that the lady stood behind defenders.

As shouts of alarm rose from the buildings around them and men dashed out ready to defend their homes if need be, the ambushers quickly broke away, disappearing around corners as swiftly as possible.

The city men dashed off in pursuit and the islander sent a few of his own to help, keeping the rest with him until the ship departed with its passengers.

No bodies lay upon the ground in the aftermath, but Arnacin did not pause for details as he hurried the group down to the harbor. There, sailors had already clambered aboard one ship, and stopping below it, Arnacin pushed Cornyo in the direction of the waiting gangplank. Cornyo did not budge at first. Looking the islander in the face, he whispered, "Thank you, Arnacin. Th–"

"Just go, or the ship will leave without you," Arnacin sighed, secretly fearing another attack should they remain too long. They had their evidence, and it had been too easy for his liking.

Still standing there, the former knight finally asked in a hurry, as if his life depended on it, "Arnacin, will you promise me... us... something?"

"What, Cornyo?" the islander exhaled in concerned frustration.

"If ever Miro offers you the throne–"

"Miro will never–"

"No, listen. You are a terrible general. You are a terrible follower, period. You're so dogmatic in your view of right. You won't compromise anything, and while that makes you a lousy underling, it would be the best anyone could ever dream for in a king. Too many rulers are weakened by fear, but you, Arnacin, would always keep righteousness first. If Miro offers, take it. I will never know a truer king."

"I am promised elsewhere, Cornyo," Arnacin softly reminded him, as a means of avoiding the real issue. "Now go."

Sadly taking a step away, the former knight added, "As you wish, Arnacin of Enchantress Island. Mira's king you may never be–officially–but I will tell you now, in front of witnesses, I never knew a king until you came."

Taking his lady's hand, the former knight dashed up the gangplank as a sailor untied the ship. Dawn glowed red on the horizon as the sails disappeared beyond the sea gates, and Arnacin only turned away as those portals were hauled shut against the ocean with him inside.

As he headed back up the street with his remaining men, another approached, gasping, "Arnacin. We caught one of the attackers."

"Does he say anything?"

"He insists we have no right to capture him. We must be brigands acting against the king's orders."

"Indeed," the islander muttered with a grim smile. "We'll take him right to Miro then, but we must make sure no one sees us."

"How are we going to do that?"

"Easy, share your armor with him and hold a knife to his back." Arnacin's wicked smile must have been infectious as he saw it mirrored around him, and they followed the guard back to the captive.

Unfortunately, the captive had accepted the order by word of mouth, with only a brief glimpse of the royal seal. The seal, however, seemed to have disappeared, and his defense of his easy belief was that stranger orders had been given.

Once Arnacin was alone with the king, Miro turned to him. "This is the price of not executing everyone guilty of carrying out the last forged orders, Islander. Whoever did it before is bolder to try again. This time the payment must be made, *unless* you have actually found anything?"

Without moving, Arnacin met the king's furious gaze. Then, after a long moment, he whispered, "I have reason to believe that it's Darien, Your Majesty. I don't have the tangible proof you want–"

Miro's raised hand halted him. "How sure are you that you have the right man?"

"Fairly certain, Your Majesty."

"Very well, then. It is time to learn what an act can achieve."

"Darien," Miro snapped as all his councilors finished assembling.

"Yes, Sire?" the councilor asked, stepping forward. If he had suddenly realized the true nature of this abrupt trial, he did not reveal it.

Coldly, the king said, "It has come to my attention that you dared invent my orders for your own gain, not once, but twice." Before the councilor could speak, the king continued, "Do not bother to deny it. Its truth has already been testified to." He was of course, bluffing, yet the councilors hardly knew that. "Last month, you attempted to rid yourself of Arnacin by convincing Mira of his desertion, while you ordered his death in such way that no one could ever trace the long chain of rumors and orders back to you. Having succeeded in remaining undetected, you grew bolder and attempted it again, for a baser goal."

He waited, noticing the murderous looks thrown behind him, where he knew Arnacin stood undoubtedly looking as dark as ever.

"Testified, Sire?" Darien finally voiced. "A snake would testify as much to his own innocen–"

"Quiet! Dare you to assume Arnacin did the testifying?"

Panic began to form in Darien's gaze, which shot to the group of lower councilors. Reading it, the king nodded. "You need not concern yourself. He whom you confided in shall not escape justice either."

As he had wished, an instantaneous gasp came from the group.

"Sire, I had no part in it!" Erlund cried. "He did all the plotting! I simply listened."

"Silence, *traitor*," Darien snapped before the king could speak. The councilor's face had turned a deep red in the full realization of the inescapable doom before which he stood. Whether he knew the king had manipulated the whole trial or not did not matter. "You've done enough."

"Indeed he has," Miro agreed, fixing the condemned councilor with his icy glare. "You are granted one opportunity, Darien, to die like a man. Are you able to do so?"

Tossing his head back, the councilor retorted, "I need not submit to your standards of a man, O King–you who allow a boy to manipulate the whole kingdom to meet his demands. What are you but the largest puppet of the *foreigner*?"

Despite the growing coldness of the king's demeanor, he continued, "Had you even eyes, you would see it. Everyone here knows how 'your islander' dares insult you publicly, and you bow to his contempt like a puppy begging for his master's forgiveness after committing an unknown crime. At least I die with the knowledge that I am far more a man than any wretch present."

"For that, Councilor," Miro growled, "you will lose your tongue as well before your hanging."

Guards closed in around the councilor and, at the king's command, they seized the condemned man by the arms, pinning him. Yanking back his head by the hair, they cut out his tongue. The councilor screamed, a tortured gurgle from his blood-filled throat and, from behind him, Miro heard Queen Rosa whimper herself.

"Take him below and tar him," the king ordered, "After they are finished, you, Darien, will stay in the dungeons as you are until tomorrow, when your life shall be ended with the rope." Nodding to the guards, Miro bid them leave to depart with their captive.

For a second, Miro was silent as the doors closed behind Darien, and then he ordered Erlund forth. That councilor, however, only moaned as his colleagues shoved him before the throne. "Apparently there is little loyalty among you," Miro commented while the councilor hastily picked himself up and whirled to face the king.

"Sire, please..."

"You may think yourself innocent, Councilor," the king interjected, "yet you have betrayed Mira all the same by your silence. Had you once taken the responsibility for warning me, I might have considered a lesser judgment. You loved Mira no more than Darien, however cowardly you were in actually acting against it. For that, you will hang with him tomorrow, if not share in the rest of his punishment."

Erlund, unlike his companion, had no words to say, and he allowed the guards to lead him away in defeated silence.

It was the custom in Mira to alter the type of hanging based on the extent of the crime. When someone reached the point of execution, Valoretta could not imagine how Mira could judge the crime any further. All the same, the law divided crimes into levels of severity, and someone condemned to death might receive the rope via the snapping of their neck or through strangulation. That day, Erlund was granted the simpler snapping. Darien was not.

Watching the latter culprit led beneath the hanging rope after the executioners had removed Erlund's body, time appeared to disappear. It seemed to her that her mother again stood beside her, whispering, "I'm sorry, Princess Valoretta, but you are not simply a princess. You are the heir to Mira and it will be your responsibility to condemn the lawless. As a queen regnant, you will need to be harsher still."

The queen might have achieved the silence Sara had not then been able to, yet she had not swayed the princess' heart. Inside her regal shell, Valoretta hated executions.

As much as Darien fully deserved all he received, she saw the way his sides moved beneath the tar and the ropes his executioners had simply wrapped around him, not wishing to touch the black pitch. She knew how his hands would likely be at his throat already if able, and she felt nauseated. Had she been queen, she might have backed down and simply seen him beheaded, as weak as enemies would deem it.

Sliding her fingers up her sleeve, she touched the wooden item she had hidden there earlier and glanced over at Arnacin, standing for once beside her. His frame was locked, as happened when his bitterness was boiling under the surface. Sighing, the princess slipped her hand into his. "Please don't watch," she muttered. "For my sake."

His shoulders moved in a long silent exhalation, yet he dropped his gaze from the gurgling culprit hanging on his rope. If only for the sake of covering the horrible sound, Valoretta commented, still facing the scene herself, "I didn't realize until now how much war has hardened you. I remember a boy who was horrified just by the thought of death."

Arnacin's only answer was a brief shrug, yet the look she saw him pass her out of the corner of her eye spoke volumes of dark unvoiced thoughts.

Chapter 20

The Prophecy

King Miro paused on the terrace, watching the guards on duty tromp in time to their own parade beat, their march filling the spring's night air with the sound of safety. From a window above, Princess Valoretta's sweet voice could be heard mingling with her harp. Between those sounds, the castle seemed completely at peace, while the bright stars blazed down as if in approval.

A smooth tread sounded behind the king and Miro turned to face his high councilor.

"Sire," Memphis insisted, his posture remaining straight despite the dip of his chin. "Should you not have retired long ago? It's five past the hour."

"Memphis." Miro exhaled in exasperation. "How can you be tired on a night like this? Doesn't the sky give you energy at just the sight of it?"

"Oh... yes," the councilor replied after a second, although his gaze did not flick upward once, but stayed fixed on some sight before him. Before the king could follow that disgruntled gaze, however, Memphis growled, "Thinks he owns the world, that one."

To the king's unasked question, the councilor pointed his well-manicured finger toward the ramparts. Only knights patrolled there and, when Miro shook his head, Memphis explained, "On the barn roof."

The barn in question sat nestled against the outer ramparts. Now the king saw there, sleeping in his cloak on its wooden roof, a black-haired figure. Smiling fondly, Miro noticed that Arnacin used only his arm as his pillow, once again proving his rugged, humble background. Even the shadows of the patrol flickering over him did not appear to disturb him under the light of the stars.

"All he wants is what you have." Memphis's growl cut into the king's thoughts. As Miro cast his councilor a sharp look, Memphis dove into an explanation, as though he thought that if he did not speak then, he never would. "Why else would he be so polite until you give him any type of license, at which point his men no longer obey any higher authority? He's a dark jackal, you know it, preying on the gullible like he does."

"Arnacin is just a boy–" Miro started.

As with Sara when she was at the end of her patience, however, Memphis huffed, "Boy, pah. A seventeen-year-old shark. A boy would not have led armies to victory the way he did, nor stand at your side and try to instruct his betters."

Miro allowed the man to finish, simply to hear his weak arguments, and then snapped. "I'm king. I will not be contradicted, and I expect you to know that."

Smoothly bowing, the high councilor mumbled, "It is only for your safety that I lose control, Sire. I apologize."

Snorting, the king turned away with a growled, "I wonder..." After a moment, he pressed, "Moreover, none of the men that I put under him have complained about him 'taking over,' as you put it. Cornyo in fact informed us that Arnacin often spent much time learning from their counsel before he would decide anything. I am told that often, although the action was on his command, much of the plan was of his men's design."

"Are you sure he is even seventeen," Memphis asked, falling back on perhaps his last argument–Arnacin's honesty.

"Does he not look it?" Despite his assurance, Miro looked again toward the figure on the roof. True, by day, he appeared much older–battle hardened, proud, with that gleam of deep wisdom in his eyes that he had possessed from the beginning–but now, in peaceful sleep...

Beside him, Memphis closed his eyes as if the sight revolted him. "He is dangerous," the councilor insisted.

Scornfully, the king studied his councilor and it felt like he saw him for the first time. Everything about him was oily, smooth and affluent. Where Arnacin's appearance spoke of simple honesty, this man took every thought to his appearance, and quite an ambitious appearance he upheld. He would not even bow anything more than his head, lest it ruin his regal bearing. It was with these thoughts that Miro finally understood all his high councilor's attacks on the islander.

"You have always wanted the throne, have you not?" the king whispered, noting the sudden, perfectly blank look he received in reply. "For years, you have made to please me in everything. Whether the council was good or bad, if I liked the sound of it, you insisted on its wisdom in order to remain my favorite. I am sad to say, you succeeded–until recently. Recently, a threat has ripped into your carefully laid plan, and you've betrayed yourself in trying to remove him. Let me tell you something now, Memphis." Barely breathing, Miro admitted, "He will receive your goal before anyone else does, and it will be because he does not try."

Raising his voice, the king called his ever-present and invisible bodyguards. As they came through the doorway, he ordered with a nod toward the councilor, "Arrest him. "

In the brief struggle that followed, the king shrugged. "I cannot keep people around who will act only for their own glory. Lock him away until I decide what to do with him."

As Memphis was dragged away, he shouted, "Mark my words. Someday you will regret having accepted that boy! Someday you'll see!"

Without a word, the king turned down the opposite corridor.

The first thing Arnacin noticed the next day was how the councilors whispered together in tight corners, cutting off as he neared, and how some completely changed directions when they saw him in order to avoid him. On some of their faces was fear, and on others, loathing.

Then Miro sent for him. The king stood alone in the throne room when the islander entered. "Arnacin," Miro greeted him. He paused as if contemplating his words, and then said, "I am in need of a new high councilor."

For a complete minute, Arnacin stood there, but no understanding would come. "What happened to Memphis?"

"I had him arrested for selfish manipulation last night. No one can swear to serve king and country and then only serve oneself."

"Why are you telling *me* this? Mira has a school training new councilors. Why are you not there?"

"Arnacin, you are not unintelligent." There was a low growl in the king's voice as he stepped closer, lowering his tone. "Stop pretending I could not be asking what I am. With this war where it is, I trust very few. I picked my councilors originally for their large array of viewpoints. I refused to have a biased reign. Unfortunately, they have grown more alike in the time since.

"That is not the issue, however. I worked with those students even before selecting them as my councilors. The most intelligent and wisest of them, I eventually placed as high councilor until such time as I had a son to fill the place. As you know, I never had a son and so he has kept his place for too long.

"Now, I need someone I already know well and trust to fill that place. You, Arnacin, with your overbearing sense of honor, will not use your council for your own gain. Will you accept the position?"

Arnacin found that he was backing away, step by slow step. He barely prevented himself from shaking his head. "You need someone who will be here after the war. I can't do it, I'm sorry."

"Arnacin..." Sighing, Miro turned back to his throne, but it seemed to the islander that he was almost using that movement to hide his expression. Once at the far end of the hall, however, the king turned back. "New arrangements will be made once this war has ended, but until then I need a councilor who I can depend on to have the good of Mira first and foremost in their thoughts. I will accept your considered answer this evening, when you have had time to think about it."

Recognizing the dismissal, the islander bowed out, but as one of the king's guards shut the door behind him, his thoughts turned to the dungeons. Could it be that Miro had just realized what Memphis was? He could have just as easily dismissed him from service, unless there were political machinations of which Arnacin had not yet heard.

If he asked Memphis about it, the former high councilor would likely answer dishonestly, but perhaps the islander could still learn something.

With that thought, he cautiously headed down to the dungeons' guardroom, hoping they would not again refuse him entrance. He could not think of a reason they would, but their grim expressions, their naked blades and spear tips glinting in the torch light, and the thought of how easy it would be to bar the door behind him made him sidetrack to his room to grab his cloak.

The truth was, he had never been below ground before. The horror stories parents told their children on the island to prevent them from exploring the mound at the peak of their island mountain did not feel like a simple tale for children when facing the idea of descending into the ground–into dungeons no less. Underground was said to be, in short, the playground of evil spirits, the heart of their chambers.

Wrapping his cloak tightly around his shoulders, Arnacin pulled its folds close before starting down. His parents had never told such stories and, when asked, they had said that the ground, the dirt and the rocks beneath them were the only things holding up their island from the sea. Underground was as much a gift as above, except that it was dangerous for a child to try digging into the many caverns said to exist in their mountain, due to collapsing tunnels, lack of light, and whatever evil dragons and enchanters alike had left under their particular mountain.

The guards merely nodded to him when Arnacin descended into the large stone room. It spanned the entire size of the keep and was broken into several sections for a mess-hall, sleeping barracks, armory and the large iron door at the far end.

Pausing, the islander heard himself ask, "Do you never come out?"

One guard nodded. Considering the game near his elbow, he had obviously been playing Molshunting with another before the islander's approach brought every single man to his feet with weapons ready. Now however, he shrugged, "Of course we do. Our guard is broken into troops of fifty. Once a month, we rotate troops. We're almost through our month of service down here. Personally, I can't wait."

"Did you need something?" another asked, clearly the one in charge as his sword motioned in the direction of the stairs. His meaning was clear–if Arnacin was not down there for a reason, he was to turn straight back up the stairs and stop distracting them.

"I came to see Memphis, if I may."

One guard, standing at attention near the large iron door leading into the dungeons themselves, bowed slightly and turned to place a key in the lock.

As the door groaned, a guard snickered, "We're supposed to keep it well-oiled, but it does intimidate the prisoners so." Giving the islander directions and a key they said only worked on the cell door and not on the prisoner's chains, the guards turned back to their game and Arnacin was left to descend the dark steps alone.

"There are lights to guide you," the guard at the door whispered and then, as the islander slipped by, he closed the door, locking it again. Hearing the click of the key, Arnacin shuddered, yet he willed his feet forward.

The depths of the castle dungeon echoed eerily and the occasional lanterns tinted the stone behind them a harsh red amid the intense darkness. Even worse, the flickering lanterns caused the patches of red to dance greedily and the shadows to shimmer like many passing ghosts. Time and again, the light caused Arnacin to stiffen, sure that something had moved, only to be proven wrong. Although the place was neither damp nor decaying, the islander felt he had never seen anywhere that made him think more of Hell than these dungeons, as he slowly descended the stone slabs, ever deeper into the silent bowels of the castle.

After what seemed like hours of twists and turns, Arnacin reached the bottom, wondering what had been so important as to bring him down in the first place. Curiosity, yes, but–he reminded himself–anything Memphis would be willing to tell him would help to advise his next steps.

Only slightly reassured that he was not just being overly curious, Arnacin started forward, berating himself for his childishness. With the directions given by the jailer at the top, seemingly thousands of stairs up, Arnacin found the correct cell, marked by the lantern hanging from a hook on the wall. Memphis sat chained on the far side of the cell. Knowing his sympathy showed in his face, Arnacin slipped in, settling himself against the wall opposite from the former councilor.

Memphis was the one who broke the silence, however. "You stole my position, I gather."

It wasn't a question, but pulling his knees to his chest, Arnacin shrugged. "It was offered to me, but I haven't agreed to take it yet. What did you do?"

The councilor laughed humorlessly. "How naive you are, boy. Learn politics for a change, why don't you! You'll need it where you're going."

"What are you talking about?" the islander asked impatiently.

"Kings guard their position jealously. They'll kill their own heirs if they think they show too much ambition. Take my advice. Leave before you're next, a targetable cockerel like you."

"I would if I could," Arnacin admitted, "not because I believe a word you've said, but because..." he dropped off, studying his knees.

"If you could," Memphis scoffed. "You ca–"

"I gave my word. Regardless of the consequences, I'll stay until my job here is finished." His answer was cold, yet Memphis didn't seem to care, his sneering smile knowing and nasty.

"Fool," the councilor finally voiced. "Your job will never be finished. Do you honestly think he will ever let you go? Leave now, while you can, while you're still permitted to visit your ship."

Terror pierced Arnacin, as if he had only been waiting for those words to prove his worst nightmare. All the same, he threw it aside knowing the councilor was a liar and manipulator. Coolly, he rose and departed with a nod.

Once in the safety of the main keep, Arnacin quickly retreated to the north-facing terrace. There, his shivers slowly calmed, yet his unease did not leave so readily. He could deny the position the king offered, yet he knew the king would consult him whether he agreed or not. That much was certain.

"Arnacin." The soft call jerked the islander from his thoughts to find Valoretta standing beside him on the terrace. Her auburn hair billowed in the sea breeze, her slender shoulders were covered only in a thin flowered mantle, and she had tucked the front of her skirt through her girdle, revealing the white gown beneath. Today, Sara had forced upon her charge a bracelet of small stones, a matching necklace, and a small band of gold that circled her brow above her cloud-blue eyes.

"Are there foreign ambassadors today?" Arnacin asked in response to her appearance, suppressing the thought that she suddenly looked rather grown-up.

"Briefly," the princess confessed. "I'm not even going to see them, though. Sara is just trying to find every excuse she can to strangle me." She laughed, "If she could, she would probably try to convince me there were foreign nobles here every day, just to dress me up."

When Arnacin only smiled half-heartedly, Valoretta pressed, "Why are you so reclusive today? I thought you would be on your ship in such nice weather."

Sighing, Arnacin dropped his gaze to the railing, running his fingers back and forth along it. "There's not really anything to do there anymore. I'm not even on it enough to swab it every day, and the repairs have all been made. I'm just..." He dropped off, but as Memphis's taunt again echoed in his ears, he glanced at the princess, asking, "Valoretta, do you know... have you heard anything... about your father's intentions after the war?"

For another minute, she studied him. Looking away, she remarked, "Father keeps his own council. It doesn't matter, though, if you are concerned about how he'll treat you after what happened to Memphis. He loves you—that I know."

Instead of comforting him, Arnacin felt slapped in the face. Dare she suggest that Miro knew love, when he called humans "savages," when he guarded his own high seat with such zeal—even Miro's choice of who and when to marry had nothing to do with real love. Well, Arnacin knew what real love, selfless love, looked like, and nothing in the king resembled it.

Whirling away, he snapped, "Royalty know nothing of love!"

Her gentle fingers brushed his arm. Sighing, he turned back, meeting the princess' sorrowful gaze. "Arnacin," Valoretta whispered. "My father refused to annul his marriage to my mother when it was impossible for her to have another child after me. It was against all political wisdom, but he loved her, and I've always loved him for it, no matter what he does. You know that, Arnacin. So why are you so vehement today? Are you not happy here?"

"I promised to help where I could. What I want doesn't matter, but I know... if even six more years pass..." He could not finish.

"Of course, the war has no right to continue, but why are you so nearly sick over it? To my knowledge, you never even found what you came to find."

"I don't care if I never find whatever it was. I left to find somewhere I could serve with every fiber of my being, and serve wholeheartedly. I wanted the side I died for to be wholly noble. Instead... I now doubt such a place even exists. It was a fool's journey from the start." He broke off his nascent rant, sighing. "Valoretta, I promised to return... I have to."

When she said nothing, dropping her gaze to her feet, he continued, "I promised my family I would return before I was twenty-five, and I'm afraid this war will never end. It's been going for decades already and, if the two promises clash, I don't know what I'll do. I'll have to break one or the other. On the one hand, how long can

I desert my mother… my sister, even my brother, yet… I could not feel very good about walking out in the middle of war either. But should not my family come first?"

Valoretta simply folded her arms over the railing. As Arnacin continued to watch her, waiting for her thoughts, she mumbled, "I feel rather jeal–" Looking up at him with a guilty smile, she stammered, "–jealous that you… that they… I mean, because they can be so certain of your return."

Still studying her, wondering what could possibly be running through her mind to evoke such random comments, Arnacin explained, "But that's what love does."

"You mean that it takes sacrifice," the princess clarified, turning her full attention on him once again.

"It does, but that's not what I meant. Love is trust and acceptance, as well as selflessness. Even if they didn't believe I'd return, by love, they would trust outwardly until it became an inward trust as well. Therefore, if I never returned, they would believe I died, whether that was the truth or not. That will be the truth, of course."

"So out of love, even the strongest force could not keep you away, except death?" As Arnacin nodded, she muttered, "Now I'm exceptionally jealous. But Arnacin, I would ask something–what would happen if that love was in two different directions?"

"I don't see how it could be."

Before Valoretta could respond to the simple statement, Sara's infuriated tones broke over them, "My Lady! Your skirt!" Paling, the princess yanked her skirt out of her girdle, letting it fall back over her garments, and turned to face her nurse.

"My delicate hands were sweaty from lifting it," she stated defensively, causing Arnacin to choke on a laugh. At the glare Sara passed him, he attempted to smooth away his smile long enough for the two ladies to leave. With them gone, he once again looked out toward the sea.

Despite his reservations, Miro convinced the islander to take the position of high councilor. After having heard about the customs and proper conduct of a high councilor from the princess, Arnacin prepared himself for the worst. For even as he agreed, he knew his conflict with the councilors would intensify.

Although a low murmur had ensued at the first sight of Arnacin standing in Memphis's position, it was not one of displeasure. On the contrary, all the nobles consented to him being there and instantly had high hopes for their further protection.

As Memphis had predicted, however, the other councilors all viewed the replacement as a greater threat and thereafter joined together to discredit their enemy. To that intensified conflict, Arnacin and Valoretta worked even harder to find an argument for peace—one that would best all opposition, however clever. As fate would have it, though, the sands of time emptied before they could find it.

Without forewarning, the doors crashed open and in walked an oddly familiar old man. As he neared, Arnacin remembered the insane man he had disturbed after becoming lost in the castle early in his stay—Mira's discarded oracle. To the islander's horror, he saw that the seer's eyes, although unfocused, had lost all cloudiness.

Before anyone could comprehend the strangeness, the seer spoke. "The war is at its end. The waves of history shall forge a new path. Mira shall crumble, her very foundations dipping into the netherworld, while Elcan shall rise."

"Impossible," Miro breathed, as if the word was wrenched from his throat without thought. "You—"

But the oracle had not finished and, likely unaware that anyone had even said anything, he concluded, "Heed this warning: Only should Mira humble herself and the Black Phantom vanquish all her king's opposition will these outcomes be thwarted."

All gazes turned to Arnacin, standing behind the king. The islander's sole reaction, however, was the closing of his eyes.

Cloudiness seeped back into the seer's pupils and, stumbling forward a few steps, he mumbled to himself, "What hall is this?

I don't remember leaving my..." Then, seeming to realize he was not alone, he snapped, "Who's there?"

"You may retire to your tower," Miro growled, a blade in his tone. No one could miss the wrath that filled the blind face at the sound of his king's voice, yet all the same, the seer bowed and left, leaving a horrified stillness behind him.

The king broke it first, snapping, "Islander!" When Arnacin stepped into Miro's line of vision, he demanded, "Where is Elcan?"

For just a moment, the islander did not reply, his gaze searching the king's own. Finally, he confessed, "It's the closest land mass to Enchantress Island, about a day's journey from home."

"And what do you know about it?"

"Practically nothing. It's split into four kingdoms or so, which have nothing better to do with their time than war over each other's thrones, and we have no desire to contaminate ourselves with suchlike."

Studying the foreigner closely, Miro persisted, "And what would it have to do with Mira's collapse?"

His own tone cooling, Arnacin probed, "What are you suggesting?"

"You swear you have made no agreement with any of their kings?"

After a heartbeat of wrathful silence, Arnacin whirled away.

"This meeting is not adjourned," the king reminded him, causing the islander to turn sharply in the doorway.

"Do you refuse to know or are you that ignorant of what reply I would give any king who dare ask me to aid their greed?" Arnacin snapped before resuming his departure.

Behind him, he heard Miro hurriedly bark, "You're all dismissed!"

Walking beside Duke Cestmir as they departed, one of the remaining nobles sighed, "That was a poor cover for the fact that the islander closed the meeting."

"It still worked in its own way," Cestmir said, in support of their king. "Everyone knows the islander could use a good thrashing, but I doubt he will ever submit enough to another to allow it. And as for death, most would say he has done nothing to give Miro a right to that, either."

"The councilors will be the first to disagree with that, particularly in light of the seer's prediction."

"Let us hope everyone is smart enough not to speak of it," the duke mentioned, "or the councilors will be the least of our worries, I fear."

Unlike Arnacin, Valoretta could not remain still for hours on end with nothing to do. Since her companion had been called away during another discussion about the wall—a dead subject in reality—she had finally pulled out a book. Hardly had she finished the first section, however, when the islander reentered. One look at his eyes told her something had happened.

Wisely ignoring that fact, she asked, "Do you wish to resume our pointless discussion?"

It seemed that he stared at her without vision before asking, "Do you know anything about how the seers would advise Mira's kings in the past?"

"Not really. Why?"

"He appeared today with a supposed prophecy," the islander growled, digging his fingers into the edge of the table in frustration.

Watching his knuckles turn white, the princess inquired, "What did he say?" Those dark eyes silently flicked to hers and, attempting to lighten what she saw in them, Valoretta joked, "The natives will win unless we return to older Miran beliefs?"

Shoving away from the desk, Arnacin strode toward the window where he stood in silence for a moment. Sighing, he then answered, "Is it common knowledge that he's blind?"

"Of course," the princess shrugged. "It's a nasty bit of superstition, but the so-called prophets were all of the same family and, according to legend, they burned every child's eyes at birth in order for them to inherit the gods' messages. If they could see, they wouldn't be able to."

Arnacin stared back at her in horror and disgust, and she pressed, "Why?"

"He wasn't blind today," the islander said in that flat way of his, causing the princess to stiffen. "In short, his message was that Mira will fall while a place near my home strengthens, unless..." Running his fingers along the windowsill, Arnacin quietly finished, "unless the Black Phantom conquers all opposition. I believe your father has deciphered it to mean he must submit to me."

"Arnacin," Valoretta gasped. "What is the seer trying to do?"

"*He* is not trying anything," the islander exclaimed, whirling back to her. "There is no natural means for him to *name* the continent neighboring my home. Not only that, but you said yourself that he has always been blind."

Silence stretched between them. Finally, licking her lips, Valoretta mentioned, "Maybe it's real. Maybe someone was trying to warn Father that he needs to start listening to your plans."

"Only you would think that," Arnacin said in exasperation. "Not only will he never listen, something like this is bound to cause division. People will fall back to their disgusting superstitions and feel obligated to rise against Miro in my name, and the price will be hundreds of their heads! Tell me that was a considerate warning."

Smiling sadly at his understanding of politics, Valoretta reminded him, "You are the one who believes in an all-powerful god, Arnacin. I would expect you to say that He might send the warning, and it is up to us to use it for good or evil."

"But it's certain evil, Valoretta. He would know they will never listen. Therefore, how could He send it?"

"I'm hardly the one to answer," the princess laughed. At his glare, she sighed, "I think we can use it to our advantage, though. It hardly matters what such a message really implied. If someone were willing to present it as being about the wall, Miro might listen." Seeing the protest on his lips, she hurriedly added, "No, listen. The thing about your neighboring continent might mean nothing more than how it will flourish once you return home, after you narrowly escape our fall if we don't go along with your wall.

It makes enough sense and, under the current circumstances, everyone will petition their agreement."

"And so you use their fears to your advantage," Arnacin growled with a knowing nod.

"It's not my advantage. It's their *lives*."

"Discarding honor has never saved lives."

"Sometimes, it has."

"No, it hasn't, and I'll tell you why," the islander stated vehemently. "You are willing to lie, twist other people's thinking for something you think 'better' for them. And, maybe, the first time, that thing *is* better for them, but now you've chiseled away at your honor, and the next time something dishonorable seems necessary, it's so much easier to chip away more for that imaginary cause. This war started because of a lack of honor. Do you fancy it will turn around through a greater lack of it? Not in my mind. If I cannot find an honest way..." He broke off, insisting, "There *is* a way to achieve peace through honor."

"But there isn't," Valoretta contradicted him. "How long have we tried? Had there been a way, that wall would be in the making already."

Obstinately, Arnacin stated, "Then peace will never be and that's the end. There is no dishonor that can obtain it. Look how many people I have injured by doing just that? Cornyo, Firth, all of Mira really."

"You've never mentioned Firth before. What happened to him?"

She saw the shields go down over the islander's eyes. Instead of answering, he said, "For the cause of your war, I've learned deceit. I've murdered women and children. I no longer wince when someone dies and I feel no sympathy for a tortured culprit. I hate what I've become, but I can't go back, and there is nothing I've gained through it."

Hissing in defeat, Valoretta's gaze dropped to the table still littered with diagrams and histories. Silence again fell in the cavern. Slowly, the princess' thoughts caught up with her gaze, and pushing aside a few books covering the object of her attention, she breathed, "We're fools, Arnacin." She paid no heed to the sarcastic glance thrown her way, instead finishing her thought. "The sea wall. The blockade against pirates."

No comprehension altered the islander's frustrated expression and she exclaimed, "Was not Memphis's excuse that a wall caused more attacks, because it meant we could not defend ourselves without one?" Laughing now, she asked, "Well, where are our pillaging pirates? I have yet to see any."

A slow smile crept across Arnacin's face and he replied, "That's only because they're invisible, Valoretta."

"That's exactly what the councilors will say," Valoretta continued his line of thought, as it seemed the sun had once again woken from a deep sleep.

Miro did not call the islander for an entire week, but then word arrived from Mira's forces that Melmoor was completely empty of savages. The king at last called Arnacin into the council chamber along with the rest of the councilors to discuss the enemy's possible reasons for leaving the woods.

As men ran out of possibilities and Miro looked on the verge of dismissing all of them, Arnacin spoke up. "Your Majesty. You possess a sea wall. Do the pirates whom you built it against now deem you weak? Do they attack all the more?"

A dead silence fell. Miro's councilors glanced from the king to the islander and back, nervously. Arnacin waited, the lift of his chin expecting attack, and Miro continued to study the speaker.

Finally, one councilor ventured, "It makes little difference either way. Unless Mira builds a wall all the way around the entire continent, someone could just go around, particularly someone who has often used the sea to his advantage." His look pierced the islander condemningly.

Arnacin did not submit. "With a wall all the way around, only a ship could..."

"Enough!" Miro roared, cutting off all argument. "I told you once never to mention it again. The next person to ever mention a wall in my presence, or out of it, will have their tongue cut out. Is that clear?"

Fire lit Arnacin's dark eyes as a million unwise words formed behind them, yet he dipped his chin with the rest, hissing, "Most clear, Your Majesty." As all the rest turned to the usual war plans, the islander asked, "I have no more suggestions to give currently, Your Majesty. May I beg your permission to leave?"

Miro regarded the islander for a moment, yet as if recognizing the tenseness and the clamped lips, he nodded, adjourning the meeting. Leading the retreat, Arnacin swept off down the halls to his ship.

Not long after, Arnacin was scrubbing the deck as he would have liked to scrub away the whole of Mira, the king and the councilors–viciously, cruelly, until his knuckles bled from the scouring. Then he sat back on his heels, his anger exhausted by the lonely, hard work, and slowly he exhaled in submission. There was nothing he could do, anyway.

All the same, as the salty sea wind whipped across his hot face, he felt his throat constrict in yearning for the open ocean so close, yet so far away. He could dip his fingers in it and still never know its freedom. That was how tauntingly near its great vastness lay, red now in the setting sun. That sky promised a wonderful morning, and therefore also promised the intense bloodshed good weather brought.

Jerking awake at the sound of hurried footsteps approaching his door, Arnacin had just enough time to register the darkness outside before someone pounded on it, calling his name.

"Stop trying to break the door down and come in," the islander groaned, sliding out of bed and pulling his top layers over his head.

"Arnacin," the squire gasped even before he had fully entered. "You're to come to the great hall at once. Duke Cestmir returned from the field earlier this morning, and he's only just come around."

Yanking his cloak around his shoulders, the islander brushed by the squire, leaving his boots where they stood. "Come around?" he asked, as the squire fell into step beside him.

"He rushed back with only a few of his men, but no sooner had they galloped into the ward then he fainted–right off the back of his horse. When he did wake, he insisted he felt fine, and he is also on his way to the king by now, I'm sure. Something horrible must have happened, Arnacin."

Wordlessly, Arnacin agreed, trying to imagine anything that would cause the regally proper Cestmir to faint.

As it was, however, Arnacin arrived in the great hall before the duke, catching the king's concerned gaze before slipping behind him. Neither spoke, and only a few minutes later, the duke himself entered with a bow. "Sire," he said, and Arnacin heard the strained note of sickness in his voice. "They have nearly reached the capital. Through the marshes."

"What?" Miro snapped, and even Arnacin felt himself pale.

Unrolling the map he carried in his hand, Cestmir pointed to the empty place in the west, marked only "Marsh." As he had said, it ended not far from where the forest, Kelwin, began. If they swarmed that forest as they had Melmoor, they would only be a few miles from Mira's capitol.

"My men were out patrolling the towns remaining on our northern borders one night when we saw a false sunrise at our backs," the duke explained. "I sent a detachment to find out why and they never returned. Then, when I moved my troop to discover the reason myself, we found a flattened farmstead–bodies left scattered among the ashes. Not only that, but I met with Sir Hadwin's forces. They also reported farm attacks behind our lines. We agreed to join forces for the time being and remained on the alert for any more strange attacks.

"Finally, we saw a group of the savages on the march and swooped in on them. They didn't even wait to meet us, retreating as soon as they heard our footsteps. We followed them–straight into the marsh. Although we followed right in their footsteps–as near as we could–our men sank. We attempted to pull them out with ropes, but those monsters poured arrows upon us from the bracken. We had no choice but to retreat. The men we tried to save were all pierced by their arrows anyway, and I immediately took a few men with me to return here, while the rest stayed to aid the other force watching the marshes.

"Your Majesty," he concluded. "You no longer employ enough men to watch all the borders you hold. Should you send us to guard one area, rest assured they will pour forth from another."

If Cestmir fainting was an impossibility, Arnacin thought it equally impossible to see Miro pace. Yet after a few seconds of dark silence, the king whirled away toward the black windows of the great hall and, after a few steps, whirled back. Repeating his pent-up movements about three times, Miro finally halted before his duke, stating, "I will return with you to the battlefield as soon as the sun rises."

Two chins shot up in surprise, yet he gave neither Arnacin nor the duke time to speak. "I wish to know the battle lines for myself. While I am gone, Princess Valoretta is the ruler of Mira. Arnacin, I leave you, as high councilor, in charge of the city's defense. Should I not return, everyone knows what to do."

Without comment, Cestmir and the islander followed him out, sharing only the briefest of grim expressions.

Standing beside Arnacin in the library, Valoretta watched the king ride out alongside his duke and the few men in their entourage. "Part of me hopes he dies out there," the islander admitted.

For a long moment, the princess did not reply. Then she whispered compassionately, "You might think that now, Arnacin, but realize that even if the war ends soon after, you could never leave."

He turned toward her in puzzlement. Uncomfortably, Valoretta walked away and picked up a book from the table, running her finger down the spine. "He put you in charge of military actions."

"Is that common for a high councilor to be given command while the king is gone?" the islander inquired after a moment of silence.

"None of this is common, Arnacin. In the first place, I am not a prince. But no. As a matter of fact, each time one ruler passes, the new monarch discharges all the old councilors and chooses new ones of his liking from Mira's university of peasants, around twenty or so."

"And what would make this occurrence so different that I would remain your captive?"

"A captive, Arnacin?" Valoretta inquired, the words cutting like a blade. Unable to meet his gaze, she answered half-untruthfully, "I assume it would be your honor that would hold you. If Miro dies, no king stands in his place, and Mira's state of warfare would only grow. Unless I destroyed Mira and decided to live as the natives, it would not settle. I'm not sure I can safely do that. Truthfully, I have put off thinking about that choice as long as possible."

She knew he was studying her, perceiving there was something she was not saying, yet she could not look at him. Her father had, by design or not, left Arnacin's life and freedom at her mercy. She could easily bind him to Mira by his honor forever if something happened to the king. To her shame, she felt excited by the prospect. If her thoughts were her fingers, they were gleefully tightening around the islander's future in a stranglehold.

So much for love. Would love ever consider denying him everything dear to him, everything that gave him breath, simply because of her selfishness?

Instead of contemplating that guilt, she finally opened her book, leaving Arnacin to figure it out himself if he could. She hoped he never would.

After returning from the field, Miro strode into the council chamber. Furiously tossing his riding cape over a chair, he unrolled a map onto the table. He did not have to wait long for his quarry, to whom he had sent a messenger before entering the room. Arnacin entered with a subservient nod; his cloak testimony to the fact that he had been outside as usual.

Hardly had he entered, however, before the king jabbed his finger at a point on the map, exclaiming, "Those rotten tribes continue to slink through our guards around the marshes and are burning our villages, scurrying back to their roost before we can strike. How are they even slipping through the guard?"

Exasperated, Arnacin said, "They know back ways, side ways, front ways, and I wouldn't put it past them to have top ways and bottom ways out of there as well. Your men can't be expected to guard every path in or out when they know nothing of the land, if there were even enough men for the task."

"Every time we try to explore those lands, we lose another hundred at least," Miro reminded him, tiring of the hidden tone of their continued debate.

Arnacin did not reply for a minute, studying the blank edge of the map, where the maker's lack of knowledge cut off at the marshes. It was challenge that lit those dark eyes, however, not defeat in the hopelessness of that ignorance. Knowing Arnacin's unconquerable determination, the king also knew that short of burning their enemy out–dangerous though that would be–they had no better choice. Even the barren plains around the marsh aided the savages.

Finally, the islander stated, "You keep trying to go in by force. Stall for now. Pull all your subjects behind your city's walls while you send someone to follow the tribes in, until that person knows enough of the terrain to return with the information. Then, and only then, will you be able to send in an army."

"And in the meantime, we cower behind our walls and starve while they pillage and burn our fields and livestock."

"If we act fast enough, starvation can be prevented. There is no better option. They are already destroying supplies."

"No better option! I can find a better option if repetitive creatures like you let me think! I'm king and I will not cower or allow the kingdom to be set upon by swine, for whatever amount of time!"

"Forget your pride!" Arnacin snapped at last. "You're losing, and there isn't any time left! Your worry should only be for the protection of your subjects, not your artificial, selfish honor!"

"Artificial? Selfish?" Miro spluttered, turning a violent shade of red. "What–!"

Yet it was like a river's dam had been yanked open and there was no stopping the ensuing flood. "If you had any real honor, I wouldn't have to tell you what your duty is and isn't–"

"Who do you think you are to tell a king–?"

"I don't care who or what rank you are–you are still human, and thus not above other people's safe–"

Arnacin had finally overstepped his boundaries. In jealous, hateful fury, Miro swung his fist, catching his ostensible enemy on the side of the head with his gauntlet. A crack seemed to echo in the room and the islander collapsed to the floor without a sound, blood trickling down the side of his head.

It seemed to Miro that he saw the islander revealed. Had not Memphis truthfully depicted him as a shrouded figure, devouring hearts with every breath he took and converting them for his own support? Now, the kingdom had been stolen by the islander, his people had surrendered wholly to him. They would act for him–breathe for him–and him alone.

Even Carpason had not gone to his last battle for Miro, but to preserve the wretch's honor! And even Miro's precious Valoretta had defied her very birthright, her father's love, before hundreds, to claim the islander as her lord! The king himself had been duped, duped until now when the Phantom had the audacity to proclaim his power and expect the king to yield. Memphis alone had known.

"Guards!" Miro snapped, hardly even glancing at the heap on the floor. As two men stepped out from behind the doors, he commanded, "Take this thieving filth to the nearest tower and have the mason seal him in. I don't need to see him to be able to deal with his treachery." Without another glance, he strode out of the room, yanking his cloak off the chair as he passed.

Chapter 21

The Black Phantom

Setting her handheld loom on her lap, Valoretta studied her nurse carefully. "Sara, I know you don't want to hear it, but where's Arnacin? I haven't fou–" Catching herself before she admitted that she was seeking the islander, the princess amended, "–seen him anywhere."

Simply lifting her eyes without moving her head, which gave her a very sharp appearance, her nurse stated, "I would suggest, My Lady, that you forget all your time wasted in that person's presence."

"Sara!" the princess exclaimed. "Just answer my question and forget how much you dislike him."

"He has left for good, chi..." Sara faltered, stumbling on the beginnings of a few more words before giving up.

"His ship is still sitting in the harbor," Valoretta stated firmly. She received no reply and in frustration she shot to her feet. "Sara, you have never lied to me. Answer me at once. Do you know where Arnacin is?"

"My Lady," her nurse whispered, her voice trembling uncharacteristically. "It will be better if you don't ask."

Feeling her heart rate increase, the princess dropped to her knees before her nurse. "Sara, please..."

Not meeting her gaze, Sara answered, "The rumor spreading about the castle is that he was killed."

"What?" Valoretta heard her own voice sound as no more than a puff of air. "Who attacked him?"

"I don't know the details, dear one," Sara moaned, her own voice tortured. Her hands trembled on her embroidery hoop. "I heard the king ordered him sealed within the keep's northeast hearth room, to suffocate or die of thirst there. I swear, I know no more."

It was as though someone else's legs trembled and failed as Valoretta thumped onto her bottom. Her mind would not function, and no sound would escape her throat. The king had ordered Arnacin's death? It was impossible.

"No!" she finally screeched, shooting to her feet and racing to the door. She did not hear Sara's call, did not notice the saddened stares she received as she flew to the indicated tower, her skirts pulled high to allow her flight. She would not, could not, believe it unless she saw for herself.

She arrived to see the tower door standing not as it normally did, but spackled over with a thick clay, its handle laying on the floor by the toe of a suit of armor, and the handle's hole filled in with more mortar.

Movement beside her caused her to jump. Their mason–whom she had seen several times bent over drawings with her islander–stood there brokenly studying his clayed fingers.

"How could you?" she screamed, barely restraining herself from launching at his throat.

"Our king gave orders, My Lady," he choked. "I'm only a servant..."

His voice trailed feebly off, and the princess shrieked, "The King's orders! Were I queen, I'd see you hanged for base treachery!"

Sadly, the mason replied, "Were you queen, My Lady, this would not likely have happened." So saying, he stumped away, his shoulders even more stooped than normal.

Valoretta flung herself against the new wall. It did not budge. As a sharp pain lanced through her shoulder, she slid down into a ball on the floor, trembling from tears for the first time in her life–angry, betrayed and lost. It was not until gentle hands wrapped themselves about her shoulders that she allowed herself to be led away, barely hearing Sara's uncharacteristically soft reassurances.

Valoretta did not sleep that night. Even the cool, strong wind blowing through her window was unable to soothe her. Her eyes and nose burned, still damp and uncommonly swollen.

Finally running her hand down her cheeks, she slid out of bed, pulling her dark robe over her undergarments. Without even intending to, she slipped through the quiet castle, straight to the sealed hearth room. Outside light flickered across her path although the moon had left for the night, and she watched its window patterns play over the corridors' floors and walls without interest.

As she came to the door, she felt her tears renew. In a flash of temper, she ripped the spearhead from the suit of armor standing nearby and attacked the clay, determined only to exact her vengeance on it. That she proceeded to do until, losing that first wave of strength and energy, she dropped to the floor in broken weariness.

She lay there curled into a ball, trembling with quiet sobs until the distant realization hit her that her knee was pressing against some kind of hole beneath the door. Gasping, she shoved her fingers into it, feeling empty space behind. It was highly unlikely that the mason had overlooked it, which could only mean...

"Arnacin," she croaked softly, but no response came. Biting her lip in frustration, she ordered, "Arnacin, keep digging. The more you help me, the faster you can escape." Her reward was the sound of soft scraping from the other side and, smiling in pure relief, she set to work on her side in earnest.

Only the early morning glow of sunrise coming through the window halted the princess' feverish work and, as it turned the clay red in front of her nose, she looked up with a start. "Arnacin," she breathed, "I'll be back tonight." Pulling herself to her feet, she hastily replaced the rather dull spearhead, dusted her skirt, pushed all the powdered clay under the door, and dashed back to her room, ignoring her throbbing shoulders.

Throughout that day, the princess strove hard to hide her burning muscles and weariness. Yet, with vengeful satisfaction, she noticed at times, looking out her window as she embroidered, her father pacing the terrace, his shoulders uncharacteristically stooped.

To her delight, the king appeared entirely beaten. She highly doubted it was the state of the war that had cast him into such weakness. In justification of her spite, she told herself he had betrayed them all–yet, to her shame, Arnacin's quips about royalty's incapacity to love haunted her.

By night, as soon as she knew the keep was still, she trod again the path to the sealed tower, finding a fresh spearhead and returning to work on the edges of the door, despite her crying shoulders. The only sound she made was the soft reassurance as she set to work, "It's me. Continue."

In the occasional silences as she briefly rested her arms, she heard a soft scraping noise of metal on stone, and over it Arnacin's rasp of hoarse panting–a dry, choking sound. In desperation, she increased the strength of her struggle against their common enemies–the door and time.

Again, she halted only when the sun's rays illuminated the door, forcing her to stop. Worrying more than the day before, she forced herself to leave, hearing as she did his weak coughs in a vain attempt to clear his throat.

Those coughs haunted her day. Restless, she paced the corridors, subconsciously biting her fingers. Without any water at all, Arnacin would likely die before he could escape, yet she knew a cup or waterskin would never fit beneath the door.

Sara passed her at one point, but with a sorrowful nod she left Valoretta to pace. Watching her nurse's disappearing back, the princess wondered if the basin of water could be filled early if she asked. But what excuse could she create to have the basin immediately refreshed after cleaning her feet, hands and neck before slipping into bed. Sara only ever refilled it for the next evening, and emptied it instantly after use.

"There is not one man I would deem capable of such a mission." The voice caused Valoretta to stop. A corridor branched off to her left and down it walked the king with one of his generals beside him. It was the general who was speaking in concern and defeat. "Those I would think able, I wouldn't trust not to sell us out."

"Who are those?" Miro asked. Neither one had noticed the princess standing there as of yet, and she listened intently.

"There are our adopted natives. Although they do not know all the secrets of their people, their hunting skills are amazing. Even if they were spotted, they are natives after all. However..."

He dropped off and the king finished, "They are natives after all, and such a mission might remind them of their blood."

"My thoughts exactly. Once they were alerted to our plan, we couldn't try again. To be honest, Your Majesty, there was only one man I would think capable of such a task whom Mira could have trusted..."

"Then we shall simply need to think of another way," Miro said, looking away and noticing his daughter for the first time. With a nod, they passed and Valoretta felt her breath leave in a pained sigh.

Once again, she waited until the castle slept before slinking out of her room. As she shut her door behind her, she felt something warm and soft brush her leg. Her breath stilled. One of Rosa's lap dogs was there, but by night, they were usually all nestled into the queen's bed beside their mistress.

She did not bend to touch it, but a soft rustle approaching told her why the dog was about that night. The queen was out herself.

Turning to Rosa, Valoretta wished she had grabbed a shawl before leaving her room. Without one, she thought it obvious that she was in a hurry to leave.

Carrying a candle, Rosa smiled softly at the princess. Instead of asking questions, however, she pulled a kerchief out from her Vemose robe and held it out. "For true love," she whispered, as Valoretta cautiously accepted it.

Cool dampness dropped over her palm and her gaze jerked back to the queen. Rosa only curtsied and turned away.

Even wonder could not keep Valoretta there a second longer, and she turned down the stairs to the only doors exiting the royal accommodations. As the guards merely opened the doors for her to pass, it occurred to her that perhaps Miro was one of the only ones in the castle who did not know about the islander's attempt to escape or her role in helping him.

Once at her self-assigned post, she shoved the wet cloth beneath the door. With that, she set to work, now whimpering slightly herself due to her painful shoulders. Despite their constant, burning complaint, she did not halt except to replace her tools when one became too dull. She now stood atop a chair, working above the door, where her companion could not likely reach. As dawn again spread its light over her work surface, she whispered, "Keep working, Arnacin. There's not much left. You'll be out by noon at the latest."

Clearing away evidence of her treachery, she added, "Come out by noon, Arnacin. Don't die before you can."

With one last look, she hastily departed, feeling weariness steal over her like incoming fog. She had not rested, except for the few times she had drifted off over her loom, for the past three days.

After all the time in his intended tomb, Arnacin's vision had adjusted well to the pitch darkness. It was with relative ease, therefore, that he attacked the hinges, sawing them off through the wood with the Tarmlin blade, which no one bothered to take from him.

As the last hinge came undone, the door thudded to the ground before crashing inward. Sunlight streamed through the gaping hole, seeming to burst through the islander's skull. In that moment of overwhelming agony, made worse by dehydration, he distantly felt fingers seize his arm.

"Here," a man's voice sighed, piercing Arnacin's head with more pain. Something was pressed against his mouth, yet the wonderful feel of water pouring down his throat ended any impulse to struggle. In some remote corner of his mind, it occurred to him what might be in that water, but he did not care.

When the flask was withdrawn, he dared to try opening his eyes again, only to quickly close them after a single glance at the streaming glow.

"Come on. You'll readjust to the light on the way," the disembodied voice stated. As firm as the grip was that pulled him to his feet, twisting one arm behind him, it also had a certain gentleness about it and Arnacin did not possess the strength or desire to resist its guidance.

Beyond his pain, he felt the sea wind coming through the windows they passed, bringing the smell of saltwater, grass and flowers with it. That and the water slowly took their effect, starting to revive him as he was led along, half-limping in weakness. Before it could take complete effect, however, he was pushed forward, colliding with hard stone. Thankfully, it was now dimmer. Looking up, he first saw Miro seated on his throne, arms folded in an attempt at his false idea of strength. Even so, unreadable emotions flickered in those eyes, controlled far too quickly to be deciphered.

Arnacin almost did not care what those thoughts were. Feeling a deep fury well up, he pushed himself to his feet, meeting the king's gaze with pure defiance, a dare for all to see.

Movement behind the throne caught the islander's attention. Standing next to the queen, Princess Valoretta seemed on the verge of speech, dark rings under her eyes and her posture one of pained tightness. Meeting her gaze, Arnacin twitched his head in warning. In reply, she glanced down, eliminating all concern from her face as she did, simply appearing mildly interested in the proceedings.

Satisfied that she would not reveal her part in the escape, Arnacin turned his attention back to the king, who was simply staring at him in silence. As the islander's baleful gaze again met the king's, Miro exhaled.

"I will not ask how you managed to escape," the king said. "I know that your continued breath is only through power a god alone could possess, as I have thought on other occasions. Therefore, Arnacin of Enchantress Island, I will tell you that only through love will I not strike you down now."

Arnacin felt his head lift in scorn at such a phrase, yet Miro did not ask for his thoughts. "No other man has ever, or will ever, defy me as you have and live to speak of it. However, in consideration of your volunteered, ever-present–"

Once again, some other emotion flickered in his gaze, and choking off, he finished shakily, "Arnacin, Son of Bozzic of Enchantress Island, you are hereby banished from Mira. Should you ever again set foot or anchor upon it, it shall be on pain of death. Let everyone take note."

With a cool, unconcerned nod, the islander turned toward the door. Yet a different tone than he usually heard in that voice halted him with a tortured whisper. "Arnacin, what made you flout all rules so freely?"

With pride he had only ever associated with his sister, dark and kingly, Arnacin turned back. "I had remained silent and patient long enough for you to wake up. Darkness consumes you and I'll have no part of it."

With that, he swept out, ignoring Miro's darkening features. Once out of sight of the great hall, however, he fled all the way to his ship, never to be seen by most Mirans again.

As soon as Arnacin had departed from the great hall, Miro barked, "You are all dismissed!" Most of the men standing there instantly bowed out, but as Rosa placed her hand on the king's shoulder, he snapped, "All of you!"

Valoretta did not need another word. Curtsying, she left and–hoping she would not be spotted–charged up to the terrace. Out in the harbor, a small ship had unfurled its sail and was turning toward the great open waters. A lump felt lodged in her throat while she pushed air slowly around it. Once again, in the space of three days, she could not think beyond the stark pain of horror, regret and loss.

"Farewell," she choked out, watching that ship's sail disappearing rapidly from sight. "You will never realize how I loved you, or how..." She angrily halted her words as sobs rose in her throat. Drawing on her long political training, she calmed herself, sighing, "It is probably better this way, but wherever you go, Arnacin of Enchantress Island, whatever you do, I wish... and... and pray that protection will follow you."

Sadly, she ran her fingers along the balustrade as the small streak of white disappeared over the horizon. Feeling a twinge of bitterness, she stated, "I'm sure your family will be happy to see your unfettered return."

Yes, Valoretta, princess of Mira, would never be part of such perfect love, and it filled her with unendurable sorrow.

THANK YOU FOR READING BOOK 1 of *The Black Phantom Chronicles*, *The Savage War*. If you enjoyed this book, please leave a review on Amazon, Goodreads or your favorite review site. It helps me reach more people so they too can follow Arnacin's journey.

Read on for a sneak peek at
Book 2 of *The Black Phantom Chronicles*,
The Eternal Struggle,
available at emeraldlakebooks.com/eternal.

Chapter 1 of *The Eternal Struggle*

The Price of Leadership

SILENCE... THE SILENCE OF IMPENDING DEATH filled the air. No light broke the thick blackness. Not even a chisel of starlight on a moonless night seeped into his tiny, entombed—could it even be thought?—coffin. Air gradually exhausted itself in the abysmal space, and Arnacin's uncontrolled shivering, his gasping breaths, the very heat of his body, betrayed him. He sat crumpled against what used to be the entrance, sealed shut out of spite. Already, as he forced sleep away, the pain of airlessness allowed no more movement than the last futile twitch of his fingers in the place a doorway had once existed.

Crack! A flash of light brought the cabin back. Something in the back of his mind told Arnacin the storm bashing against all four walls was reality. His trembling body, however, insisted that the sound was wishful thinking, a last hope granted before he died in darkness.

For hours on end, it was impossible to discern either tomb or storm as reality. Yet, as the world in which the cabin existed stopped rolling on storm waves, Arnacin bolted for the door and yanked it open. He ran until he stood on the far side at the dipping prow in the settling waves. There, as the vision of his tomb dissolved back into memory, Arnacin shivered for another reason—weak relief.

So his life had been since his exile from Mira. Yet, until the storm, he had dreamed of finally going home. At least he had been traveling in a homeward direction due to the navigations of his heart, not his head. Home was not in actual dreams, for he rarely slept anymore; even when complete exhaustion washed over his thin frame, he could only doze beneath the stars, where the cold only permitted fitful rest.

Now, in the renewed sun after the passing of the storm, Arnacin looked up at his sail—the sail that would remain limp since the storm stole its brace. Without the wind against the sail, his ship could only drift with the current, and neither food nor water would last that agonizingly slow voyage.

There were no alternatives. He was doomed to die at sea, for no one would come across his ship out in the middle of the vast expanses of water and sky. Even if they did, whom would he trust? Even Valoretta had betrayed him. Yes, he had wanted her to keep her part in his escape secret, but she had chosen not to stand up for him at all. Considering her disloyalty, he knew, as he had come to realize these last few months, there was not a soul on whom he could rely.

"My lady," Sara called from down the corridor. "A rider will be here in another moment."

Quickly hiding the rough wooden key in her sleeve, Valoretta met her nurse before the older woman could reach the little alcove where the princess had been sitting.

"I told the gatekeepers to send him to the great hall when he arrives," Sara continued.

The princess shook her head. "I'll meet him in the outer ward." Lifting her skirts, the princess raced toward the outside, wishing to catch the messenger as soon as he rode in. She heard the weary footfalls of her nurse, simply plodding behind with no word of dissent.

Valoretta caught up with the messenger just as he was turning up the keep's stairs. "What word?" she gasped, even as the flushed messenger began talking.

He dropped to one knee. "My lady... I'm sorry. Miro was struck down. His remaining troops sent me back while they still drew breath to warn you, but they didn't expect to live. Those that stood remained to hold the savages back for as long as they could. This morning, I noticed a false sunrise toward Fortress Corguman while I rode."

"Our last fortress," Valoretta breathed, her skin icy, the perspiration from her mad dash suspended in little droplets down her back. With a flash of pain, she thought of all those senseless deaths. There was no turning back now though. Looking up at the walls, the princess, now ruler of Mira, calmly ordered, "Go into the city and make it known that it's time to evacuate Mira. Tell the ship captains they must allow our evacuees."

Wearily, the messenger bowed and left to do as bidden. "Sara," the princess sighed without turning around, her gaze returning to the retreating messenger. "Make sure the people know they are to take only what they most need. I will start with the nobility. I doubt we have much time."

"Is that your decision? Have you not thought of another solution?" Sara's tone was beaten, but unsurprised.

Turning to her nurse, Valoretta admitted, "My waking hours have been consumed with little else. This end has been likely for a long time."

"But there is nowhere to go, my lady. No kingdom will aid us, and there is no unclaimed land we can sail to."

"I know... Yet we must go as individuals and integrate into other kingdoms. I see no other way to hope for life."

Sara's gaze flicked to the ground, but she stubbornly asked, "Do you intend to win Mira back someday, once her people are safe?"

"Never, Sara. It should have been evacuated long ago. Mira has proven greedy, unjust and immoral. If and when we find safety, we must start anew."

"My Queen," Sara intoned with a gracious curtsy far deeper than Valoretta had ever seen from the older lady. Then Sara hurried off, and Valoretta shook aside her feeling of complete dread and immense loss. Only resolution could pull them through.

Subscribe to my newsletter at
emeraldlakebooks.com/blackphantom
to be notified when the next book in
The Black Phantom Chronicles
is released.

Acknowledgments

THIS BOOK WOULD NOT BE possible without my parents, who let me dream, and my siblings, without whom I would never be the person I am today.

Thanks also to my Sherman critique group, past and present, and the Realm Makers tribe for how they have sharpened my craft and opened doors to the writing world.

And to the people who have had endless patience with me and Arnacin: Tara Alemany and Stephanie Warner. I'm more grateful than I can say.

About the Author

Esther Wallace is a writer and a freelance illustrator, who holds an associate's degree in graphic design and animation.

Her flash fiction piece, *Princess Herona and the Dragon*, won the Georgia Peach Award (third place).

Coming from a large family, Esther began writing fiction to entertain her younger siblings and share her creativity with them. Likewise, she shared all the most stirring books she read.

Her favorite stories are those that ask the most difficult of questions. She likes it even better when she can encourage other people to discuss those things with her or at least to ponder on their own.

Esther enjoys hearing from her readers. If you'd like to contact her or invite her to your next book club meeting, visit emeraldlakebooks.com/wallace.

CPSIA information can be obtained
at www.ICGtesting.com
Printed in the USA
BVHW042245011122
650929BV00001B/5